HATTIE'S STORY

SEABURY SERIES COLLECTION: BOOKS 4-6

BETH RAIN

Copyright © 2022 by Beth Rain

Sandwiches in Seabury (Seabury: Book 4)

First Publication: 28th February, 2022

All rights reserved.

Copyright © 2022 by Beth Rain

Secrets in Seabury (Seabury: Book 5)

First Publication: 30th April, 2022

All rights reserved.

Copyright © 2022 by Beth Rain

Surprises in Seabury (Seabury: Book 6)

First Publication: 30th June, 2022

All rights reserved.

No part of this book may be reproduced in any form or by any electronic or mechanical means, including information storage and retrieval systems. Except for use in any review, the reproduction or utilization of this work, in whole or in part, in any form by any electronic, mechanical or other means now known or hereafter invented, is forbidden without the written permission of the publisher.

Published by Beth Rain. The author may be contacted by email on bethrainauthor@gmail.com

CHAPTER 1

Pebble Street Hotel,
Seabury,
Devon

My Dearest Hattie,
I hope you're well. I know it's been an age since we last spoke, but I wanted to say how sorry I was to hear that your restaurant has closed. I know how many hours you put into that place and how much your work means to you. Marco's a fool not to take you with him to his new place. You always were the real talent there and, if you ask me, it's his loss. You mark my words, he'll realise that very soon.

I've always been so proud of you, Hattie. There's nothing better than being able to brag about my great-niece - one of London's top chefs! I know that it probably doesn't feel like it yet, but I've no doubt that this change will end up being a brilliant leap forward for you. It just needs to work its way out in the wash first, you'll see. Don't let Marco's short-sightedness dim your light – this is what you love and what you were born to do (and I'm not just saying that because you're family!)

Now then, I've got a proposition for you. I'm not sure if you've heard my news yet - but I've bought The Pebble Street Hotel! It's probably the most extravagant and impulsive purchase of my entire life – but I honestly couldn't be happier with my decision. Even though it's going to take some getting used to, I can't exactly say that it's a random choice on my part. I love my home here and, when the opportunity arose, I found that I couldn't turn down the chance to own it myself. The thought of going through the whole legal rigmarole to stay in my flat like I had to when Veronica took possession of Pebble Street sent shivers down my spine! Now I never have to worry about all that ever again.

How it came about is a very long story and I won't bore you with it here - (I think it will be better shared in person with a nice bottle of red wine on the table between us!) - but I've got grand plans for the old girl. In particular, I want to start serving evening meals again. Pebble Street used to be very well known for its food back in its heyday. There's nowhere to eat here in Seabury of an evening – not once The Sardine closes – and I think it's time to change that.

This is where I hope you might come in.

I would love it if you might consider coming to work for me here at The Pebble Street Hotel. Or - I should say – with me. As Head Chef you'd have full control of the menu, the kitchen, the restaurant and all things foodie. Between the two of us, I think we could really get the old girl back on her feet and make something very special here.

I'm guessing that you've probably been inundated by job offers since Marco dropped you. With your talent, vision and drive, they'll all be desperate to snap you up. On top of that, I know that Seabury doesn't exactly offer the bright lights of the big city, but I wanted to ask you anyway - even though I know in my heart that the answer is likely to be no.

Don't worry - I'm under no illusions. I know a Head Chef position here can't even begin to compare to working in a fancy London restaurant. I also know that helping out your old uncle isn't the same as working with a rising celebrity like Marco Brooks. But – here's the thing – I just thought, if you fancied a change and were feeling up to the challenge of creating a menu from scratch and building something new and exciting - well, the job's yours!

I would love nothing more than to have you here in Seabury. It would be like old times! Remember how much you used to love spending your summers here as a child? Well, maybe you didn't love the hotel so much – who did with the dreaded Veronica at large - there was no getting away from her awful food, was there?! But I know you loved the town and the beaches. You were always surrounded by friends when you came to stay - everyone looked forward to seeing you.

Not much changes here. Seabury still has a strange kind of magic about it, and very few people move away once they settle. That's why I think this plan is so exciting. It is *a change – but hopefully, it'll be a change back to the good old days!*

Anyway, please have a serious think about my offer. There'll be a nice ensuite room here at the hotel for you as part of the job, but I'm sure we could find somewhere else for you to stay if you'd prefer.

If you decide that it's not for you, or you've already accepted another offer and plan to stay in London, I completely understand – and you're not to worry about it one little bit. Like I said above – that's honestly the answer I'm expecting. But I had to ask, Hattie! Just like when I bought the hotel, there's no way I can pass up the opportunity to try to lure you back to Seabury after all these years.

I look forward to chatting about it all with you if you'd like to – and of course, I wish you all the luck in the world with whatever you decide to do next. I've no doubt you're about to start work at some famous restaurant... but I stand by what I said to my old friend Charlie the other day when we were talking about you – I'm offering you this job because I can't imagine anyone more perfect for it!

Much love, as always,
Uncle Lionel

P.S please forgive the letter rather than a telephone call, but I didn't want to spring this all on you and not give you plenty of time to think it over!

CHAPTER 2

Hattie was exhausted. Actually, no – scratch that. Exhausted didn't even begin to cover how she was feeling. This was on the same level as her seventh birthday when she'd been so tired, she'd face-planted into a big bowl of apple crumble and custard. This was the kind of tiredness that made you want to curl up into a ball have a good cry. Hattie glanced around her. If it wasn't for the fact that there were still two other passengers sharing her train carriage, she'd probably give in and do just that.

Instead, Hattie rested her forehead against the window and did her best to ignore the dull ache that was creeping up her legs from the soles of her feet.

This was her third train of the day, and she'd had enough. Stupid. Bloody. Trains. Of course, it really didn't help matters that she'd managed to miss the one and only "fast" train to Plymouth. She'd been so close to catching it... close enough to watch the blasted thing pull away from the platform at Paddington as she'd hurtled like a dodgem car through the dithering crowd.

After a frantic chat with a very bored woman on the customer services desk, she'd managed to piece together the details of various connections that would take her as far as Dunscombe Sands. Dunscombe was one of the larger resort towns just along the coast from Seabury, and it was as close as she could get to it by rail. Frankly, it would have to do.

The journey had already taken several hours longer than it should have. She'd endured a very chilly wait for a delayed connection at her first stop. Then she'd followed this with a mad, sweaty dash at the next station so that she didn't miss her final connection.

Now that she was on her last train of the day – a tiny two-carriage affair - Hattie was running on empty. She was feeling even worse than when she'd set off – something she hadn't realised was physically possible.

Hattie closed her eyes for a split second and felt the instant pull of sleep. No. That wouldn't do at all – one little snooze and she'd be halfway across Cornwall before she knew it. She sat forward abruptly and rubbed her eyes hard.

Reaching for her bottle of water, Hattie took a tiny sip before glancing at the luggage rack above her, compulsively checking on her case for what must have been the tenth time. Yup – there it was, exactly where she'd left it - the single, lonely suitcase that held the handful of items that constituted her "life". Eighteen months in London, and all she had to show for it was now riding along in that little black case above her head.

It had come as quite a shock when she'd realised how few possessions she'd managed to accumulate – but then, it shouldn't have come as that much of a surprise. There hadn't exactly been much opportunity – or point – in making her flat feel like a proper home. It was just a convenient place to fall asleep for a couple of hours before hot-footing it across London and heading straight back into the kitchen again.

Hattie had been so sure that all her hard work would pay off. Her commitment. Her diligence. Okay, so it hadn't been her own restaurant – that was the ultimate dream - but being such an integral part of Marco's place had made her feel like she was on her way, like she was on the cusp of something huge.

Marco Brooks. Mercurial chef. Wunderkind. Official git.

Marco was a legend in his own lunchtime, and he had the whole city talking about him. The thing was, he'd always promised her and the rest of the team that his success was their success. She'd bought into it, hook, line and sinker. She'd loved being part of something so exciting, and for a while there it had felt like nothing could hold them back.

As it turned out, she'd been right – nothing *could* hold Marco back – including the promises he'd made to them all. One swishy job offer later, and he dropped them without even flinching.

The minute Marco had signed on the dotted line, he'd casually wandered into the kitchen, gathered them all together and told them that he needed new inspiration and motivation. His old team? Well, they'd just hold him back. He wouldn't be needing them. He wouldn't be needing *her*. There hadn't been the slightest hint of an apology either. Nothing. Nada. Zilch.

Hattie winced and took another sip of water, though she struggled to swallow it. It was like sand in her mouth. She simply couldn't think about Marco and what he'd done without a jolt of pain running through her. All that hard work – for nothing.

'Bastard!' she muttered under her breath, frowning at her own bedraggled reflection in the window as the fields flashed past on the other side.

Hattie couldn't get over the fact she'd been such an idiot. She should have seen something like this coming, shouldn't she? The fact that she hadn't suspected a thing – not even for a second - well, it just made it a whole lot worse.

SANDWICHES IN SEABURY

When Lionel's letter arrived, her heart had lifted at the idea of getting away from it all. That was seconds before it sank again under the crushing weight of her failure. Because - she had to face it - running off to her great uncle's hotel wasn't exactly a triumphant career move, was it? It would be like admitting defeat, and Hattie refused to be defeated.

She'd spent several days at war with herself. Her heart kept yelling "yes – do it!". Moving to Seabury would solve so many problems. It would give her a place to live and, even better, a place to lick her wounds in peace. But her head? Her head kept stomping its angry little foot and shouting "no" – because moving to Seabury would be the biggest cop-out in the history of mankind. She should be busy talking to head-hunters and looking for a new position in the city. She needed to capitalise on her excellent reputation while people still remembered who she was. She definitely *shouldn't* be disappearing off for a break at the seaside!

The problem was that Hattie simply didn't have the energy to start from scratch again. Not after the hours she'd spent working to build Marco's reputation. Marco's restaurant. Marco's future. The thought of having to do it all over again while getting used to another delicate ego and fiery temper . . . well, it was just too much.

In the end, she ignored both her heart and her head and let her exhaustion make the decision for her. She would move to Seabury - just until she felt better. If it meant that she could help Uncle Lionel out at the same time - brilliant.

Hattie had expected to be more upset when it came to leaving London behind, but she hadn't felt a thing as she'd handed back the keys to her flat. As for saying goodbye to her life there… well, it had been one reality check too far when she'd realised that there wasn't a single person outside of work that she'd felt the need to say goodbye to.

No life. No friends. No job - and without that – no Hattie.

Hattie felt her lip starting to tremble and she bit it hard. She had a sneaking suspicion that if she gave in to tears, she might not be able to stop. She wasn't a cry-baby. It wasn't her style. But right now, she'd simply had enough.

She swallowed hard and stared around the carriage in a desperate attempt to distract herself from her doom-laden thoughts. Two seconds later, she promptly gave it up as a bad job. The guy opposite her was fast asleep with his hat pulled low over his face. The little old lady over in the corner was still busy knitting the longest scarf she'd ever seen in the most lurid shade of green. She'd been at it ever since Hattie'd hopped on the train.

Hattie sighed, boredom settling heavily on her shoulders as she went back to staring out of the window. Surely they must be nearly there by now? It was already mid-afternoon, and she was desperate to get off the train.

She glanced at her watch. She should be in the kitchen right now, making a start on the evening's prep – not on a train to her childhood holiday haunt! She sighed again and blinked hard. Bloody Marco throwing a bloody depth charge into her bloody life.

At long last, with the screaming screech of breaks on rails, the train finally ground to a halt. Hattie grabbed her handbag and pulled the strap over her shoulder. At the same time, a block of lead settled in her stomach. She should be in the kitchen. In her restaurant. In London.

This officially sucked.

Hattie unfolded from her seat with some difficulty. Every single one of her joints seemed to be locked up from being cramped into the tiny space for so long. She reached up and hauled her suitcase down from the rack, grunting at the weight of it before dumping it unceremoniously on the floor. She tilted it onto its wheels and began to shove it towards the carriage doors.

Doing her best not to stumble as the waves of tiredness ramped up a notch, Hattie hefted her case down the steep train steps onto the tiny platform. She put some distance between herself and the train before pausing to look one way and then the other.

It was a short platform. The station itself was a minuscule, white-painted, wooden affair that was very clearly closed. Other than the bright, blinking lights of the self-serve ticket machine that stood against the wooden wall, the place looked like it belonged in the 1950s.

'Toto, I've a feeling we're not in Kansas anymore,' she muttered.

What on earth was she doing here?

This really did have to be the worst day of her entire life. All her dreams of running her own restaurant had gone up in smoke, and here she was with her tail between her legs, running off to hide in Seabury.

She had to face facts – she'd never been further from her dream than she was in this moment. She'd given it everything she had, and what did she have to show for all those hours quite literally slaving away over a hot stove? Precisely zero. All those hours. All that work. Wasted.

Hattie blinked hard. She guessed that this was what "rock-bottom" felt like. The only thing that could make things any worse right now would be if she fell in love. That would be a disaster. The icing on the cake, the cherry on top, the thunderbolt from the blue that would prove to be the nail in the coffin. Love didn't have any kind of a place in her life. Not while she was still chasing her big dream. It would just get in the way.

Hattie let out a little laugh that sounded more like a sob. Considering there hadn't been the slightest sniff of romance for years, at least she knew she was worrying about nothing.

She gave herself a little shake, stood up straighter and tried to let the train-weariness leave her body. It was like trying to pull her feet out of quick-drying cement. It was time to make her way to The Pebble Street Hotel before she fell asleep right here on the platform edge.

Wrapping her fingers firmly around the handle of her suitcase, she headed towards the station exit and made her way out onto the little side street behind.

'Balls.'

She stared up and down the narrow stretch of road, but there wasn't a taxi in sight. There wasn't even a rank where she could wait for one to appear. Hattie frowned. She'd simply have to look for another way to reach the end of her journey.

There might not be any taxies in sight, but there was a big old bus parked a little further along the street. It looked more like it belonged at a vintage fair or steam rally than here, outside the station. Hattie guessed that it was probably some kind of tourist attraction – but maybe there'd be someone on there who could help.

As she made her way closer, she stared at its glossy red curves. It looked strangely familiar. In fact, it looked exactly like the bus that had trundled along Seabury's seafront all those years ago. The one she liked to race while waving to the driver in his smart flat cap. He'd always waved back to her before making his way to his final stop at North Beach. From there, he'd head over to Nana's Ice Cream Parlour for a treat before making his return journey.

A shiver ran down Hattie's spine. She suddenly felt like she'd stepped back in time. Memories of those long, hot summer days on Seabury's beaches pushed their way past her worries, floating to the surface and bringing an unconscious smile to her face.

Despite how tired and sad she was feeling, a little bubble of hope lodged in Hattie's chest. It was time to get to Seabury. Her memories were calling her home.

CHAPTER 3

The sight that greeted Hattie as she approached the open door of the old bus wasn't exactly what she'd been expecting. Instead of an ancient, flat-capped volunteer ready to greet her with a handful of leaflets, she was faced with two long, denim-clad legs that led to a pair of scuffed old trainers resting on the dashboard. The driver's top half was completely hidden behind a massive newspaper.

Hattie stood for a moment, wondering whether to disturb him. Well, she couldn't stand here forever – it was time to ask for some directions – and this looked to be her best bet. She cleared her throat.

Down went the pair of feet and up came a rather surprised face from behind the newspaper.

'Hi!' said Hattie.

'Hullo,' said the guy, staring at her in surprise and

reaching up to push a tousled mop of blond, beachy waves out of his face. 'I'm sorry – I didn't realise you were there.' He looked her up and down. 'You look... lost?'

Hattie gave a little shrug and tried to ignore the heat that was rising to her face. If only he knew how accurate that was!

She stared at him as he got to his feet. He was long and lean, with a definite twinkle in his eye. Hattie swallowed. What had she just been telling herself? Don't fall in love. So the fact that this random stranger's nice, friendly smile was making her stomach do strange things set alarm bells ringing.

If she wasn't so tired, she'd probably burst into tears right now out of sheer confusion. Instead, she just kept staring at him, hoping against hope that he might have something sensible to say – because she sure as hell didn't.

The guy quirked an eyebrow at her as he ambled down the steps and joined her on the pavement. He looked to be about her age and, like the bus, was . . . strangely familiar.

'Erm,' she mumbled at last, unable to stand the silence any longer, 'can you tell me where I can find the . . . erm . . . *normal* bus stop?'

'Not sure about normal,' he laughed. 'Where are you off to?'

'Seabury.'

'Then this *is* the normal bus stop,' he grinned.

SANDWICHES IN SEABURY

'I mean a proper bus. Not a tourist one,' she muttered, feeling awkward.

'This is the one and only bus to Seabury,' he said, 'though, as you can see, there's not much call for it at this time of year!'

'Oh,' said Hattie, glancing up at the bus windows. Sure enough, it was empty.

'If I'm being completely honest – there's not much call for it at any time of year. No one really comes to Dunscombe and then wants to go on to Seabury!' he said.

Hattie shrugged again. 'I missed the train to Plymouth, so I had to come here.'

'Ah – that explains it,' said the driver. 'Well, you're in luck – I can take you to Seabury.'

Hattie let out a long sigh of relief. 'Great. Okay, so what time do you leave?'

'Anytime you want,' he said with a little shrug.

Gah! She wasn't in the mood for cutesy banter. 'I'm serious, I just need to get-'

'Where in Seabury are you headed?' he interrupted.

'The Pebble Street Hotel,' said Hattie.

'Oh. My. Goodness!' he said, looking her up and down.

Hattie took an involuntary step backwards.

'You're Hattie Barclay, aren't you?' he said.

Hattie raised her eyebrows. 'Yes?' she said, not sounding quite so sure about the fact as she usually did.

'I *thought* I knew your face! Lionel mentioned you were on your way. We just didn't really expect to see you so soon – the last time I saw him he said you were coming at the weekend?'

'Yeah, well - I needed to get out of London,' muttered Hattie.

She wasn't being deliberately rude, but she didn't really want to get into the finer details of her imploded life right now. Not in front of this random stranger, at least. She didn't know him, after all, and the last thing she could do with was the whole of Seabury discussing her arrival. Though, from what he'd just said, it sounded like it might be a bit late for that already.

'I'm Ben,' he said, holding his hand out for her to shake.

Hattie looked at him in surprise but then, out of sheer automatic, British politeness, took it.

She didn't know if it was because she was so tired, but as she stared into Ben's blue-green eyes, something kindled inside her. The memories of long distant days, summer sun, and eating ice cream on the beach came rushing in again.

'Do we know each other?' she asked, frowning.

'Well,' he chuckled, 'I was about to ask if you remembered me! We used to play together when you came down here on holiday.'

Hattie's jaw dropped in surprise.

Oh crap.

This was bad.

Really bad.

'Ben Yolland?' she breathed.

So, it was definite then. Coming back to Seabury was the worst idea in the entire world.

Hattie remembered Ben only too well. She'd been in love with him from the moment she'd met him as a kid – mesmerised by his sandy, tousled blond hair and the golden freckles that used to bloom across the bridge of his nose where the sun kissed it.

Hattie peeped at his face. Yup, there they were – still there even though it was only late February – a sprinkling of freckles underneath his crinkling, kind eyes.

By the way her heart had started pounding and her hand was now sweating in his, nothing much had changed. Two decades might have passed since those summer days on the beach, but it seemed that Ben Yolland still had a strange effect on her.

'Sorry,' she said, quickly dropping his hand and nervously tucking a strand of hair behind her ear. It was a childish gesture and by the sly smile Ben was giving her, it looked like it was one he hadn't forgotten.

Hattie cleared her throat awkwardly. 'So, Ben,' she said, grabbing the handle of her case and beginning to drag it towards the door of the bus.

'Here, let me!' said Ben, quickly taking the

handle from her, hefting the heavy case up the steps and easily lifting it onto the old-fashioned luggage rack.

'Erm, thanks,' she said, following him in a strange kind of daze. 'So, erm... you drive buses now?' She could have kicked herself – what a stupid question. Of course he drove the bus - why the hell else would he be here?

Ben just grinned at her. 'Well, to be honest I'm just doing a favour for my old dad today. He usually drives the bus, but he's at the dentist.'

'Oh,' said Hattie, feeling even more stupid for some reason. 'Poor him!' she added lamely.

Ben shrugged. 'It's just a check-up, but I said I'd cover for him.'

'Oh,' said Hattie again.

She'd forgotten what it was like down here. Everyone shared everything about everybody. She'd been here a matter of seconds and already knew that Ben's dad was at the dentist. No doubt the entire town and everyone who lived within a ten-mile radius would know that she'd lost her job. Lost her dreams. She'd been completely deluded that she could come down here to escape her worries – the whole of Seabury would be in on it!

She just needed to go to sleep in a darkened room for as long as humanly possible. Maybe when she woke up, everyone would be kind enough to let her forget that she was a big, fat failure for a while.

'So – one ticket to Seabury?' asked Ben, settling himself back into the driver's seat.

'Yes. Single please,' said Hattie, coming out of her daze and rummaging in her pocket for her wallet.

'You know,' said Ben, 'a return ticket would be cheaper.'

'I don't want a return,' said Hattie. 'I'll have a single please.'

'Or I could give you an extended return if you'd prefer. That's if you want to stay longer than three days – but then that does cost a bit more than a single.'

'I'll just have a single please,' she repeated, doing her best not to grind her teeth or growl at him.

She didn't want a return. She didn't *need* a return. Her life was too much of a cock-up to ever want to go back to it. She wanted to hide. Preferably under a big fluffy duvet. She didn't want to think about returning to London.

'But the return is cheaper than a single,' he repeated slowly, looking at her as if she wasn't quite getting the message.

'Uh-huh. I'll have a single please,' she repeated for the third time.

'O-kay,' said Ben, looking bemused, 'message received. The lady wants a single.'

Hattie dug around in her wallet for the correct fare, doing her best to avoid making eye contact with him. In just a minute or two, she'd be able to disappear towards the back of the bus and this decidedly awkward and unexpected blast from the past would be over.

'So, erm – where in Seabury do you stop?' she asked, wondering how far she'd be forced to trudge with her case until she reached the hotel.

'Wherever you need me to,' said Ben with a smile as he triumphantly handed her a little paper ticket. 'It's not like I've got passengers coming out of my ears here,' he added, gesturing back at the empty bus. 'I can drop you right to the hotel if you'd like?'

'Perfect.' At least that was one bit of good news. 'Right outside the hotel would be great.'

'Alright then!' said Ben. 'Grab that seat there and you can fill me in on what's been happening in the last ... oh ... twenty years!' he grinned.

Hattie let out a resigned sigh. So much for being able to sneak off for a quick snooze on the back seat until they reached Seabury!

With one last wistful glance towards the back of the bus, she plonked herself on the front passenger seat, close enough to chat to Ben. Even in her exhausted, sad and befuddled state, her treacherous heart was doing a little jig about the fact that he wanted to talk to her. Ben Yolland wanted to talk to *her*. She could feel her inner eight-year-old squirming with pleasure.

'Right – all aboard!' said Ben, turning the key in

the ignition and letting out a little whoop as the bus rumbled to life.

Hattie bit back a smile. This really *was* a bit like time travel – Ben was still the same happy, cheery, unashamedly sunny little boy she remembered from all those years ago. Only now... he wasn't so little, was he?

Hattie did her best not to ogle Ben as he carefully navigated his way out of Dunscombe Sands. Instead, she kept her eyes trained on the quaint cottages and narrow streets that soon gave way to views of the Devon hills and deep, coastal valleys as they flitted past the windows.

'You know,' said Ben, breaking the silence at last, 'everyone in Seabury's really excited that a proper chef's coming to town!'

Hattie peeled her eyes from the window and glanced at him. Her stomach performed an involuntary back-flip.

'They are?' she said weakly.

'Of course!' laughed Ben. 'Lionel hasn't stopped talking about it for days – ever since you agreed to come!'

Hattie shot Ben a weak smile as a sinking sensation took over from the backflip. This news should make her happy, shouldn't it? The fact that she was heading somewhere where people were looking forward to her arrival should be a boost! So why did she suddenly feel so wretched?

It didn't take a genius to work that out though. The simple fact of the matter was that she wasn't intending to stay in Seabury long-term. No matter how much she dreaded going back to London, she was just in Seabury long enough to regroup, get her head back together and give Lionel a hand at the hotel while she was at it. When it came time to leave, would she have to break Lionel's heart, just like Marco had broken hers?

'I can't wait to get started,' said Hattie weakly.

'Once more - this time with energy!' said Ben, glancing at her quickly with his eyebrows raised.

Hattie forced a smile onto her tired face.

'You just need an ice cream from Nana's and the feel of sand between your toes again,' said Ben. 'It'll be fine, you'll see. Seabury will work its magic on you.'

Hattie gave him a stiff little nod. The last thing she needed was for Seabury to work its magic on her. After all, there was no way she'd ever reach her dream of running her own restaurant if she stayed working in a small seaside hotel that no one had ever heard of, was there?

CHAPTER 4

'There ya go!' said Ben, plonking her case down on the pavement in front of The Pebble Street Hotel and turning to grin at her.

'Thanks so much,' said Hattie awkwardly. She wasn't used to gorgeous men coming over all chivalrous around her – but then, she was that exhausted she didn't have the energy to argue.

'Well, Hattie Barclay,' said Ben, shooting a cheeky grin at her as she did her best to bite back a yawn that was fighting to escape, 'it's been lovely catching up with you! I guess I'll be seeing you around.'

Hattie nodded dumbly and watched as he turned, bounded up the steps back onto the bus and settled into his place behind the steering wheel.

Hattie raised her hand and waved as he pulled the lever to close the doors with a gentle *clonk*. She was surprised to feel a sharp pang of regret as she watched him pull away and head towards North Beach. Despite her current status as *officially the most knackered person in England*, part of her wished that she could have stayed gossiping with Ben a little bit longer.

After the initial awkwardness had passed, the journey from Dunscombe Sands had turned out to be a cheerful, sunny end to a long and painful journey. Ben had chatted away about summers long gone by as they'd whizzed through the early-spring lanes towards Seabury.

It hadn't taken long before they'd both reverted to the eight-year-old's banter that had been the mainstay of their summers so long ago. Ben's company had awoken some long-dormant memories of the fresh sea air ruffling her hair and the feeling of sand between her toes. As she watched him drive away, she found she wanted to hear more – to remember more.

Hattie sighed. Ben had said "see you around" but somehow, she guessed that wasn't very likely. Her heart sank and for a moment the urge to burst into tears reappeared out of nowhere, nearly overwhelming her.

Hattie took a deep, steadying breath, and as her lungs filled with salty sea air, her heart lifted again. She felt a bit like she'd turned into an emotional yoyo. But this *was* Seabury after all, not London. Everyone bumped into everyone down here – so she was *bound* to see Ben again, wasn't she? From what she remembered and from the stories Lionel had told her over the years, this was a tiny town full of people who thought of themselves as some kind of weird, extended family. With any luck, it would be almost impossible to avoid him!

This realisation stirred Hattie into action. It was time to get inside the hotel and have a rest. She was exhausted – and as much as she'd enjoyed catching up with Ben, the idea of making small-talk with any more of Seabury's inhabitants when she was struggling to string a sentence together wasn't appealing.

Things were already bad enough. It was the first time Ben had seen her in two decades, and she probably looked like she'd been dragged through a hedge – or, in fact, a whole forest of hedges – backwards. What a lovely impression to leave him with!

Picking up her case, she strode down the short path towards the front door of the hotel. Grasping the large, brass knob, she turned it. It didn't budge. It was either locked . . . or maybe just stuck? She gave it another shove for good measure, but it was a no-go. Definitely locked.

Taking a step back, Hattie looked around and only then noticed the sign that had been blu-tacked into the front window. In a bold, black script someone had typed *Under New Management*. Underneath this, scrawled in blue biro were the words *Sorry - we're closed.*

All she wanted to do was crawl into bed and fall asleep – preferably for several weeks – but now it looked like she'd have to go and hunt Lionel down first.

She doubted it'd take her too long to find him. He was bound to be on one of the beaches or, failing that, in The Sardine. Hattie glanced at her watch. Hmm, given the time of day she had a sneaking suspicion that one of the beaches was more likely. The question was, which one should she try first?

The Pebble Street Hotel was slap bang between them, sitting proudly in the middle of Seabury with The King's Nose extending out into sea behind it. This grassy, rocky outcrop separated the two beaches. Hattie could just as easily head straight to the pebbly shores of North Beach or work her way back along the road towards West Beach, with its coating of golden sand.

West Beach had always been her favourite as a kid. There had been nothing better than stripping off her shoes and socks and leaving them in an abandoned heap while she dug her feet into the soft mounds of warm sand. Hattie could remember paddling up to her knees, watching mesmerised as the gentle waves lapped at her skin.

That settled it. She'd try West Beach first – but she was damned if she was going to drag her case all the way there and back again. She'd leave it here, nestled down under the short hedge that separated the hotel from the pavement. This was Seabury after all - no one was going to pinch it.

Straightening up, Hattie made her way back onto the pavement and turned towards West Beach. Maybe if she couldn't find Lionel there, she'd nip into The Sardine. Her uncle always spoke so fondly of the little seafront café. Right now, she could do with a cappuccino if she was going to have to wander all over town searching for him.

Hattie set off at a pace, but as the gentle sea breeze smoothed back her hair and she listened to the gulls calling overhead, her mission felt a little bit less urgent than a few seconds ago.

It had been a really long time since she'd last visited the town – not since those magical summer holidays in fact - but very little seemed to have changed. The air still had its trademark, salty tang that felt like a balm to her frayed nerves. She could hear the sea calmly shushing itself as she wandered along.

Hattie paused briefly, wrapping her hands around the metal railings that separated the pavement from the drop down onto the beach. She raised her face to the blue sky and stood for a moment just watching the white, fluffy clouds drifting lazily along as the gulls wheeled on the wind and called to each other.

When was the last time she'd stood still like this and just watched? She honestly couldn't remember. Hattie let go of the railings and wrapped her arms around herself, trying to find a bit of extra warmth against the breeze that was whipping up from the sea. When they'd passed The Sardine on the bus, she'd noticed a few customers lingering at its pavement tables. She suddenly had a newfound respect for those brave souls. It might be late February, but the air still had a chill to it.

Hattie rubbed at her arms and wished she'd thought to grab her jacket from her case before she'd set off on this wild goose chase.

'Time to get moving!' she muttered. Standing around looking at the view was all well and good – but not so great if you turned into a human popsicle while you were at it!

Hattie dropped her hands, still unable to tear her eyes away from the waves. Then a cold – slightly wet – nudge at her fingertips made her jump.

Peering down, she found a large, rather fluffy dog staring straight back at her. Hattie broke into a delighted smile as his amber eyebrows wiggled slightly above his soulful, dark brown eyes.

'Who are you?' she cooed, offering the back of her hand for the giant, fluffy newcomer to sniff. He was absolutely massive and made her think of a big, friendly bear as he snuffled at her hand before giving it a lick. 'You taking yourself for a walk?' she asked, glancing around to check if there was an owner anywhere in sight. But no – it was just her and this big black, white and tan fur-ball.

'Where are you off to, eh?' she said, stroking the huge, glossy head gently and earning herself several wags of the dog's feathery tail. Her fingers found a collar and she bent low to read the little disc attached.

'Stanley?' she asked. The dog wagged his tail harder. Hattie looked back down and spotted a mobile number on the back of the little disc. Stanley took a few steps away from her before turning back as if to ask - *are you coming, or what?!*

'Okay – let's see if your owner is down on the beach,' she laughed – as that's clearly where he was going. 'If not we'll go and get my mobile out of my case and I'm dobbing you in!'

The dog just stared at her, politely waiting for her to catch up.

The minute the pair of them reached the first set of steps that lead down onto West Beach, Stanley scurried down ahead of her and hurtled along the sand at top speed, darting straight towards the sea, his tail wagging madly.

Hattie couldn't help but giggle as she watched him pile into the water, jumping over the waves and snapping at seaweed before beginning to swim in earnest.

'Rather you than me, Stanley lad!'

The call came from one of two deckchairs that were placed a little way down the beach towards the shoreline.

Hattie grinned. She'd recognise that voice anywhere – it *had* to be her Uncle Lionel and – even better - it sounded like he knew her furry walking companion.

'Stanley – don't you go getting too far out now!' called the occupant of the second chair.

Hattie looked down to where Stanley was now blissfully splashing through the waves, having reluctantly turned back towards the beach. She began to make her way towards the chairs, and as she drew nearer, she saw that both gents were wrapped in blankets and wearing woolly hats. They each had a steaming mug of coffee and seemed to be tucking into whopping great big slices of cake too. To finish off this idyllic little scene – there was a painter's easel complete with canvas set up in front of each of them. Clearly, her uncle was in the middle of giving a painting lesson to his companion.

A huge part of Hattie wanted to sneak up on the pair of them so that she could check out their paintings without being spotted, but right at that moment, as if sensing her presence, Lionel turned his head and spotted her.

'Hattie!' he cried, his face splitting into a huge smile. He scrambled out of his deckchair with some difficulty, sending his blanket flying and knocking over the thermos flask that sat at his feet in the process.

Hattie returned his smile with interest and

hurried forward to give her great uncle a hug. He'd always been like a grandad to her, and as he wrapped his arms around her, Hattie found herself surrounded by the scent of paints and turps and varnish and oils. It smelled just like her uncle had always smelled - of childhood and happiness.

Hattie had to swallow down an unexpected lump of emotion as Lionel pulled away and peered into her face.

'All okay?' he asked gently.

Hattie nodded quickly and rubbed her eyes, willing the tears not to fall. 'All okay,' she said with a wobbly smile. 'It's so good to see you.'

'You too, my dear! I wasn't sure when you were going to arrive – sorry I wasn't there to greet you but I'd promised Charlie a little lesson.'

Hattie peered at her uncle's companion and recognised him instantly as Charlie Endicott. She might not have seen him since she was a little girl, but Lionel's best friend still had the same kind face, gnarly hands and bushy eyebrows he always had.

'Charlie,' said Lionel, 'this is my niece - or my *great*-niece, I should say. Hattie.'

'Well, well, well. You're all grown up, eh lass?!' said Charlie, giving her a warm smile, his eyes crinkling at the corners.

'It's been a while,' said Hattie, feeling a slight pang of guilt as she reached out and shook Charlie's hand across her uncle's vacated chair.

'That it has. So, you've come back to be our new, super-duper chef I hear?' said Charlie.

Hattie felt the warmth rise to her face despite the chilly breeze that was still blowing up from the sea.

'Erm,' she said uncertainly. 'Well, yes.' She wasn't really sure what else to say. 'What are you both working on?' she said, deciding to change the subject and nodding at the half-finished paintings on the easels.

'Your poor uncle's trying to teach me to paint,' said Charlie with a rueful grin. 'I keep telling him he's on a hiding to nothing, but he refuses to give up.'

'Charlie is doing brilliantly,' said Lionel, with a smile, patting his friend firmly on the shoulder. 'He's just having a little bit of trouble with his sea and sky all blending into one, that's all.'

Hattie looked over Charlie's shoulder at his work in progress. 'I like it,' she said.

Charlie turned and grinned at her, giving her his patented nod of approval that she recognised from all those years ago.

'Anyway,' said Charlie, 'I think that's enough painting for me for today. Hattie, it's lovely to have you back. Now, I'd better go and retrieve Stanley from the sea before he manages to find a seal to play with.'

'Who does he belong to?' asked Hattie, watching Stanley as he paddled around in circles, dragging a piece of seaweed with him.

SANDWICHES IN SEABURY

'He lives with Kate – up at The Sardine,' said Lionel as they watched Charlie striding down towards the water's edge.

'Ah! So, he isn't far from home, then!' said Hattie in relief. 'He just appeared and kind of escorted me down here!'

Lionel laughed. 'Sounds like our Stanley. He might live with Kate – but that dog is welcome everywhere he goes. He's probably the most popular resident in Seabury!'

'I can understand that,' said Hattie with a smile which turned into a huge yawn without any warning.

'My poor girl,' said Lionel, throwing a concerned glance at her. 'You must be so tired after your trip. Let me quickly pack our things up here and we'll get going. I won't be a moment – Charlie's got his truck, so he'll load everything in the back and drop it over later – after he's walked Stanley to the café!'

Hattie nodded, wrapping her arms around herself again. She felt a bit guilty for breaking up their lesson, but the waves of exhaustion were back with a vengeance and not even the lovely blue sky, sea air nor the sound of the gulls was going to be able to keep her awake and on her feet for much longer.

'All set,' said Lionel a few moments later as he pulled an old duffel bag onto one shoulder. 'Here,' he said, and taking Hattie's hand, he tucked it into the crook of his elbow. 'Let's get you home.'

CHAPTER 5

Hattie was certainly grateful to lean on Lionel's arm as they made their way back up the beach. Every step across the sand was taking some serious effort, and her ears had started to do some kind of funny ringing thing.

'It really is very good to see you,' said Lionel, 'I know you said you might come early, but I hadn't really expected you to arrive until the weekend.'

Hattie smiled sleepily as Ben's words came back to her. 'Yes,' she said, 'Ben already mentioned that.'

'Oh, you've bumped into Ben already?' said Lionel, looking delighted. 'Well, nice to see where your priorities lie, young lady,' he laughed, elbowing her playfully in the ribs. In her befuddled state, the gentle nudge nearly knocked her flying.

'Ben first and *then* your old uncle! So, did he

remember you from when you were little?' he asked, curiously.

Hattie nodded, unable to stop the treacherous smile from spreading across her face. 'Yep, and I remember him too.'

'Of course you do!' chuckled Lionel, letting go of her arm so that he could bound up the little stone steps that led off the sand and onto the pavement. He turned back at the top and offered Hattie a hand, which she took gratefully.

'What's that supposed to mean?' she puffed, finally finding the steadying influence of the pavement beneath her feet.

'I seem to remember you were head over heels about him when you were little!' said Lionel. 'You'd come back to the hotel after a day out and about running riot with your little group of friends, and all I could ever get out of you was *Ben this* and *Ben that!*'

'Whatever you do, don't you dare go spreading that little rumour around Seabury!' muttered Hattie shooting a warning glare at Lionel that she promptly spoiled with a grin.

'As if I would!' said, Lionel, looking affronted before winking at her. 'Anyway, there would be no point spreading it around - everyone remembers you and Ben!'

'That's a real comfort!' laughed Hattie, squeezing Lionel's arm as they ambled their way back towards the hotel.

'I have to say,' said Lionel, hastily changing the subject, 'thank you so much for accepting my offer and coming back to Seabury. I'm so excited that we're going to be working on this project together.'

Hattie nodded, and a swoop of something ominous went through her. Nerves? Dread? Disappointment? She was too tired to be certain, but she didn't want her uncle picking up on it, that was for sure. She forced a smile and nodded. She wasn't exactly sure that "exciting" was the word she'd use, but working with Lionel should offer her a little bit of peace and quiet. Something controllable, with a distinct lack of egotistical maniacs to deal with. When she thought about it like that, the whole thing sounded pretty blissful!

'I can't believe Veronica's gone,' she said, deciding to change the subject onto something safer.

'You and the rest of the town,' said Lionel. 'She caused quite the ruckus, I have to say.'

'Why?' asked Hattie, her eyes lighting up. She'd heard a part of the tale from her uncle already but couldn't resist getting the full story of the downfall of her childhood nemesis. Veronica had waged a long and furious war against her little band of friends, determined to put a stop to as much of their summertime fun as possible.

'Oh, she went and did a runner just before a wedding she'd booked at the hotel!' said Lionel. 'She'd just started to do the place up a bit. From what

I've been able to gather since, she promptly ran out of available funds and decided that the best way around it all was to make off with the bride and groom's hard-earned cash!'

'What happened?' gasped Hattie.

'What always happens in Seabury?' laughed Lionel. 'The entire town came together. The bride and groom had a wedding to remember – even if it wasn't *quite* the one they'd been expecting… and then I ended up buying a hotel!'

Hattie laughed. 'Something tells me there's quite a lot more to the story than that.'

'Well, now you come to mention it,' chuckled Lionel. 'But I'm guessing you need a rest and maybe even a cup of tea before I fill you in on all the little details?'

Hattie nodded. She did her best to stifle another huge yawn that came out of nowhere.

'How was your journey anyway?' asked Lionel. 'Nice and easy?'

'Bloody awful,' she said, raising an eyebrow. 'I missed the train to Plymouth.'

'Ah! That explains how you ended up in Dunscombe Sands then! I was wondering how you'd already managed to catch up with young Ben considering he's covering for his dad on the bus today.'

'Yep, I got a private tour all the way back to Seabury,' she said.

'That's not so bad then,' grinned Lionel. 'Right, here we are.'

They'd reached the front of The Pebble Street Hotel, and Hattie paused, watching as Lionel pulled a large old key from his pocket. 'What did you do with your luggage?' he asked.

'It's right there, under the hedge,' said Hattie. 'I thought it would be safe.'

'Well, yes, of course! This is Seabury,' he said, staring at her single case.

Hattie caught the concerned look on his face.

'Is that it?' he asked. 'Just the one bag?'

She nodded, feeling defensive. 'Yep, all my worldly possessions fit in this single suitcase.' She jutted her chin out defiantly. Somehow, admitting that sad fact out loud made her want to cry again. She couldn't meet her uncle's eye. Crikey, she needed to get a grip on herself!

She knew Lionel was one hundred per cent on her side – but she also knew that he'd be looking at her with pity in those kind old eyes of his, and right now she couldn't handle it. Normally, she'd be ready to defend her life choices of all-work-and-no-play, but after what had happened recently, nothing felt quite so certain anymore.

'Anyway,' said Lionel, 'let's get you inside and get that cup of tea. I want to show you around!'

He fitted the key into the lock and, with a clunk

followed by a long, low groan from the old hinges, pushed the door open.

Hattie dragged her case behind her into the foyer and stopped dead as the decades fell away again, just as they had when she'd spotted the old bus earlier.

Stepping inside The Pebble Street Hotel brought such a strong flood of memories cascading back that it nearly floored her. She could almost feel her old crabbing bucket in her hand instead of the handle of the suitcase. When it wasn't full of unsuspecting crabs, she'd fill it with shells from West Beach, a special pebble or dried starfish from North Beach, and maybe even a windmill from Doris at the Post Office. She'd loved those colourful windmills. In fact, she still did.

She peered around her. It was clear that her uncle had done his best to clean and clear everything up a bit – at least out here in the reception. But even from this vantage point, Hattie could see that the hotel had seen better days and would need quite a lot of TLC to get it back up to scratch.

Though the hallway floor gleamed and the reception desk was fairly clear of junk, there was an empty quality to the place. Maybe it was simply the current lack of guests that gave it this slightly abandoned air.

That said, Hattie's enduring memory of entering the hotel on her way up to her uncle's flat was the smell of Veronica's awful cooking. She'd always done her best to hold her breath as she ran upstairs –

taking the steps two at a time in a bid to outrun the stench of over-cooked cabbage.

'I know she's not quite at her best, but I've got great plans for the old girl,' said Lionel, patting the wall gently, as if trying to spare the hotel's feelings.

'It always was a beautiful building,' said Hattie, choosing her words carefully, 'but . . . it is an *awful* lot for you to do on your own, Lionel.'

'Haha, see that's my cunning plan!' he said, with a grin and a triumphant clap of his hands. 'Now that you're here, I'm not on my own, am I?'

Hattie smiled at her uncle while doing her best to ignore the sinking sensation somewhere near her heart. She adored Lionel and hated the idea of letting him down. Staying at The Pebble Street Hotel wasn't her long-term plan, but leaving would feel like abandoning him.

Sure, she'd be here to help him get things going, but there was no way she could stay in Seabury for too long, not if she wanted to save her career. No one would take her seriously as a chef if she spent too long in a town no one ever came to.

'Anyway,' said Lionel, 'Veronica had already got some of the work in the dining room done before she did her runner. That's where we held the wedding. So the flooring in there's been restored beautifully and everything's has had a lick of paint. That's probably the least grotty of all the rooms.

'What used to be the old Breakfast Lounge has

also been tidied and had a good clean. We pilfered bits of furniture from around the rest of the hotel. It's all a little bit mismatched, but it works okay. But the rest of it . . . well, the rest of it's still a total mess, if I'm honest… and that's just this floor. Don't even get me started on upstairs!'

Hattie nodded along but, by this point, she was feeling totally dazed. She'd love nothing more than to explore the entire hotel with her uncle, but maybe after she'd had a chance to sit down. Or preferably lie down. In a darkened room. Under a blanket. For a few weeks.

'I really want to bring back some of that old-school charm the place used to have,' said Lionel. 'Do you remember that touch of elegance it used to have? You could still just about feel it here even after Veronica had got her claws into the place. Ooh yes, I've got big plans for the old girl, but it's all going to take some time.'

Hattie nodded, glancing around her. She wondered if she could maybe just sink down onto the wooden chair behind the reception desk and rest her eyes for a moment. It was now as much as she could do to keep them from drifting closed.

'Oh Hattie,' said Lionel as he turned to her, his eyes widening, 'you must be exhausted.'

She must look an absolute state to elicit that kind of look! Hattie shrugged, desperate not to upset her lovely uncle, but she knew she'd been rumbled. There was no way she could disguise how knackered she felt.

'I'm so sorry,' said Lionel. 'Here's me rambling on when what you really need is a sit-down. Come on, let me take you up to your room – we'll do the grand tour when you've had forty winks!'

Before she could stop him, Lionel had eased her case from her unsuspecting grip and was on his way up the stairs. Hattie was just about to argue that she'd love to have a look around first, but instead her shoulders slumped, and she gave in. With what felt like a huge effort, she started to follow him up the stairs.

'Here we are,' said Lionel, coming to a stop in front of the door to room 13 on the first floor.

Hattie eyed the tarnished number, and in her bleary, barely-awake state hoped against hope that it wasn't an omen for her time here in Seabury.

'I hope you'll like your room,' said Lionel, pulling a small key from his pocket and unlocking it for her. 'I've done my best to make it as comfortable for you as possible. It's got one of the better mattresses - Charlie helped me bring it down from the top floor. I don't think it's been used much, to be honest with you.'

Lionel pushed the door open and then stepped back to allow Hattie to go ahead of him. She took two steps into the room and then stopped. It was full of light and fresh air. The window, which was still open a crack to let in the breeze, faced out to sea.

Abandoning her case, she wandered over and looked out. She could see The King's Nose and had views right over West Beach to one side and North Beach to the other. Looking down, she spotted a marmalade jar full of wildflowers sitting on the window sill. Hattie smiled and reached out a finger to brush a tiny purple bloom.

'I picked those for you earlier,' said Lionel.

Hattie turned to him with a smile.

'I love them, thank you!' she said.

'I want you to feel welcome here. This is your home now, Hattie!'

Hattie swallowed hard. There it was again, that little squirm of discomfort in her stomach. She really needed to talk to Lionel about her long-term plans or, more to the point, her lack of long-term plans when it came to Seabury – before things got any further. But she simply couldn't face it right now.

'Thank you for asking me here,' she said, 'and for believing in me.' She felt her lip starting to wobble and bit it.

Lionel smiled at her and patted her gently on the shoulder. 'I'll leave you to get some rest,' he said. 'If you need anything at all, just let me know.'

The minute Lionel had closed the door behind him, Hattie stripped off her shoes, jeans and jumper.

Leaving them in a heap on the floor, she crawled up onto the bed. Within seconds she'd wriggled down under the duvet cover and snuggled into the mound of fluffy pillows. Her eyes drifted closed as the sea started to sing her a lullaby.

CHAPTER 6

Hattie let out a monstrous yawn, stretching her arms above her head before falling back onto her ridiculously comfortable bed. That had to have been the longest sleep of her entire life. It had certainly been the deepest.

She guessed that was the joy of being out of the city and next to the sea again. Nothing quite sent you off for a long, hard sleep like the sound of the waves breaking just below your bedroom window.

Hattie was so warm and cosy, she was seriously considering rolling over and nabbing another ten minutes of snooze time. She'd been having a wonderful dream that was already beginning to melt away. Just ten more minutes… But no! It was time to get up and figure out exactly what she'd let herself in for here at Pebble Street.

Hattie scrambled up to a sitting position, hugging

her knees to her chest and peering around her brand-new bedroom. She hadn't really taken it in when she'd arrived – she'd been too tired and eager to finally fall into bed. But now, with the soft morning light making its way around the edges of the curtains, she was able to take stock a bit.

The room was clean and bright, but there was no getting away from the fact that it was all a little bit tired around the edges. Both the curtains and the carpet were looking a bit threadbare, and it could certainly do with a lick of paint and some new soft furnishings to tart it up a bit.

Hattie hopped out of bed and wandered through to the ensuite. Hmm – this had seen better days too. One good thing - the bath was absolutely massive! She was looking forward to testing that out with the longest, bubbliest soak she'd ever treated herself to! At least there was a plug for both the bath and the sink – clearly brand new – and a stack of fresh, new flannels and towels on a little chair near the door.

Hattie went over to the basin and peered down at the soap on the old-fashioned dish. Although it was still wrapped in some kind of waxed paper, it must have been left over from the hotel's previous incarnation – it was ancient! But then, soap didn't go off… or did it?!

Deciding not to risk it, Hattie dashed back through to the bedroom, unzipped her case and grabbed her wash bag where she'd stashed her bathroom basics. Right... it was time to brave the shower.

She hopped tentatively into the bath, pulled the curtain around her and turned the large silver tap. The shower-head began to trickle lazily and Hattie laughed – clearly, the water pressure was still just as bad as it had been when she was a kid. At least the water warmed up relatively quickly though.

Drying herself on one of the voluminous new towels was a bit of an ordeal. It might be super-fluffy, but it seemed to be simply moving the water around rather than actually drying her off at all. Hattie would gladly put money on the fact that she'd probably air-dry faster.

Finally, it was time to pull on some fresh clothes. She didn't really have many – she'd spent most of the last eighteen months in her chef's whites. Her case contained a selection of tee shirts and a couple of pairs of jeans. She quickly pulled some on and then added her big old slouchy day-off sweater over the top. There – she was ready to face the world!

Hattie marched over to the window, drew the curtains and let out a gasp. She *really* hadn't appreciated how beautiful this was at first glance! She had the most amazing view over The King's Nose, the two beaches and the sea. It couldn't be further from the petrol station and the cemetery that her place had overlooked back in London.

With a huge smile spreading over her face, Hattie

wrapped her arms around herself and did a little jig as she watched the waves lapping gently at the pebbles of North Beach. She never thought she'd be back in Seabury after all these years – but here she was – and it was time to make it her home, even if it was just for a little while.

Hattie dashed for her bedroom door. Now that she wasn't partially comatose, she couldn't wait to have a proper look around.

As she reached the wide staircase that led down to the ground floor, she eyeballed the bannister sadly. It was covered in layer upon layer of paint. Gutted! This bannister had some serious memories attached to it - mainly ones at dizzying, high speed as she'd slid down the glossy wood all the way to the floor below. It used to drive Veronica mad – but then, that had been half the fun.

If only she could give it a go now – but Hattie had a feeling that the layers of paint would act a bit like Velcro on her skinny jeans. Shame!

Instead, she took the stairs two at a time. The question was, where was she going to find Lionel? She wasn't entirely sure what time it was, but it had to be fairly early in the day. Fingers crossed he hadn't already disappeared off out and about. Though, if he had, she had a sneaking suspicion that if she headed over to The Sardine, he was bound to turn up before too long. She'd start with the Breakfast Lounge and go from there.

Hattie made her way down the hallway, sticking her head into various rooms as she went. There was no doubt about it, although Lionel had clearly done his best to tidy the place up a bit, it still had an air of neglect about it. It looked like it had been cleaned through recently but definitely didn't look like it was ready to receive guests.

Hattie peeped in at the dining room as she went past. It did look to be in a much better state than the rest of the place – and it was *huge!*

The idea of filling this space with diners made her stomach flutter with nerves. She needed to find Lionel and get him to fill her in on exactly what his plans were – before she went into hyper-panic mode! Crossing the hallway, Hattie pushed the door open and stepped into the Breakfast Lounge.

The room wasn't quite as grim as she remembered. Her enduring memory of it was of Veronica's PVC tablecloths, a carpet sticky with the residue of years of dropped prune syrup, and filthy windows that were practically opaque.

Like the rest of the downstairs, it looked relatively clean. The windows had certainly been given a good wash – and she could only assume that the carpet had too, given that she hadn't yet lost a shoe to the prune-glue of years gone by.

There was an odd mishmash of furniture piled into the far side of the room – a couple of sofas, some dressing tables, an old writing bureau and an empty clothes rail. The walls were lined with the same ghastly pictures she remembered from childhood – terrible prints in garish colours. This side of the room was a lot clearer, and only held a couple of small tables.

'Hattie, there you are,' said Lionel, getting to his feet from behind the one nearest the large window and grinning at her. 'Can I tempt you with a little breakfast?'

Hattie sniffed the air enthusiastically. There was nothing quite like the scent of fresh, buttery toast when your stomach was growling. She strode quickly towards her uncle, nodding.

'Yes please!' she said, settling into the chair opposite him, 'I'm absolutely ravenous.'

'Well – I'm not surprised!' said Lionel, uncovering a rack full of warm, fresh toast. 'You *have* been asleep for two days!'

'Give over!' chuckled Hattie.

'I'm serious,' laughed Lionel. 'You arrived on Tuesday afternoon and it's now Thursday.'

Hattie stopped dead in the action of pilfering two massive slices of toast. 'I slept for *two* whole nights?'

Lionel grinned at her and nodded. 'We were about to send in a search party. You've been asleep for so long I was starting to get a bit worried! I got Ethel to look in on you yesterday – just to check you were okay. I hope you don't mind…'

'Mind? Of course I don't!' said Hattie, wide-eyed.

SANDWICHES IN SEABURY

'Hey – is that where the mystery cup of tea on my nightstand came from? And the Rich Tea biscuits?' she asked, suddenly remembering the random midnight-feast she'd discovered.

'Sounds about right,' laughed Lionel. 'I wouldn't normally do that – but you were so quiet I wanted to check you hadn't come down with some kind of lurgy.'

Hattie shook her head, feeling mortified.

'Anyway – Ethel told me that you were out for the count – sound asleep.'

'I'm so sorry,' said Hattie. 'I can't believe I slept straight through like that.'

'Don't apologise! You must have desperately needed the rest to sleep that deeply.'

Hattie nodded. 'I don't think I realised how tired I was, to be honest.' She smothered one of her toast slices in thick, yellow butter and took an embarrassingly large bite.

'Well – it's good you've had some kip. And there's no pressure or rush for you to get started. Have a break for a few days first.'

Hattie shook her head furiously, chewing as fast as she could so that she could tell her uncle that she couldn't wait to get started – but Lionel just laughed.

'You haven't changed,' he said, pouring her a cup of tea from the old-fashioned brown pot on the table. Hattie couldn't help but notice that both of their teacups were chipped – and the plate that was holding her toast had a fine crack across it.

'Thanks,' she said, picking up her tea and taking a sip. As she did so, she eyeballed her cutlery – it was tarnished and could do with a good clean and polish. Actually, what it *really* needed was dropping straight into the nearest bin.

'I know not everything's quite up to scratch,' said Lionel, clearly noticing that she was taking in every little detail. 'The whole hotel's in a pretty poor state. Veronica basically ran the place into the ground – especially towards the end. But I've got a plan – and that's why I asked you to come!'

Hattie didn't say anything. She didn't want to stop him in his tracks, so she nodded encouragingly as she made a start on her second slice of toast.

'As I said in my letter – I want to start serving evening meals here again. It'll bring people back. I mean, I've had a few visitors since I bought the place, but most people were happy to cancel when they found out it was going to be closed for a while.'

Hattie swallowed quickly. 'Wait – you *have* had some guests? What did you serve them?'

Lionel ducked his head slightly. 'Sandwiches,' he muttered.

Hattie's jaw dropped.

'In my defence,' said Lionel, before she could respond properly, 'they were very nice sandwiches. The bread was always fresh, and I made sure they always had a choice. The cheese was from a local farm just down the road. There were the classy ones with extra tomato, and then there were the ones with chutney. Plus, I had the really fancy ones with-'

'Don't tell me,' interrupted Hattie, 'with both tomato *and* chutney?'

'How did you guess?' he said with a sheepish smile. 'But I always made sure there was plenty of it because Veronica was a mean old trout, and I never wanted to be like that!'

Hattie reached across the table and patted her uncle's hand. 'Don't worry,' she said with a soft smile, 'you couldn't be even if you tried!'

'Thank you,' said Lionel, returning her smile. 'But I was never a chef. It's as much as I can do to manage to feed myself if I'm honest. I don't know anything about kitchens and all that malarkey. I've tended to get most of my grub over at The Sardine when I can.'

'Well,' said Hattie, leaning back with a sigh having already cleared her cracked plate, 'you don't need to worry about that now I'm here.'

'Thank heavens,' said Lionel with a grin.

'Question is – what am I going to find in the kitchen, eh?' she said, raising her eyebrows and preparing to hear the worst.

'Well, I can't pretend it's in a very good state,' Lionel sighed. 'The WI ladies blitzed it before the wedding – so it *looks* presentable on the surface.

Mike and Kate prepped a lot of the food in there, so the counters were cleaned down properly.'

'Well, that's got to be a positive start!' said Hattie, surprised that there was some good news.

'Don't get too excited,' said Lionel, his bushy eyebrows pulling together. 'I haven't ventured into the cupboards – and don't even get me started on that freezer – I dread to think what might be in there. Knowing Veronica, maybe a few bodies…'

Hattie spluttered and Lionel shot her a rueful smile.

'Look,' he said with a sigh, 'if it would be alright with you, I'd just really love to hand the whole sorry mess over to you to deal with as you see fit. The kitchen's your domain – your territory – and I want you to be completely happy with it. Of course, if I'm asking too much, I do understand.'

'It's not a problem,' said Hattie. She could feel the excitement blooming inside her. This would give her the chance to do things her way. Just the way she liked it. 'I like a challenge.'

CHAPTER 7

After breakfast, Lionel walked Hattie to the kitchen door. She'd never been inside it before. As a kid, it had been Veronica's lair – not that the woman had ever done any real cooking. She was notoriously stingy. When her menu said *rasher of bacon* it meant just that - one measly rasher.

If you opted for the cooked breakfast, you'd be treated to your one rasher along with the dubious delights of an egg that was old but just about edible… if you were lucky. On the side there would be toast, never bread – because then you'd be able to tell just how stale it was.

Veronica had one serious superpower though. She'd been able to cut a slice of bread so thinly that you could see your hand through it.

'Are you sure you want to start on this today?'

Lionel asked her again. 'It's your first day here… well… second, technically, as you were asleep for your first day.'

Hattie smirked at him. 'You're never going to let me live that down, are you?'

'You'd better believe it!' he laughed. 'Anyway, are you sure you want to start working straight away? You know, there's plenty of time if you'd prefer to take a few days off – get reacquainted with the town… unwind a bit?'

Hattie shook her head. Now that she was standing outside the kitchen – *her* kitchen – the excitement was surging in her stomach. She loved nothing more than a challenge and this would take her mind off everything that had happened back in London. She had a purpose again – even if, right now, that purpose was de-scuzzing the kitchen of The Pebble Street Hotel!

'I'm sure,' she said with a grin. 'And you really don't mind me doing what I need to do?'

'Mind? I'll be delighted!' said Lionel. 'This is your space now, Hattie. You're in charge. Make it your own. Do what you want.'

'Brilliant,' breathed Hattie.

'And… well… put it like this,' said Lionel, giving her a cheeky wink, 'I don't think you can make it any worse.'

Lionel gave Hattie a quick pat on the shoulder

followed by little salute before he disappeared back into the depths of the hotel. She took a deep breath and turned to stare at the closed kitchen door again, fighting a childish wriggle of fear that Veronica might be behind it. Of course, she *knew* that Veronica was safely on the other side of the world in Australia. Nevertheless, all these memories of the old trout were making her question why on earth she'd looked forward to summer holidays in Seabury so much.

Hattie took another big, deep, calming breath. If she was going to make a start she needed to get in there!

'Here goes nothing,' she muttered and pushed her way through the heavy door.

She paused and let the breath go in a long, slow whistle. On first appearances, it really didn't look that bad in here. It seemed to be relatively clean and tidy... but she wasn't going to let first impressions fool her. She'd been in enough kitchens to know that what she was looking at right now was just the superficial stuff.

If she really wanted to know how bad things were, the fridge was the place to check. If it was bad in there, then it was almost guaranteed that the rest of the kitchen would be a catastrophe too.

Hattie tiptoed over towards it as if trying not to alert Veronica's ghost to her presence in the kitchen, and gingerly opened the door.

'Huh!' she muttered, staring in surprise. It wasn't as bad as she'd been expecting. There was virtually nothing in there - a bottle of milk, some lovely looking local cheese, a bowl of fresh tomatoes and a jar of what looked to be homemade chutney. There was also a half-drunk bottle of Upper Bamton white wine sitting in the door.

Hattie sniffed. Bleach. It didn't take a detective to figure out that the fridge had been tidied up relatively recently. On closer inspection, there were stains on the plastic shelf at the bottom where something had dripped and rotted onto it. It must have been something strong to bend the wire shelves and melt the plastic like that!

Right. Riiiiiight. This was all clearly worse than she thought. The fridge might be clean and have some basics, but that probably meant the rest of the kitchen hadn't been touched. If the disaster-zone wasn't waiting for her in here, it must be elsewhere…

Hattie eyed the cupboard doors suspiciously. Dare she? Oh yes – she dared! Her fingertips were practically tingling, desperate to start throwing things away and get scrubbing.

She pulled open the door to the nearest set. Ah-ha – bingo. It was packed to the gunnels with an assortment of boxes, tubs and jars.

Hattie grabbed a couple of packets at random and pulled them down, wrinkling her nose at the weird combination of dust and grease they left on her fingertips. Okay – so supposedly the one in her right hand was meant to be oats. Nice and simple. She twisted it around, searching for the sell-by date. Ah. Right. More than a decade out of date. Opening the top of the pack of cornflakes, she grimaced. It was full of little beetles.

She plonked both packets down on the counter and pulled out more items, unearthing a rich seam of jars. Some of them had mould growing on the inside. Others had mould growing on the outside. She had to admit – it was all rather colourful and pretty – in a totally gross way!

Well – that decided it then. Everything was going to have to go. She started lifting jar after jar down, inspecting each one at arm's length. Some of them appeared to have dried up altogether and others had a congealed mass at the bottom that looked nothing like what was described on the label. In fact – the whole thing looked like some kind of ongoing science project. It was time to take urgent action!

Hattie turned and stared around the rest of the room. There had to be some rubber gloves and a roll of bin bags around here somewhere, didn't there? She crossed to the sink and opened the cupboard underneath. Bingo! There was all sorts of random rubbish piled up in there, but right at the front sat a fat roll of bags and a new pair of gloves still in their pack. God bless the WI – she guessed these were probably a leftover gift from their pre-wedding-blitz.

Reaching into her pocket for a hair elastic, Hattie pulled her chestnut mane back into a messy bun. Next, she tore several bin bags from the chunky roll and pulled on the marigolds, ready to get cracking.

Then, without further ado, she unceremoniously loaded the entire contents of the cupboard straight into the bin bags. Normally, she'd scrupulously wash all the jars out and make sure everything was separated so that it could be recycled properly. But desperate times called for desperate measures, and she quickly decided that this lot posed too much of a biohazard for that kind of behaviour.

As soon as it was empty, Hattie surveyed the cupboard. The shelves were sticky with goodness knows what. It could be anything – and didn't really bear thinking about – especially given how long they'd probably been like that. It would all need to be disinfected.

Before emptying the rest of the cupboards, Hattie decided to man-up and take a look inside the chest freezer. She knew that Lionel had been joking when he'd mentioned the possibility of dead bodies. That didn't stop her from wanting to check that there wasn't the potential for some awful horror story loitering in her new kitchen. The science experiments had been enough for her nerves to deal with!

Hattie tugged on the handle and struggled to force it open. Eventually, it gave way with rather a lot of crunching, and she peered inside with some trepidation.

Okay – the good news was that there didn't seem to be any bodies in there. Instead, there was more snow than the arctic and the entire thing looked like it was frozen solid. From the little patches of bags she could see through the top layer of snow, it seemed to be full of garden peas. Bags and bags of them. Who knew what was underneath – it'd be a while before she'd be able to tell!

Hattie knelt down and followed the sticky power cord back until she found the socket and promptly unplugged it. She'd leave the top propped open and it could begin to defrost – though heaven only knew how long that would take. She guessed she'd better source a whole heap of towels to soak up the mess once it got going though!

Hattie turned back to the cupboards and was just about to launch into emptying out the next set when the hairs on the back of her neck prickled. She whipped around, only to find that she had company.

'You look busy, dear!'

The woman, who was standing framed in the doorway, was holding two large cake tins and staring at the three black bin bags Hattie had already filled.

'You must be Hattie,' the newcomer continued, placing the tins down on a relatively clear patch of worktop. 'I'm Ethel.' She held out a hand and smiled as Hattie quickly whipped one of the already-grubby marigolds off so that she could shake it.

'Nice to meet you,' said Hattie.

'Lionel told Charlie that you like to get stuck in, but this is taking it one step too far, don't you think?' she laughed. 'I can't believe he's put you to work on your first day.'

Hattie smiled and shook her head. 'Ah, we can't blame Uncle Lionel for my workaholic tendencies. The minute he told me he had no idea what might be lurking in here behind the scenes, I couldn't resist getting started!'

'I can see that!' said Ethel, eyeballing the bags again, clearly impressed with her progress. 'Charlie thought you might need an extra pair of hands to get things sorted out in here… I just wasn't expecting to wait for two days for you to wake up before I could meet you properly!'

Hattie could feel herself starting to blush. She really wasn't going to live that down any time soon, was she? 'Thank you for checking on me yesterday – and for the cup of tea!' she said sheepishly.

'My pleasure, dear. Anyway, it's understandable. You needed a proper rest, what with everything you've had to deal with in London.'

Hattie felt her insides squirm. How many people had Lionel shared her disastrous career implosion with?

SANDWICHES IN SEABURY

'Now then,' said Ethel, tactfully changing the subject, 'I wasn't sure what kind of cake you prefer, so I made two. One's walnut and the other one is a sponge with raspberry jam - I can't stand strawberry so I always use raspberry - even though the pips get in your teeth.'

Hattie watched as Ethel popped the top off both cake tins. She had to work hard not to start dribbling on the spot. Then she noticed there was already a hefty slice missing from the walnut cake.

'Ah,' said Ethel with a wry smile, 'that was Charlie, I'm afraid. Walnut's his favourite and I told him not to – but that was yesterday, and he'd already been waiting a day to get his hands on a piece, poor thing, so I didn't have the heart to say no again this morning!'

Hattie grinned. 'I'd never begrudge Charlie a piece of cake! Do you know him well?'

This was the most subtle way she could think of to find out what the story was. Ethel had been here a matter of minutes and had already mentioned Charlie a handful of times.

'As well as anyone in the world,' said Ethel softly. 'I'm his fiancé!'

'Oh wow – congratulations!' said Hattie, trying to imagine old Charlie getting down on one knee and failing miserably.

'Thank you dear!' said Ethel, and then catching Hattie's curious glance towards her ring finger she grinned and shook her head. 'No ring yet, but I did get a very nice bunch of onions instead!'

'Onions?' laughed Hattie. 'Well, that does sound more like Charlie…'

'Indeed,' said Ethel. 'It's all a bit difficult to explain really.' She paused and Hattie watched as she smiled softly to herself.

'Sounds perfect,' said Hattie gently.

'It was,' said Ethel. 'Now then, enough of all that, we've got work to do.' She started to roll up her sleeves. 'What's on the agenda.'

Hattie shrugged, feeling slightly overwhelmed for a second.

'All I know is that I won't be able to settle until everything in here has been emptied, cleaned and organised!' she said.

Ethel nodded. 'I'm guessing there's nothing in those cupboards worth keeping?'

Hattie shook her head. 'You should have seen some of the things I just pulled out of the first set – I swear some of it's been in there since Veronica bought the place!'

Ethel nodded. 'We did our best in the limited time we had before the wedding back in the autumn. In reality though, that was just a case of making sure it looked clean and presentable and that there were a few clean surfaces to work with. I didn't dare look in the cupboards – I don't think anyone else did either!'

'Can't say I blame you,' laughed Hattie, 'it's a

whole new layer of vintage in there – and not the good kind! I'm dreading having to sort the chest freezer out.'

'It'll be fine love. We'll just tackle it together,' said Ethel. 'Now then, point me in the direction of a pair of rubber gloves and tell me where you want me to start!'

CHAPTER 8

There were now two rows of full bin bags lined up by the kitchen door and the sink was full of steaming hot water, brimming over with frothy suds.

While Ethel had got busy soaking, washing and stacking every plate, saucer, cup and utensil she could get her hands on, Hattie had doused the shelves and cupboards with detergent. Whatever was stuck all over the surfaces, it was proving to be stubborn and uncooperative so she'd left them to soak – it was time for them to think about what they'd done wrong.

Hattie threw her rag into a bucket full of disinfectant, stripped off her gloves and washed her hands at the sink before scuttling over to the table. She couldn't resist it! She tugged the top of one of the cake tins off and promptly tucked another slice of Ethel's divine sponge cake into her face.

'Mmmmmmmnnnnnnn,' she groaned.

'Alright there, dear?' laughed Ethel, turning to look at her.

Hattie grinned, but she couldn't do much other than nod as her mouth was full to bursting with jam, cream and the lightest sponge cake she'd ever tasted. Okay, so that groan may have verged a little bit too close to the obscene end of the spectrum for polite company – but that was Ethel's fault for making such amazing cakes.

Popping the last bite of the slice into her mouth, Hattie closed her eyes for a moment and placed her hands on her hips, rolling her shoulders to ease out the cleaning-induced kinks. She took in a deep breath, then opened her eyes and surveyed the scene.

Between them, they'd managed to empty out every single cupboard. Everything that had once been deemed as "edible" was now firmly tied up in the black sacks by the door, ready to be taken out to the big bins around the back.

Everything else they'd unearthed – tins, bowls, gadgets, cutlery – was spread around the kitchen on the table and counters. Each item had either already been scrubbed to within an inch of its life by Ethel - or was next in line.

The freezer hardly looked like it had changed at all. It wasn't surprising really – they basically had their own private iceberg to deal with there. Hattie guessed it would take at least a few days – if not a week or more - to completely defrost. She was already dreading what she'd find in its innermost depths when that did happen. Whatever it was would create a pretty unholy soup!

In terms of what she had to work with when it came to actually doing some cooking... well, it was fair to say that Hattie was feeling more than a little bit apprehensive. The cooker was ancient – so old, in fact, that it looked like the hotel had been built around it. She'd given it a very nervy test-run, and miraculously the oven and all the burners seemed to work.

Hattie had removed the shelves and they were now in the middle of having a damn good soak to get rid of the decades of debris that had welded onto them. There would probably be the need for a bit of scraping and scrubbing later – but at least it was a start.

Now that things were feeling decidedly less icky in here, Hattie felt ready to at least start thinking about the next hurdle. Creating a menu. The problem was, she needed to start over with some fresh... everything!

Hattie turned to watch as Ethel took an enormous Brillo pad to the blackened bottom of a jam saucepan. 'Where around here would be the best place for me to get my hands on some new ingredients?' she asked. 'I need everything. I know I can grab the basics anywhere, but what about fresh produce?'

'Well, love,' said Ethel, looking up and giving her hands a quick shake before stripping off the Marigolds, 'Veronica used to get deliveries from the nearest supermarkets. They'd turn up in their little vans, either from Dunscombe Sands or Bucklepool. They're the two nearest towns - though it depends on whose directions you trust as to which one is *actually* closest to Seabury.

'Charlie always says it's Dunscombe, but I'm not so sure – I think he just prefers going there because it's a nicer drive.'

'No wonder Veronica was always so stingy with food!' gasped Hattie. 'That's got to be the most expensive way I can think of to run a business like this. Using supermarkets instead of wholesalers or buying direct from producers is an insane idea!'

Ethel nodded. 'Well, yes, but Veronica didn't actually pay for very much of what she had delivered. She was always in dispute with the shops about what was on the vans. She'd claim that half of it was missing – until both shops realised that she was having them on and banned her from using their delivery services!'

Hattie grimaced. 'Blimey, that takes some doing!'

'Well,' said Ethel with a wry smile, 'I'm sure you remember what Veronica was like!'

Hattie nodded. 'So, what did she do then?'

'She'd just drive herself to one or the other of

them and raid their bargain sections, stocking up on whatever was cheapest. She had this big old car, and she'd fill the back with stuff. I bet it's still around here somewhere. Everyone used to see her coming and would practically dive off the road to get out of her way. She was an awful driver!'

'Well,' said Hattie, 'even if she was raiding the offers aisles – it's still a ridiculous way to run a business.'

She paused and gave an involuntary shudder at the idea of trying to create a menu with ingredients sourced solely from the supermarkets. It would be a total nightmare! 'Anyway,' she said, 'I need exciting ingredients – fresh... unusual... a bit different...'

'I don't know about unusual,' said Ethel, 'but if it's fresh you want, why don't you start up at the allotments? My Charlie's president of the association up there. I bet he'd be able to help. Veronica never much liked fresh vegetables – she always complained that they were covered in mud and had things living on them.'

'Oh, for heaven's sakes,' laughed Hattie.

Ethel rolled her eyes. 'Yup – all that fresh food right on her doorstep and she chose to ignore it in favour of the pre-packed rubbish from the big shops. She completely turned her back on the allotments. It was a real shame. But I bet the plot holders would love to work with someone who actually wants to use their produce!'

'You really think so?' said Hattie. She couldn't help the note of doubt that had crept into her voice. From what she remembered of the allotments, they were pretty small and basic.

'I know so!' said Ethel. 'Charlie provides The Sardine with a lot of their fruit and veg, but there's always more than Kate needs. Besides, there are loads of other growers up there. They're always looking for someone to use their goods!'

Hattie laughed. 'Why on earth do they grow the stuff if they haven't got any use for it?'

'It's a *passion* thing,' said Ethel. 'Have you ever met a baker who stopped baking just because they weren't sure who was going to eat their next cake?' Ethel threw a sheepish nod towards the two cake tins she'd brought with her.

'Okay,' said Hattie with a laugh, 'I get your point!'

'Think about it,' said Ethel, her eyes gleaming. 'What could be better than serving delicious food made from fresh, local produce?'

Hattie nodded slowly. 'Okay – I'll give it a go.'

'Good,' said Ethel, giving her an approving nod. 'Now then, Charlie's up there today. Why don't you go and talk to him about it? I'm sure he can fill you in on who grows what, and what's available when.'

Hattie nodded again, a small flicker of excitement kindling in her stomach. 'Okay. Good plan. I remember where the allotments are.'

Ethel grinned at her. 'Of course you do! You'd be

up there every summer holiday – where else could you scrump apples and eat your fill of fresh strawberries, eh?'

Hattie squirmed, feeling like the naughty eight-year-old who'd never quite been caught. 'You remember me?' she asked.

'Of course I do!' said Ethel. 'And I'm betting everyone else in Seabury will remember you too. You were a right little terror!'

'Aw no,' laughed Hattie, not sure whether she was being told off or complimented.

'In a nice way!' Ethel added hastily. 'We all used to look forward to your visits – even the plot holders. Well... sort of. They all knew you were related to Lionel, so a few strawberries here and there didn't really bother them. I think they all liked to see you enjoying your summer holidays – running around like the wild tearaways you were!'

Hattie smiled. Everyone here had always been incredibly kind to her as a child – even if she'd had a decidedly wild streak. Her and her little band of friends had certainly run riot. The sea air and swimming had meant they were always ravenous, and the allotments had provided a veritable feast.

There had been strawberries – red, shiny and still warm from the sun. They picked apples straight from the tree and shined them up on the legs of their shorts. And there was nothing better than stripping peas straight from the pod with your teeth. They'd always slipped under the fence – giggling at their bravery – only to dash away again, their pockets bulging, at the first sign of an adult.

'It's nice to have you back again, you know,' said Ethel with a soft smile. 'It's been too long.'

Hattie looked at her for a long moment. 'I'm not sure how long I'm going to stay, you know,' she said quietly.

Ethel simply shrugged. 'Give it some time, love. Seabury might grow on you.'

Hattie let out a long, slow breath. It didn't need to grow on her. Hattie adored Seabury – she always had. The problem was, this was the kind of place where her kind of dream came to die.

She gave herself a little shake and stared around the kitchen, trying to take her mind off the fact that sooner or later, she was going to have to let Lionel down. But not today. Today, there was still work to be done.

They'd been at it solidly for hours and had achieved loads already, but there was still so much to do before she could even *think* of actually cooking anything in there. It suddenly felt quite overwhelming again.

'Why don't you get on and head straight up to the allotments now?' said Ethel, who'd been watching her closely. 'You look like you could do with a change of scenery for a little while.'

'But there's still so much to do here,' said Hattie.

'Nothing that can't wait. I'll get the rest of this lot cleaned and dried by the time you get back. I'm certain you'll feel better for some fresh air and a good walk after being cooped up in that room of yours for so long.'

Hattie grinned at Ethel. She did have a point. After a whole morning of scrubbing and soaking and throwing things away, she was feeling more than a little bit bent out of shape. Perhaps a walk would do her good.

'Now then,' said Ethel briskly before she could change her mind, 'there's a cupboard off the side of the sitting room near the front door. It's full of old wellingtons. I'd have a look in there and find yourself a pair if I were you - there's bound to be some that will fit you. It can get a bit muddy up at the plots.'

After double-checking that Ethel really didn't mind being left with the rest of the washing up - which led to Ethel practically manhandling her out of the kitchen – Hattie went to investigate the boot cupboard like a good girl.

Just as Ethel had promised, when she opened the wooden door – which creaked like it hadn't moved in years – she was faced with a massive jumble of wellies. There were all sorts – from kiddie sizes to massive men's pairs. There were a few reds, yellows and blues in the mix, but the pile was mainly sludgy greens of varying shades. All of them must have been left behind by their owners many, many years ago.

Hattie thought it was kind of sad to see them lying there in a pile – along with a colourful layer of plastic buckets and spades, deflated armbands and snorkels. It was like time had frozen in here - a reminder of how the old hotel had once buzzed with life and activity.

Hattie swallowed a strange swell of emotion. Even if she wasn't here very long, she really did hope that she'd be able to help Lionel breathe some life back into the place.

It took her quite a while to find *one* boot that fit – let alone two – but eventually, Hattie found a battered old pair that were the right size. She pulled them on and grinned. They could have been made for her. Like the hotel, they had seen better days, so she wouldn't be jumping in any puddles to test them out, that was for sure!

CHAPTER 9

Halfway up the hill towards the allotments, Hattie remembered exactly why she'd always needed a feast of strawberries by the time she got to the top. It was a hell of a climb!

The memory of the warm summer sun beating down on the back of her young head made her pant for a bottle of water she hadn't thought to bring with her. She paused for a moment, took off her coat and tied it around her waist.

Hattie turned and peered back down towards Seabury for a moment. Nothing much seemed to have changed – it was pretty much how she remembered it. That in itself was so different to London where there was building work everywhere – constant change, and traffic, and noise. Here there was just the sound of the waves and the seagulls.

She stretched her arms out to the side, suddenly realising that her shoulders were already less tight. It must be something to do with the magic of the sea air. Now, if only she could find the ingredients of her dreams up at the allotments, she'd almost feel like she could relax. Almost.

Hattie turned and set off up the hill again, keen to get to the plots and see what Charlie might have to show her. The thing was, it wasn't exactly the time of year for fresh produce, was it?! Plus, what could such a small patch of mud really have to offer her to cook with?

She was used to being able to lay her hand on whatever ingredients took her fancy and creating fairy tale concoctions to tempt the fussiest of pallets. The best she could hope for here would be a jus of carrots and a timbal of broad beans.

Marco would hate the place! His food was all about structure and balance. It had to look good piled high on an expensive white plate. He'd insisted on taking photographs of every single dish he created – and how it looked was more important than how it tasted. The light had to be just right, and every element had to be placed to perfection.

Hattie didn't think about cooking that way – but she'd soon learned that if she wanted to get anywhere, that was the way she had to think. It had worked for Marco after all. In fact, it had worked so well that she was now out of a job and marching around Seabury in a pair of borrowed welly boots on the hunt for a half-decent cabbage.

Hattie let out a sigh. Despite the blue sky overhead and the beauty of the sea glistening below her – she couldn't help the deep sting of disappointment at the way things had turned out.

By the time she turned in at the allotment gates, Hattie was sweating buckets. Was it really this unseasonably warm or was she just out of shape, having done next to no cardio for over a year and a half? She had a nasty feeling it was the latter.

Closing the gate carefully behind her, she made her way around the hedge. It looked like the plots were in much better shape than she remembered from when she was a kid. Most of them were beautifully dug, carefully edged and clearly much loved.

Still, she couldn't really take it all in. She had no idea what any of it meant. She was used to having everything delivered straight to the restaurant looking perfect. Maybe she was a bit like Veronica after all? Perish the thought!

'Hello!'

A grinning, whiskery face appeared around the corner of the nearest painted shed. Well – it hadn't taken her very long to find Charlie – just as Ethel had promised!

'Nice to see you up and about!' he said, his eyes twinkling.

Hattie smiled at him. Of *course* he knew she'd

just spent more than twenty-four hours solidly in bed. Of *course* the whole of Seabury knew. For a split second, she craved the anonymity of London life.

'Anyway,' said Charlie, 'I think I'd better apologise.'

'What for?' said Hattie in surprise.

'Pilfering a slice of your special "Welcome to Seabury" cake that Ethel made for you. I *am* sorry… but I couldn't help myself,' he grinned.

Hattie laughed. 'There was more cake there than I could manage in weeks! So, you're forgiven. Besides – I'm a sponge kinda girl!'

'Ah well, that's okay then,' said Charlie, plunging his hands into the giant rain butt that stood next to his shed and giving them a vigorous scrub in the icy water. 'Walnut's always been my favourite, though quite frankly, I'll tuck into anything Ethel makes!'

He took his hands out of the water, gave them a quick shake and then snagged what looked to be an ancient, filthy tea towel that was hanging from a hook under the eaves of the little shed.

'How's it all going down at the hotel?' he asked. 'Did Ethel arrive in time to give you a hand?'

'She certainly did!' said Hattie. 'She's like a human whirlwind. I'm so grateful! It would have taken me days to do everything on my own. Anyway – she suggested I came up here to ask for your help.' Hattie felt a sudden swoop of nerves, even though Charlie's warm, open face was smiling at her from under his flat cap.

'Anything I can do, you just ask!' he said.

'Well,' said Hattie, 'I need to start sourcing ingredients for my new menu...'

Charlie clapped his hands together, looking thrilled. 'Well then, you've come to the right place, my girl!' he said. 'Where do you want to start?'

'Potatoes?' asked Hattie.

'It's as good a place to start as any,' said Charlie. 'If you get your variety of potatoes right, it's going to make a huge difference to your dishes.'

Hattie nodded, doing her best to keep her face straight. She thought *she* was fanatical about getting the right ingredients – but she had a feeling she'd met her match when it came to veg.

'Now,' said Charlie, 'have you heard of Pink Fur Apples?'

'Pink Fur Apples?' repeated Hattie, feeling lost.

'They're a type of potato,' explained Charlie. 'Ancient variety, beautiful flavour, almost nutty. I've got some in storage. They're not very popular these days because they're irregular shapes – all knobbly and not very big – but mark my words, they can't be beaten for flavour. When they're fresh, they're lovely as salad potatoes but at this time of year I've got them stored away safe and sound. Little bit of extra work to prepare but the flavour is worth it!'

Hattie smiled. 'I'd love to give them a try!' she

said. 'And how about actual apples? Not of the pink fur variety?'

'Ah – of course you'd ask about them,' chuckled Charlie. 'I remember what you were like as a kid - you couldn't leave that tree alone. One of the earliest for coming ripe I've ever known – and perfect for you and your little gang to raid towards the end of your long summer holiday!' Charlie stopped, pulled out a spotty hanky from his pocket and wiped a tear of laughter from his eye. 'Nearly gave poor Mr Morris a heart attack, you kids and your antics.'

'Oh don't!' breathed Hattie, looking mortified.

Charlie was still laughing though. 'We always loved seeing you up here. Honest. Lionel used to give us the heads-up when you were due to arrive in town so we could all make sure we picked what strawberries we wanted to keep. You were always welcome to the rest.'

Hattie grinned at him, shaking her head. She could remember the fizz of excitement as she shoved an apple in each pocket and grabbed a handful of sun-ripened strawberries before hot-footing it back towards the fence. There would always be a scramble with Ben and the others as they all attempted to be first through the gap in the hedge - their pockets bursting with goodies.

'It's changed a bit up here since then!' said Hattie, looking around at the well-tended plots.

'Oh yes!' said Charlie, nodding. 'We've widened all

the paths quite a lot, and there must be at least a dozen or so new plots at the bottom there since you were last here,' he added pointing down the hill.

Hattie nodded. That explained why it felt so much bigger than she remembered it!

'We've got big plans for the future too – we're going to open up some more plots a little bit further up the hill soon. We've got people up here growing all sorts now – and so much expertise, you wouldn't believe!'

Hattie couldn't help marvelling at his excitement. This was clearly his favourite subject.

'Anyway,' laughed Charlie, 'sorry! Get me going talking about this place and you could be here for years.'

'I don't mind,' smiled Hattie, realising that she really, truly didn't. It was lovely to listen to someone talk about something they loved so much. It reminded her that was exactly how she felt about cooking – or had done before it had turned into such a shit-show.

'You know,' said Charlie, giving her a friendly pat on the shoulder, 'most of the plot holders remember you from when you were a kid.'

'Uh oh,' laughed Hattie.

'Not at all,' said Charlie. 'They all want to help in any way that can – even Mr Morris! Actually, going back to your question – yes, he's got plenty of apples stored away. Not from your favourite tree – being such an early harvest – but he's got some lovely, sweet eaters all wrapped in newspaper and stored in boxes in his shed. And some cookers too – it was a good harvest last year.'

'That sounds brilliant,' said Hattie.

'I can vouch for how tasty they are – Ethel uses them in her cakes – she likes to use a mixture of both. Anyway, if you want some I can ask Mr Morris for you next time I see him.'

'Perfect, thanks Charlie!'

'It'll be like old times – you making off with half his crop!' Charlie winked at her, and Hattie couldn't help but grin back at him.

'Now,' she said, crossing her fingers, 'what I'm really going to need to get my hands on are some fresh herbs. I've got to design the whole menu from scratch, and I like to build my recipes around the flavours. It would be good to know what I can get my hands on without having to visit one of the supermarkets for some basil flown in from Peru!'

'Nothing worse,' muttered Charlie, looking scandalised. 'I don't know what the world's coming to, I really don't. But never fear,' he added, his frown disappearing, 'I've got just the man for you. Come on!'

Hattie slipped and slid in her borrowed boots as she navigated the muddy path. Charlie led the way, heading diagonally down the hill towards a large polytunnel that sat on the far side of the allotments.

SANDWICHES IN SEABURY

As they drew nearer, Hattie could see that there were strings slung over the roof, weighted down with bricks at either side.

'Ah,' said Charlie, when she asked what they were for, ''tis to keep it from being blown away. The winds can get a bit excitable up here at times.'

'Really that bad?' asked Hattie, now staring at the great rocks at the corners of the tunnel that appeared to be playing the part of massive anchors.

'Oh, aye!' he nodded, 'you should have seen it at Christmas. There was this storm that blew the town Christmas tree halfway to America. People have been finding the decorations for miles around. Luckily, we'd all prepared up here pretty well – better to be safe than sorry!'

'Wow,' said Hattie, eyeballing the sea, which was currently a calm, forget-me-not blue with gentle peaks just about visible as they caressed the beaches. It was hard to imagine such a stormy scene just a few months ago.

'Come on, then,' said Charlie, leading Hattie inside the tunnel.

'Wow!' said Hattie again, coming to a standstill. The place was absolutely packed with tray upon tray of tiny seedlings.

'Hello?' Charlie called into the mini jungle in front of them.

'Be right with you!' came a shout from somewhere near the far end of the tunnel, behind some layered growing beds that looked like they held some larger, more mature plants.

Hattie was about to say something to Charlie when she spotted a man coming towards them, picking his way through the pots. Her jaw dropped. She recognised those freckles!

'Hattie – this is Ben,' said Charlie, his eyes twinkling. 'Though of course you two already know each other.'

Hattie gave him a dazed little nod.

'This is his polytunnel. He grows the herbs around here – if you want it, I can guarantee you Ben's your man.'

Hattie looked up into the friendly, grinning face and swallowed hard.

'Fancy seeing you here!' said Ben with a warm smile. 'Did you sleep well?'

CHAPTER 10

'Ben, this is Hattie Barclay – the new chef at Pebble Street!' said Charlie, grinning between Hattie and Ben. 'Hattie, this is Ben Yolland. He's your man for herbs.'

'Hi Hattie,' grinned Ben.

Hattie couldn't believe how warm it was in here. She could feel the flush rising to her face and uncomfortable prickles were starting to run down the back of her neck.

'We… erm… we already know each other,' she muttered to Charlie, who was still smiling at them both with a twinkle in his eye.

'Oh – I know,' he said. 'You two go way back. So – I'll leave you two to it, then! See you soon Hattie. Ben.'

Charlie tipped his cap at them both and scuttled

off, looking more than a little bit pleased with himself.

Hattie turned back to Ben and gave him an awkward smile, tugging at the neck of her jumper in a vain attempt to let a bit of fresh air in. Goodness, she was warm! Or maybe it was just the fact that Ben was standing so very close to her. He seemed to be staring too, which really didn't help matters.

Okay, maybe he wasn't staring... maybe he was just waiting for her to say something. She took a deep breath of the humid air, trying to pull herself together. It was sweet and intoxicating - a mixture of basil, coriander, parsley, and higher notes that were more lemony. It was all very green... very alive! The onslaught of sensation didn't do much to calm her down, and she blew a strand of hair off her hot face.

'I'm looking for some herbs,' she said at last. It took quite an effort. For some reason, the words seemed to tumble out without a lot of air behind them. Maybe it was just the fact that there wasn't much air available in the polytunnel to start with.

Ben smiled at her. It was a nice smile – all golden skin, crinkling eyes and cute freckles. Hattie took a moment to soak it in – but it did absolutely nothing to help the breathless feeling.

'Well,' said Ben at long last, 'you've come to the right place. I've got all sorts of stuff on the go!'

Hattie nodded, tearing her eyes away from his to look around the tunnel.

'Most of the larger stuff is companion planting to limit the pest damage on my herbs – plus a few bits salad leaves and bits I've grown for myself. The rest of the herbs are all babies at the moment – not much bigger than seedlings – but they should be ready for you in a couple of weeks.'

Hattie nodded. 'What have you got?'

Ben started to lead her in between the various trays of seedlings, pointing them out as they went.

'Dill, parsley, basil, coriander… you name it, I've probably got it in a tray in here somewhere. That's the joy of having the tunnel – I can start my growing season really early and keep going really late too.'

Hattie shrugged. 'I don't mind that they're tiny. I prefer using micro-herbs anyway. They've got a better flavour when they're small and tender.'

'Ugh,' said Ben, coming to an abrupt standstill and pulling a face at her. 'You're not one of *those* chefs are you?'

'What do you mean?' said Hattie, feeling her spine stiffen slightly.

'You know, the ones that are all about how things sound on the menu – like *micro-herbs*. One of those that cares about how it looks more than how it tastes – all piled up on a stupid white plate and then painted with different colour squits so that when it comes to the table it's half cold and practically impossible to attack with a knife and fork…'

'I-' Hattie started, but promptly gave up. Ben was still mid-rant.

'I mean, seriously,' he continued, barely taking a breath, 'I think a lot of chefs have lost their way. It isn't about food anymore. It's not about whether there's enough to satisfy someone after a long day's work. All they want is something to take a picture of – I mean, *how* are you supposed to eat something like that?!'

Hattie stared at him. She could hear the note of amusement in Ben's voice. Clearly he was joking - sort of - but she couldn't help but see the similarities between what he was saying and the kind of food Marco had served. The kind of food *she'd* been serving. His honesty had her rattled. He'd just described the kind of cooking that she'd been working on perfecting for months.

'People go out to eat to experience innovation and new taste experiences,' she challenged him.

Ben chuckled and shook his head. 'People go out to eat because they're hungry – not because they want some kind of weird foam all over their plate.'

Hattie huffed. She'd made an awful lot of foam when she'd been working for Marco. It wasn't that it was *her* kind of cooking, but it was what was expected - what you had to produce if you wanted to get anywhere in the foodie world.

'Ah man!' laughed Ben. 'You *are* one of those, aren't you?' he paused and nudged her playfully in the ribs. 'You're going to cover everything in spinach foam and diced dandelion leaves! Seriously, I hope you're not expecting us all to eat that?' he giggled.

Okay, so he was now *definitely* joking – but Hattie didn't feel much like laughing. The thing was, *she* might not try dicing dandelion leaves, but Marco sure as hell would have if there had been a decent photo at the end of it.

Maybe this wasn't the place for her after all. So - Ben might have some herbs here, but she didn't need this kind of attitude while she was working on designing her new menu. He clearly just didn't understand.

Maybe she *should* go over and check out what was available in the supermarkets instead. But then… she'd have to catch the bus out of town, and what was the betting that it would be driven by Ben again too?!

Hattie stared hard at her boots and then glanced around her, trying to figure out the best way to extricate herself from this uncomfortable, hot, stupid polytunnel before she lost the plot.

Suddenly she realised that her eyes had lingered too long on the brown streaks of earth that trailed down the denim hugging Ben's thighs. Hattie quickly looked away again, catching his eye as she did so.

She *really* needed to get out of here, the heat was getting too much for her to bear. She hadn't said anything in far too long now. Hattie forced a smile back onto her face.

'Okay – maybe I'll come back in a couple of days when I've had a bit more of a think about what I need,' she said tightly. In her head, she was busy making a silent vow not to bother. If everyone in Seabury turned out to be like Ben, her style of cooking was going to go down like a fart at a brass band rehearsal.

Well… fine. She'd just have to pull out all the stops and make them realise their mistake. She'd make them take her and her food seriously.

'You okay?' said Ben, looking at her in bemusement.

'Absolutely,' she said in a forced, cheery voice that made her sound like an old-fashioned schoolmistress. 'Lots to do. Must dash!'

Hattie reversed out of the polytunnel at speed, doing her best not to look at Ben as she did so – but right at the last moment she caught the look of pure confusion on his face. Clearly, he had no idea why she was beating such a hasty retreat.

Hattie breathed a sigh of relief as soon as the fresh air hit her face – but it didn't do anything to get rid of the sharp shard of hurt that seemed to be lodged in her chest. Well, one thing was for certain - Charlie had been wrong. There was definitely nothing in *there* that could help her.

Without a backwards glance, Hattie hurried towards the lower end of the allotments and took a shortcut through the hedge. She knew she was being rude, but she really didn't want to have to talk to Charlie on her way out. She could do without any playful banter about her and her childhood crush right now. All she wanted to do was get out of here as fast as humanly possible.

As soon as she reached the pavement, Hattie dug her hands into her jeans pockets and began to trudge back down the hill towards the hotel.

What would someone like Ben know about fine dining, anyway? If he had his way, he'd probably be all for keeping Lionel's sandwiches on the menu! Or fish and chips served up in newspaper. Not that there was anything wrong with a sandwich or fish and chips - but it simply wasn't why she was here!

She'd show him. She'd show them all what could be done by someone who actually knew how to design a menu.

Hattie jutted out her chin, clenching her jaw in determination. She'd really have to up her game to impress everyone down here. Okay, so there might be some hesitation to begin with, but she knew she'd be able to win everyone over eventually. And even if she couldn't source all the ingredients locally, she could at least make sure the food would look presentable.

Maybe she should start by trying out some of Marco's signature dishes. After all – he wouldn't know that she was serving them. He was too busy opening his swanky new restaurant in the city, so he'd never find out. Hattie had been cooking those recipes for eighteen months and had each one down to perfection. She knew exactly how they should look, how to balance them on a plate – as well as what wines they were best served with.

Finally - it felt like she had the beginnings of a plan. Though, she might have to travel a bit further afield than Dunscombe Sands to get her hands on some of the more obscure ingredients. Frankly, she'd never really seen the point of putting gold leaf in food – but then, it seemed to work for her old boss, so why shouldn't it work for her? Seabury wouldn't know what had hit it!

Maybe she could persuade Lionel to give her a bit more budget to play with for the ingredients. They hadn't actually discussed the money side of things yet – but if she was going to wow this sleepy little backwater, she'd need the right tools for the job.

On that note, there were plenty of things besides the ingredients that would need updating and modernising if she was going to make this an experience to remember – just like Marco's place had been in London. She'd show Ben who was right!

CHAPTER 11

*H*attie stormed back into the kitchen of The Pebble Street Hotel leaving the doors swinging wildly behind her. Rather than calming her down, the walk back into town had just managed to add fuel to the bad mood that had started in Ben's polytunnel. By this point, it had brewed up into a veritable storm.

She stared around her new domain, wishing that there was something, or someone, to take it out on – but everything was quiet. Hattie wasn't normally one of those people who felt the need to throw pots and pans around, but right now, the idea of picking up the giant jam saucepan and hurling it at the stupid, snow-filled chest freezer was definitely feeling like a valid option.

Growling quietly to herself, Hattie leant both hands on the counter for a moment and took a few deep breaths with her head bowed. She needed to get a grip. She had too much to do for this kind of nonsense. She tightened her fingers against the surface, watching as they turned white.

Stupid Ben. What would *he* know about anything? He was just a... a... a stupid idiot. A stupid freckly annoying idiot who didn't know anything.

Hattie snorted at herself. It appeared that she was still eight years old when it came to being angry with Ben, as well as when it came to fancying the pants off him.

Straightening back up, Hattie moved over to the counter nearest the sink. She needed to take control. She needed to do something positive – otherwise she was going to obsess for the rest of the day.

Her eyes ran over the plates and cutlery set out on the surfaces. Ethel had washed and dried everything up, just as she'd promised, and set it all out for inspection. It was in a sorry state.

Hattie's eye wandered across each plate, taking in the chips and cracks as she went. In fact, there didn't seem to be a single item that was whole and undamaged.

Ethel had clearly done her best with the knives and forks, polishing them up as much as she could - but that didn't cover the fact that they were all bent and battered. Some of them were so tarnished that not even a thorough polishing had done much to save them.

Hmm. Things were actually worse than Hattie had originally realised. When they'd been turfing this lot out of the cupboards earlier, she'd hoped that some of it might be salvageable at least. Unfortunately, it looked like the whole lot needed to be dumped in the bin. Damn it!

At the far end of the ranks of knackered crockery, Hattie spotted one of Ethel's cake tins. She made her way over to it, prized the top off and gave a little sigh of pleasure – it was the remainder of the sponge cake from earlier. She was just about to cut herself a slab – purely medicinal, of course! – when she noticed the note sitting next to it on the counter.

Seeing as you like the sponge best, I've taken the walnut cake home for Charlie – he'll be starving when he gets home! I'll be back a bit later on. Ethel x

Right. If Ethel was coming back, Hattie needed to do something... *anything...* to get herself out of this funk before she returned. There was no way she was going to treat Ethel to a dose of her grouchiness after everything the poor woman had done for her today. After all, it wasn't *her* fault that Ben was a stupid, thoughtless-

Hattie shook her head. It was time for her to take some positive action rather than wallowing in the disaster that had been her trip up to the allotments.

She'd get something useful done and then treat herself to a piece of cake as a reward!

Dashing upstairs to her room, Hattie rummaged right to the bottom of her suitcase before finally pulling out her old red notebook. This was where she kept all her ideas and recipes. Marco had always laughed at her – preferring to keep his ideas on an iPad – but this was one thing Hattie could never give up. This notebook was her most prized possession, and she'd be lost without it.

Hurrying back out of her room, Hattie took the stairs two at a time and dashed back down to the kitchen. Grabbing a pencil from the windowsill, she opened her notebook to a fresh, blank page. It was time to take stock of the situation.

First things first – the restaurant itself. The dining room was way too big. They clearly didn't have enough plates and cutlery – especially not in a salvageable state – to lay all the tables that would be needed to fill that space. In fact, she wasn't even sure that they *had* enough tables.

On top of that, Hattie somehow doubted they'd be able to fill a space as big as the dining room with enough covers to make it worthwhile. Somehow, she didn't think that the denizens of Seabury were *quite* as keen on the idea of a spot of fine dining as Lionel was hoping.

No. She couldn't risk it. They would do better to start with a smaller space and fill it, rather than having one or two people feeling like billy-no-mates stuck in the middle of a huge, empty space!

Maybe the Breakfast Lounge would be a suitable alternative – at least at first. It was about the right size and relatively clean. Sure, they'd need to remove the furniture and make a few changes in there to bring it up to scratch, but that seemed more manageable than attempting to fill the dining room with hungry people night after night.

Then, of course, there was the kitchen itself. She couldn't be expected to cook up wonders in here, given the state it was in. If she was going to do this properly, she'd need to start with a clean slate. That would mean a new fridge – and freezer – plus a cooker. The old one might work but it looked like it could be fairly temperamental.

Hattie bent over her notebook and added these to what was already turning into quite a lengthy shopping list – and she was nowhere near finished yet!

Of course, she'd *definitely* need new crockery and cutlery. There was no way anyone should serve food to the public on the cracked and chipped collection they currently had. She'd get some condiment pots for the tables too – something designer – something that made a statement. They'd need new tablecloths and linen napkins - not too fancy, but beautiful quality.

Hattie straightened up and peered around the kitchen before bending straight back over her notebook. There was no way she was going to be able to do this without a dishwasher! Then, of course, she'd need a washing machine for the linens. Ooh, and one of those mixers with lots of attachments like Marco had. That thing had been brilliant! Sure, she might not get around to using all the bits that came with it at first, but in the long run, it was bound to be a better investment to get the full set straight away – then she wouldn't have to hunt down the right parts later!

Of course, there was something else a chef couldn't be expected to work without – sharp knives. She'd been gutted at having to leave all her favourites behind at the restaurant in London.

'Hello dear!'

Ethel's cheery voice made Hattie jump, and she turned just in time to see her bustling into the kitchen.

'Sorry I was so long – I nipped into The Sardine to drop a few things off. What are you working on there?'

Hattie shot her new friend a smile and quickly finished adding a couple of extra items onto the end of her long list. Her bad mood had evaporated as she'd worked and flickers of excitement were starting to creep back in.

'I've just been making a list of all the bits and pieces I'm going to need to get my hands on to get things going,' she said, picking up the notebook and handing it over to Ethel. 'Have a look! Is there anything I've missed?'

Ethel took the notebook, and her face became serious as her eyes ran down the page.

'Hattie love,' she said slowly, 'I think we'd better go and sit down for a second. I've got something important to tell you.'

Hattie raised her eyebrows at the expression on Ethel's face, and her stomach squeezed. That didn't sound good.

'Maybe I should have told you earlier,' sighed Ethel. 'I just wasn't sure if you already knew or if it was even my place to mention it… but now's definitely the time. Come on.'

Ethel led Hattie out into the breakfast lounge, and they took a seat at the table next to the large windows.

'What is it?' asked Hattie, dread lacing her words. She wasn't sure she could deal with bad news after the day she'd just had. What if there was something wrong with Lionel? Hattie swallowed a lump of fear as her imagination threatened to run riot. She willed herself not to start panicking.

'Well,' said Ethel, 'I'm probably not really the right person to tell you all this… but it's clear Lionel hasn't, so…' She paused and looked intently at Hattie for a moment. 'Have you and Lionel discussed budgets yet? Finances? Any of that?'

Hattie let go of the breath she was holding.

Money? Ah, okay. Not her favourite subject, but not a total disaster either. She shrugged awkwardly. 'Not really.'

'Well, dear, you should know that when your uncle bought Pebble Street, he sunk his entire life savings into getting his hands on the place. There's very little left over.'

Hattie nodded slowly. She hadn't really given it much thought until now.

'So,' said Ethel, watching Hattie as the news started to sink in, 'he isn't likely to have the money to spend on half the things on your list. Ingredients? Yes. Refurbishing everything?' Ethel just shook her head.

Hattie nodded slowly as she took in what Ethel was telling her. The list she'd just made was pointless. A dream rather than a possibility. There wasn't any point in asking her uncle for the budget to buy it all. Hattie knew Lionel – he would desperately want to help. He'd want to please her, and it would make him miserable not to be able to.

'I hope you don't mind me filling you in a bit,' said Ethel, looking worried. 'But it's not fair to you if you're basing your plans on something impossible.'

Hattie shook her head quickly. 'I'm really grateful,' she said. 'Honest!' she added, seeing Ethel's doubtful face. 'I actually feel a bit stupid. I should have realised what the situation was. I should have *asked!*'

She dropped her eyes to her notebook on the

SANDWICHES IN SEABURY

table in front of her and scanned the list again. It looked ridiculous to her now she knew the situation. Sure, these things would be so *nice* to have – but asking for them would cause a ridiculous amount of stress and upset.

Here she was with her big ideas - but they weren't what Lionel really had in mind. Or what he or The Pebble Street Hotel needed, come to that.

And yet…

She stared at the list again. There was no denying the fact that there were a few things on there that were essential.

Hattie let out a sigh. 'I'm just going to have to do the best I can with what we've already got, I guess. Then – if we're successful and things start to take off a bit – we might have some funds to spend in the future… when things ease up a little bit.'

Ethel smiled at her and nodded encouragingly. Hattie did her best to look like she wasn't disappointed. Clearly, she wasn't doing a very good job of it though as Ethel's face creased into a frown.

'What's up?' Ethel asked gently.

Hattie chewed her lip. 'We're going to *have* to replace some of the basics. There's no escaping it. That's not me being one of *those* chefs,' she added quickly, Ben's comments from earlier still ringing in her ears, 'but we just can't serve food to the public on cracked and chipped tableware!'

Ethel nodded and as Hattie watched her, she was

sure she could see an idea brewing behind those kind old eyes.

'You know,' said Ethel slowly, 'there might be *something* we can do. About some of it at least.'

Hattie stayed quiet, waiting for Ethel to fill her in. If she was being honest, she was completely wiped out. It wasn't so much the cleaning and scrubbing that had done it, but the constant ups and downs of the day.

First, there had been the allotments and Ben's attitude to her kind of cooking – and now there was this new discovery. There wasn't any cash to get things off the ground here at Pebble Street, and Hattie didn't have the answer.

She wasn't really sure she could handle another wild-goose chase today. She was just about to suggest to Ethel that whatever plan she was concocting might have to wait until the morning when she caught the purposeful gleam in Ethel's eye. Hattie had a sneaking suspicion that it would take a stronger (and stupider) person than her to turn Ethel down when she was in full flow.

'Right Hattie,' said Ethel, getting to her feet and clapping her hands. 'Get those muddy wellies off. We're going to visit someone, and I really don't want you leaving muddy footprints all over her carpets too!'

Hattie widened her eyes in horror as she followed Ethel's gaze down to her filthy, borrowed boots that were still firmly in place. Then she spotted the line of muddy footprints that she'd tracked through from the kitchen.

'Oops,' she said sheepishly, feeling like a naughty eight-year-old again – especially when she realised she'd probably left a muddy trail all the way up to her bedroom too.

Ethel laughed. 'Don't worry – I'll show you where the hoover and mop are kept when we get back!'

CHAPTER 12

'You're being very mysterious!' said Hattie, practically trotting to keep up with Ethel. They marched along the seafront of West Beach, past The Sardine – whose little pavement tables had been brought in for the evening – and then turned up a narrow side street.

'Not at all,' laughed Ethel. 'I'm just not sure if Rose will be in – though at ninety-three years old, she does tend to be in more than she's out!'

'Erm… are you going to tell me why we're going to meet this Rose?' said Hattie, feeling more than a bit confused. As much as she was enjoying this magical mystery tour of the back streets of Seabury, she was knackered. Ever since meeting Ethel that morning, it was a bit like she'd been swept up by a whirlwind.

'Well,' said Ethel, pausing to let Hattie catch up with her before continuing to stride up the hill, 'Rose Blanchford used to work at The Pebble Street Hotel. She was a chambermaid there ever since she was a girl – and she was one of the few members of staff who survived the big clear-out that happened when Veronica bought the place.'

'Blimey, she must have worked there for years!' said Hattie.

Ethel nodded. 'Oh yes – decades! An awful lot of people lost their jobs when Veronica took over – some even had to move away. It was a really bad time for the town. But Rose stayed put.'

'But… why are we going to see her?' asked Hattie, still confused. It wasn't that she didn't *want* to meet Rose – but maybe it would be better when she wasn't coming off one of the most frustrating, emotionally charged days she'd spent in a long time.

'Patience, grasshopper!' laughed Ethel, turning into the tiny front garden of a pretty white cottage and knocking loudly on the door.

Hattie opened her mouth to ask more questions but promptly closed it again as someone inside the cottage started unlocking the door. The next thing she knew, a tiny woman with wispy, white hair was peering out at them. She gave Hattie a quizzical glance before her face cracked into a huge smile at the sight of Ethel.

'Hello, Rose,' said Ethel, beaming back at her. 'Sorry to turn up unannounced.'

'My favourite kind of visit!' said Rose happily. 'Can I interest you in a pot of tea? Maybe a bite of cake?' As she said this, she raised her eyebrows at Hattie. 'Who's this one, then?'

'Rose, this is Hattie Barclay,' said Ethel, 'she's the new chef at Pebble Street!'

'Well well well!' said Rose.

Hattie felt like she was being x-rayed as the old woman looked her over from her head right down to her toes. She was suddenly intensely grateful that Ethel had made her change out of her muddy boots.

'Tea sounds wonderful,' said Hattie nervously.

Rose beamed at her. 'I've got cake too!' she said, beckoning for them both to follow her inside.

As Hattie paused to slip off her shoes in the hallway, she couldn't help but wonder how long it would take before Seabury managed to turn her into a piece of cake.

Following Ethel into a neat little sitting room, Hattie found herself surrounded by the gentle ticking of about half a dozen clocks. As she perched on the old sofa she looked around trying to locate them all. There was a tiny, gold carriage clock under a glass dome on the sideboard, a vintage cuckoo clock on the wall next to the window and a handsome, dark wooden mantel clock above the fireplace.

As Rose reappeared bearing a tray laden with a floral teapot and three matching bone-china cups in saucers, Hattie tried to get back to her feet to help, but the squashy sofa seemed to have half-eaten her, making it impossible to move fast enough. It didn't seem to matter though - the old woman's hands were probably steadier than her own, and within moments she had set everything down and begun to pour for the three of them.

If Ethel hadn't already told her that Rose was in her nineties, Hattie would have guessed that she was at least twenty years younger.

'There we go,' said Rose, handing them each a cup and then heading back towards the kitchen. 'Two ticks – I've got my cake subscription box from The Sardine! Young Sarah brought it over for me yesterday and I've only had the chance to try the apple-crumble cupcake so far.'

A minute later, she came back and offered a selection of cakes to Hattie, who looked down in wonder at the little gems staring back at her from the box. With a murmur of thanks, she helped herself to a rosy-red macaron in the shape of an apple.

'Good choice,' said Ethel, approvingly.

'Now then,' said Rose. 'What can I do for you both? I'm sure you didn't just turn up for the cake!'

Hattie smiled but thankfully Ethel saved her from having to speak around the huge bite of chewy, appley goodness she'd just taken

'Well, Rose… I was wondering if you'd be willing

to share with Hattie what you told me a little while ago?'

'What did I tell you?' said Rose, raising an eyebrow at Ethel.

Hattie smiled. Rose was fooling no one – she clearly knew exactly what Ethel was talking about, but for some reason was stalling.

'You know,' prompted Ethel, with a smile. 'About the things you saved from Veronica?'

'Oh... that,' said Rose, a mischievous twinkle in her eye. She peered hard at Hattie, who did her best to smile back while under such intense scrutiny. Eventually Rose gave her a little nod. 'Hattie Barclay, you say?'

'That's right,' said Ethel. 'Lionel's great-niece.'

'Well, in that case,' said Rose, 'I guess there's no harm in letting her in on the secret!'

'Secret?' said Hattie, looking from Rose to Ethel and then back again.

'Well,' said Rose, 'I *may* have hidden a few things when Veronica took over at the hotel.'

'Things?' said Hattie.

Rose nodded. 'I only did it because I was fairly certain that Veronica would sell them otherwise.' Rose paused and took a sip of tea. 'I didn't steal them or anything!' she added, her face serious. 'But those things belonged at Pebble Street – where they'd always been.'

'But...' Hattie shot a quick glance at Ethel to

check that it was okay to ask questions. Ethel gave her a little nod. 'But *what* things?' she asked.

'I can't remember!' laughed Rose. 'It was a very long time ago. But hopefully, they'll still be there, where I left them.'

Rose got to her feet and headed over towards the sideboard. Hattie watched her in confusion as she picked up an old, china ornament of a black cat. She gave it a good shake and it rattled loudly before several objects dropped out of the hollow figurine into Rose's hand.

'Here,' said Rose, gesturing for Hattie to hold out her hands – which she did so on autopilot. Rose promptly tipped about a dozen tarnished keys into her cupped palms. 'These are for some of the cupboards at the hotel where I locked up bits and pieces for safe-keeping.'

Hattie stared at the pile of keys for a moment and then watched as Rose eased herself back into her chair and took another gulp of her tea.

'Now then – when you go hunting around, you'll probably need someone with a screwdriver to get into some of those cupboards. Veronica's idea of cleaning was to paint everything over in cheap gloss paint – and I know at least a couple of them were painted shut in the process. Especially as she thought the locks were broken or the keys were missing!' she laughed.

SANDWICHES IN SEABURY

'I know someone who might be able to help,' said Ethel.

Hattie shot a look at her, but before she could think too much about who Ethel had in mind (as *if* she didn't already know!), Rose reached across and patted Hattie's hand, making her jump.

'You know,' she said, 'I remember you from when you were little. I have to say, I'm having a hard time believing that this lovely young woman sitting in front of me – drinking nicely from her teacup instead of slurping out of the saucer – is the same little girl who used to tear around the hotel!'

Hattie pulled what she hoped was an apologetic face.

'Oh yes,' laughed Rose, 'I remember you alright. I used to be the one who made all the beds – and I've never seen anything quite like yours. I used to have to shake the sand out of your sheets every morning. And remove all the bits of seaweed!'

'I'm *so* sorry!' said Hattie, cringing at the memory of quite how wild she'd been as a child, as Ethel shook with laughter next to her.

'Don't you worry, my girl!' said Rose. 'You were a breath of fresh air in that place. I'm very glad that you've come back.'

Hattie smiled at Rose. She didn't know if it was the emotional rollercoaster of the day catching up with her again or just the fact that she'd eaten way more than her monthly quota of cake – but a lump had formed in Hattie's throat and it was proving difficult to swallow.

Fighting to keep her emotions in check, she watched as Rose got to her feet again and retrieved a pair of reading glasses, a piece of paper and a pen from the sideboard.

'Right,' said Rose, looking over at Ethel. 'It's time to get down to business. You might have the keys but some of my hiding places will be harder to find than the others!'

Hattie watched in awe as Rose began to sketch a perfect treasure map of the hotel – with Ethel's help and input here and there. Rose knew precisely the number of steps in each staircase – and how many paces it was to get to each of the hiding places where she'd stashed things.

'How do you remember all this?' asked Hattie in wonder. The little map had already turned into a detailed blueprint a diamond thief might be proud of.

'I walked the corridors of The Pebble Street Hotel for more than sixty years. I know that place like the inside of my slippers – and I loved it almost as much – at least until Veronica got her hands on it.'

'Weren't you afraid that Veronica might find any of your hiding places and start to ask questions?' asked Hattie, as she watched Rose add more details to the map.

Rose shook her head, not taking her eyes off the drawing. 'That woman never had an ounce of curiosity about anything. She was just interested in making as much money as possible by doing as little work as she could get away with.'

'Sounds like Veronica to me,' muttered Ethel, draining her teacup and placing it down on the saucer a little more forcefully than was strictly necessary.

'Well, quite!' said Rose. 'I knew her better than most people in the town after working for her for all those years.'

'Poor you,' said Ethel with a scowl.

Rose shrugged. 'Did you know that when it came time for me to retire – years and years after I should have done, I might add – she didn't even give me a thank you card?'

'You're joking,' gasped Hattie.

Rose shook her head. 'Absolutely nothing. So, you see, I haven't once felt bad about hiding these things away from her. Not even for a minute. In fact – if I'm honest, I'd rather forgotten about it all until Ethel reminded me!'

'Well,' said Hattie, 'I'm really grateful to you for sharing it with me… whatever the treasures are!' she added with a grin.

'I hope it will all come in useful, Hattie,' said Rose. She folded the map carefully in half and handed it to Hattie, holding her eye for a long moment. 'I'm not sure there's much of anything when you put it all together – just odd bits and pieces that I squirrelled away without her ladyship noticing. I did it for the best – and I hope you don't think I'm a bad person for doing it.'

'Not at all!' said Hattie. 'I remember Veronica – trust me, I understand. But thank you – seriously. Every little thing I can get my hands on will help me… and Lionel… get Pebble Street back on its feet.

CHAPTER 13

Hattie drummed her fingers on the table in front of her. She felt like a kid on Christmas morning waiting for her parents to get out of bed so that she could start opening her presents.

She clutched Rose's hand-drawn treasure map in her hand and stared impatiently at the door. She'd taken up position at the reception desk in the foyer at least half an hour ago.

On their way back to the hotel the previous evening, Ethel had promised her that she'd speak to someone about coming to help with any painted-up cupboard doors. The minute they'd said goodbye and Hattie was safely back inside the hotel however, she'd decided to take matters into her own hands.

Hattie had a sneaking suspicion that Ethel was planning to send Ben around for the job – and that was the last thing she needed right now. He was firmly on her shit-list and she didn't want to spend any more time with him than she had to – at least until she'd got more of a handle on what she was going to do about the Pebble Street menu.

So, after a quick search on her phone, Hattie had booked her own handyman for the next morning.

Now he was five minutes late and Hattie was starting to climb the walls! She plunged her hand into her pocket and drew out the handful of well-worn keys Rose had entrusted to her the day before. She couldn't *wait* to find out what they would reveal.

With a sigh, she laid the map out on the table in front of her and stared at it again. Now that she was looking at it in the hotel without Rose to point out the finer details over her shoulder, she was having a hard time making much sense of it. Just as she was starting to worry that she might have called the handyman to the hotel on a wild goose chase, the front door creaked open and Hattie leapt to her feet.

'Oh,' she said, the smile of greeting falling from her face, 'it's you.'

Ben stepped into the reception. He had a toolbox in one hand and the other one was raised – half in greeting, half in surrender. A little smile tugged at his lips as his eyes met hers.

Bloody typical. The one person she didn't want to see.

'What are you doing here?' she demanded. 'I'm waiting for a handyman to show up.'

'Yeah… that'd be me,' said Ben.

Hattie shook her head. 'No – definitely not. I spoke to the guy last night.'

'Yeah, he can't make it,' said Ben apologetically. 'I said I'd fill in for him.'

'Of *course* you did,' sighed Hattie. Suddenly her stocking full of presents she'd been so eager to unwrap had just turned into a bunch of coal.

'Anyway,' said Ben, wandering over towards her, 'I was glad to be able to help him out because I wanted to see you after yesterday. I wanted the chance to apologise for what I said in the polytunnel.'

Hattie raised her eyebrows and did her best to glare at him, even though he was standing close enough to her now that the woody scent of what must have been his shower gel was wafting over her, making her feel decidedly weak at the knees in spite of herself.

'I'm not a chef, Hattie,' he said quietly. 'I don't know what I'm talking about. Sometimes I go off on one and like to have a bit of a rant about things – but I'm really sorry if I hurt your feelings.'

What could she do? With those eyes looking quite so disarming and that innocent smile beaming at her… of *course* she had to forgive him. Besides, he had a toolbox with him and she really *did* want to find out what was in these hidey-holes!

'It's fine,' said Hattie. 'Sorry I disappeared so suddenly.'

Ben shrugged. 'No worries. Right – let's get to it, shall we? Ethel told me last night that you might need my help – so I've brought along every long-handled screwdriver I could find!' He paused for a second. 'Actually – that's all I've got in here,' he said, waggling his toolbox at her. 'I just wanted to look the part. Most of the time I just make things up as I go along.'

Hattie snorted. Somehow she didn't believe that was entirely true. 'So – has Ethel filled you in on everything on already?'

'I promise I didn't jump on the job on purpose!' said Ben, still sounding like he thought he might be in trouble. 'I just happened to bump into her last night, so when Mark rang me to tell me he had an emergency this morning and couldn't make it over to you, I knew what we'd be up to. That's all, I swear!'

Hattie grinned at him. 'Hmm, so not the Seabury mafia at work behind the scenes?'

'No. Well maybe a little bit,' said Ben. 'Kidding!' he added quickly when she scowled at him. 'So, anyway, where's this treasure map old Rose drew for you?'

Hattie pointed at the desk where the map still lay.

'Why the face?' he said, noticing that she was frowning at the piece of paper.

'Honestly? I'm struggling to figure it out now I'm back here. It made sense when I was looking at it with Rose and Ethel – but I can't make head nor tail of it.'

'Can I take a look?' said Ben.

'Be my guest,' said Hattie, angling it so that he could get a proper view of it while trying to keep her breath steady.

Ben Yolland was standing right next to her! She gave her inner eight-year-old all of ten seconds to go giddy before pulling herself together as best as she could. They had work to do!

'Okay,' said Ben. 'I think I see what she's done. It's like she's drawn it with the floors flattened out. They're kind of in one big squiggle along here?' he drew his fingers across the drawing. 'Running from bottom to top?'

Hattie nodded. That sounded about right. 'Yup – and she's marked the locations of all the hiding places with these arrows.'

'Great!' said Ben. 'So we just need to start at one end of the hotel and work to the other.

'Sounds like a plan,' said Hattie.

'So, top to bottom… or bottom to top?' said Ben, wiggling his eyebrows at her.

'I beg your pardon?' spluttered Hattie.

'Top floor first or ground floor first?' asked Ben with a cheeky wink.

'Top,' said Hattie, shaking her head. 'We'll start up there and work our way back downstairs to the lobby.'

The pair of them climbed the stairs to the top floor, and after angling the map this way and that, they navigated their way to where the first arrow indicated a hiding place.

'X marks the spot!' said Ben, tracing his finger in a giant x over a small cupboard that was built into the wall there.

Hattie let out an excited squeak. The cupboard door had been papered and painted over – not with any care at all - but it meant that it was completely sealed up. It looked like it had been like this for many years.

Ben opened his toolbox and Hattie quickly discovered that he'd been joking about the collection of screwdrivers and nothing else. He took out a Stanley knife and, egged on by Hattie, ran it around the edges of the door, cutting through the layers of paint and paper.

'Here,' he said, 'I'll chip away at the hinges if you want to have a dig at the lock with this?' he handed her a small, sharp screwdriver. It was the perfect size and shape to pick at the paint and paste that had gummed up the keyhole.

Pretty soon, she'd dislodged enough of the rubbish to fit a key in the lock, and after trying four of the keys from her pocket with no luck, the fifth fitted a treat. After a little bit of resistance, it turned, and with some coaxing from Ben wielding one of the long-handled screwdrivers, they managed to get it open.

Hattie peered inside, holding her breath. There, on a shelf, was a bundle wrapped in an old pillowcase. She reached in and carefully drew it out. It was heavy and soft in her arms. Peeling the case open, she gasped. It held a stack of beautiful tablecloths. They were practically new. They needed a wash to freshen them up – but other than that, they looked to be in perfect condition.

'Hey look,' said Ben, reaching out and flipping back a couple of layers of the linens. He pointed to the words *"The Pebble Street Hotel - Seabury"* that had been beautifully hand-embroidered on the cloth. 'I bet they're all like that!' he said excitedly.

'Well,' said Hattie, beaming at him, 'that's not a bad start to the treasure hunt, eh?'

'I don't think I've ever seen anyone quite so excited about a bunch of table cloths!' laughed Ben.

'Just you wait until you see them on our tables at opening night,' said Hattie. 'Then you'll understand.'

'Well,' said Ben, 'how about we go looking for the next hiding place?'

Hattie nodded excitedly.

In the next spot – a larger cupboard that was masquerading as a stretch of blank, painted wall, they found half a dozen plates with The Pebble Street Hotel monogram on them. Hattie was instantly smitten with them – even if she knew they wouldn't really be that useful as there were so few of them.

The next arrow took them to an innocent-looking ledge with a top that turned out to be hinged.

'Sneaky little hidey-hole!' laughed Ben, as he flipped it open without having to do any kind of work on it. It hadn't been painted in or locked, but by the line of dust and grime it left behind on its surroundings, it was clear that it hadn't been opened for decades.

'Okay – I take it back about this not being a proper treasure hunt!' gasped Ben, as he reached his arm all the way down into the hole.

'What is it?' said Hattie, struggling to contain her excitement as she tilted her head, trying to get a sneaky peek of what lay inside.

'Silver!' said Ben, pulling his hand back out and passing her a couple of forks.

'Two forks,' said Hattie, doing her best not to sound disappointed. She took one from him and turned it over. Sure enough, it was hallmarked, and the handle was beautifully engraved with the hotel's name.

'Erm…' said Ben, who'd been fiddling in the cubby hole while she'd been inspecting the slightly tarnished treasure, 'not exactly two forks, no!'

Hattie watched as Ben very carefully pulled his hand back out of the hole for a second time, dragging yet another pillowcase through the opening.

'That's not full of…?' gasped Hattie.

'Yep!' said Ben with a delighted grin, plonking the package on the floor.

Hattie knelt down to inspect the heavy bundle. Sure enough, the pillowcase was crammed with more engraved, hallmarked silverware. There were enough knives, forks and spoons for every eventuality.

'Rose was right,' said Hattie, shaking her head. 'This lot would *definitely* have been worth something to Veronica! She'd have sold the lot if she'd known it had existed.'

Ben nodded, wide-eyed.

As they worked their way along the map, it didn't take long before the pair of them had unearthed a load more of the monogrammed plates – at least enough to serve a full breakfast lounge. Then there were matching, monogrammed milk jugs and a snowy stack of what looked to be brand new, embroidered linen napkins.

There was stuff hidden all over the place – Rose was a squirrel alright. It was just a marvel that it had been there all this time, waiting to be rediscovered. Thank heavens Rose had such an incredible memory!

Very soon, they had to start leaving their discoveries where they found them – they simply couldn't carry all the goodies with them as they bounded from hiding place to hiding place.

'I can't believe this is the last one!' said Hattie,

eventually coming to a halt on the landing above the lobby with Ben in hot pursuit.

'Not a bad haul, eh Hattie!' laughed Ben, plonking his toolbox down and eyeing the cupboard door in front of them. 'I wonder what we'll find in here.'

Hattie shrugged. This one looked like it was a lot bigger than all the other hidey-holes they'd checked out so far. Unlike the others, it wasn't painted over but had a sign on the door. "Cleaning Materials. Authorised Personnel Only."

Hattie could only imagine that Veronica would never have bothered to look inside.

'Doesn't look like there's much for me to do with this one,' said Ben.

Hattie nodded, drawing the keys out of her pocket and trying one in the lock. It didn't fit. Damn. She'd been doing her best to keep a mental note of which ones she'd already used – but they were all so similar it had proved to be practically impossible.

It took two more attempts before she managed to find the right key. As she turned it, the lock gave a satisfying *click*, and the door swung open.

Hattie stood stock still for a second and just stared. There were literally dozens of beautiful condiments sets staring back at her – probably solid silver by the look of them.

As she bent closer, she spotted some candlesticks further back on the shelves. Okay – so maybe they'd be a bit much for the breakfast lounge – but they *were* lovely all the same.

'Oh, my!' said Ben.

'I know!' squealed Hattie. 'Just loooook!' She wriggled with excitement at this new find and started to bounce up and down on the landing carpet. With everything they'd discovered, it really did feel like Christmas morning and she couldn't stop herself from laughing and jumping like an excited kid.

And then – without quite knowing how she managed it, she'd pogoed and toppled straight into Ben's arms.

They grinned at each other for a moment as he held her steady. Hattie felt her heart still jumping in her chest, even though she'd frozen in place, captivated by Ben's beautiful eyes and surprised smile. The feeling of his arms around her was doing something strange to her insides.

Hattie swallowed. This shouldn't feel quite so good, should it? In fact, what was she even thinking? What was she *doing?!* This wasn't good at all. She wasn't at Pebble Street to fall in love – that was meant to be the last thing on her mind!

Just as she was about to panic, Ben gently set Hattie back on her feet and stepped away from her.

'Erm... fancy going for a celebratory coffee in The Sardine?' he asked, his voice casual as he picked up his toolbox.

Hattie stared at him dumbly for just a moment,

watching as he rubbed at the back of his neck with his spare hand. Then her brain kicked back into gear. She nodded quickly.

'Sure. Great!' she said.

Anything that meant there would be a table between her and Ben had to be a good idea right now!

CHAPTER 14

The little café was packed to the gunnels, and as she followed Ben inside, Hattie found herself surrounded by a large group of soggy, dripping women. They all seemed to know each other, and they *definitely* knew Ben. He was treated to "hellos" and hugs as they slowly made their way through the crowd.

'The Chilly Dippers,' said Ben, turning back to her with a grin. 'Seabury's mad wild swimming tribe!'

'Yeah,' said a waitress as she edged between Hattie and Ben in order to reach the table the Dippers were crowded around. She placed her tray down carefully. 'You've got to watch what you say around this lot, or they'll have you roped in before you can say *brrr!*' she laughed.

'We go in at least once a week!' said a woman with a smiling face as she wrung out her plait before picking up a hot drink and wrapping her hands gratefully around the mug. 'You're always welcome to join us!'

Ben laughed and quickly shook his head.

'Told you,' muttered the waitress, rolling her eyes good-naturedly at Hattie. 'I'm Lou, by the way. I'm guessing you must be Hattie?'

Hattie nodded, not bothering to ask how she knew. This was Seabury, and clearly a new face in town made it pretty obvious who you were.

'That's Sarah over there,' she said, pointing to the other young waitress who was behind the counter cranking out a line of perfect coffees from an ancient, ornate machine. Sarah raised her hand and Hattie returned her smile before pulling out a chair at the only available table.

Ben fought his way around to the other side and squeezed into the chair opposite her, just as a familiar and rather damp dog appeared next to Hattie.

'Hello,' she grinned, reaching down to stroke Stanley's head. He promptly leaned his entire weight against her trouser leg, and she felt a large, damp patch start to bloom on the denim. 'Erm, I'm guessing Stanley's a member of the Chilly Dippers too?' she said.

Ben nodded. 'Oh yes – you can't keep that hound out of the sea for five minutes!'

Hattie patted Stanley's soggy head again,

wishing that she was wearing her borrowed wellies – at least that would have kept a tiny part of her trousers dry.

Stanley let out a blissful sigh and lay down, curving himself around her chair and effectively making sure that she was a prisoner there until he decided to move.

'I'll get the coffees,' chuckled Ben, realising that she was now a captive of the big, fluffy mountain.

Watching as Ben headed over towards the counter, Hattie sniffed the air and her stomach grumbled. The delicious aroma of fresh soup was coming from the stove and seemed to have woken up her appetite.

Ben was back in moments, placing a perfect cappuccino in front of her. 'Here you go.'

'Thanks,' she smiled at him gratefully. 'I almost called over to you to swap my order for a bowl of soup – it smells amazing!'

Ben nodded, taking a sip of his coffee. 'Kate always makes sure there's freshly made soup for the Dippers after their swim – it's February after all!'

'Perfect way to warm up!' nodded Hattie.

'I think it's vegetable today… not sure what's in it exactly but knowing Kate it'll be a right mixture – all fresh from the allotments, of course!'

Hattie glanced enviously at the gaggle of damp women who were now tucking into bowls of the scalding soup as well as slabs of crusty bread.

'Well Hattie,' said the one nearest to her, 'it's lovely to see you again, I must say!'

Hattie stared at the woman for a moment and then realised that she recognised her face.

'Doris?' she gasped. 'From the Post Office?'

'The one and only,' said Doris with a grin. 'You always used to come and see me for those little windmills whenever you visited.'

Hattie nodded, her eyes sparkling. 'And a packet of skips! I can't believe you remember me.'

'How could we forget you,' laughed one of the other women, 'right little tearaway you were – and running around with this one,' she added, nodding at Ben. 'Well, there was no keeping tabs on you lot.'

'Shame Kate's not in here at the moment,' laughed Ben, 'she was usually in on most of the trouble!'

Hattie gasped. 'Kate? As in the owner of this place is the same Kate from back then?'

Ben grinned at her and nodded.

'The one with the red dungarees I always wanted?' said Hattie. 'I can't believe she never moved away!'

'I don't know about the red dungarees,' chuckled Ben, 'but no – she never moved away – at least, not for very long!'

'Wow,' said Hattie. Lionel had been right, there did seem to be something about Seabury that kept people here. The thought made her feel suddenly uncomfortable, and she took another sip of her coffee to mask her confusion.

'So,' said a tiny woman who was wearing a beach towel like a toga and sipping on her bowl of soup whilst wearing a bobble hat, 'what are you going to be cooking up over at the hotel when you open up the kitchen?'

Everyone fell silent and turned to face Hattie, and she squirmed slightly under the attention. 'Well,' she said, shifting awkwardly in her seat and shooting a quick look towards Ben, 'I haven't made any firm plans just yet – I've got to talk it all through with Lionel. Then when we're ready to open, we'll make sure everyone knows.'

There were nods around the table, and thankfully, within seconds most of them were chatting away again and the focus had eased off her a bit.

'Hey Ben,' Doris called over, 'why don't you tell our lovely new chef what you think about food that's been messed about with!'

Hattie glanced at Ben and couldn't help but smirk at his discomfort. He was busy doing his best to pretend he hadn't heard what Doris had just said, but he'd sunk low in his seat and was looking decidedly shifty, clearly wishing the ground beneath him would swallow him whole.

'Is there anything else I can get for you both?' asked Lou, stepping in to save the day at just the right moment. 'I've still got a bit of soup left if you're interested?'

Hattie shook her head. 'Thank you – but the coffee is perfect. I really need to get back over to the hotel soon – there's so much to do.'

'Well, said Lou, 'if you need a hand at all, I could always do with a few extra hours. No pressure or anything.'

Hattie smiled at her. 'Thanks – I'll definitely bear that in mind. There might be an opening for some waiting staff, but it won't be for a few weeks yet.'

'Great! Ben knows how to get hold of me if you need me – or just pop in here.' She looked down at Stanley who was still cosied up to the base of Hattie's chair. 'Come on you – you've trapped poor old Hattie at the table!' she laughed.

Stanley slowly got to his feet and plodded over towards the Chilly Dippers, demanding titbits from their plates. He munched on a proffered piece of bread before going into a full-body shake that splattered several of them with spray from his damp coat. Given that most of them were still wet from their swim, it didn't seem to bother them in the slightest.

Hattie turned back to Ben and smiled at him, suddenly feeling a bit guilty that she hadn't paid much attention to him since they'd arrived. Maybe that was a good thing. After all, she didn't want him getting the wrong idea – especially after landing in his arms *quite* so dramatically at the hotel. The last thing she was looking for was romance – whether holiday or otherwise.

Though, as he grinned at her and pushed his beachy hair back off his face, Hattie couldn't help but admit to herself that, if she *was* in the market for a fling, then Ben Yolland would be in a lot of trouble.

Hattie cleared her throat. Suddenly the muggy warmth of the little café felt a bit claustrophobic. It was probably best for her blood pressure as well as her sanity if she didn't think too much about having a fling with Ben!

As if picking up on her awkwardness, Ben promptly drained his coffee. 'Right, Hattie, sorry to love you and leave you,' he paused a moment, wincing at his choice of words. 'Erm, what I mean is – I'd better go. I promised Dad I'd cover for him on the bus again for a couple of hours this afternoon.'

'Oh, right,' said Hattie, smiling at him brightly. 'Well, thanks for your help today.'

'My pleasure,' said Ben, struggling to his feet in the cramped space and easing out from behind the table. 'I'll see you around – just shout if you need more help breaking into things!'

He winked at her, and before she had the chance to say anything else he'd disappeared, leaving her sitting alone.

The minute he was gone, Hattie decided it was time to leave too. The little café suddenly felt too hot and too noisy. She was now craving a bit of calm -

some peace and quiet to ease her frayed nerves. She levered herself to her feet with some difficulty.

'Off so soon?' asked the tiny Dipper in the towel.

'Well, lots to do,' she said, navigating her way through the group and doing her best not to step on anyone's toes.

'It was lovely to see you, Hattie!' said Doris.

'Lovely to meet you,' several of the others chorused.

'Don't leave me with this lot!' laughed Lou, grabbing Hattie's hand in mock entreaty. 'They're trying to convert me to their insane swimming ways!'

'In that case,' said Hattie, 'I'm out of here before they start in on me!'

Hattie left the café with a huge smile on her face and was followed outside by a friendly chorus of goodbyes. It might be a little bit loud, mad and noisy, but there was something incredibly cosy about suddenly finding herself a part of such a close-knit community – even if it was only temporary.

The minute she was outside, the sea breeze started to cool her flushed cheeks. Okay, so "cool" might be the wrong word for it! This was flipping freezing! Hattie snuggled into her cardigan as much as she could as she crossed the road.

Staring down West Beach, she shivered slightly. The sea was grey and looked decidedly unwelcoming. The Chilly Dippers were clearly completely insane to voluntarily swim in that!

Hattie had always enjoyed swimming when she was younger – but she was pretty sure the sea had never looked anything like this back then! It had always been a beautiful, sparkling blue under a sunny summer sky.

If she was honest, she couldn't even remember the last time she'd had a swimming costume on, let alone gone for a dip. As Hattie thrust her hands into her pockets, desperately seeking an extra bit of warmth, she had to admit that right now she had no intention of doing anything to rectify that. They could do their best to rope Lou in, but there was no way the Dippers would convince her that a swim in the sea in February was a good idea. They had to be kidding!

CHAPTER 15

Hattie stared longingly at the painted bannister for a moment. She'd love nothing more than to start the new day with a slide down to the bottom floor - Veronica's love of gloss paint really had sucked a whole lot of joy out of life! She let out a sigh and bounded down the stairs instead.

She was due to have breakfast with Lionel. She'd already filled him in on the successful treasure hunt she'd enjoyed with Ben the day before. After getting back from The Sardine, she hadn't been able to resist nipping up to his flat. For one thing, she'd felt the need to apologise for the various patches of damaged wallpaper and scratched paint they'd left dotted around the hotel. Ben had already promised that he'd come back at some point to neaten everything up.

Far from being worried about any damage they'd

done in getting into the cupboards, Lionel had been intrigued and thrilled in equal measure. He remembered many of the items from Pebble Street's heyday and was over the moon that they'd been saved from Veronica's clutches.

Hattie swung around the corner and bounced into the breakfast lounge, only to find that Lionel had beaten her to it once again – and already had stacks of toast and a pot of tea waiting for her on the table.

'Well, you certainly look full of the joys of spring!' said Lionel, beaming at her.

Hattie returned his smile and dropped a kiss on top of his head before taking the seat opposite him. 'I've just had a good sleep and a chance to recover from the Ethel-shaped whirlwind I was subjected to yesterday,' she laughed.

'Yes – she is a bit like that, isn't she?' said Lionel with a wry grin. 'Our Charlie's got his hands full there!'

'I reckon you might be right!' said Hattie. 'But she's lovely. So's Charlie.'

Lionel nodded. 'I'm really glad you've had the chance to meet everyone already – Rose, Lou, young Sarah over in The Sardine - and the Chilly Dippers too!'

'Blimey, how did you know about that?' said Hattie. She was pretty sure she'd avoided mentioning her après treasure hunt coffee the previous evening. She buttered a piece of toast and ripped into it with enthusiasm – all this sea air was giving her a mighty appetite!

'It's a small town, Hattie. News travels fast!'

'I'll have to remember that,' muttered Hattie, thinking of Ben's arms around her as she toppled into him, and thanking her lucky stars that there hadn't been anyone else around to witness it. 'I have to say, it's lovely that everyone has been so welcoming – even the people who remember me as a kid.'

'Why wouldn't they welcome you?' said Lionel, looking puzzled.

'You remember what I was like!' she laughed. 'I think someone used the word "feral" to describe me once. Just about sums it up, I guess.'

'Ah now, you weren't that bad,' said Lionel, looking at her fondly. 'You had a lot of spirit and liked to be out and about running free with your friends. Nothing wrong with that – it's as it should be.'

Hattie smiled at her uncle gratefully. She knew she couldn't have been easy to deal with. She had a fair memory for just how naughty she'd been.

'So, Hattie,' said Lionel, picking up his teacup and peering at her over the rim, 'have you had any thoughts on your menu yet? I can't wait to hear what you're going to cook in that kitchen!'

Hattie shook her head, her heart sinking ever so slightly. 'You know, I'm still not sure.'

Lionel smiled at her. 'That's okay. There's plenty of time. I'm just excited to hear your ideas!'

Hattie nodded. 'Well, at least now, thanks to Rose, we've got our beautiful tableware to use on opening night, and the lovely linens!'

'I still can't believe that was all here, hiding right under our noses,' said Lionel, shaking his head in wonder.

Hattie nodded. She breathed a little sigh of relief that Ethel had managed to warn her before she'd shown him her ridiculous wish-list. She hadn't mentioned it to her uncle, and that was the way it was going to stay. Sure, there was still a great deal of things that needed to be sorted through in the kitchen, and many of them would need replacing – but that was something she'd have to deal with gradually.

'I'm not going to set a date for our grand reopening until you're ready,' said Lionel, watching her tuck into yet another slice of buttered toast.

'Brilliant, thank you!' said Hattie gratefully. That was definitely a relief. She needed to get cracking on developing the menu – but at least this gave her a little bit of wiggle room while she worked.

'It's not a problem – you don't need any extra pressure while you're figuring everything out.' He paused and topped up both their cups of tea from the pot. 'Now then, before I forget, I should tell you that I'm going away for a few days.'

'Oh?' said Hattie in surprise. She wasn't sure how she felt about being in the hotel on her own so soon.

'Not for long,' laughed Lionel, catching the moment of child-like panic on her face. 'I'm off to stay with my friend at Upper Bamton vineyard for a few days. I've been buying their wine for ages and now that I own the hotel – well, it's the perfect opportunity to put a slightly larger order their way.'

Hattie nodded, looking interested.

'Don't worry, it won't be anything too extravagant, just a few bottles here and there to try out with various things.'

'Sounds good,' said Hattie.

'I'm really looking forward to it - I'm taking my knitting with me!' said Lionel with an excited smile. 'Apparently, there are plans afoot for a knitting club over there. I haven't had the chance to talk knitting with anyone for ages. Charlie's a dear lad, but all he wants to talk about is vegetables. Even when we're painting, he talks about the blasted things!'

'That sounds about right!' Hattie laughed, thinking of how easily Charlie got into his stride when she'd been chatting to him up at the allotments.

'I was only asking about the menu because if you had any dishes nailed down, I could have chosen some wines to go with them. But it doesn't really matter – all their wine is excellent.'

'Is that the stuff you've got in the fridge?' she asked, remembering the bottle sitting in the door.

'That's the stuff!' said Lionel. 'You should try some – help yourself! I've always liked that lovely dry white with fish.' He paused, his eyes going a bit misty. 'I haven't had a nice bit of fish in forever, you know. Veronica barely ever served it. She said the smell of it cooking would hang around in the curtains for days!'

'What… these curtains?' said Hattie, smirking at the ancient hangings that had seen better days.

'I know – fit for the bin, aren't they?' said Lionel with a little shudder. 'I think it's their age that can be blamed for making them smell, not the fish!'

Hattie stared at her uncle.

'What?' he said, raising his bushy eyebrows.

'Fish!' said Hattie, hitting herself on the forehead.

'What about it?'

'Seabury. Just like the name suggests… we're surrounded by the sea!' said Hattie.

'Just noticed that have you?' said Lionel in amusement.

'Why didn't I think of it before?' said Hattie, ignoring her uncle's sarcasm. 'I'm such an idiot. This is the perfect place to open a seafood restaurant.'

'Oh!' said Lionel, catching on.

'What do you think?' she asked, crossing her fingers in her lap. Because now the idea had dawned on her, she *knew* it was the right thing for Pebble Street.

'I love it!' said Lionel. 'But-'

'Aw,' said Hattie, 'why does there always have to be a "but"?'

'Well – there might be a problem. See, the local fishermen used to deliver directly to the hotel, but Veronica-'

'Don't tell me,' interrupted Hattie with a frown, 'Veronica didn't pay them properly, used to complain about the quality, and they stopped coming?'

'Pretty much exactly what I was going to say,' nodded Lionel. 'She'd whine and complain about it not being fresh or full of bones – and it wasn't long before they'd had enough of her. You might be able to persuade them to return – but it might take a bit of diplomacy.'

'But Veronica's long gone,' said Hattie.

'Yes, but in a small town like this, the bad memories linger. It's like they're attached to a building or a business rather than the idiots who ran them.'

Hattie nodded. That didn't sound good – because it meant yet another hurdle they'd have to overcome before people would come back to the hotel as paying customers.

'Don't look so disappointed,' said Lionel gently, clearly thinking her mind was still on fish rather than panicking about the bigger picture. 'You know, the local fishermen supply the fish van that comes around town once a week.'

Hattie lifted her head. That sounded promising. 'Where do they stop?' she asked.

'The far end of North Beach – near Nana's Ice Cream Parlour. In fact – it's the right morning for it.' He quickly glanced at his watch. 'If you hurry, you might just catch them – no pun intended!'

Hattie scrambled to her feet. 'Thanks for breakfast!' she shouted, rushing for the door with a backwards grin.

'I'll see you in a couple of days!' Lionel called after her.

Hattie gave him a quick wave over her shoulder before zooming down the hallway and snagging her handbag and jacket from where she'd dumped them on the front desk. Then she bolted for the front door.

Taking the pavement at a bit of a trot, Hattie turned towards North Beach. She felt like a bit of an idiot. Why hadn't she thought of serving fish at the hotel sooner? It should have been the first thing that came to mind – especially as they were constantly surrounded by the sight and sound of the waves crashing against The King's Nose. If it was any more obvious, it would be silly!

As she strode along, ideas began bubbling away in Hattie's head. It was like someone had pulled a blindfold away from her eyes. Charlie had been telling her about those wonderful Pink Fur Apple potatoes of his – and they might be just the ticket for the dish she now had in mind.

'Please don't let me be too late!' muttered Hattie, as she squinted, trying to see if she could spot anything that looked remotely like a fish van at the far end of the seafront… but she was still too far away to tell. Reluctantly, Hattie broke into a jog. She couldn't bear the idea of missing the van now – she had a recipe she wanted to try out!

CHAPTER 16

As she dashed along the seafront, Hattie couldn't help but notice a new addition to the familiar shops she remembered from when she was a kid. New York Froth was definitely a newcomer. Blimey – that must have been a bit of a shock for The Sardine when it opened its doors!

It looked like a pretty swishy café, and it was massive in comparison to Kate's tiny place. Hattie wondered how long it had been open. No matter how hard she tried, she couldn't for the life of her remember what had been in that shop when she was little. Even though it was clearly new, somehow New York Froth looked like it belonged there.

Nothing else at this end of town looked like it had changed much though. There were still double yellow lines everywhere and nowhere to park. The beach hadn't been tidied up at all. Not that it was scruffy – just nice and ordinary. Undomesticated. The perfect way for a beach to be.

Sure, the sea wall looked like it could do with a bit of care and attention – but then, as far as she could remember – it had always looked like that.

Hattie paused for a moment to catch her breath. She stared across the sea towards the point where the lighthouse stood. She hadn't been outside this much for months. Maybe even years.

The temptation to strip her shoes and socks off and head down to the sea for a paddle was huge – but no, she mustn't! She had somewhere she needed to be. Besides – it was February, the sea was probably freezing, and she had no idea what kind of state her toenails were in!

Hattie hadn't paid much attention to her feet in a long time. After all, you didn't tend to think about them much when you were working in a boiling hot kitchen all day. The only time she'd spared them a thought was when she was trying not to drop anything on them - like a sharp knife or pan of oil – and last thing at night when she finally fell into bed after a long shift and was busy wishing they'd stop aching!

When she was fully in command of her breathing again, Hattie set off with her eyes glued to Nana's Ice Cream Parlour way ahead of her. Now, there was a place that was full of memories! She stared at its sunshine-yellow frontage. It was a bit like seeing an old friend after decades apart. It didn't look like it had changed at all – which came as something of a relief. When they were kids, they'd called it "Bananas" – creatively enough. A great deal of her pocket money had been spent inside its bright and welcoming walls.

Hattie smiled to herself as the memories came flooding back – of ice-cream dollops toppling from wafer cones and landing on bare feet. It had happened more than once. That was the problem with being a kid always in a hurry – eating ice cream was a bit of a danger sport. Still, she seemed to remember that the feeling of vanilla ice cream melting all over your bare foot on a hot summer's day was actually quite pleasant – after you'd got over the wobbly lip that came from losing your ice cream in the first place!

Somehow, Hattie very much doubted that it was the same *Nana* who served up the ice creams now. She'd been a grey-haired granny figure all those years ago. She could only imagine that someone else had probably bought the business by now – in a way, that made it even more impressive that it hadn't changed at all.

If this was anywhere but Seabury all these shops would be long gone. The frontage would probably have been pulled down and turned into blocks of flats with parking and "stunning sea views" that would sell for hundreds of thousands of pounds.

There would be concrete everywhere. But luckily, this *was* Seabury. From what her uncle had told her, the place resisted change and development with a ferocity that was admirable.

Hattie knew she should be all for developments that would bring new customers and more money into the little town, especially given the feat she was attempting in opening the Pebble Street restaurant back up. But, right now, surrounded by so many precious memories from her childhood, she was grateful that Seabury was exactly the way it was.

Hattie could completely understand why Lionel loved the place so much. Of course, he loved it enough to move here for good. She had other plans though. This was just a bit of a working holiday – something to do until she could get herself back on track. The only thing was… she wasn't entirely sure what that meant just yet.

Hattie had jotted down a few ideas in her notebook on the train on the way down here, but they didn't seem to mean much to her when she'd taken a peep at them up in her new bedroom. Of course, it *would* help if she could read her own writing – that train had been particularly bumpy. Clearly, they hadn't improved the train tracks to Dunscombe Sands over the years! She'd figure it all out eventually… she had to!

By the time Hattie drew level with Nana's Ice Cream Parlour, she was puffing hard and out of breath again. The good news was – just around the corner she could see a little white fish van.

She hurried over to it. It was obvious that she was rather late in the day – the beds of ice were practically empty and the fish had almost sold out. Hattie peered around looking for the driver, but there was no one to be seen.

'Hello?' she called tentatively.

'Be right with you!'

The familiar voice drifted to her from around the front of the vehicle. She hadn't managed to wipe the smile off her face before Ben appeared. He was wearing a white coat and his blonde waves were tucked into a rather fetching hair net. He looked vaguely ridiculous – but Hattie couldn't help noticing that he somehow managed to look incredibly cute at the same time.

Ben came to a halt and grinned at her, and Hattie found herself momentarily lost for words.

'I'm just standing in for a friend!' he said. 'This isn't my actual job.'

Hattie snorted. Bus driver? Handyman? Fishmonger? There really was no end to this man's talents!

'Not your actual job?' she repeated, grinning at him.

'Well,' he shrugged, 'it is, and it isn't. I fill in most Tuesdays and Thursdays. Sometimes I help out on the boats too. Anyway, it's a nice surprise to see you!'

'Thanks,' said Hattie, suddenly feeling weirdly shy.

Ridiculous. 'I didn't know about this van until just now, otherwise I'd have come earlier – it's clearly popular!'

'Oh yes. All the fish is freshly landed – if it wasn't for the point over there, you'd practically be able to see where everything was caught!' he laughed.

Hattie nodded. She could see that what he was saying was true. The few bits of fish that were left were super-fresh. The same quality seafood in London would have cost an absolute fortune.

'All this lot was pulled from the sea this morning,' said Ben, proudly. 'Sorry there's so little left.'

Hattie shrugged. 'Don't be – I take it as a very good sign.'

Ben nodded. 'Is there anything you want?'

Hattie looked everything over again. 'Yes please – I'll take all the white fish you've got left.'

'You've got it!' said Ben, beginning to wrap the fillets. 'Working on your new menu?' he asked, not taking his eyes off the job in hand.

'Yup,' said Hattie, an excited smile spreading over her face. She couldn't wait to *finally* start working on the perfect set of dishes to launch Pebble Street back into the world. There was enough fish here that she could try out the recipe she'd been dreaming up. The only thing was, with Lionel away, she was going to need a willing guinea pig to test it out on.

'Hey… Ben?' she said before she could chicken out.

'Yes Hattie?' laughed Ben, handing a large paper bag full of wrapped fish over to her.

Hattie swallowed. How on earth did this guy have the ability to make her feel so nervous while wearing a white coat and hairnet? She quickly decided to take the plunge before she wussed out completely.

'I don't suppose you'd fancy dropping around to Pebble Street for some food this evening?' she gabbled.

'I'd love to,' said Ben.

'I mean, it's not like a date or anything!' Hattie added quickly. The moment the words were out of her mouth she could have kicked herself. Why? *Why?* She always turned into such a solid gold plonker when she was nervous. 'What I meant to say,' she said more slowly, 'is that I'm trying out a new recipe for the menu and I'd love it if you'd be my test audience.'

There. Disaster averted. Kind of.

'I'm flattered,' laughed Ben. 'And yes please, that sounds lovely.'

'Great. Brilliant.' Hattie smiled at him. 'Now, what do I owe you for this lot?'

She handed over the cash, quietly congratulating herself on not managing to *completely* balls the whole thing up.

'See you later then,' she said.

'Yeah. Erm – what time?' said Ben.

'Six-thirty work okay for you?' she said, her heart

hammering even though she was doing her best to keep her voice cool and casual.

'Looking forward to it,' he said.

Hattie turned away and couldn't resist swinging her little paper bag as she strode back down the seafront towards The Pebble Street Hotel. She had all day to get her plans in place. The table would be beautiful and the meal plated up to perfection.

Now she'd show Ben Yolland what real cookery was!

CHAPTER 17

After leaving Ben that morning, the rest of the day had gone by in a haze of activity. Hattie had taken her precious fish back to Pebble Street and placed it in the fridge for later. Then she'd grabbed a couple of empty cotton tote bags and practically route-marched up to the allotment. Her mission was to find Charlie and the other ingredients she'd need to create her masterpiece that evening.

She'd been in luck. Charlie had happily taken one of her bags and filled it to the brim with Pink Fur Apple potatoes from one of his wooden storage crates. Hattie was really excited to give them a try – they were firm and a beautiful colour, still dusted with the dried soil they'd been lifted from. Of course – the real test was yet to come - the proof would be in the cooking. She'd just have to work around the comedy knobbly shapes they came in.

She'd then asked Charlie where she might be able to find Mr Morris to beg the use of some apples. Charlie had taken her straight over to Mr Morris's plot, explaining that he was in his own shed right at that moment. Hattie had felt like fate was on her side at last.

Despite their turbulent history and memories of having to chase Hattie and her friends away from his apple trees every summer, Mr Morris had greeted her like a long-lost granddaughter. This time, she'd asked Mr Morris nicely if she could have some of his apples rather than scrumping them, and the old man had been more than happy to oblige.

He treated her to a bagful – half of cookers, half of eaters – just like Ethel liked to use. Then he'd patted her gently on the cheek with a large, calloused hand and told her how proud he was of the young woman she'd become. This had promptly made her well up and want to gather the old man up into a hug.

After thanking both men profusely, Hattie made her excuses and ambled towards the lower end of the allotments in the pretence that she was going to hop through the gap in the hedge. The moment she was sure they'd both turned their backs - disappearing together towards Charlie's shed to share a pot of tea - she'd snuck into Ben's polytunnel, closing the doorway carefully behind her.

Knowing that Ben was out and about in the fish van, she'd felt braver than usual - confident that she wouldn't bump into him while she was up to no good. She needed to pilfer a couple of things from his stash of herbs and salad leaves he'd grown for his own private use. She was fairly sure he wouldn't mind – after all, he'd be the one enjoying them when they were cooked and presented to perfection!

After getting back to the hotel, Hattie had pulled out her notebook. She finally knew exactly what she was going to cook, and she wanted to make sure it was all written down and worked out to perfection. Tonight, she would be serving fish and chips followed by apple crumble and custard – all with a twist. She would be cooking this meal London style. Marco would be proud.

There would be tiny strips of fresh fish in tempura batter with triple-fried Pink Fur Apple chips served with salsa verde and wilted leaves. Then, for dessert, she would craft tiny castles of apple crumble that would be dished up with three perfectly proportioned dollops of egg custard surrounding it. Absolutely divine!

There was one thing she'd decided to do differently to normal – she'd resist the urge to pile the food in the middle of the plate in an elaborate structure. That would show Ben that she'd listened to his rant the other day and taken it on board.

Right. It was finally time to get cooking.

Hattie stared around the steamy kitchen and pushed back a wayward strand of hair with her forearm. Somehow, she'd managed to use every pot and pan in the place. She was so used to having someone there to wash up after her when she was cooking that the amount of mess she'd left in her wake had come as quite a shock.

Things were a bit different here in Pebble Street, that was for sure. Hattie was working on her own – but she soon found that she really didn't mind. It was just lovely to be back in her element again.

She let out a happy sigh, a huge smile spreading over her face. Working in here just felt so easy and natural to her – even though she was having to use such antiquated equipment. Of course, it would be lovely to have some of the gorgeous gear that she was used to from the restaurant – but at least this way she could show the world that she wasn't all about gadgets. She would show them that Hattie Barclay could cook world-class cuisine under any circumstances – even with ordinary ingredients - and the results would be spectacular.

Hattie had been enjoying the process so much that she'd rather lost track of time. It wasn't something she was used to in a working kitchen. There were usually orders flying in all over the place and instructions being yelled left, right and centre with precisely zero niceties added on. Obviously, things were a bit more relaxed in here.

If Hattie was being honest, she'd been apprehensive about working solo at first – she hadn't been sure how she'd react. She was so used to working in cramped conditions, surrounded by other people all moving at the speed of light to get food cooked, plated to perfection and out the door in record time. But this... well, this was bliss – and weirdly, pretty relaxing!

'Hello? Anybody in there?'

Hattie whirled around only to find Ben's head poking around the kitchen door.

'Hi!' she said with a grin. 'You're early!'

Ben shook his head. 'Nope! Bang on time,' he waved his watch at her as if to prove the point.

'Blimey,' gasped Hattie, 'I don't know where today's gone. I completely lost track of time! Don't worry,' she added hastily, 'everything's ready!'

'Brilliant,' said Ben, edging fully into the room, 'I'm absolutely starving. There's nothing like getting up at five in the morning followed by a day full of sea air to get the appetite up.'

'Have you been working all day?' asked Hattie with her back to him, carefully plating up the meal.

'Yup,' said Ben. Fish van this morning, then the bus again for dad for a couple of hours. Then I went up to the allotments for a while before getting a call from Lou down at The Sardine asking if I could fix Trixie their tricycle. She had some problems with the brakes on their delivery rounds this morning – not what you need around here with these hills! Anyway, it's all sorted now.'

'Thank heavens for that!' said Hattie as she turned to Ben. 'Now, why don't you go through and take a seat in the Breakfast Lounge, and I'll play waiter?'

'What, wait in there on my own?' laughed Ben.

'No – I'll join you when you're all set and settled,' said Hattie.

'Nah,' said Ben with a grin. 'Let's make life easy and eat in here, then we can chat while you finish up!' He slumped into one of the chairs at the little wooden table near the door. It was probably the only spot in the entire kitchen that Hattie hadn't covered with dirty pots and pans.

Hattie frowned. This wasn't quite what she'd had planned... but Ben was her guest. If he wanted to eat in here, then they would eat in here.

'Let me get you a glass of wine,' she said.

Ben shook his head. 'Better not. I think I'd better eat something first otherwise I might come over all unnecessary!'

Hattie nodded. 'Fair enough.' She quickly laid two places at the table, and then brought the beautifully arranged plate of food over to him. It looked wonderful, even if she did say so herself. She'd used the monogrammed plates the pair of them had found, and the whole thing just looked balanced to perfection.

However, the moment the plate touched the

kitchen table, Hattie knew she'd made a mistake. Ben looked at the meal, then back up to her, his eyes wide.

Hattie stared back.

'Erm, is there any bread?' asked Ben.

'No,' Hattie shook her head stiffly.

'Oh,' said Ben.

Just like that, the easy banter they'd managed to find disappeared into thin air. Things were suddenly as awkward between them as they had been when she'd backed out of the polytunnel following his cooking rant. This time, though, there was no running away.

'Sorry,' muttered Hattie, 'I've made a bit of a miscalculation, haven't I?'

Ben shrugged, clearly not knowing the right thing to say.

'It looks good though, right?' said Hattie.

Ben peeped back up at her and shrugged again. 'Yeah, but where's the rest of it?'

Hattie looked down at the two tiny, battered fish fillets and the little stack of perfectly golden chips. They barely filled a quarter of the plate. To top things off, the salsa verde looked a bit like a squashed slug now she came to think of it – and the wilted leaves she'd been so proud of had disappeared into almost nothing.

She looked at Ben and saw that he was staring past her towards the little turrets of apple crumble that stood waiting on the counter. Hattie quickly went to step in front of them to block his view – but then stopped herself. It was already too late.

Ben's face broke into a huge smile. Hattie watched in horror as his lips started quivering, and he desperately tried to stop himself from laughing.

He failed.

Miserably.

Once Ben had started to laugh, he simply couldn't seem to stop himself.

Hattie stared at him, determined to be angry. She managed to last all of five seconds before she started to giggle as well. Ben's laugh wasn't one of those mean, jeering sounds. It was full of joy – and completely infectious.

After several minutes, Ben finally managed to hiccup himself back to sanity, holding his ribs as Hattie wiped at the tears of laughter that had trickled down her face.

'You know,' said Ben, 'I think I'd quite like that glass of wine now!'

Hattie grinned at him and headed straight for the fridge. She returned to the table with the bottle and two glasses and poured them both a large glass of wine.

Ben picked his up and lifted it towards her. She smiled at him as she chinked her glass against his and took a sip. Lionel was right, this Upper Bamton stuff really was very nice.

'Can I make a suggestion?' said Ben, as he took a gulp of wine and then cleared his tiny portion of food in about two mouthfuls, 'do you think we can try that again?' he said, pointing at the empty plate. 'Maybe I could help!'

Hattie bit her lip and turned to survey the devastation that was her kitchen. Why not?! She still had fish left, a pan of parboiled potatoes and plenty of stewed apples.

'Sure!' she said, going over to the side and lobbing a spare apron at him. 'I've got everything we need – and a bit more crumble mix will only take a few minutes.'

Ben got to his feet and pulled the apron over his head. 'Can I suggest *a lot* more crumble mix?' he said, looking sadly at the tiny puddings she'd prepared.

Hattie's chin started to tremble and before she knew what was happening, they were both laughing again. As she watched Ben double over, fighting for breath, she decided that he really was a very annoying man... but she couldn't help but like him... a lot.

CHAPTER 18

Carefully lowering the remaining fish fillets into the new batch of batter, Hattie made sure they were coated to perfection. She glanced to her side where Ben was in charge of chopping up the parboiled potatoes for the chips.

'I think you've done enough for the whole of Seabury there!' she laughed.

'Well,' said Ben, reaching for his wine glass and taking a huge sip before carrying on with the job in hand, 'you suggested double the original amount!'

'And that's more like twenty times,' she said, shaking her head.

'You always did like to exaggerate,' smirked Ben. 'It's more like four times.'

Hattie stuck her tongue out at him before heading over to the sink and washing the batter off her fingers.

'More chips,' said Ben. 'Bigger chips. Always better. None of this measuring each one and whittling it down into a matchstick. And that's still not going to be enough fish,' he added, pointing at the fillets.

'Well, that's all there is left,' laughed Hattie, rolling her eyes at him before grabbing a mixing bowl and beginning to weigh out the ingredients for more crumble topping. 'You know, I could have fed a party of six people in the restaurant with the amount of food you're planning to pile on your plate!'

'Well, in that case, all six of them would have needed a large bar of chocolate when they got home to stop them from starving,' said Ben.

Hattie leaned over and gave him a sharp prod with her long, wooden spoon. Ben let out a little growl and threw a tiny bit of potato at her.

'Oi!' she laughed. 'Unless you want an all-out food-fight…'

Ben raised his hands in surrender, laughing as he shook his head. 'Please no, I'm too hungry for that! I need to eat something quick before I get all weak and feeble!'

'Okay,' chuckled Hattie, taking pity on him, 'let's get those chips frying!'

'I'll be right back!' said Ben, dashing from the room as Hattie began to lower the potatoes into the golden, sizzling oil.

She nodded, not taking her eyes off what she was

doing. Once they were all in the pan, Hattie turned only to see Ben sidling back into the room. He was carrying one of the candlesticks they'd found upstairs, along with a freshly laundered tablecloth and some of the silverware.

'Let's do this properly, shall we?' he said with a grin.

Between them, they set the table and Hattie even managed to rustle up a couple of candles from the box she'd discovered in the cupboard under the sink. Presumably, they'd been stashed there in case of a power cut. She lit them, one at a time, from the gas-ring on the hob and placed them carefully in the gleaming silver holder. The table looked beautiful – incredibly proper in amongst the devastation that was now the kitchen.

'Alright, Mr Yolland,' said Hattie. 'Sit yourself down.' She placed his wine glass next to his setting on the table and topped it up.

Ben did as he was told and took his place at the table, while Hattie dished up the newly prepared feast.

When she brought the plate over to him laden with golden chips and perfectly fried fish – along with a good dollop of salsa verde on the side - Ben actually let out a whimper. No matter how hungry he was though, he managed to wait for her to join him with her rather smaller portion of food.

'Tuck in!' she said with a grin.

That's exactly what Ben did. Hattie couldn't believe the amount of food he managed to put away in such a short space of time. Hattie couldn't help but be impressed that he managed to finish it all and secretly wondered whether competitive eating might be his true calling.

There hadn't been much conversation while they'd both groaned their way through the delicious meal, but as they sat finishing Lionel's wine off between them, Ben grinned across at her.

For a moment Hattie was spellbound as the flickering candlelight glittered in his eyes and picked out the golden highlights in his hair. The man, the table, the food, the candles. It was all incredibly romantic.

Uh oh.

No.

Not romantic, just… nice.

'I haven't had so much fun in a kitchen in ages,' she said shyly.

Ben laughed. 'That's because you didn't have to get your ruler out to check the length of each chip.'

'Oh hush, you!' said Hattie, giving him a kick under the table.

Ben promptly got to his feet and then, in slow motion – or at least that's how it felt to Hattie – he leaned across the table and planted a kiss right on her lips.

It was over long before she would have liked it to be – but it took Hattie an age before she could find her voice again. She sat staring at Ben in surprise, lips tingling where his had pressed against them just moments before. She was more than a little bit shell shocked – but more than anything else, she just wished he'd do it again.

'Just wanted to say thank you,' mumbled Ben, a sheepish smile on his face. 'For cooking.'

'You did a fair amount of it yourself!' she croaked.

Ben grinned at her. 'I'm not a chef. I'm just good with quantity!'

'The more the better?' said Hattie.

'If in doubt, double it,' he said, then raised his eyebrows and tilted his head. 'Actually, I take that back. In your case, it needs to be more like quadruple it.'

'Clearly, I've got a few things I need to change before I suit a Seabury customer,' she sighed. 'Pretty much everything, in fact.'

'No, Hattie,' said Ben gently, shooting her a wink, 'they already like everything about you – they just want more of it!'

∽

Hattie dug her toes deeper into the sand and let out a huge sigh as the crashing of the waves invaded her senses. She willed the sound to give her two seconds of respite from reliving those moments with Ben the previous evening. She still couldn't quite work out if the entire night had been a complete disaster or one of the best evenings of her life.

Hattie had woken up, desperate to feel the sand between her toes. The minute she'd climbed down the steps onto West Beach, she'd stripped off her shoes and socks and left them in a heap where they landed. By this point, she could barely feel her toes any longer. Late February in Seabury was far from tropical.

Still, she couldn't imagine a better way to start the day than a quiet walk along the beach. It certainly beat all the noise and bustle, people and worry that had invaded every waking moment in London. Sure, there were one or two people on the beach – mainly the early morning dog-walkers – but they all said hello as they wandered past. In London, she'd always kept her head down, doing her best to blend in and to go unnoticed – but here she felt free to greet the day with her head held high.

Hattie couldn't believe that so much had changed for her in just a few short days - losing her job, being invited to work at Pebble Street, uprooting her entire life and moving to Seabury. No wonder she'd arrived and then promptly gone to sleep for what had seemed like an age. Now here she was trying to make sense of it all. If she was honest, she was still trying to work out whether it was a dream or a nightmare.

Then, of course, there was Ben. Her mind had been circling back to him ever since last night – like it was on some kind of torturous loop. Ben had kissed her – and not just once! He'd done it again in the doorway of the hotel as they'd said good night. For someone who had basically never been out of Seabury, Ben certainly seemed to know what he was doing… just another skill to add to the list of things he was good at.

Hattie sighed, watching as her feet sank into the damp, soft sand with every step she took along the water's edge. Hadn't she promised herself that she wouldn't fall for anyone down here? What was this then… the beginnings of a holiday romance? Would that really be so bad? It couldn't turn into anything serious. Sure, her career was on hold for a little while, but she would need to go back to it before too long.

She didn't dare let herself think too much about what it would be like to settle down with someone here in Seabury. That wasn't for her. Not right now, at least. Maybe when she got to be as old as Lionel.

Hattie shook her head. She felt mean for even thinking that. She had no idea how old Lionel had been when he'd first arrived in town. Did it even matter? All she knew was that this was the perfect place for him – but it wasn't the right place for her – not for long, anyway.

Hattie paused and stared impatiently out to sea for a moment. She felt like there were two invisible sides of herself at war in her head – the one that had fallen back in love with this tiny seaside town after just a handful of days, and the other – that wanted to chase the dream of owning her own restaurant and dazzling the critics.

As she watched the waves, a boat appeared around the end of The King's Nose. Slowing down, it came a little closer to shore before the driver cut the engine and waved at her. Hattie broke into a massive grin and waved back. It was Ben.

'Hey Hattie!' he yelled against the breeze.

'Where are you off to?' she called back, trying to ignore just how happy she was to see him again.

'I've got to go and rescue Stanley! He's made friends with a seal and is headed for France!'

Hattie started laughing.

'Can I see you again later?' he shouted at the top of his voice.

It didn't take her a second to think about it. 'Of course!' she called back. 'Dinner again?'

Ben gave her two thumbs up, and even from this distance, she could see the huge grin on his freckled face. 'More chips please!' he yelled.

Laughing again, Hattie watched as Ben started up the engine. She waved madly as he set off. He turned and grinned at her over his shoulder, raising his hand in farewell as he sped off around the far point.

Hattie stood watching the spot where he'd disappeared for several minutes, unable to wipe the smile from her face as she wriggled her toes into the damp, cold sand.

Maybe life was simpler than she thought? It might be worth sticking around for a little while to find out. After all, it could be fun…

THE END

SECRETS IN SEABURY

SEABURY - PART 5

CHAPTER 1

*H*attie Barclay was quickly discovering that living in a hotel room had some unexpected perks. For instance, she loved the fact that her great uncle Lionel delivered the Sunday papers right up to her room and left them outside her door every week. Sure, they were always a little bit late, but what difference did that make in the grand scheme of things? It might be Wednesday already, but that didn't mean she couldn't enjoy a good read in bed before starting the day, did it? After all, you couldn't have everything, could you?

Things at The Pebble Street Hotel were fairly eccentric, but frankly what else could you expect with Lionel Barclay in charge? Besides – she adored her uncle for all his little foibles, and she was quickly falling head over heels in love with the hotel too.

Jumping back into bed, Hattie riffled through the

various sections of the chunky paper, spreading them out across her duvet as she searched for the food supplement. Ah ha! There it was.

She grabbed the glossy magazine and settled back into her pillows, taking a deep, steadying breath before beginning to scan through it. She didn't know why she was so nervous – what difference did it make to her what they'd printed about Marco Brook's new place? She didn't have anything to do with her old boss anymore, after all.

Hattie had been waiting to get her hands on this newspaper since Sunday afternoon when Laura, one of the pastry chefs at her old restaurant in London, had sent her a text about it. Apparently, Marco's new restaurant *Number 14* had been reviewed by their notoriously vicious food critic – and according to Laura it was "unmissable reading".

Hattie wasn't one hundred per cent sure what that meant, but she did know that Marco was *persona non grata* with all his old staff after he'd sacked the whole lot of them en masse before buggering off to his new restaurant. Somehow, she couldn't imagine it was going to be anything good.

Marco Brooks was rude, precious and obnoxious. He also had one of the worst tempers she'd ever come across in a kitchen – which was saying something. But after eighteen months of hard graft, putting up with all his rubbish because she thought it would get her one step closer to her dream of owning her own place one day – Hattie simply couldn't shake the feeling that her name was still connected with his somehow.

Flipping hurriedly through the pages, her heart started to pound way too hard for this early on a Wednesday morning. She was being ridiculous… this had absolutely nothing to do with her.

'Stop being an idiot,' she muttered, her heart still racing, making her feel clammy and slightly sick. Then she let out a breath she hadn't realised she'd been holding. There. She'd reached the review.

For a minute, she couldn't tear her eyes away from the single yellow star that topped it. Oh dear – this might be even worse than she'd suspected.

Hattie let her eyes drift to the critique underneath. She read the first few lines and winced. It made for painful reading right from the word go. Starting out with the restaurant itself, the reviewer criticised everything from the décor and the lighting to the *"dreadful, disinterested and ill-informed staff."*

'Hah!'

Just like that, her nerves morphed into something that felt more like vindication, and she was unable to stop a little smirk from sneaking onto her face.

He deserved it. It bloody well served him right for dumping the incredible team that he'd had at his old place. He had treated them like rubbish the entire time they'd worked for him – but they'd been a brilliant bunch – knowledgeable, experienced and flawless in the way they kept that place running.

Marco had promised to take everyone with him when he moved on to *Number 14* but had then dumped them all without a backwards glance.

'Looks like it's come back to bite you on the bottom, doesn't it, you miserable sod?!' Hattie muttered as she glanced at the artsy photograph of Marco in his chef whites that accompanied the piece. She wrinkled her nose at his shaved head with the ridiculous orange topknot. Pretentious git.

Hattie didn't dwell on it for long though – she wanted to get to the bit about the food.

"Due to an oversight, I left it rather later than I'd intended to book a table for my party. Fully expecting to be disappointed, I was surprised to find that Number 14 had any space left for us on what should have been a busy Friday night. On arrival, it turned out that the restaurant was practically empty. Now, having sampled the menu and the atrocious level of service diners can expect, I'm no longer surprised at its lack of customers - in fact, I'm now surprised that there were any there at all ... something that won't be true for very much longer, I'm sure."

Hattie blew out a breath.

Ouch.

She quickly skimmed down to the next section where the critic got his teeth into his favourite subject. After just a few sentences, she started to cringe again.

"Brooks has somehow created a menu that manages to be plain and stodgy at the same time as being annoyingly tricksy. It's minimal and old-fashioned, but not in a good way. The dishes are bland, flavourless and overcooked."

Seriously – ouch! Could this get any worse?

Her eyes flew over the next few lines and the words there made her want to hide under the pillows in some kind of shame-by-proxy.

"A once-rising star in the culinary firmament, everything pointed towards the fact that Marco Brooks was going to be a name destined for greatness. Sadly, it looks like he has boiled over."

'Oh, bloody hell!' squeaked Hattie, flipping the magazine closed and flinging it away from her in case that kind of criticism was catching. She wriggled back down in her bed and burrowed under her duvet.

Poor Marco.

Nah. Balls to that. Poor Marco indeed!

She gave herself a little shake and let the horror of the bad review leave her body. It had *nothing* to do with her. Marco had made sure of that. The guy was a complete tool who didn't deserve a single ounce of loyalty or respect after the way he'd treated them all. The way he'd treated *her*.

Hattie felt the familiar swell of indignation fill her chest. She'd put so much energy and effort into his restaurant over the eighteen months she'd worked with him, and he'd cast her aside without a moment's hesitation. Well, it certainly looked like he was getting his comeuppance, didn't it?!

Under the privacy of her duvet, Hattie allowed a little smile to cross her lips. She knew it wasn't the done thing to gloat, but she felt justified in taking just a second to revel in Marco's downfall.

She didn't give into it for long, though. It was a total waste of energy when she had a busy day ahead of her here at Pebble Street. Popping her head back out from her mound of fluffy bedding, Hattie peered around her, feeling a sudden rush of warmth and love for the place.

The room was already beginning to fill up with shells and interesting bits of driftwood she'd collected during her brief walks on Seabury's two beaches. Her apartment in London had been so lifeless and practically half the size. She didn't miss it for a second. This might be just a room in a hotel, but it already felt more like home than her old place ever had.

Hattie let out a little snort of laughter as the food critic's words popped back into her head.

Plain.

Stodgy.

Tricksy.

Man, she didn't miss working for Marco one little bit. He'd always had this habit of getting in the way. Whichever way she turned and no matter what she was doing, he was there ready to trip her up.

Marco had spent more time wanting to photograph the food than actually doing any cooking - that bit was usually left up to her. As was the buying, all the preparation... oh, and the cleaning down afterwards. Well, it certainly looked like he was in the process of discovering just how much she'd really done for him, didn't it?!

Hattie sat up and shuffled towards the edge of her bed. It was time to put Marco Brooks out of her mind. That was all firmly in the past. She was in charge of the kitchen at the hotel – and she was determined that she was going to make a success of it, even if most people would never know it existed.

Swinging her legs over the edge of the bed, Hattie stretched then slumped slightly, letting out a huge sigh. That was the one fly in the ointment, wasn't it? The only bit about being here in Seabury that niggled away in the back of her mind and sapped the joy out of things. Being here meant that her dream of having her own, successful restaurant would remain just that – a dream.

Ah well, right now wasn't the moment to dwell on what she couldn't have. There was so much to be done that there wasn't really a moment to lose... even though she'd love nothing more than a pot of tea and some toast in bed right now. Not today though.

Today was all about securing herself some waiting staff for their opening night at the restaurant, and she had Lou from The Sardine turning up for her interview before too long.

Hattie and Lionel had discussed it at length. Funds were tight, but they'd decided that they couldn't do without someone in to help them. If they could lend a hand in the lead up to the big night too – all the better! It was happening in just over a week, and Hattie was already a bag of nerves. What she needed was someone steady, calm and experienced to help make sure everything went off without a hitch.

If this had been London, she'd have had CVs from hundreds of applicants willing to work long hours for very little pay. That had always been the way of it at Marco's place – hundreds of applicants willing to sell their souls, all for the pleasure of being able to say that they'd worked for Marco Brooks.

She'd always wished that she could have given them a sneaky heads-up that Marco was *not* a nice person to work for. He had an appalling temper and treated his waiting staff like dirt. Hattie was determined that she would *never* behave like that towards her staff. That wasn't the kind of kitchen she intended to run. Still, that didn't mean she could magic applications out of thin air. This was Seabury after all, not London!

Luckily, Hattie remembered that one of the waitresses over at The Sardine had mentioned that she'd be interested in some shifts if they became available. She reckoned that Lou would be just about perfect for the job – which was just as well really, as she was the only applicant!

Rose Blanchford had said that she wouldn't mind helping out if there was a problem, but Hattie had gently declined her kind offer. Given that the former Pebble Street chambermaid was now ninety-three, Hattie thought that she deserved an invitation as one of her guests of honour - rather than ask her to put her pinny back on for the evening!

Right. It was time to start the day. Hattie gave her mattress one last loving pat, got to her feet and wandered over to pull open the curtains.

It was cold and blustery outside. The sea was grey and all stirred up as it swirled ominously around the rocky outcrops of the King's Nose. Hattie peered over towards the pebble-strewn North Beach, which was completely empty, and then turned her eyes towards the sandy shores of West Beach.

'You're kidding me?!' she breathed.

Hattie watched in mild horror as half a dozen or so of the Chilly Dippers, Seabury's wild-swimming group of nutcases, marched their way down the beach towards the water. Clearly, they were about to brave the waves. She couldn't quite make out exactly who they all were from here, but she was pretty certain that one of them was Lou!

Hattie stared harder. Yep – it was definitely Lou – wearing a plastic swimming cap of some sort. Well, this had to be the weirdest form of interview preparation she'd ever come across, but each to their own!

Hattie snorted with laughter as she watched them wade into the forbidding waters. They were laughing and splashing about having a great time. Odd lot!

'Ouch!' squeaked Hattie as a massive wave hit Lou dead in the face. Her prospective member of staff promptly disappeared from view under the agitated water for a few seconds before three of the other Dippers came to her rescue, reaching down and hauling her back to her feet. From what Hattie could make out of Lou's body language as she tried to regain her balance, it didn't look like she was enjoying the experience of being pummelled by the waves very much. The rest of them were a completely different story, however.

Hattie shook her head and gave an involuntary shiver. Yep. They were definitely more than a little bit nutty!

CHAPTER 2

Hattie closed her bedroom door gently behind her as she made her way out into the hallway - and promptly broke into a huge grin. This happened every single morning when it dawned on her that she no longer had to face the dreaded commute across London to get to Marco's restaurant. Her kitchen was down just a few flights of stairs, and she could practically sleep-walk there if she needed to.

Not that getting a good night's sleep was any kind of problem here in Seabury. The fresh sea air and sound of shushing waves beneath her bedroom window made sure that Hattie slept long and deep, no matter how stressed she might be.

As she wandered towards the main stairwell, Hattie admired the fresh coat of paint that had appeared on the walls of the corridor. The hotel had changed quite a bit over the last couple of weeks and there was always something new to discover. Ben was working his way through the building like a whirlwind.

What had started with him patching up the little bits of damage the pair of them had caused during their treasure hunt had quickly turned into a full-building facelift. It was typical of Ben really - if he knew something needed doing, he wouldn't rest until it was done. Basically, the whole of Pebble Street needed something doing – so poor old Ben was unlikely to get any rest for quite some time!

Everything was a work in progress as he dashed around redecorating, restoring and recarpeting. He'd already worked wonders, but there was still a long way to go.

Usually covered in a fine film of wood shavings and a generous splattering of emulsion paint, Ben barely ever stood still. Although it meant he was super-busy, Hattie secretly loved the fact that there was so much for him to do at the hotel - because it meant she got to see him every day. It might be just brief moments snatched in between jobs, but at least it was something.

Hattie felt a tingly glow sweep through her. The little boy she'd played with every holiday when they were kids had turned into a kind and ridiculously gorgeous man. Every time she caught a glimpse of Ben, bending low to fit a piece of new carpet or stretching up to fill a bit of cracked ceiling plaster, Hattie's heart flipped. It took all her willpower not to turn into a daydreamy teenager every five minutes with him around.

Ben Yolland had very quickly become one of the main reasons that being here in Seabury wasn't quite the disaster she'd expected it to be. She just hoped that after opening night, things might settle down a bit so that they could actually spend a bit of quality time together. Time that didn't involve paint brushes or discussing light fittings!

Hattie paused as she arrived at the top of the vast, sweeping main staircase that led down to the ground floor. She grinned as she ran a finger lovingly over the smooth curves of the newly stripped bannisters. One of the first things Lionel had asked Ben to do was to get rid of the layers of horrid gloss paint from the long sweep of wood. Now it was back to its fully polished mahogany glory that Hattie remembered sliding down as a child. Oh, how she'd love to do that again.

Why not?!

Maybe it was time to reclaim a little bit of her youthful naughtiness!

Hattie hesitated, throwing a glance over her shoulder. It was still fairly early, and it didn't sound like there was anyone else around... but she shouldn't, should she?! She was a grown-up. She had so much to do...

It was a difficult temptation to ignore, though… in fact, it would be a waste of all Ben's hard work if she didn't make the most of it. And that would just be rude, wouldn't it?!

She didn't want to appear ungrateful.

And, after all, no one was around to see…

Throwing caution to the wind, Hattie hopped onto the bannisters, threw her whole weight against the rich, glossy wood and started to slide, gaining speed by the second. She shot around the corner and pelted down towards the ground floor.

'Whhhhheeeeeeeeeee!' she squealed, her inner eight-year-old going wild as her heart thumped.

The bump of the newel post as she reached the ground floor nearly toppled Hattie from the bannisters, and a delighted giggle escaped as she clambered down… only to find Lionel waiting for her. He had his arms crossed, one eyebrow raised in rare disapproval.

Uh oh!

Hattie blushed, feeling like a naughty kid. What made it worse was the fact that her uncle was standing in exactly the same spot Veronica used to lie in wait for her. That woman had been like a trap door spider, ready to jump out and start yelling at the slightest hint of any fun going on in her establishment. Miserable old bat.

'I knew you wouldn't be able to resist,' sighed Lionel.

Hattie shot him a sheepish grin and then relaxed as she caught the twinkle of amusement in his eyes. Her uncle couldn't be more different from Veronica if he tried! Now – as long as he didn't start asking her about the menu for their opening night, she might just get away with-

'How's the menu looking for the big event?' asked Lionel.

Balls.

Hattie straightened the sleeves of her jumper and pushed her hair back out of the way, trying to buy some time. 'Erm... it's still a bit of a work in progress,' she said. Then she sighed. She knew she owed it to Lionel to be completely straight with him. He deserved that, at the very least, after everything he'd done for her. 'I don't know, it all feels a bit up in the air... like the rest of the hotel.'

Lionel patted her kindly on the shoulder. 'Don't worry about the hotel, there's plenty of time for all that to come together.'

Hattie nodded, horribly aware of her heart thudding in her chest. She wished she could blame it on her slide down from upstairs, but she knew this was more to do with the fact that her to-do list was looming large.

For some reason, she was finding it hard to make decisions and finalise anything. She was usually so confident in the kitchen – clear and decisive - but this new menu was proving to be an absolute nightmare to pull together.

The trouble was, Hattie was desperate for Seabury to fall in love with her cooking, but to do that, she knew she needed something different from what she was used to serving in London. She'd learned that lesson the hard way when she'd cooked for Ben the first time. The worthies of Seabury wouldn't be swayed by fancy ingredients and tiny portions. She needed to be bold and brave and go her own way... but that was proving to be far scarier than she could have imagined.

'Now,' said Lionel. 'I don't want to pressure you in any way, but the breakfast room is already filling up with bookings and I want to make sure that I don't end up having to feed my guests sandwiches again!'

Lionel let out a barking laugh, which Hattie did her best to emulate, though she felt her heart rate kick up another notch.

'Don't worry,' she said with a forced grin, 'it won't come to that!'

'I know, my dear,' said Lionel with a grin. 'I have complete faith in you.'

Hattie nodded, trying to swallow her fear. She had loads of ideas for the menu jotted down in her precious notebook – she'd been brimming over with plans after the pair of them had agreed that Pebble Street was going to be a fish restaurant... but she just couldn't make those final decisions. What if it just wasn't enough? What if no one liked her food?

Not for the first time, she sent up a little prayer of thanks that she'd made the decision to go with the much smaller breakfast lounge for their opening night. The dining room was vast – and the thought of *that* being filled with hungry guests waiting to judge her new menu would have sent her completely potty by now.

If she was being totally honest, using the breakfast lounge hadn't been entirely her decision. If they'd gone for the dining room instead, there simply wouldn't have been enough plates, serving dishes or even spoons to go around. Add to that the fact that half the chairs were rickety and awaiting repair and they could have had a disaster on their hands. The last thing they needed was for their guests to be dumped unceremoniously on the floor as they waited for their puddings!

Hattie made a mental note to ask Ben to sort out the chairs - though there was no way she could expect him to get around to them in time for opening night. He already had way too much to do as it was.

'Shall we take a look at the breakfast lounge?' said Lionel.

Hattie nodded, suddenly feeling like she was being led to the gallows. She followed her uncle through the doorway and looked around despondently. She really wanted to be in love with the space that was about to become their new restaurant, but it still needed so much work. She just couldn't picture the final outcome.

The wallpaper was grubby, and Hattie really wanted to get rid of the huge rug that covered the floorboards. She'd never liked carpets in restaurants – they just didn't make any sense to her. On top of that, they'd need to remove all the random bits of furniture out of here too.

'You know,' said Lionel, clearly sensing her low mood, 'it's amazing how much a splash of fresh paint on the walls can work wonders…'

Hattie nodded. 'Yep – it definitely needs it and there's just about time to make sure it's aired in here before opening night if we get on with it.'

Lionel nodded encouragingly.

'And I'm going to get rid of those awful pictures Veronica put up!' she continued, pointing at the garish prints that lined the room. 'That's okay with you, isn't it?'

'Absolutely!' said Lionel. 'You're the boss, Hattie.'

Hattie smiled. She might be the boss, but at times it didn't feel much like it. There were plenty of things that she knew needed doing – but she also knew they would have to wait. Money was tight and they simply didn't have the funds to do everything. At least, not yet.

For instance, the curtains in here looked like they

were the same ones from when the hotel had originally opened its doors – and she'd love to replace the ancient light-fittings too. Still – they'd get there eventually. After all, they'd managed to come up with some ingenious solutions when it came to the rest of the hotel.

The carpets on the stairs had been so worn as to be dangerous, so after a couple of days of asking around, Ben had managed to source a whole bunch of mismatched offcuts that various local companies had gladly gifted to Lionel. With a bit of careful cutting and laying, the staircase now boasted a different colour and pattern every couple of treads. It looked ridiculously funky – and way more intentional than it had any right to be.

Perhaps if Hattie could commandeer Ben for a couple of hours to help her in here, they'd finally get somewhere. If they could just get rid of the rug, paint the walls and generally make it feel more like a restaurant it might give her the kick up the bum she needed to start finalising the menu.

'Maybe Lou will be able to help me get things in here up to scratch,' said Hattie, giving the curtains a final glare before turning back to her uncle.

Lionel smiled. 'Isn't her interview today?'

Hattie nodded. 'Yep – that's if she doesn't drown first. It looks like the Chilly Dippers finally got their hands on her.'

'Lord save and protect her,' laughed Lionel. 'Well,

I hope it works out. Lou's a gem – I think she'll fit in really well here.'

'Me too,' said Hattie nodding.

She was pretty sure Lou would be perfect – she had impeccable references from Kate for starters. Like her, Lou hadn't been in Seabury all that long, but it was clear that she was very well-liked. Hattie agreed with her uncle, she thought Lou would fit in a treat… the weird, icy swimming thing notwithstanding. But then, this *was* Seabury - everyone here was just a tiny bit nutty.

'Let's just hope she won't mind rolling up her sleeves and getting stuck in straight away,' sighed Hattie.

'Knowing Lou, she'll be delighted. Let me know how it goes, won't you?' said Lionel.

Hattie smiled and nodded.

'Right, I'll leave you to it – sounds like you've got your hands full.'

The minute Lionel was out of sight, Hattie let the smile slide back off her face. For just a moment she allowed herself to feel the full weight of everything she needed to do. There was a serious amount of work to be done before she could pull off the perfect opening night.

Being in charge of everything foodie here at The Pebble Street Hotel wasn't quite what she'd been expecting when she took the job. There was a lot more DIY, maintenance and clever budgeting involved than she would have ever guessed.

'You've got this, Hattie,' she muttered to herself, staring around the room for one last time before going to get her list of questions ready for Lou's interview.

Of course she could do this. She just had to pick a place to start and work from there.

CHAPTER 3

The minute Hattie pushed her way into the kitchen, she felt more confident. Even if she was having a bit of a nightmare with the menu, this was her territory. This was where she knew what was what. Sure, she'd recently developed the annoying habit of double-guessing herself – even when it came to cooking – but at least in here, she was back on firmer ground.

The kitchen was all spotlessly clean now, thanks to Ethel's help with her initial blitz. Hattie'd thrown all the old food away, along with anything that was too broken or worn to use. She'd even managed to replace most of the basics – making sure that her limited budget went as far as she could possibly stretch it.

Sure, she'd love nothing more than to be able to add some of the gadgets she'd been used to back in

London, but it was definitely a case of "make-do" for now until things got off the ground.

The good news was that they hadn't come across any signs of infestation in the place – no mice or, even worse, rats had been in here. She'd been relieved, but not particularly surprised. Veronica had been so mean with her food that there would have been precious little for the blighters to eat if they had come to visit.

Still, Hattie had taken a certain amount of satisfaction in stripping the kitchen back to its bare bones. All the cupboards had been emptied, bleached and then washed out more than once with scalding hot water.

It was definitely coming together. She had everything where she wanted it and she was starting to learn steps that went with her new workspace. There was a dance that went with every kitchen. The one in London had included many hasty back-steps to avoid Marco and his blasted camera. Not here though – this kitchen was a blissful one-woman performance.

Hattie pulled a high stool up to one of the counters, grabbed her notebook and a pencil and glanced at the clock. Lou was due to arrive in five minutes. She had just enough time to run through the questions she'd already jotted down and add a few more.

Hattie was keen to pick Lou's brains about ideas for the breakfast lounge. Sometimes a fresh perspective was all that was needed. Perhaps she could come up with some suggestions on how to make the space a bit more presentable in a short space of time... with no budget!

Exactly five minutes later, a knock on the door made Hattie's head snap up. Lou had arrived right on time for her interview.

Hattie did her best not to stare... or giggle...

Lou definitely had an odd take on what might be considered suitable attire for a job interview. She was wrapped in a large, purple towel. The straps of a light blue swimming costume peeped out from underneath it, crisscrossing the mottled, slightly blue skin of her shoulders. She was wearing a pair of wellington boots on her feet and on her head sat a swimming cap with pink, plastic flowers all over it.

Hattie leapt to her feet just a beat too late to be polite and held out her hand.

'Hi Lou,' she said, forcing her voice to remain steady. It was quite a job considering how much she wanted to laugh right now. 'Erm... thanks for coming in.'

Lou nodded stiffly and took her hand.

Bloody hell, her fingers were-

'S-s-s-s-o-r-r-r-y!' stuttered Lou through purple lips. 'I'm f-f-f-f-r-e-e-e-z-z-ing!'

Hattie nodded in agreement. The woman's fingers were blocks of ice. 'Can I get you a hot drink?'

'Y-y-y-e-s-s p-p-l-e-a-s-s-s-e!' shivered Lou.

Hattie quickly made her way over to flick the

kettle on. Unless she managed to thaw Lou out, this interview was going to take quite a while to complete.

'Have a seat,' she said, turning back to Lou with a smile and pointing to the second stool at the counter. Lou dropped gratefully onto it without saying a word.

Hattie sighed. The poor thing had clearly had the wind knocked out of her as well as being cold to the bone. She realised that it was probably up to her to make small-talk until Lou warmed up a bit – she definitely wasn't up to it in her state.

'So,' said Hattie, lifting down two mugs and adding a teabag, 'how was the water?'

'R-r-r-o-u-g-h-h!'

One word was clearly all Lou could manage. Hattie placed a steaming mug of tea in front of her and watched as she wrapped her blue-tinged fingers around it gratefully.

'Give me two secs,' said Hattie.

She dashed for the door. There was no way she could watch Lou shiver for another second – it was making goosebumps appear on her own arms. She grabbed the big old fleecy jacket she'd left on the back of the chair in reception. It was the one she always threw on for a bit of added warmth whenever she headed down to one of the beaches.

'Here!' she said, striding back into the kitchen and throwing the jacket around Lou's shoulders. She could practically feel chilly waves rolling off her prospective member of staff.

'Thank y-y-o-u-u!' said Lou, snuggling gratefully into the extra layer. Her teeth were now officially chattering. Hattie quickly realised that this interview was going to go nowhere fast.

'Look, Lou,' she said, making a swift decision, 'you need to go home and sit in a warm bath for about a week!'

Hattie saw Lou flinch, and she had a feeling that she would probably try to tell her that she was "absolutely fine" – if only she could get the words out past her shivering lips. Hattie held up a hand to save her the effort.

'You can come back later when you've recovered,' she said, giving her a smile. She already knew that she was going to offer Lou the job. There was no point keeping her here and stringing this out any longer – at least, not when hypothermia was a serious risk! 'You've got the job if you want it.'

'Y-a-y-y. T-t-t-h-a-n-n-k y-y-y-o-u!' said Lou, greeting the news with a big shivery grin, followed by a nod. 'I d-d-d-o-o-o n-n-e-e-d to g-g-o h-h-h-o-m-m-m-e!'

'You're welcome,' said Hattie. 'Now get going and warm up properly before you get sick.'

Lou nodded and went to peel the fleece off again, but Hattie quickly shook her head. 'Oh no you don't!

Bring it back another time – you need it more than me right now!'

~

As soon as Hattie had seen a shivering Lou back out through the front door, she headed straight back to the kitchen, grabbed a bucket and began to mop up the sea-watery footprints Lou had left all over the kitchen floor – along with quite a lot of sand and several bits of seaweed.

It had certainly never been like this when she'd worked in London! Just the thought made her grin. Sure, Lou had been frozen, virtually monosyllabic and turning blue – but Hattie couldn't help but like her. She just hoped she'd made the right decision!

'Hello you!'

Hattie's head shot up only to find Ben peering at her around the kitchen door.

'Hi!' she said, straightening up and leaning on the mop. 'Just the man I wanted to see!'

'Oh yes?' he said, coming fully into the room and shooting her a grin that stole her breath away. How did he manage to do this to her every single time they were in the same room?

His sandy, messy beach hair was tucked back behind his ears, perfectly showing off the sprinkling of freckles across his nose and cheeks. Ben really was just as gorgeous as he'd been when they were kids, and she was just as head-over-heels about him as she had been all those years ago. Not that she could tell him that, of course. Because that would mean whatever this was between them was serious. And it couldn't be serious because she had no idea how long she was going to stay put in Seabury.

Hattie let out a quiet, quivering breath that was actually a full-blown, lusty groan inside her head.

'Erm, earth to Hattie?' laughed Ben.

'Huh?' she said, dazedly wondering what she was doing holding a mop.

'You said you needed to see me?' he raised his eyebrows at her, and she was sure she could see a naughty twinkle going on in their depths. Damn it – it was bad enough that he made her feel like this every time he was in the same room – the last thing she needed was for him to *know* what she was thinking when she zoned out!

'Right... right!' she said, trying to pull herself together. 'I need to get the menu for the opening night finalised. I was wondering what veggies are available up at the allotments. I... erm... I didn't really take it all in last time I was up there!'

She winced slightly at the memory. The first time she'd headed up to the allotments, she'd got into an argument with Ben about what "proper" cooking meant and had left in high dudgeon. The second time she'd visited, she'd snuck into his polytunnel and pilfered a bunch of ingredients. To be fair, they'd been for a meal she'd been cooking for him, but still…

'Well, it's still pretty early in the season,' said Ben, 'but there are some bits and pieces coming ready. I've got plenty of herbs just about ready for a haircut if you need any. And some of the other plot holders still have some winter veggies in storage – though they're coming to an end now too. I think your best bet would be to have a word with Charlie and he can ask around for you.'

Hattie nodded, feeling even more confused than before she'd asked. Somehow, it didn't sound particularly inspiring – but there might be something up there that might spark off her imagination and help her finalise her menu.

Hattie was keen to work with the growers at the allotments if she could. She didn't really want to have to head out of town to one of the big shops. That was the mistake Veronica had made – she'd gone for inferior ingredients that were then poorly cooked. Hattie would rather cook with seasonal, local ingredients if she could.

'I'm just going to have to get creative!' she said, feeling a spike of determination mingle with the nerves that had been swirling in her gut for days now.

Ben smiled at her and nodded. 'You definitely need to come up for another visit and have a look at what's available. You'll get a better feel for it up there.

The Sardine seem to be managing to find plenty for their vegetable soups!'

'Yeah,' chuckled Hattie, 'I think poor old Lou could have done with a bowl of Kate's soup this morning rather than coming over to see me instead.'

'What happened?' said Ben, raising his eyebrows.

'The Chilly Dippers got their hands on her. *Why* she'd agree to go swimming in the sea just before an interview is beyond me...'

'You try having to repeatedly say "no" to that lot,' laughed Ben, 'it's practically impossible after a while!'

'Have you ever been in with them?' she asked, trying not to get too swept up in the image of Ben in a pair of swimming shorts.

Ben shook his head. 'Nah. They've asked me loads of times, but I always tell them I'm too busy. Tends to be the truth anyway, luckily! Doesn't sound like our girl had her excuses nicely lined up, though!'

'Poor Lou!' laughed Hattie. 'She was in a total state. She was shivering so badly she could barely hold the cup of tea I made. In the end, I gave her an extra layer to wear and sent her home to warm up.'

'Good call,' said Ben. 'Don't worry, she'll be back. The Chilly Dippers all have to be a bit mad – but she'll soon get used to it.'

Hattie nodded. 'She's got the job anyway. I really like her – so does everyone else – so it's a no-brainer really.'

Ben nodded. 'She's great. Just gets on with

everyone and fits in. Just what you need. Someone who gets stuck in with very little drama.'

'As long as you don't count this morning,' said Hattie with a grin.

'Well, quite!' said Ben. 'Oh – Lionel mentioned you might need a hand with some bits and bobs in the breakfast lounge?'

Hattie nodded. 'If you've got any time to spare? If not, I'm going to rope Lou in as soon as she's back in the land of the warm-blooded.'

'I've got a couple of hours this afternoon if that's any good?'

'You have?' said Hattie, unable to mask the relief in her voice.

'Sure!' said Ben. 'I've got to wash the bus with dad and then I've promised to fix someone's toilet. Oh – and I need to nip up to the allotments and make sure the polytunnel hasn't been blown away or lain siege to by a bunch of slugs… but that's a fairly quiet morning really. As soon as I'm done, I'll come back and get stuck in.'

Hattie grinned at him. 'That would be amazing.'

'Righty-ho! I can't stop for a cuppa,' he said just as she opened her mouth to offer him one.

The next thing she knew, he'd disappeared.

And then he was back.

'Forgot something,' he said.

Striding over to her, Ben threaded his fingers into the hair at the nape of Hattie's neck and caught her lips in a swift, warm kiss. Hattie closed her eyes, breathing in the smell of sea spray and the outdoors mixed with the faintest hint of paint.

And then he was gone again, leaving her reeling and rather grateful that she could still cling to the mop for a bit of support.

Hattie blinked and shook her head. Ben Yolland had a kind of magic about him that could make her forget every single one of her worries – for a moment or two at least.

CHAPTER 4

It was early afternoon when a hectic knocking at the hotel's front door brought Hattie skittering out from the kitchen. She'd been completely lost in menu planning and was feeling more than a little bit dazed by the interruption.

She opened the door to find Lou getting ready to hammer on it again.

'Hi!' said Hattie in surprise. 'You look... warmer!'

'And I've got more clothes on,' snorted Lou, looking mildly mortified as she handed the fleecy jacket back to Hattie.

Hattie took it with a smile and beckoned for Lou to follow her inside.

'I'm so sorry about this morning,' said Lou. 'I got ambushed by the Dippers and I couldn't really say no because I did say I would give it a go and I don't know if you know what they're like but it's practically impossible to worm out of anything around that lot and I didn't want to chicken out.'

Hattie raised her eyebrows. She had a feeling her new member of staff wasn't aware that she'd just entered full-blown auto-witter and had said all that in one breath.

'Anyway,' said Lou, clearly unable to give in to a single moment of silence, 'now that I've warmed up – it was actually really… invigorating? Not that I want to go in again. Not until August anyway. Maybe I should get myself a wetsuit… though I don't like the idea of squeezing in and out of one of those and having all my wobbly bits on show for everyone to see. None of the others wear wetsuits and I'd hate to be the odd one out. I don't know how they do it.'

She paused.

'I really don't.'

She paused again.

'I'm so sorry. I've just developed verbal diarrhoea, haven't I?!'

Hattie chuckled and nodded as she watched Lou go a bit pink. Finally quiet, she was looking at her awkwardly, as if unsure what to say next.

'Well,' said Hattie, taking pity on her, 'if a morning dip in the sea can do this for you, maybe I should try it myself. I reckon I'd get so much more done!'

Lou broke into a grateful smile. 'Happy to make

the introductions,' she said, raising her eyebrows playfully.

'Let's wait until after opening night, shall we?' said Hattie, as a swoop of unease ran through her.

'Lots to do?' said Lou, going serious.

'You've no idea,' said Hattie with a heavy sigh.

Lou nodded, stripped off her coat and dumped it on the back of the chair at the reception desk. Then she stashed her shoulder bag underneath it as if she'd been doing this for months. Rolling up the sleeves of her jumper, she turned back to Hattie.

'Right,' said Lou, a determined look on her face, 'what can I do to help?'

'Now?' said Hattie. 'As in, you want to start today?'

'If you need me?'

'Oh, trust me, I need you,' Hattie laughed. 'Follow me.'

She led Lou down the hallway and into the breakfast lounge. Just the sight of it did its usual trick of making her feel instantly deflated. If Lou could help her to transform this space – even slightly – maybe it would kickstart everything else too.

'Welcome to the restaurant,' she said flatly.

Lou nodded, looking around with interest. 'It could be really nice,' she said carefully. 'Lovely light, nice view…'

'And so far, that's about it,' Hattie laughed. 'But as nice as the dining room is-'

'It's huge!' said Lou, finishing her thought for her.

'Precisely. So, to begin with, this is what we've got to work with,' said Hattie.

'How can I help?' said Lou again.

Hattie glanced at her and the sincere look on Lou's face had some kind of instant, magical effect on Hattie's stress levels. She felt the weight that had been resting on her shoulders lift ever so slightly.

'Maybe we could start by taking these bloody awful pictures down,' said Hattie. 'They've got to go – they're hideous!'

Lou nodded in agreement. 'Got a ladder?'

'Yep. Ben's left his stepladder leaning against the wall by the toilets. I'll grab it!'

Within moments, she was back.

'We'll take it in turns,' said Hattie, positioning the steps and climbing straight up them, leaving Lou down below ready to take the ugly picture from her as she lifted it down.

The frame was ancient and dusty. The minute Hattie disturbed it, the plaster around the picture hook started to crumble, sending a shower of dust down onto Lou as it threatened to come out of the wall.

'Watch your eyes!' said shouted.

Lou turned her face away just in time and then reached up to take the frame from Hattie.

'Next!' said Hattie, climbing back down.

'Actually, this is a one-person job, don't you

think?' said Lou. 'I'll do this. The ladder's completely safe and there's no point you standing underneath and getting plaster in your hair!' She reached up and picked a chunk out of her own ponytail with a laugh.

'Okay – you're on,' said Hattie. 'Just pile them up over there by the door so that we can take them around to the bins once you're done. I'm going to shift those chairs and tables to the side so that I can start rolling this carpet out of the way at the other end of the room.'

'Sounds like a plan,' said Lou, shifting the ladder to the next horrible print and bounding up it.

Hattie made her way over to the far end of the room and started stacking the spindly chairs that were currently set around the two little dining tables they had in there. She'd only been at it for a couple of minutes when a deafening crash made her jump.

Whipping around, she was relieved to see that Lou was still safely balanced at the top of the ladder, but the frame she'd been about to lift down had just crashed to the floor. It had managed to miss the slightly softer landing the rug would have provided and had hit the bare strip of floorboards instead.

'You okay?!' gasped Hattie, hurrying over. Her heart was pounding with the shock.

'I'm fine,' said Lou. 'I'm so sorry, the hook just slipped straight out of the plaster!'

'Don't worry – it's no great loss!' said Hattie, staring at the frame on the floor. A few shards of glass were poking out from underneath. 'They're all going in the bin anyway.'

Lou climbed back down the ladder. 'I'll clear this up before we go any further,' she said, bending down and flipping the wooden frame over, clearly expecting to find a halo of glass to deal with. 'That's weird!'

'What?' said Hattie, willing her heart rate to calm down.

'Look – most of the bits of glass are being held back by the picture!'

Hattie crouched down next to Lou. Sure enough, Veronica's horrific print was torn in a couple of places, pierced by slivers of glass that were poking through from behind.

'The pictures are taped on top of the glass!' said Lou in surprise. She reached out and gingerly took hold of a torn flap of paper.

'Careful you don't cut yourself!' said Hattie as Lou pulled at it, releasing several jagged splinters onto the floor.

'Would you look at that,' laughed Lou, peering at the back of the print she'd just torn in half.

'Looks like Veronica cut them out of a magazine or something,' said Hattie. She stared down at what looked like an advert for some dreadful piece of "collectable" china that would never be worth the ridiculous "special offer" price. 'Classy!' she chuckled.

'Looks like it was just a cunning way to get out of

dusting!' said Lou, pointing at the lower edge of the frame where a grubby bit of glass had survived the fall. She wiped her finger through the ancient layer of dust. 'Look at this though!' she said, tearing the rest of the awful print away and carefully setting a couple of large bits of broken glass aside.

Hattie raised her eyebrows in surprise. Lou had just revealed an old black and white photo of the front of a building. Reaching over, she took the entire frame in both hands, upended it to shake any remaining glass onto the floor and then turned it back over for a closer look

'That's the front of the hotel!' said Lou.

Hattie nodded, pointing at a narrow line of typewritten text that had been added to the photograph across the bottom.

The Pebble Street Hotel. 1951.

'Wow – cool!' said Lou. 'I wonder if any of the others are the same?!'

Hattie's eyes lit up. 'Let's find out!' she said. Straightening up she retrieved the pile of frames that had already been set aside for the bins.

'They've all been taped on!' said Lou, excitedly, helping Hattie to lay them out across the floor.

Within minutes, the pair of them had ripped all the gaudy prints clean away from the glass, only to reveal a series of stunning black and white photographs.

'These are amazing!' said Lou, staring down at them all.

Hattie nodded. She was feeling slightly queasy at just how close they'd come to throwing all this precious history in the bin.

A few of the photos showed the outside of the hotel and views of Seabury, but the majority of them were shot inside Pebble Street. In fact, most of them seemed to have been taken inside this very room when it was absolutely packed with people.

'The Pebble Street Pudding Club?' said Lou, reading a little typewritten note at the bottom of a photograph that showed a whole host of expectant faces sitting around circular tables. They were all grinning into the camera and each of them had a spoon in hand. 'Ever heard of it?'

'Nope,' said Hattie, gazing at the photograph, a little tingle of something travelling down her spine.

'Heard of what?' Ben's voice at the door made both of them turn to him. 'Blimey!' he said, spotting all the frames laid out across the carpet. 'Where did that lot come from?'

'The walls,' said Hattie. 'Veronica had taped those horrible prints right over the top of these!'

'Wow,' breathed Ben, going from one photograph to the next.

'Aren't they gorgeous?' said Lou.

SECRETS IN SEABURY

'You know you can't throw these away now, right?' he said. 'I mean, this is history – they need to go back on the walls where they belong!'

'Totally agree,' said Hattie, nodding, watching Ben going from one frame to the next.

'Wait a minute!' he said, crouching down for a closer look at a photograph of half a dozen revellers crowded around one of the circular tables. 'That's my grandparents! And I'm sure that's old Rose Blanchford back in the day... and I'm not sure who this is, but the face is very familiar...'

'There are still a couple more to uncover!' said Lou, pointing at the last few frames hanging on the walls at the far end of the room.

Before Hattie could say anything, Ben had grabbed the ladder and he and Lou were carefully removing them and bringing them over to join the others.

'You do the honours!' said Lou, eagerly nudging Hattie into action.

Hattie knelt down and picked at the crusty old cello tape. Tearing the prints off, she revealed each photograph in turn.

The first one was a picture of a woman holding out a vast pudding in front of her. The caption below it read *The Famous Pebble Street Pudding. Voted best pudding in Seabury three years in a row.*

'I know who that is,' said Ben.

'Who?' said Hattie, turning to him in surprise.

'That's the old cook. She used to work here in the days before Veronica bought the place and sacked everyone.'

'Thank goodness that hook dropped out of the wall,' said Lou, 'we'd never have known about these otherwise!'

The next two frames showed hordes of people devouring the pudding – along with captions the captions *coming back for thirds* and *leave enough space for the pudding – you won't be disappointed.*

Hattie's strange tingling sensation was getting stronger. She was intrigued by this unexpected slice of history they'd unearthed.

'I wonder what this pudding was?' she murmured, looking at the happy, excited faces from all those decades ago. She wondered what it must be like to have people coming from far and wide just to eat at the hotel. 'Maybe Lionel will be able to tell us something about them.'

'Doubt it,' said Ben, 'these were taken long before his time here… though I do know who we can ask!'

'Who?' said Hattie, a surge of excitement leaping in her stomach and taking her by surprise.

'Mrs Scott, my old school headmistress,' said Ben.

'That prickly old bugger?' said Lou in surprise.

'You know her?' said Hattie.

Lou nodded. 'She's popped into the Sardine a couple of times. She gets the cake subscription box. Prefers to have it delivered though, I don't think she likes coming into town much. She's a bit... set in her ways?'

Ben shrugged and then nodded. 'Just about sums her up.'

'But why would she know anything about these?' asked Hattie.

'Because that,' he said, pointing to the picture of the old cook holding out the mysterious pudding, 'is her mother.'

CHAPTER 5

'I feel bad for leaving Lou to sort out that mess while we skive off!' said Hattie, following Ben in the direction of North Beach. 'It's only her first day!'

'We're hardly skiving,' laughed Ben, tucking the file of photographs more securely under his arm as he went. 'This is serious culinary research!'

Hattie grinned as Ben took her hand. She couldn't help but be excited about the strange twist her day had taken. The pair of them were off on an adventure to find out more about the mysterious Pebble Street Pudding Club.

It had been Ben's idea to take the rest of the afternoon off and visit Mrs Scott. Hattie knew she shouldn't have agreed – not with all the work there was to be done – but she couldn't ignore the feeling that this was somehow important.

Lou had suggested that they take some of the old photographs along to show Mrs Scott – especially the ones of her mother. So, they'd carefully removed them from the frames and gathered them into a folder, which Ben had then insisted on wrapping in a sheet of plastic for some reason.

They'd left Lou clearing up plaster dust and broken glass. She didn't seem to mind though. She'd ushered them off, stating that she was excited to get stuck into cleaning up the old frames and finding out which ones needed mending before they were reinstated on the walls.

Hattie had the sneaking suspicion that Lou might get excited about most things… perhaps that wasn't such a bad trait.

'Hattie?' said Ben, peeping sideways at her as they trudged along.

'Yeah?'

'Can you swim?'

'You seriously can't remember after spending so many summers in the sea with me as a kid?' she huffed in mock indignation.

Ben grinned at her. 'To be honest, you did so much splashing about that I was never sure if you were floating, standing with your feet on the bottom, or actually swimming!'

Hattie punched Ben's arm. 'I can swim,' she pouted. 'Why?

'You'll see,' said Ben.

'And why are we heading down onto the beach?' she added, following him down the steps onto the pebbles of North Beach. 'I thought Lou said that Mrs Scott lives a little way out of town?'

'Oh, she does,' said Ben, as he led her towards a little boat that was pulled up onto the beach. On reaching it, he quickly removed the cover, rummaged around in the back and then handed her a life jacket.

'What's this for?' asked Hattie.

'What do you reckon?' laughed Ben.

'What are you up to?' countered Hattie.

'Well, there are two ways to get to Mrs Scott's house. We could go by road, and it would take twenty minutes or so to get there. Or we can take the boat. It takes less than half the time to get there by sea.'

'By sea?' she echoed faintly.

'Yep,' Ben nodded, helping her on with the life jacket before patting the side of the little boat. 'We're going by boat... unless you want to walk?'

Hattie shook her head, unable to say anything.

'Great,' said Ben, leaning over the side of the boat and carefully stashing the precious file of photos inside one of the benches. 'Right – help me push her down to the shoreline and I'll do the rest!'

Rather reluctantly, Hattie put her shoulder against the boat and following Ben's guidance, helped him to push it into position. As he helped her to hop on board, she suddenly didn't feel quite so sure that she wanted to go on this adventure after all. Maybe she should have sent Lou along instead.

'Cheer up!' laughed Ben, throwing his shoes over the side. 'Worse things happen at sea!'

Hattie stuck her tongue out at him and then held on for dear life as he pushed the boat out into the water before hopping in, his feet and legs glistening with salty water. Clearly this was the reason Ben always wore shorts!

Thankfully, the sea had calmed down since she'd spotted Lou and the Chilly Dippers battling the waves earlier. There was no way she'd be up for a boat ride if there was any chance of them getting battered all the way there.

This wasn't so bad, was it? She peered at the water beyond The King's Nose, but even that was fairly calm at the moment. Hattie took a long slow breath, willing herself to calm down a bit. She couldn't remember the last time she'd been out in a boat. In fact, she wasn't sure if she'd *ever* been out in a boat.

Goodness, she hoped she wasn't seasick. That would be so embarrassing! She was sure she wouldn't be, but you never really knew about these things, did you?

'Okay?' asked Ben, shooting her a wink.

Hattie smiled brightly and nodded.

'Tide's changed and the wind has backed.'

'Right,' she murmured, nodding as if she knew

what the hell that meant. She kept nodding as he spouted a bunch more nautical terms that she didn't really understand, surreptitiously wrapping her fingers around the edge of her perch.

As Hattie watched Ben guide them easily out to sea, she started to relax a bit. He had a practised, skilful air about him, and clearly knew what he was doing - much to her relief.

Hattie blew out a breath and eased back onto her seat a bit further. Now that she trusted Ben not to dump them both straight into the water at any given moment, she could start enjoying the ride. This was almost... relaxing.

Well... *kind of*. Hattie's fingers were still wrapped tightly around the edge of the bench and her knuckles went white with every little swell the boat skipped over. She wasn't about to loosen her grip though - she was convinced she'd fall in if she did.

Hattie glanced at Ben, meaning to ask him how long he'd owned the boat. She promptly forgot all about her question and scowled at him when she saw the look on his face. He clearly thought it was very funny that she had a death grip on her seat – but at least he had the good grace to hide it. Mostly.

Hattie watched suspiciously as the hint of a grin crept through now and then - right at the corner of his mouth. But he had a nice mouth... and lovely eyes... maybe she was just imagining it...

Nope, that was definitely a smirk trying to break

free… or perhaps it was just sea spray getting in his eyes.

Stop overthinking this!

Hattie squeezed her fingers even tighter, gripping her seat hard, not because of another unsettling swell but in an attempt to make herself appreciate this very Seabury experience. She needed to lighten up, sit back and enjoy the ride as much as possible.

It was pretty incredible to get to see the town from this different perspective and Hattie tore her eyes away from Ben and peered back towards the shore. Seabury looked smaller than she imagined – and far more remote. It was cradled in the arms of the surrounding hills, with the old lighthouse standing sentry on the point. She could see the ordered lines of the allotments high up on the hill, and the tiny dots of sheep grazing the distant fields.

Seabury disappeared from view as Ben motored around the next headland, and they left the lighthouse behind them too. Soon they were whizzing through a series of smaller, tree-lined bays. Hattie could see little pebble beaches, but no houses at all.

'It's gorgeous!' she yelled to Ben when she finally trusted her voice to work properly. He grinned at her and nodded.

The boat slowed as they passed through a series of rocky outcrops and Ben guided them into another tiny bay. Hattie could see a little stone quay ahead with steps leading up from the water.

Ben puttered the boat at a leisurely speed towards the steps until they were right up alongside them. Then, like a human gazelle, he leapt lightly from the boat onto the steps and tied it safely in place.

'Here,' he said, holding out his hand and helping her onto the blissfully solid and stationary stone steps.

'Thanks!' said Hattie, finding her feet in a far less graceful manner than Ben had done. 'So – how exactly do you know your way here quite so well?'

'Easy,' laughed Ben, 'I used to travel this way to school every day! Mrs Scott used to be my old head-teacher. The old school closed years ago, and she bought the building. I think there were only four or five kids that went there towards the end! Anyway, she lives there now.'

'Wow!' said Hattie, trying to imagine coming to school by boat every day. 'Was it much bigger when you went there?'

Ben shook his head. 'Not really, no! Kate from The Sardine was in the same year as me. You've met her, right?'

Hattie nodded. 'Hasn't she just moved into the lighthouse?'

'Yup, that's her,' said Ben, taking her hand and leading her along a path that wound its way into the trees 'And you've probably met Stanley by now too? Her big bear of a Bernese Mountain Dog?'

'Stanley was actually my Seabury welcoming

committee,' laughed Hattie. 'He was busy taking himself for a walk down to the beach when we bumped into each other.'

'That's our Stanley!' said Ben, squeezing her fingers and making her toes curl. 'We're nearly there, look.'

Hattie peered ahead of them. The pathway they were on felt magical – like it was leading into another realm rather than towards an old schoolhouse. A gateway was nestled between the trees a little way in front of them.

'There it is,' said Ben as they reached the gate and paused for a moment. They were looking at the old school playground. It was a small, paved area that still boasted some worn markings in bright paint – relics of ball-games past. The house beyond still looked very much like a school, and Hattie half expected to hear a bell calling the pupils in from playtime.

'I feel like I'm late for assembly!' laughed Ben, opening the gate for her.

They made their way towards the front door, and Ben knocked loudly. Hattie held her breath as they waited, listening intently for any signs of life inside.

Eventually, they heard the sound of approaching footsteps followed by a chain being drawn aside. Then a face appeared. A slightly annoyed, unsmiling face.

'Yes?'

The old woman was upright, and her grey hair was scraped back in a tight knot at the nape of her neck. Even if Hattie hadn't known that she'd once been a headteacher, she was pretty sure she would have guessed. This was clearly not a woman to be crossed!

'Mrs Scott!' said Ben, beaming at her.

Mrs Scott stared at him for a beat or two before recognition dawned on her face.

'Benjamin Yolland. What on earth are you doing here? You rarely showed up on time when you were *meant* to be here!' she said, raising a wry eyebrow.

Ben grinned. 'I've brought someone to see you, Mrs Scott.'

Hattie smiled at how formal he was being. Clearly calling his old headmistress by her surname was a habit he'd never grow out of.

'And you are?' Mrs Scott asked, turning her beady eye towards Hattie.

'I'm Hattie,' she said, standing up a little bit straighter under the scrutiny. 'I work at The Pebble Street Hotel.'

'So?' said Mrs Scott.

'I wanted to ask you about these,' said Hattie. She took the folder of photographs from Ben, removed the plastic and held them out towards the old lady.

Mrs Scott took the photographs as if on autopilot and opened the folder. For just a moment, her mood seemed to soften – then she cast a suspicious glance at them both.

'I guess you'd better come in,' she said, clearly resigning herself to the fact that she had visitors whether she wanted them or not.

Mrs Scott turned on her heel and headed back into the house and Hattie and Ben hurried to follow her indoors.

Ben took the lead and Hattie couldn't help but smile as she watched him gaze around his old school, his eyes wide. She guessed that childhood memories must be flooding in.

'I feel like I should go to my peg and hang up my bag and coat!' he whispered, making her laugh.

They passed a glazed door on their right, and Hattie peeped inside only to find that it was one of the old classrooms – now empty of desks but still pretty unmistakable for what it was.

'I don't go in there very often,' said Mrs Scott, catching her looking. 'It's a big room and difficult to heat. I live in the rest of the building – the old kitchen and cloakrooms. I've always found it really rather cosy.'

Hattie smiled at her and nodded.

Mrs Scott led them into a little sitting room that might have been the original staff room and indicated for them to sit.

'Would you like tea?'

It was definitely more of a statement than a question and it was clear to Hattie that they were going to drink tea with Mrs Scott whether they wanted to or not.

Their hostess took a little while to make the tea, but the pair of them didn't dare chat while they waited. Instead, they both sat there with their hands folded in their laps, completely silent. Hattie was careful not to look at Ben for fear of getting the giggles. She had the distinct impression that Mrs Scott wouldn't be past handing out detentions if she found them misbehaving.

Returning with a neatly arranged tea tray that held matching cups, saucers, teapot and milk jug, Mrs Scott placed them down carefully on a little side table.

'I don't have biscuits,' she said, beginning to pour. 'I don't believe in them.'

'That's okay,' said Hattie in a tiny voice, taking her cup and saucer. 'Thank you.'

'Now, cake's a different matter,' said Mrs Scott, handing Ben his tea next. 'But I don't have any at the moment. I'm waiting for my next box from The Sardine. I think Sarah's due to deliver it tomorrow. You came on the wrong day,' she finished with an accusatory tone.

'Sorry about that,' said Ben with a grin.

Hattie took a sip of tea to stop herself from giggling. For a second there, she'd caught a definite glimpse of the eight-year-old she'd met all those years ago.

'Anyway, you're here now,' huffed Mrs Scott, picking up her own cup and taking a delicate sip. 'So, we'd better get this over with.'

CHAPTER 6

Hattie shot an alarmed look at Ben, but he just smiled back and gave her an encouraging nod. He seemed completely at his ease in spite of their hostess's obvious displeasure at their arrival. She took a deep breath and turned back to Mrs Scott with a smile.

'We found the photographs, and about a dozen more, when we were working in the Pebble Street breakfast lounge this morning,' she said, nodding at the folder that was now sitting next to Mrs Scott's chair. 'They'd been covered up,' she added, not quite sure how to explain.

Mrs Scott didn't look in the least bit surprised. 'I'll bet that was Veronica's doing,' she huffed.

'Yes, we think so,' said Hattie, nodding. 'They were still in the frames but had these awful prints taped over the top of the glass.'

'Idiotic woman,' said Mrs Scott, taking a disapproving sip of tea.

Ben snorted. 'You could say that.'

Mrs Scott threw him a tight smile. 'But what's this got to do with me?' she asked.

'Hattie wanted to find out more about the Pebble Street Pudding Club,' said Ben easily. 'There are little captions on each of the photographs and several of them show The Pebble Street Pudding Club in 1951. I told her you'd be the best person to ask as I recognised your mum.'

Mrs Scott's smile relaxed a little and she reached for the folder. Flipping through the pile, she paused to stare intently at each image.

'I recognise nearly all of these faces,' she said, clearly lost in memories. 'Some of them were locals and some of them visitors – but all of them loved The Pebble Street Hotel. Mum was the cook there for years and years – basically her whole working life. I'm guessing Benjamin told you that?' she glanced up at Hattie.

Hattie nodded, not wanting to say anything that might stop her in her tracks.

'Well, when I was tiny, we used to live in the cook's rooms in Pebble Street's attic.' She flipped through the photographs again and drew out the one of the woman holding the massive pudding. 'That's my mother. I remember this one being taken. I wasn't supposed to be out of bed, but I knew the club was happening that night and I wanted to see everyone, so I snuck downstairs!'

'Can you tell me about the Pudding Club?' said Hattie.

Mrs Scott peered at her for a moment as if she was trying to decide how much to tell her.

'People loved it. They came from all over the place – and mum was always right at the heart of it.' She ran a gentle finger over the photograph. 'You'd have thought the extra work would have been too much for her, but she loved it. She adored the hotel and cooking her puddings for everyone.' Mrs Scott paused and turned to one of the other photographs. 'Look – I'm in this one!'

Hattie leaned closer and, sure enough, there at the edge of the image was a glimpse of a tousle-headed little girl clutching a moth-eaten teddy bear.

'Mum eventually retired, of course. That was shortly before... before the gentleman from London moved into the suite.'

'Lionel?' said Hattie.

'Yes. Him,' said Mrs Scott, her voice tight with some kind of emotion. She paused and took a long sip of tea.

Hattie wondered if perhaps talking about her mother was proving to be difficult for Mrs Scott and was just trying to figure out how to change the subject when she continued.

'We'd moved out of the hotel years before that, of

course. I did hear on the grapevine that he bought the hotel after Veronica left? I really can't imagine why – the place is full of bad memories for me.'

'How come?' asked Hattie in surprise. The photographs showed so much happiness – jolly evenings full of fun and laughter and pudding! 'I'm sorry,' she said quickly. 'You don't have to answer that!'

Mrs Scott frowned and shook her head. 'After mother retired, Veronica bought the hotel. She found out about the Pebble Street Pudding. That's it there, in the photos. It was legendary – award-winning… practically mystical,' she smiled softly, but two seconds later her face hardened into a scowl. 'Veronica decided that she wanted the recipe. She said that as the owner of the hotel, it belonged to her.'

'But that's ridiculous!' said Hattie.

'Yes, I quite agree – but that didn't stop her from hounding my poor mother. Veronica never gave up, never left her alone, not even when she was extremely frail and in her last few days.'

'Horrible woman,' muttered Ben.

Mrs Scott nodded, a fierce look on her face now. 'Mother never did give her the recipe. She'd never actually worked for Veronica, but she hated the way she'd treated the staff. They'd been like our extended family, and Veronica just sacked the lot of them. No, mother didn't like her one little bit, so no matter what Veronica did – all the ways she tried to trick her - mum kept that recipe secret.'

Mrs Scott paused and took a long, shaky breath. After a few seconds she looked back up, and Hattie felt herself pinned to the back of her chair with the intensity of the woman's stare.

'And now you're here for precisely the same reason, I'm guessing? No doubt you want the recipe too.'

Hattie held up both hands and shook her head. 'No, seriously – that's not it at all.'

'Plenty of other people have badgered me for it over the years, you know, and I've told them all exactly the same thing. It's the same answer I've got for you too. No. You can't have it.'

Hattie shook her head again. 'That's really not why I came to see you,' she said steadily, willing Mrs Scott to believe her. 'I just wanted to hear a bit about the history of the hotel. I'm going to put the photographs back up where they belong on the walls of the breakfast lounge so our guests will be able to enjoy them when we reopen.'

Ben nodded enthusiastically next to her, but Mrs Scott just let out a mistrustful little huff.

'I want people to be able to see what the place looked like back in its heyday,' said Hattie, 'back before Veronica took over.'

But it was clear to Hattie that she was now fighting a losing battle. It would take more than just a few words to convince Mrs Scott that this wasn't just some kind of sneaky plan to winkle the Pebble Street Pudding recipe out of her. The old woman had completely clammed up and was now clearing away the tea things, even though they'd only half-emptied their cups.

Taking their cue from Mrs Scott, and not wanting to distress her any further than they'd already managed to, Hattie and Ben made a move to leave. They barely had the chance to thank her for her hospitality before they found themselves back out in the playground with the door closed firmly behind them.

∼

Hattie felt a sense of gloom settle on her shoulders as Ben took her hand as she climbed back down into the boat. She was pretty sure her mood had nothing to do with the grey clouds that had gathered overhead.

'You okay?' asked Ben, untying the rope and then clambering down after her.

Hattie nodded and shrugged at the same time, making Ben smile.

'It's just… I hope we didn't upset her. Mrs Scott, I mean. She was so happy to see those photographs at first – but then they just seemed to stir up so many bad memories for her. I don't know... I feel really bad. I didn't mean to make her feel like that.'

Ben nodded as he started to guide the boat gently back out of the little quay. 'We weren't to know how she'd react. I'm sure she'll be fine – especially when she realises that you really weren't trying to steal that recipe. Like Lou said, she's a funny old stick. She never used to be like that, though.'

'Really?' said Hattie in surprise.

Ben nodded. 'I always liked her as a teacher. I mean – she was really strict, and I did have a habit of rubbing her up the wrong way a bit, but that was completely my fault. She was right - I didn't always show up when I was meant to – not when there were fish to catch and those stones with holes in to find and an endless blue sea to swim in. Being a teacher in Seabury must have been a tough gig, come to think of it!'

Kate laughed, thinking of the tearaway version of Ben she'd met as a child. Bare-footed, freckly and always with a pocket of things he'd found on the beach.

'Yeah,' said Ben, 'she was strict but always really lovely. She always wanted to know how us kids were getting on, even after we'd left the school. But then she seemed to change. The old school closed... and now she barely ever comes to town. Sounds like she goes into The Sardine occasionally, but I don't think she's set foot inside the hotel since before Veronica took over.'

Hattie nodded as she watched Ben effortlessly guide the boat through the rocks, cutting a path through the dull, grey waters back towards Seabury's beaches.

'I wish she'd been up for chatting about it all a bit more, though,' said Hattie sadly. 'I wonder what that pudding tasted like… though I completely understand about her wanting to keep her mother's recipe a secret.'

'Well,' said Ben, 'as it was a pudding from the fifties, I can imagine it might have been pretty rich.'

Hattie nodded. 'Yeah. Probably wouldn't appeal much to a modern audience anyway. But wouldn't it be wonderful if we could have a Pudding Club at Pebble Street again one day…'

Ben grinned at her and nodded. 'Count me in! I'll be your first customer.'

'You know, I think I'll talk to Lionel about it,' said Hattie. 'Maybe after the opening night though – there's so much still to be sorted out and I don't want to give him another thing to worry about!'

Hattie went quiet for a moment, staring down at her hands as her own set of worries landed squarely back on her shoulder. Time was starting to run out. She really shouldn't have gone off on this wild goose chase with Ben – especially when it had turned out to be such a dead end. She didn't know what she'd been thinking, but she really needed to focus.

It had been lovely to spend a bit of time with Ben, but Hattie would be glad to get back onto dry land again – even if that meant that she'd finally have to grow up and finally make a bunch of decisions she'd been putting off. She didn't think Lionel could wait much longer for the finalised menu before he got super-fidgety. Frankly, neither could she.

Hattie needed the chance to cook a couple of test runs. Then they needed to choose the wines. Why was this all proving to be so difficult when it used to be second nature to her? Maybe she was just over-thinking everything.

'Hattie - look,' said Ben, his low voice bringing her back to the present.

She glanced up at him and then followed his pointing finger to the swirling water at the side of the boat. A seal stared directly back at her from just a few feet away.

'Oh my!' she breathed, completely captivated. She watched for a few moments before the seal dipped back beneath the waves. 'I thought that was Stanley there for a second,' she laughed, turning back to Ben.

'Just as likely,' said Ben, 'just not this time. I've picked Stanley up out here plenty of times – he does love to swim with the seals. Bet that was one of his mates!'

Hattie grinned and turned back to the water just

in case there was any chance their new friend might resurface again. To think - she'd been so lost in her worries that she'd almost missed it. She promptly made a vow to herself to enjoy the moment a bit more. The little encounter had reminded her what a wonderful place Seabury was – even if there *were* a few characters around her that she was finding it a little bit tricky to work out!

CHAPTER 7

'Oh my goodness,' said Hattie, 'you've done an amazing job!'

'Thanks boss!' Lou grinned at her.

The pair of them wandered along the back wall of the breakfast lounge where Lou had propped up the newly cleaned and polished frames for inspection. The glass gleamed, the wood had a beautiful, warm glow to it and the photographs that had remained in their frames looked even better than she remembered.

'Right – all we need to do now is pop these back into the empty frames and tape them in ready to be re-hung!' said Hattie.

'Lionel popped his head in earlier and came back with a reel of tape from his art supplies, and a roll of wire to replace the knackered string they were hanging from,' said Lou. 'He suggested we reinforce the backs too – just so there aren't any disasters when we put them back up.'

'Brilliant!' said Hattie. 'So, we've got everything we need to sort these out?' she said, waving the pile of photographs she'd taken to Mrs Scott's place.

'Sure have,' said Lou. 'I would have put the others back on the walls, but I guessed there was no point as you're planning on painting in here?'

Hattie nodded. 'Let's get these guys back in their frames,' she said, 'then maybe we can get the room ready so that we can start painting in the morning?'

'I'm up for that,' said Lou.

'Perfect,' said Hattie gratefully.

Between them, they dragged one of the little tables over to the window so that they had plenty of light to work with.

'So, did you have any luck at Mrs Scott's?' asked Lou curiously.

Hattie let out a sigh. 'Not really. I think she enjoyed seeing the photos of her mum – but there's something about the hotel that really seems to stir up bad memories for her.'

'That's a shame,' said Lou. 'I've only met her a few times – not exactly one of life's chatterboxes, is she?'

Hattie shook her head. 'You could say that.'

'So, no luck finding out about the pudding club thingy?'

Hattie shook her head again. 'Not really. She said it was super-popular and clearly remembered quite a lot about it, but then she clammed up. She seemed to think I was only there to steal her mum's recipe. I mean, of course I'd have loved to hear about the pudding, but that's not why I was there. Anyway, I think she's planning on taking that recipe to the grave.'

'Shame,' said Lou.

Hattie shrugged. 'I don't really blame her – it sounds like Veronica really gave her old mum a hard time about it for years after she'd left the hotel.'

'Wow. So much drama over a pudding!' laughed Lou, carefully placing one of the photographs into a newly-cleaned frame.

'Well, people do get mighty cagey about their creations,' said Hattie, watching as Lou made sure the mount was square before she started to tape a backing board in place.

'It's a pity, though,' said Lou. 'It would have been nice to find out a bit more, wouldn't it?'

'Yeah,' sighed Hattie. 'I must admit, I came out of there feeling pretty low about everything... this whole opening night's creeping up on me a bit.'

'Just think,' said Lou, nodding at the old photographs, 'all this history in front of us... and you're the next chapter!'

Somehow, the thought just added to the weight Hattie felt like she was carrying around.

'You know,' she said, reaching out and helping Lou to smooth a bit of tape down, 'I never imagined that I'd end up in Seabury. I had my life all mapped out. I was going to open my own restaurant – that was my ambition. My dream. But somehow, I ended up here instead!'

Lou nodded. 'Same here really. I just landed in Seabury on a whim and never left!'

'What brought you here in the first place?' asked Hattie curiously.

'A cheating, rat-bastard of a man,' said Lou with a dry laugh.

'Husband?' said Hattie.

Lou shook her head. 'We'd been together for aeons, but never tied the knot. Thank goodness, I guess.' She paused and sighed. 'Anyway, I needed a change of scenery and came to Seabury, and everyone here was so lovely that I decided to stay. And now… well there's nowhere else in the entire world I'd rather be.'

'Really?' said Hattie. 'This is it for you?'

Lou nodded enthusiastically. 'Working at The Sardine practically saved my life. I love it there, and now I get to work here too? I mean, I'm just incredibly lucky.' She beamed at Hattie. 'Anyway, sorry… I've just gone off on one as usual. I've got to say… and I hope you don't mind… but I think it's great that you and Ben have got so close so quickly!'

Hattie felt the blush hit her cheeks without any kind of warning. She quickly turned to grab another empty frame to work on. She wasn't really sure that she was comfortable chatting to a member of staff about this stuff. She'd never have done it in London!

Hattie gave herself a quick mental slap. She *had* to stop doing that. This wasn't London, this was Seabury. Things were different here. People here were friends. And friends chatted.

'Erm... thanks,' she said, not really knowing what the right response was. After all, it had been a *very* long time since she'd had a friend to chat with.

'You know,' said Lou, shooting her a naughty look, 'I must admit I did consider going after Ben myself a couple of times. I mean – he *is* super cute. But if I'm honest, I prefer a slightly older model... and besides, he never stays still long enough.'

Hattie let out a surprised laugh.

'You know what I mean?' said Lou. 'I don't know where he gets his energy from, I really don't. The man never sits down!'

'It's true,' said Hattie with a giggle.

'Well... good luck to you dating the Duracell bunny. He might be cute, but I don't think this old woman could keep up,' Lou chuckled, pulling a length of tape from the reel and securing the back of the frame she was working on. 'I like my men chilled. Not that Ben isn't... but I like long, lazy lie-ins wrapped in each other's arms. And leisurely lunches. Dark hair too... though I don't mind me a silver fox these days.'

As Hattie listened to Lou witter on about her

ideal man, she realised that her own experience was woefully limited. So much so that she didn't really have a "type" – unless you could count Ben Yolland as an entire category by himself.

Hattie had been working in kitchens ever since she'd been allowed to get a Saturday job. There just hadn't been much time for boys. Men. Relationships. Her handful of previous attempts at romance had been short-lived – grabbed between long shifts and ridiculous working hours.

Things were even worse when she'd started working for Marco. There simply hadn't been time in the day for *any* kind of personal life -sleeping for example - let alone nurturing a relationship. She'd been so focused on getting ahead, and Marco had taken advantage of that by heaping responsibilities onto her shoulders. Then he'd promptly dropped her. Hattie'd always known that he was a self-centred twit, but she couldn't help feeling angry with herself for not spotting how it was all going to end up.

'I've not really given much time… or thought… or effort to the whole *relationship* thing,' said Hattie, pulling a face. 'I mean, is that bad? I just poured myself into my career.'

'No – that's *not* bad!' said Lou, turning to her with a serious look on her face. 'I mean, look at this amazing opportunity it's prepared you for.'

Hattie scrunched her face up.

'What?' demanded Lou.

'It's just… this is just a blip. I'm just helping Lionel out. I really need to get a plan together and get back to London. I need to work towards getting my own restaurant. That's *always* been the dream.'

Lou crossed her arms and blew out a long breath.

'What?' It was Hattie's turn to demand this time.

'Well… it's just…' Lou paused. 'Hm, maybe I should keep my gob shut. It's only my first day!'

'Spit it out,' laughed Hattie.

'Well… okay fine. It's just - you've already got your own restaurant - here at Pebble Street!' said Lou with a little shrug.

Hattie opened her mouth to argue… and stopped. Because, of course, Lou was right. She'd never really thought of it like that before for some reason.

'Huh,' she said, frowning.

She was in charge. Lionel was relying on her, and she had total control of the kitchen – the menu – the restaurant.

Hattie stood stock still. She felt sick with the sudden, sinking sensation that she was on the verge of blowing this incredible opportunity. All because she'd been so busy chasing some vague notion that she had to be in London for her dream to come true.

'Why don't you forget about the big city?' asked Lou, her voice gentle. 'Start right here – where you don't have to work for assholes.'

Hattie's mind was reeling, but she managed a tiny nod of agreement. Because Lou was right. She was living her dream already – but she was so obsessed with how it was *supposed* to look that she was in danger of messing it up. Hell, at the rate she'd been going, she was in danger of missing it completely.

'I'm so sorry,' said Lou, a sheepish look crossing her face. 'I know I'm blunt. I can't seem to help it… that's me all over.'

'Don't apologise!' said Hattie quickly. Because right at that moment she was intensely aware that she'd hired the perfect person. Doses of common sense like that were worth their weight in gold. 'You're totally right. I do have the chance to do everything I've been dreaming of - right here at Pebble Street!'

Lou nodded, looking relieved. 'Yep.'

'Argh!' Hattie let out a frustrated growl.

'What?' said Lou, looking alarmed.

'I've wasted so much time already!' said Hattie.

'Hardly,' laughed Lou. 'You've only been here a matter of weeks.'

'Exactly, I should have the menu all sorted out and finalised. And this place should be ready,' she added, gesturing around the room.

'Okay – number one – don't worry about this place,' said Lou firmly. 'We'll have the restaurant ready before you know it.'

Hattie nodded. With Lou's help and with Ben on hand too, it wouldn't actually take long to transform the breakfast room.

'But the menu,' she sighed. 'I just can't get a handle on it. It has to be special. It has to have that…' she looked for the word, rubbing the tips of her fingers together in mid-air as if searching for something. 'That…' She let out an annoyed huff. 'It's hard to put into words. There needs to be something really… unique about it.'

Lou pursed her lips and shook her head. 'You're still thinking like you're working for that asshat in London,' she said. 'Look – you've already decided on it being a fish restaurant, right?'

Hattie nodded morosely.

'And that's perfect!' said Lou. 'Look outside. We're surrounded by the sea. And just up on the hill, there are the allotments.'

'But it's just so… basic,' sighed Hattie. 'I've been cooking bloomin' fish and chips for Lionel and Ben for days. They love it, but I have to move on and do something different. Marco never cooked the same dish for more than a few days in a row.'

Lou shook her head again, clearly starting to get frustrated. 'There you go again – thinking like Marco – thinking about how he'd do things. It's time to think like Hattie for a change! Forget all the ridiculous, exotic ingredients that are just there for show. Concentrate on real food that tastes amazing. Local vegetables. Fresh fish from just outside the windows. Blimey Hattie – you'll be able to measure the distance your ingredients have travelled in footsteps!'

Hattie was staring at Lou in a daze, suddenly aware that she'd stopped talking.

'You done?' she said. She felt like she'd had her mind completely blown in the last few minutes.

Lou nodded. 'I'm sorry. I was doing it again – I should have shut up ages ago. I'm just the waitress – you're the chef. You know what you're doing. It's just an opinion…'

Hattie quirked a smile at her, but Lou kept ploughing on.

'Sometimes I let my opinions get the better of me.'

'Seriously Lou, I don't mind,' laughed Hattie. 'In fact, everything you just said makes so much sense – and I really needed to hear it. You're right. I've been stuck because I keep letting thoughts of Marco squash my own instincts and ideas. What's wrong with good, old fashioned, fresh-from-the-ground vegetables?'

'Exactly!' said Lou, nodding enthusiastically.

'What's wrong with fish, fresh from the sea?'

'Exactly!' cheered Lou with a little fist-pump.

'What's wrong with cabbage?!'

'Exa- … erm… everything?!' said Lou, dropping her hand and crinkling her nose.

Hattie laughed again. It was official – she loved Lou already.

'So, you good?' said Lou.

Hattie nodded. 'Thanks to you, I think I'll be okay.'

'Get on with you!' laughed Lou, giving her a playful nudge.

'Oh, and just for the record,' said Hattie, 'there's no such thing as *just* a waitress!'

Lou grinned at her.

'You know – it *would* still be great to have something special to make the opening night go with a bang though, wouldn't it?' said Hattie, looking along the line of newly re-framed Pudding Club photos.

'Beautifully cooked food and a restaurant full of happy people,' said Lou, pointing at the smiling faces in the photographs. 'What more do you need?'

Hattie nodded. Perhaps Lou was right about this too. Whatever happened, she vowed to bring smiles like that back to The Pebble Street Hotel.

CHAPTER 8

The next morning, Hattie pulled on her coat and trainers and headed out on a mission. It was time to visit the allotments again – and this time, she wouldn't be looking to pick holes in the place. She felt quite shame-faced when she thought about her first visit. She'd gone there expecting to be disappointed and then promptly got into that stupid argument with Ben.

This time Hattie meant business, and she wouldn't be letting thoughts of Marco Brooks impact anything to do with *her* new menu for the diners in *her* new town.

With any luck, some of the plot holders would be around when she got there. She really hoped that she might bump into Charlie too – which was a fairly good bet considering he spent most of his life on his plot or in his little shed. Hattie could really do with tapping into his decades of experience and love of veg. She needed to know what she could realistically expect in terms of seasonal goodies. The burning question was – would the Seabury allotment gang *really* be up to the task of becoming the main produce supplier for The Pebble Street Hotel?

Yesterday had been such an eye-opener, and the more Hattie thought about it, the more she realised that Lou had been right. Honest food cooked to perfection simply wouldn't require any gimmicks to make it work.

Hattie marched through Seabury at speed and tackled the steep hill that led out of town towards the allotments with gusto. She'd woken up that morning mid eureka-moment. She finally knew why she'd been double guessing herself and struggling to finalise her menu. It stemmed from the moment she'd decided to make Pebble Street a fish restaurant.

Yes, it had been her idea in the first place, and *yes* – it was still a bloody good idea! But Hattie realised that she'd been wrestling with the decision ever since she'd agreed on it with Lionel. She hadn't been able to stop herself from resisting it - discounting it and picking holes in it - all because Marco thought fish was boring. Hattie puffed out an annoyed breath as one of his particularly memorable rants about cooking seafood came back to her.

What's the deal with all these bones? Food shouldn't

come with fins and scales and eyeballs! And what's with the frickin' smell. You'd never get this with a steak!

But Marco's main issue with serving fish was actually far more simple - he could never get a good photograph of a fillet. Stupidest reason in history – but that was Marco all over for you! He thought fish just looked ordinary no matter what he did to dress it up. He'd tried a few exotic combinations and on one memorable occasion, he'd even attempted using a novelty cookie cutter in an attempt to make it look more "edgy". Of course, the fish-in-the-shape-of-willies experiment had ended in disaster.

Stupid man and his stupid photos. Most of them were complete fakes anyway. Lentils that weren't actually cooked – just rubbed in a drop of olive oil to make them look shiny. Egg yolks that weren't as golden as his photos would have you believe – they'd had their real yolks removed and replaced with apricots in syrup. Yep – the whole thing was ridiculous.

Hattie shook her head. She couldn't help but marvel at what a complete idiot her old boss really was. It was hard to believe that the man was revered. Some people truly idolised him. Hell, even she'd been all starry-eyed – especially at the beginning. But now she'd had some distance, Hattie could finally see that, just like his food, Marco Brooks was all style and no substance.

Coming to a field gateway set in the hedge, Hattie paused and leaned on the top bar. She gazed at the gorgeous clumps of bright primroses that lined the hedgerows, kept company here and there by frothy white heads of wild garlic. Maybe she should pop back up here and forage some for Pebble Street's new menu – after all, what could be more seasonal? It had a lovely, soft flavour too… Not now though. She needed to get up to the allotments.

Hattie stripped her jacket off and tied it around her waist. She'd positively flown up that hill this morning… funny how thoughts of Marco were fuelling her purposeful stomp. She wanted him out of her head before she got to the allotments, though. He deserved no place in her new plans. Taking one last look out over the fields, Hattie took a long, deep breath in, and as she blew it out, she resolved to put thoughts of her old boss behind her.

Hattie barely registered the rest of the hill – she was lost in ideas for her new menu, a huge smile plastered across her face as the realisation hit home that she really could serve anything she wanted to.

Climbing over the old stile next to the five-barred gate that led into the allotments, Hattie hurried along the path that curved around the corner towards the plots. Everything looked completely different to when she'd been up here last – even though that was just a week or two ago. She had a sneaking suspicion that it wasn't the allotments that were different - it was her.

The beautifully tended patches of earth looked

full of promise and positively bursting with menu inspiration for the future… if only she knew what all the tempting shoots and unfurling leaves actually were!

'Hattie lass!'

Hattie grinned and strode forward to greet Charlie. Hallelujah! Her unwitting veggie-guru was bent over the rainwater barrel at the corner of his shed, giving his hands a thorough wash.

'Hi Charlie!' said Hattie.

'What brings you here?' he asked, shooting her a friendly smile. 'Looking for Ben?'

'Not really,' Hattie shrugged, though the thought of snatching a couple of minutes with Ben in his polytunnel was certainly tempting. But right now, she needed to keep her mind on her mission. This morning was all about her new menu.

She watched with amusement as Charlie set to work with a nail brush, scrubbing hard – though it looked like he might be fighting a bit of a losing battle.

'That's pretty thorough for you!' she laughed, nodding at his hands.

Charlie smiled. 'Ethel reckons I've always got grubby hands, so I'm doing my best to smarten my act up a bit and keep them clean for her.' He paused, drew his hands out of the chilly water and inspected his fingernails. 'Nothing much I can do about them being as tough as a pair of old leather boots though –

I've been gardening for sixty-odd years, I'm not going to have soft hands after that long, am I?'

Hattie shook her head. 'Unlikely,' she agreed.

'Anyway, I've got a feeling she rather likes them like this!' Charlie added with a naughty wink, grabbing an old tea towel from a nail on the side of the shed and wiping his hands dry. 'Hmm,' he said, giving the towel a critical look, 'might be time for a fresh one.'

'You think?' Hattie laughed. The old towel was the exact colour of the soil that filled the raised beds on Charlie's plot. There was barely a clean patch left and she could only just about make out the navy-blue stripe that ran down the side of the cloth.

'I've got plenty,' said Charlie. 'Ethel gives me all the ones she's going to throw out – and she gets through a fair few, I can tell you. Two seconds, I've got a whole stack in the shed.'

Charlie disappeared inside his brightly painted sanctuary for a moment, leaving Hattie to peer around the sunlit allotments. How she could have thought that this place was anything other than a treasure trove, she had no idea. Well – she did – she'd been playing the dumbass city-girl to a tee. Thank heavens for Lou knocking some sense into her!

There were verdant lines of new shoots and sprouts everywhere. All she needed was a touch of Charlie's specialist knowledge and she'd have menu ideas coming out of her ears!

'So, to what do we owe the pleasure?' asked Charlie, reappearing with a new towel – this time with a yellow stripe – and hanging it on the rusty nail. 'Are you after a plot? We're pretty full, but I'm sure we can figure something out…'

Hattie shook her head and held up her hands. 'I wouldn't have the first clue, I'm afraid, and I'm going to have my hands full with the hotel.'

'Aye, I bet you are!' said Charlie, his face serious.

'No. What I'm after is a run-down of your veggies up here. Your potatoes are amazing – I already know that – but I'm finalising the menu and I want to use local produce.'

'Well, that's good news in itself,' said Charlie, looking pleased, 'that you're not going the Veronica route, I mean.'

Hattie snorted. 'Not a chance! I'm not getting my ingredients from the supermarket! We've decided to focus mainly on fish and seafood – and I need the veg to go with it!'

'Veg we can help with. Ooh, I do love a decent bit of fish,' said Charlie, looking interested.

'I guess the question is – do you think you guys would be able to keep the hotel supplied on a regular basis? And if so – what does everyone grow up here?'

'Definitely,' said Charlie with a decisive nod. Then he stretched his arms wide. 'And what *don't* we grow?!'

Hattie grinned. 'I like the sound of that! I already know about Ben and his herbs…'

'Of course,' said Charlie.

'But what else can I get my hands on? I mean, Ben said it's a bit early in the season still…'

'Well, this is the perfect time of year for you to be asking, if I'm honest. There will be more and more available as the year goes on anyway, but if you let us know what your plans are and what you're likely to be needing – there's bound to be someone up here who's already got some on the go or will be interested in growing it specially for you!'

'Really?' said Hattie, surprised. 'You think the others would be willing to do that?' She realised that she was still struggling to rid herself of the image of a bunch of old stick-in-the-muds who just grew spuds, onions and prized cabbages.

'Absolutely,' said Charlie. 'Some of us like to grow a bit of everything and then others focus on their favourites. For example, Mabel only grows broad beans. That's it. That's her thing. But then there's the newest couple who like to experiment with all sorts. Last year they grew these amazing giant pumpkins and a whole bed of edible flowers. Kate and Sarah used quite a few for their cakes at The Sardine, and they were right popular, I can tell you! There's always something special to be had up here.'

'Fantastic!' said Hattie, her mind racing with possibilities.

'If you know what you're going to be needing, why don't you let me have a list over the next few days and I'll get this bunch on the job. You wait – they'll be planting up the seeds before you know it. And I can vouch for all of them – they produce the best veg for miles around without any nasty chemicals. All you have to do is wash the dirt off and you'll be good to go!'

'I'll do that,' said Hattie excitedly. 'Thank you so much, Charlie.'

'Well, thank you for asking us,' he beamed at her. 'Now, why don't you come along with me, and I'll introduce you to some of the others?'

CHAPTER 9

*H*attie stared at the massive pile of grubby veg on the kitchen table. Overwhelming? Yes! Exciting? Absolutely!

She hadn't been able to wipe the goofy smile from her face ever since she'd got back to The Pebble Street Hotel. Considering Ben had warned her that there probably wouldn't be very much available just yet, the plot holders had been incredibly generous with goodies for her to experiment with. Charlie had ended up giving her a lift back down into town - there was no way she'd have been able to carry everything down the hill on her own.

Hattie placed her hands on her hips and slowly circled the table. All she had to do now was make some sense of this epic pile...

'Hattie?' Lou gave a light knock at the kitchen door to get her attention.

Hattie looked up, shaken out of her veg-induced trance.

'Hey Lou - look what I got up at the allotments!'

'Fab!' said Lou, casting a quick glance at Hattie's spoils. 'Erm – there's someone here to see you.'

'Ben?' said Hattie distractedly, wondering why he hadn't just bounded in here like he normally did.

Lou shook her head. 'It's Mrs Scott.'

That got Hattie's full attention. 'Mrs Scott?' she repeated.

Lou nodded. 'From the look she gave me, I'd say that you're in trouble! What did you say to her when you went to her house?'

'I… we…' stuttered Hattie.

'You're gonna get deteeeeentionnnnn!' crowed Lou.

Hattie rolled her eyes. 'Where is she?'

'In the breakfast lounge,' said Lou. 'Want me to give this lot a wash while you're getting told off?' she added, pointing to the veg-mountain.

'That'd be great, thanks,' said Hattie.

She made her way out of the kitchen as quietly as she could and peered around the open doorway of the breakfast lounge. Hattie was surprised to find her unexpected visitor actually smiling as she looked at the newly re-framed photographs.

'I remember when most of these were taken,' said Mrs Scott without turning around. She clearly still had her teacher's peripheral vision and knew when there was a nervy kid behind her waiting to be told off!

Hattie moved to stand beside her, and Mrs Scott shot her a quick smile that completely transformed her face - the stern lines softened and became kind and gentle.

'They were taken by an old man who had a Brownie box camera,' she said, turning back to the photographs and staring fondly at the one of her mother holding out the Pebble Street pudding. 'I can't believe they survived all these years.'

Hattie nodded but didn't say anything. She didn't want to break the spell that had somehow got the cranky, ex-headmistress talking.

'I missed these two being taken,' Mrs Scott continued, working her way along the line. 'I had chickenpox. And I remember the ones of the outside of the hotel because I had to go to the dentist that day, and the photographer was just finishing up when we got back.'

Hattie followed Mrs Scott as she made her way along the entire row of photos, listening to her reminisce about each one. She couldn't help but marvel at the old woman's memory. It seemed that she could remember exactly where she'd been standing when each of them had been taken – mostly just out of shot having snuck down to join the festivities when really, she should have been fast asleep upstairs.

As they reached the last frame, Mrs Scott turned to face Hattie.

'I think I owe you an apology,' she said.

Hattie raised her eyebrows.

'Look, I didn't really take on board that you were related to Lionel when Ben brought you to see me. I thought you were just another eager chef who'd come to beg me for my mother's recipe.'

Hattie shook her head quickly, but Mrs Scott held her hand up, clearly wanting to get the words out now that she'd started.

'I'm sorry that I was curt with you, but I'm afraid that's just my way. I'm old enough to know that it's one of my many faults – and old enough to know that it's one I'm never likely to master!'

'I do understand, though,' said Hattie quickly. 'And I *really* didn't come about the recipe.'

Mrs Scott shook her head. 'I realise that, my dear.' She paused again. 'You know – I remember exactly what you were like as a child when you used to visit. Funny, feral little thing you were with your wild hair, causing havoc wherever you went.'

Hattie pulled an embarrassed face. It wasn't the first time she'd been told this since coming to Seabury

'You always gathered a vast gang of other children around you – the ones I used to teach at the school as well as other holidaymakers you somehow roped into things!'

'I've calmed down a bit since then,' said Hattie, shooting her guest a smile.

Mrs Scott patted her awkwardly on the elbow. 'I actually find it quite encouraging that you've grown into such an able and *seemingly* normal adult... though first impressions can be deceptive.' Mrs Scott's eyes lit up, making Hattie laugh.

'I'm about as normal as a workaholic chef can get,' she said.

'Well then. I've been thinking. Now that the hotel belongs to Lionel – and his *grandniece*, of all things, is running the kitchen - well, I think it is time to hand the recipe back over to you.'

Mrs Scott paused but Hattie found that she couldn't say anything. She just stared at her in complete shock.

'I've been thinking about it ever since your visit, and it feels right. My mother dreamed it up in your kitchen all those years ago – and I think it's time for it to come home.'

Hattie realised that her mouth was hanging open and quickly shut it.

'I think... I think she'd want it to be like this,' Mrs Scott added, glancing at the photograph of her mother again and giving a little nod. 'I'm going to let you in on this secret, Hattie – but you have to promise me that you'll not tell another soul!'

Hattie nodded her agreement straight away. She wanted to pinch herself, just to check that she hadn't slid sideways into some kind of alternate dimension, but she didn't dare – not with Mrs Scott watching her intently.

Hattie realised that she was waiting for verbal confirmation that her mother's secret was going to be completely safe.

'I promise,' said Hattie quickly. 'Just me.'

'Well then,' said Mrs Scott with an approving nod. 'In that case, we have a deal. But just *telling* you won't help – it's a complex mixture of ingredients and methods, and a complete nightmare to make at the best of times.'

'Okay…' said Hattie, feeling like she was about to be inducted into some kind of ancient cult.

'Here,' said Mrs Scott, crossing the room and picking up a basket she must have brought with her. 'I've got a sample with me for you to try… if you'd like to?'

'I'd love to!' breathed Hattie.

'I have to say,' said Mrs Scott, 'I do wonder if it might be too rich these days… too full of cholesterol and all that nonsense. But try it and see what you think.'

She pulled a Tupperware container from the depths of the basket.

'I'll just grab some spoons!' said Hattie, dashing towards the door. In her excitement to taste-test the mythical pudding, she crashed headlong into her uncle.

'Oops! Sorry Lionel...' she said, steadying them both with her hands on his arms. But Lionel wasn't looking at her at all. He was staring straight over her shoulder, looking very much like he'd just been struck by lightning.

'Mary?' he said quietly, gazing at Mrs Scott as if she was some kind of ghost. 'What are you doing here?'

Hattie watched him in surprise and then turned to catch an identical look of shock on Mrs Scott's face - before it was quickly covered up by a dose of stoic, old fashioned good matters.

'Lionel,' she said in a steady voice, nodding at him in greeting. 'I was just having a meeting with Hattie about the Pebble Street Pudding.'

Hattie watched her uncle nod in slow motion. She'd told him all about the photographs and the pudding club – but it was clear by his reaction that there was more than just the hotel's history at play here.

'We were about to try some of the pudding,' said Hattie quickly, hoping to ease the strange atmosphere a little. 'I was just going to get us some spoons.'

'Jolly good,' said Lionel, his eyes still glued on Mrs Scott as if she was a mirage. 'I'd better leave you-'

'Would you care to join us?' asked Mrs Scott, cutting across him.

'I…' Lionel paused and then nodded with a small smile. 'Thank you, that would be lovely.'

Hattie was just about to subtly leave them to it for a moment when Lou appeared in front of her, brandishing four spoons.

'Couldn't help but overhear you were looking for these!' she said with a grin.

Hattie rolled her eyes at the cheeky look on Lou's face.

Lou's grin just widened even further. 'You don't think I'm going to miss out on all the fun, do you?'

'Get a move on, then,' said Hattie, beckoning her into the breakfast lounge.

The four of them crowded around the table in front of the large window, and Mrs Scott carefully set the Tupperware box down in the middle. She removed the lid to reveal a moist, spongey, chocolatey, fudge-crumbly concoction that seemed to defy description.

Hattie sniffed deeply, getting wafts of spice and brown sugar.

'Choose your weapon!' said Lou, breaking the spell as she held out her handful of cutlery.

They each took a spoon and then stood with them suspended above the box, none of them wanting to be the first to disturb the masterpiece inside.

'Oh, for goodness' sake!' said Mrs Scott after about thirty seconds where none of them made a move to dig in. 'All at the same time, then?'

Hattie nodded eagerly along with the others and as one, they took a spoonful each. She couldn't help but notice that Lou's spoon was considerably larger than everyone else's.

'What?' demanded Lou, catching her eye and feigning innocence as she lifted the heaped spoonful towards her mouth. 'I just picked up the nearest spoons I could find! Shall we, then?'

Hattie closed her eyes and tasted the pudding. It was as if time stood still. It melted... and was both chewy and crunchy at the same time.

'Oh mmmmm,' she murmured, knowing she shouldn't be attempting to speak around her mouthful, but equally completely incapable of keeping her delight to herself.

'You like it?' came Mrs Scott's voice.

Hattie opened her eyes and nodded enthusiastically. The other two were making a series of noises that would be practically impossible to spell. Mrs Scott's face broke into a huge smile.

Hattie took another spoonful and popped it in her mouth. It was absolutely delicious. She could identify a few of the ingredients – but it was impossible to put her finger on what they all were. There was definitely sugar, and allspice... flour, of course... but then there were various other things that she couldn't immediately place.

It took a matter of minutes before they were

reduced to scraping crumbs from the edges of the box – the pudding having already vanished.

'You're going to show me how to make that?' said Hattie. She felt like she needed to double-check that this wasn't some kind of mean trick, and that had been the one and only time in her life she'd get to taste heaven.

Mrs Scott nodded. 'You. And only you,' she said seriously.

'Well, there you go then,' said Lou, 'there's the showstopper you've been waiting for. That'll knock everyone's socks off, to be sure.'

'The missing ingredient,' said Lionel, nodding his head and shooting a sideways glance at Mrs Scott.

'I can't wait,' said Hattie, and for the first time since this adventure had started, she truly meant it.

CHAPTER 10

There was a strange sense of unease in the hotel after Mrs Scott had taken her leave and headed home. Hattie couldn't put her finger on it – but *something* felt off-kilter.

Lou was her usual chirpy self, but Lionel... well, there was definitely something up with her uncle, and Hattie was pretty sure that it had something to do with their recently departed visitor. Mrs Scott had left more than a few questions unanswered when she'd headed home, taking her empty Tupperware box with her.

What on earth had that strange moment she'd shared with Lionel been about? They clearly knew each other – which had come as a huge surprise to Hattie. The way Mrs Scott had spoken about him during that first, awkward visit had made her think that they were relative strangers.

Hattie knew that she probably shouldn't pry, but there had been a flicker of *something* between them, she was sure of it.

'Lou, are you happy to finish getting the room ready for painting?' she said.

'Sure!' said Lou. 'I'll get the dust sheets down and yank the tables out... anything else?'

'Mask off the light-fittings if you get a sec?' said Hattie.

'No problem!' said Lou. 'You off to play with your heap of veggies?'

'Actually, I need to have a quick word with Lionel,' said Hattie. 'About the opening night,' she added quickly.

Lou didn't need to know that anything was amiss. Hattie trusted her, but the last thing she wanted to do was unwittingly start any kind of gossip about her lovely uncle – especially if she was right and there really *was* some kind of history between him and Mrs Scott that he'd rather keep quiet.

'I think he said something about heading down to North Beach with his sketchbook,' said Lou.

'Great, thanks!' At least that would save her half an hour of hunting him down!

Grabbing her jacket, Hattie headed out of the hotel and briefly turned her face to the glorious sunshine. She'd been so busy dashing around, she'd almost forgotten that a beautiful spring day was doing its thing right outside the hotel door.

Turning her steps towards North Beach, Hattie hurried along the pavement. She wasn't really sure *what* she was going to say to Lionel, but she had a feeling that he might need someone to lean on right now. There had been something in his eyes when he'd spotted Mrs Scott – something that looked suspiciously like an old hurt lurking deep beneath the surface.

Sure enough, as she hopped down onto the pebbles of North Beach, Hattie spotted Lionel standing near the shoreline. His sketchbook was still tucked tightly under his arm, and he was staring out to sea, lost in thought.

Hattie made her way straight towards him. When she was about ten paces away, he turned to her – and appeared to be completely unsurprised to find her standing there.

'It's ancient history,' he said with a sad smile before Hattie even had the chance to figure out how she was going to broach the subject.

'Okay…' said Hattie, not sure whether this was a warning that he didn't want to talk about it any further, or whether it was an invitation to ask questions.

'Many years ago, I proposed to Mary – Mrs Scott. She turned me down.'

Hattie's eyes grew wide. If she hadn't known what to say before, she *definitely* didn't now!

'She didn't give me a reason as to why,' said Lionel

with a sad sigh, turning to stare at the waves again. 'I haven't seen her in years. I thought she might have moved away. It was a bit of a shock, seeing her like that, standing in my hotel!'

'I bet!' said Hattie faintly. 'I'm so sorry – I had no idea.'

Lionel turned to her, and Hattie did her best not to flinch. Her uncle looked haunted. She'd never seen Lionel looking anything other than one hundred per cent confident and content – but the look on his face right now broke her heart.

Hattie reached out and gingerly patted his arm, and after just a second, Lionel took her hand and tucked it into the crook of his elbow.

'Thank you, my girl,' he said, his voice gruff.

Hattie snuggled into her uncle's side and rested her head on his shoulder. She didn't say anything, wanting to take the cue from Lionel. If he needed to change the subject, she wasn't about to stop him.

'You know,' sighed Lionel, 'I'm still getting used to the idea of owning my own hotel just as much as you're trying to acclimatise to having to run your own kitchen for the first time!'

'I hadn't thought of that,' said Hattie quietly.

'Oh yes – 'tis quite they eye-opener, eh? Quite scary for both of us?'

Hattie nodded, feeling the tweed of Lionel's jacket against her cheek. She didn't know why, but the knowledge that they were both in this together was intensely comforting.

'I'll let you in on a secret,' said Lionel. 'I keep imagining that this all some kind of dream – and that Veronica's about to reappear at any moment and spoil everything.' He let out a long sigh.

Hattie lifted her head to look at him, and he shot her a small smile.

'I'm okay – just being a daft old git, that's all,' he said. 'It was just never very easy living at the hotel when Veronica was there. All those years under the same roof as someone who wanted any reason to get rid of me. She was always finding new ways to make my life a misery.'

'That's awful!' said Hattie. 'You always made such a joke out of it when I was a kid – you cast her as a pantomime villain. I guess I never thought about how horrible it must have been for you to have to deal with that every day.'

'Good!' said Lionel, firmly. 'That's exactly as it should be – I didn't want you worrying your little head with such things. It was bad enough that you had to come into contact with her ridiculous behaviour at all. I thought it would be best if we tried to laugh about it. Anyway, at least most of her little tortures were short-lived.'

'They were?' said Hattie in surprise.

'Oh absolutely,' Lionel nodded. 'That woman had

no patience or determination. She always gave up too soon!'

'And you never considered leaving?' asked Hattie curiously.

'The only time I ever thought about it seriously was when I lost Mary. I came pretty close then – I thought living in the same town would be just awful.'

Hattie nodded, though she was cursing herself for inadvertently leading them back to the topic of Mrs Scott.

Lionel let out a long breath. 'I love Seabury. I always have. It didn't take long for the good memories to start outweighing the bad. I loved my rooms, loved the view, and loved the people. All my friends were here. There was no one back in London I really cared about, and I had nowhere else to go – so I stayed.'

Hattie wrapped her arm more tightly around him, blinking hard as her eyes grew hot. The last thing she wanted to do was start crying. She just wished that she could say something that would help her uncle – but how could she when she still didn't really know the full story?

'Don't look so blue! It's been a pretty wonderful life here,' said Lionel, giving her a smile and tugging at her arm so that they began to amble along the pebbles. 'And now you've come to help me out – and I couldn't be happier to be sharing this adventure with you!'

Hattie returned his smile, and for the first time, she didn't feel the familiar rush of guilt at the thought that she'd be hot-footing it back to London at the first opportunity. At long last, she could see that being here in Seabury and working with him at The Pebble Street Hotel was exactly where she was meant to be.

'I think you'll find that it's *you* helping *me* out!' she said, her voice coming out husky. 'I just hope that I can repay you for your faith in me someday.'

'There's nothing to repay, Hattie,' he said. 'You are an incredible chef, and I think that between us we can make The Pebble Street Hotel come alive again. Between us, we'll make it forget that Veronica ever darkened its doors. Deal?'

'Deal,' said Hattie, squeezing his arm tightly.

'Oh, that reminds me!' said Lionel, coming to an abrupt stop and fidgeting around in his jacket pocket. 'I almost forgot – I've got something here for you.'

Hattie looked at him in surprise as he placed a set of car keys in her hand.

'Just in case you fancy driving yourself around rather than having to go by Ben's boat. You're going to need to get out and about, and you can't rely on the bus – that thing's so random it's like trying to catch an agoraphobic unicorn.' He paused. 'That's if you can drive, of course?'

'I can!' said Hattie. 'Not sure how I found the time to learn... but I did!'

'Don't get too excited,' said Lionel. 'The car belonged to Veronica. It's in one of the garages at the back of the hotel – though I'm not exactly sure which one. It was included in the sale. I've got no idea if it goes or not – but maybe you could get Ben to take a look at it when you find it. It's done a lot of supermarket runs and I know for a fact that she never got the thing serviced – so by this point it might be a total scrapper. Still, it's worth a try, right?'

'Thank you!' said Hattie, jingling the set of car keys with excitement. 'Shall we…?' she pointed back towards the hotel.

Lionel nodded, and they turned to start walking in that direction.

'Oh – by the way, Charlie's over the moon about you using the allotments for all our veg,' he said.

'He told you?' laughed Hattie.

'Was it a secret?' asked Lionel.

'Not at all,' said Hattie, shaking her head. 'But Lou's only just washed the mud off everything - he was quick!'

'Well, it's exciting for them - Charlie was full of it on the phone!' said Lionel with a smile. 'I told you about the bad blood Veronica caused up there. Fresh local veg from the allotments? It's about as far as you can get from how she ran the place.'

'Good!' said Hattie firmly.

'Indeed!' agreed Lionel. 'Anyway, I had trouble getting Charlie off the phone. You know what he's like when he starts talking about veg! His theory is that it's the sea air that makes the quality of their produce up there better than any you'll find anywhere else.'

Hattie giggled. She could just imagine the lecture poor old Lionel had probably had to endure. 'Hm – I think Ethel would argue it's the ridiculous amount of time Charlie and the rest of them spend up there.'

'I think you're right,' said Lionel. 'She hasn't got a hope of changing him though.'

'I don't know about that,' said Hattie, thinking of Charlie scrubbing his nails and using a fresh towel just because Ethel had mentioned it. 'People do all sorts of things for love.'

'That they do,' said Lionel, and Hattie was horrified to see the smile drop from his face and the sad, lost look returning.

'Erm, Lionel...' Hattie paused, making her uncle's eyebrows shoot up in question.

She hesitated. She really didn't want to bring Mrs Scott back into the conversation when it was clearly such a painful subject, but equally, she didn't want to risk a second nasty surprise for her poor uncle.

'Spit it out, Hattie,' said Lionel.

'It's just... Mrs Scott promised that she's going to come back to Pebble Street to give me that recipe and show me how to make the pudding. But... well, if it'll make you uncomfortable, I could always head over to her house instead?'

'That's alright,' said Lionel, smiling at her gratefully, 'I think I'm a bit old to play the lovesick teenager, don't you? It was a shock seeing her again after all this time, that's all, but I'll get over it.'

He patted her hand, and Hattie recognised it as a gentle but firm full-stop to the conversation.

CHAPTER 11

'Come out, come out, wherever you are!' mumbled Hattie as she made her way towards the old garages at the back of the hotel.

She'd already had to wait longer than she'd planned to go in search of Veronica's old car. The minute she'd returned from her stroll on the beach with Lionel the day before, Ben and Lou had commandeered her, and the three of them had spent the rest of the afternoon getting the breakfast lounge painted at long last.

Hattie had hoped that she might get the chance to slope off when they'd finished for the day, but there was still the veggie-mountain in the kitchen to tackle. By the time she'd worked her way through all that, she was in no fit state for anything other than a bath to get rid of all the paint splatters - and then bed!

But the early-morning sunshine had peeked around the sides of her curtains and woken her up at sparrow-fart. Rather than lounging around in bed, Hattie'd bounded up, determined to make the most of the extra couple of hours to go in search of her new chariot.

Hattie'd never been into the old garages that stood at the back of the hotel before. As a kid, they'd been grubby, cobwebby places where you were pretty likely to bump into Veronica, so she'd always given them a wide berth. Right now, though, the idea of having her own transport and the ability to go adventuring in the lanes beyond Seabury proved to be enough of a temptation to explore them at last.

Hattie eyeballed the cracked, red paint of the little door in the side of the first garage. She hoped there weren't too many spiders in there! She quickly grabbed the handle before she wussed-out and gave it a push. The door didn't budge - the wood was clearly warped and stuck in the frame.

Hattie rolled up her sleeves. No way was she going to let a door stop her in her tracks this morning – not after she'd left her cosy bed quite so bloomin' early!

Grabbing the handle again, she threw her entire weight against the door. It flew open with an ear-splitting whine of wood-on-wood, making her stumble into the dusty space beyond.

'Balls,' muttered Hattie.

All that effort and there was nothing to find in there but a tower of dried-up paint cans and a couple of pieces of broken furniture that didn't look like they would be good for anything other than a bonfire.

The next garage turned out to be exactly the same – apart from the fact that the door worked properly and there wasn't any rubbish stacked up there.

Hattie approached the third and final garage with her fingers crossed. The car *had* to be in there, didn't it? Unless Lionel had been mistaken and Veronica had used it in her hasty escape from Seabury. But then, she had the keys, so-

She pushed the door of the third garage open and let out a little cheer. She'd found it.

In front of her was a large, ancient Swedish estate car. Boxy and far from streamlined, it had obviously seen better days. There were scrapes and bumps all over it and, going by the twigs sticking out of the bumpers, Hattie guessed that Veronica hadn't been a stranger to regular close encounters with the local hedges.

She circled the car, giving it a gentle pat here and there as if it was an abandoned horse.

'Don't worry,' she whispered, 'I'll be nice to you!'

She squeezed around the back and peered through the grimy windows. The back seats were down – and judging by the thick layer of rubbish - it looked like that was their permanent position. Hattie wrinkled her nose. She really hoped that Veronica had taken everything perishable out of there before she did her runner!

Gingerly, she opened the boot for a proper look. It was a mess. There was a thick layer of old carrier bags, receipts and chocolate wrappers. It was clear that the old car had seen plenty of use. The carpet was grubby and torn and the whole thing could certainly do with a thorough clean, but that wasn't exactly a surprise – it echoed the state Veronica had left the hotel in. Still – there wasn't much point in spring cleaning the old thing if it didn't run.

Hattie decided to bite the bullet and give it a go. It would be amazing to have some transport – but there was no point getting her hopes up just yet, was there? Not if the car was just destined to be towed to the scrap yard.

She unlocked the front door and after brushing some mud and ancient crumbs from the seat, she took her place behind the wheel.

'Blimey!' Hattie laughed, fiddling around with the plastic wheel to give her legs a bit more space. Veronica must have driven everywhere with her nose practically pressed up against the windscreen.

Adjustments made, Hattie popped the key in the ignition and, sending up a little prayer, turned it.

'That's my girl!' she squealed, as the old car started the first time as if it had just been sat here waiting for her to come to the rescue.

Right – now, what were the things you were meant to look out for again? The tyres had all looked okay – though she'd need to double-check their pressures at some point. There were no plumes of white smoke coming from the exhaust... no red warning lights on the dash. Against all odds, it was all looking pretty positive.

Hattie reached forward and wiped the dust off of the dash with her fingertips. Huh, she had a full tank of fuel too – who'd have thought?! There were many, *many* thousands of miles on the clock – but frankly, these cars were built like tanks, weren't they? It'd probably be fine for buzzing around, collecting local ingredients, wouldn't it?!

Well, there was one way to test out that theory – maybe she should take her for an early-morning spin. She needed to remind herself how to drive after so long – and what better time to do that than first thing in the morning? There wouldn't be anyone else around...

Hattie hesitated. Maybe she'd be better off waiting until Lou turned up for work so that she could come with her and show her the way... or... well, she *could* just set off and hope for the best. She was a grown-up after all – in charge of her own kitchen... her own destiny!

Hattie let out a giggle at herself for being ridiculous. She was going to do it... what was the point in waiting?

Deciding to act before she thought better of it again, Hattie put the old car in gear and gently pulled away. She was definitely glad that the garage was nice and wide so that she wouldn't have any problem reversing back in here when she got back.

After a bit of embarrassing bunny-hopping down the Seabury seafront past West Beach and the still-closed Sardine, Hattie took the road up the hill past the allotments. When she got to the junction at the top, she hesitated.

She didn't have a map with her – but how hard could it be? All the roads around here were narrow, single-track affairs and she was pretty certain that she'd be able to remember *some* of it from her trip on the bus here with Ben – that had only been a few weeks ago, after all. Sure, she'd been pretty tired at the time, but she was bound to have taken some of it in.

After a moment's indecision, Hattie pulled out, turned left, and she was off! It didn't take her too long before she started to get the hang of things and slowly but surely felt like she could ease off her white-knuckled death-grip on the steering wheel.

Very soon, she found herself sailing through unfamiliar, open countryside with the sea disappearing in the rear-view mirror. Hattie tried to keep a mental note of where she was going.

Left... right... right... another left...

Ah sod it, she gave up! Deciding to relax and

enjoy the ride, Hattie wound down her window and felt the cool morning air dance across her face. This was freedom, alright. Zooming through the country lanes before everyone else was up, with a menu to finalise and her own restaurant to prepare for opening night.

To think that she'd been so set on working in London – stuck in a hot kitchen day after day. Not that the kitchen at Pebble Street was that much different – but it *felt* different! She was in charge. And now that she knew exactly what she was doing… nothing could stop her.

Hattie took a moment to thank her lucky stars for Lou. Despite her rather unusual interview - which obviously could have gone a whole lot better - she was a breath of fresh air. What made Lou even more special in Hattie's eyes was the fact that Marco would have hated her. He would *never* have hired her. He had strict rules on what his waiting staff were allowed to say and what they should look like – and he *really* didn't like them to smile at customers.

'Get out of my head!' Hattie muttered.

She didn't work for that plonker anymore. She could do what she liked, and it was liberating. At long last, she was finally realising that she'd stepped out of Marco's shadow for good.

'Wooooop!'

Hattie's ecstatic cheer echoed around the inside of

the old car as she trundled along yet another lane lined with high, sappy green hedges.

Her sense of exhilaration didn't last for very long. Hattie realised that while she'd been ruminating on her old boss, she'd stopped paying any attention to the various twists and turns she'd been taking, and now she was hopelessly lost.

'Balls!' she muttered.

How had she let that happen so quickly? And *why* on earth were there no road signs around here?

After a few more minutes of driving randomly around in circles, hoping that something might give her a clue as to where she was, she realised that one stretch of green lane looked like all the others.

Right, she'd just have to pull over and try to retrace her steps – otherwise, she could be driving around these damn lanes until judgement day!

Hattie swerved into a gateway and was just about to commence a fifty-three-and-a-half point turn when she spotted the fish van driving towards her. She tucked the nose of the car back into the gateway and watched as it approached.

Much to her confusion, the moment the driver spotted her, they put their foot down, putting on an insane burst of speed before slamming their breaks on again.

'What on earth…?!' muttered Hattie in surprise, as the van then crawled up alongside her.

'Ben?' she said, half-laughing as she wound down his window.

'You frightened the living daylights out of me!' said Ben, running his hand over his face.

'Why?' demanded Hattie, watching his weird reaction with some amusement.

'I thought you were Veronica there for a second!' he said.

'Well, obviously I'm not,' said Hattie.

'Obviously...,' said Ben. 'Besides, if you were, you'd be in a ditch or half stuck in a hedge!'

'Was she that bad?' laughed Hattie. 'I did wonder. This old thing is covered in bumps – and there's half a bush lodged in the back bumper!'

'Yes. She was *that* bad,' confirmed Ben with a nod. 'The woman was a lousy driver. Anyway, what are you doing out here so early?'

Hattie looked at him for a long moment and then realised she didn't really have a choice in the matter but to admit it. 'I'm lost,' she said.

She watched as Ben manfully bit back a laugh.

'*How* on earth did you manage that?!' he asked.

'There aren't any buildings... or street signs... and it all looks the same,' said Hattie, a hint of a whine appearing in her voice.

Ben shook his head. 'You're only two minutes outside of town, you know.'

Hattie had to admit that she was impressed. He was still holding the laughter at bay. Almost. A little snort escaped, and Ben quickly clapped his hand to his mouth.

'Quit it!' said Hattie, poking her tongue out at him.

'Come on,' said Ben, revealing his wide grin as he put the fish van back into gear, 'I'm heading back down into town. Why don't you follow me – if you've had enough adventuring?'

Hattie nodded. As much as she'd love to continue her magical mystery tour of the lanes, she was pretty sure she'd end up driving around the same circle for days without someone to give her directions back into town.

'Right!' said Ben. 'Follow me – but don't be too surprised if other drivers pull over.'

'Why?' said Hattie.

'They'll be getting out of your way,' laughed Ben. 'Everyone around here knows this car and they'll all think you're Veronica just like I did! It was always safer to dive into a hedge when she was coming at you!'

'Ah man!' sighed Hattie, rolling her eyes. 'And I was just starting to fall in love with this old girl,' she said, giving the steering wheel in front of her a tender pat.

'Well, maybe it would be a good idea to get it repainted then – just to stop people from having a funny turn whenever they see you coming!'

'Paint her?' said Hattie.

Ben nodded. 'I might know someone who's available to do it.'

Hattie raised an eyebrow. 'That's you, isn't it?' she laughed.

'Might be!' he said, and with that, he put his foot down and sped off.

CHAPTER 12

There was a visitor waiting for Hattie when she arrived back at the hotel. Practically as soon as she was inside, Mrs Scott ushered her into the kitchen and closed the door behind her. Hattie turned to her visitor with amusement, only to find that she was carrying a suitcase so large that it looked like she was moving in for a week.

'Is that door closed?' Mrs Scott asked briskly, nodding at the back door that led directly outside.

Hattie nodded.

'We need to make sure we can't be disturbed!' said Mrs Scott.

Hattie raised her eyebrows. 'There isn't a lock...' she said, thinking for a moment that her guest might be joking. One look at her stern face told her otherwise, however. Hattie glanced around the kitchen and then, grabbing the mop and bucket, she took them over and wedged the inner door shut.

'There,' she said, dusting her hands together, 'that'll stop anyone coming in.'

Mrs Scott glared at it for a moment before nodding in satisfaction. Then she strode over to the back door and flipped the latch.

'Right,' she said, letting out a sigh of relief and shooting Hattie a smile, 'here we go.'

Hattie quickly washed her hands and then joined Mrs Scott at the kitchen table, helping her to heave the large case up onto the surface and then watching as she popped open the lid.

Hattie peered inside. It was full of ingredients – and all of them looked fairly normal. Nothing really stood out as odd or unusual – not like when she'd worked with Marco and all the ingredients had been peculiar and hard to come by.

'Makings of the Pebble Street pudding,' said Mrs Scott, 'remember - this is for your eyes only.'

Hattie nodded, matching the serious look on Mrs Scott's face.

'Do you have the recipe with you?' she asked, looking in the suitcase again, expecting a printout – or at least a handwritten list of measurements and instructions.

Mrs Scott shook her head. 'There isn't one,' she said, lifting her chin proudly. 'It's all in here,' she added, tapping her temple. 'I sincerely hope you've got a good memory, young lady, because I don't want you writing this down. Okay?'

Hattie's eyes grew wide. Blimey, this really *was* like being inducted into a cult. A pudding cult. The mad urge to giggle rose in her chest, and she had to clear her throat as an excuse to let it out.

'Agreed,' said Hattie, hoping that she was up to the task of committing this pudding to memory.

'I'm serious,' said Mrs Scott in a warning tone. 'You've got to pay attention to the details – there are quite a few ingredients and getting the measurements right is crucial. They're a bit… odd.'

'Odd?' said Hattie.

Mrs Scott nodded. 'Mother had some pretty strange methods of getting them right!'

Hattie just nodded. She had no idea what was about to happen, but she had to admit that she was intrigued. She watched as Mrs Scott stared around the newly organised kitchen for a moment - her sharp eyes taking in every little detail. Hattie found that she was holding her breath, waiting to see if she'd passed the test.

'I may be wrong, but I believe you'll have the necessary skill to keep up!' said Mrs Scott.

Hattie had to bite her lip to stop a nervous giggle from escaping. Clearly, Mrs Scott thought that she was being nice, but Hattie could see that her visitor still had some doubts as to whether she was up to the task.

'Erm – thank you,' said Hattie at last.

'I must say, it sets my mind at ease to see this room so clean and tidy. My mother was an amazing cook, but she certainly wasn't one for order. I guess that's why the recipe is the way it is – completely eccentric – but it works and that's all that matters.'

Hattie nodded.

'Right, let's begin!' said Mrs Scott.

Hattie had to watch intently as the weighing and measuring commenced. Mrs Scott hadn't been kidding - there were some fairly wacky measurements involved.

A teaspoon and three fifths.

An ounce and a bit.

'One eggcup full?' said Hattie.

'Yes,' sighed Mrs Scott. 'I do always wonder about the size of the egg cup she used. They're not exactly standardised, are they?!'

'Hang on a minute,' said Hattie, dashing over to one of the cupboards. She'd stashed a bunch of items in there when she'd been cleaning the kitchen with Ethel. These were the things that she couldn't imagine that she'd ever use, but they'd been too beautiful - or too quirky - to get rid of.

'What about this one?' she said, straightening up and handing the ornate eggcup to Mrs Scott. 'I think these have been at the hotel forever. I kept them because I remembered them from when I was a kid.'

Mrs Scott turned the little blue and white egg cup

in her hands, holding it up so that the light glinted off of the gold edging.

'I would say it's exactly right,' said Mrs Scott, shooting Hattie one of her rare, full-beam smiles. 'I wouldn't be surprised if this is exactly what mum used when she came up with the recipe. After all – she invented it in this kitchen!'

Hattie felt a strange, tingling sensation go through her. It was as if the past, present and future were coming together right here in the kitchen. Maybe this pudding did have something a little bit magical about it after all.

∽

'Right-ho!' said Mrs Scott at last. 'That's everything… apart from the secret ingredient.'

'I thought the whole thing was secret?' laughed Hattie.

'Oh, it is. But this is *the* secret ingredient,' said Mrs Scott seriously.

Hattie watched as she went over to her coat and retrieved a glass jar from one of the deep pockets.

'Honey?' said Hattie in surprise.

'Not just *any old* honey,' said Mrs Scott, placing the jar carefully down on the table. 'This is from the hives on the King's Nose.'

'As in… wait… as in *that* King's Nose?' said Hattie, pointing through the back window towards the craggy, grassy outcrop that extended out into the sea behind the hotel.

'Do you know of any other King's Nose?' said Mrs Scott dryly.

Hattie shook her head. 'No – but… well, I didn't even know there were hives out there. I thought it was council land. I thought it was up for sale!'

Mrs Scott nodded. 'Right on both accounts. Even so – this is King's Nose honey. And without it, the pudding just isn't the same. I've tried it and it's good – but not phenomenal. Will you do the honours?'

Hattie nodded and, taking hold of the jar, managed to unscrew the lid with some effort.

'Now,' said Mrs Scott, taking the jar back and raising it high above the vast mixing bowl they'd been using, 'this takes the place of a lot of sugar.'

Hattie watched carefully as Mrs Scott poured a generous glug of honey directly from the jar into the mix. She did her best to gauge exactly how much she was adding but found herself lost in the silky-smooth stream as it flowed from the jar, the colour of rich caramel.

'Wow, it smells amazing,' said Hattie, taking in a deep breath.

Mrs Scott deftly cut off the stream and with a practised curl of her wrist, managing not to waste a single drop.

'It's the sea lavender and brambles that give this honey its distinctive taste. It's almost salty,' she said, screwing the top back on and proceeding to mix the honey through the rest of the batter.

Hattie nodded, not taking her eyes off of what was going on in front of her. There was no way she wanted to lose track of proceedings this late in the game!

'You know,' said Mrs Scott, 'I can still remember the smell of this pudding baking in here when I was a little girl. It used to waft through the whole hotel and send everyone a bit crackers. They all wanted to get a taste! Now – pass me the tin!'

Hattie fetched the wide baking tin she'd already carefully greased and lined and placed it down on the table for Mrs Scott.

'Thank heavens you've still got the same old oven in here!' she said, wasting no time in pouring the batter. 'Glad to see you had the sense not to come in and rip it out just because it's old!'

Hattie nodded. She didn't want to say anything, but the oven really was ancient and ideally, it should be replaced. The only thing that had saved it was Lionel's current lack of funds – but she decided that now might not be the best time to mention it. Not when everything was going so surprisingly well.

'Right, Hattie, get that oven open so that the baking can begin!'

The pair of them let out identical sighs of relief as soon as they'd closed the oven door on the pudding.

'Good job!' said Mrs Scott with a laugh, checking the time on her wristwatch.

'You're the one that did everything!' said Hattie, watching as Mrs Scott made a quick mental calculation as to when the pudding would be ready.

'Well, hopefully you've got it all safely stored up here for next time?' said Mrs Scott, tapping her temple again.

Hattie nodded. 'I think so.'

'That's my girl,' said Mrs Scott approvingly.

For just a moment, Hattie felt as if she was the feral eight-year-old again, getting praised by the stern headteacher.

'Now then,' said Mrs Scott, fetching a dishcloth and beginning to efficiently wipe down the work surface and clear everything to the side of the sink to be washed up, 'we need to talk about ingredients.'

'I thought we already had?' said Hattie, confused.

'I mean – shopping for ingredients. You can pick most of them up just about anywhere, but I'd like it if you'd spread them out over a few different shops. That way no one can follow the recipe.'

'They wouldn't!' said Hattie. 'Would they?'

Mrs Scott nodded. 'You'd better believe it. It's been tried before!'

Hattie felt her mind boggle slightly. Even if she didn't quite believe that anyone would go to *that* extent to steal the recipe, it was hitting her again what an honour it was that Mrs Scott was trusting her with it at all.

'I can definitely do that,' she said warmly.

'Good girl,' said Mrs Scott. 'Now, you might have some trouble tracking down the honey from Mr Eaves – but if you do, I have a few more jars that I can let you have as long as this pudding turns out well. Now that I've seen you in action today, I'm feeling confident you've got what it takes!'

'Thank you,' said Hattie, smiling.

'Right,' said Mrs Scott, as she swept up the last stray patch of flour with her cloth and promptly dropped into one of the chairs at the kitchen table. 'Now we wait – so yes please, I'd love a cup of tea.'

Hattie grinned at her and turned to pop the kettle on. 'Tell me more about the Pudding Club.'

'Well,' said Mrs Scott, 'it used to bring people to Seabury from all over the place. It just seemed to catch people's imaginations – and they'd come back time after time. Some of them never missed a club night – it was like a badge of honour. They were wonderful times, and this old place just came alive.'

'Why did it stop?' asked Hattie, pouring a cup of tea for them both. She was already having to do her best not to start dribbling. The kitchen was starting to fill with the most amazing smell coming from the oven.

'It started to decline in popularity after my mother retired,' she said sadly. 'Someone else took over who wasn't as good with puddings. Like all these things, they have their moment in the sun.'

She let out a sad sigh, and for a moment Hattie wondered if it might be about something more than the end of the old Pudding Club.

'The pudding's smelling glorious,' she said, trying to lighten her new friend's mood.

Mrs Scott nodded. 'It's the honey, you mark my words,' she said. 'You know, there was always some debate about whether this signature pudding was actually a pudding at all… or whether it was a cake!'

'Well,' said Hattie, with a little laugh, 'I guess it could be a cake… but surely if you serve it in a bowl… it automatically becomes a pudding?'

Mrs Scott smiled at her fully now. 'That was exactly my mother's take on it too. You know – you do have a very important decision ahead of you.'

'Oh?' said Hattie, taking a sip of tea to mask the little spike of nerves.

'Will you serve it with cream, ice cream or custard?'

'How did your mum serve it?' she asked curiously.

'Well, ice cream was never quite so widespread back then – so it tended to be the other two options, depending on the time of year. But this time around, it's up to you to make the choice!'

'Blimey, the pressure!' laughed Hattie.

'You *could* always serve both, of course, but I'd

advise against it. Giving people choice just confuses them,' she said with a decided frown.

'I'll have to give it some thought,' said Hattie.

'And now,' said Mrs Scott, peering at her wristwatch, 'we are very nearly there.'

Hattie followed Mrs Scott over to the oven. She held her breath as they both waited, watching the second hand of Mrs Scott's wristwatch as it ticked closer to the moment they'd been waiting for.

'Right,' said Mrs Scott, picking up the thick set of oven gloves. 'Now!'

Hattie opened the oven door and Mrs Scott deftly retrieved the tin and placed it carefully down on the counter.

They stood side by side, peering at it for a moment in complete silence.

'What do you think?' said Hattie, barely able to breathe.

'Flawless,' said Mrs Scott with a smile.

CHAPTER 13

The perfect pudding was already disappearing – one spoonful at a time.

As soon as Mrs Scott had done a taste test and given it her seal of approval, she'd packed her suitcase of ingredients back up and headed home via the back door, refusing another cup of tea. In fact, the urgency with which she made her escape made Hattie think that Mrs Scott wanted to avoid running into Lionel again if she could help it.

It seemed that Lionel had been lurking with a similar thought in mind. The moment Mrs Scott had disappeared through the back door and Hattie had removed the mop-bucket barricade from the inner door, he appeared - as if by magic. Sniffing the air hungrily, he gladly accepted Hattie's invitation to join her for a second taste test.

Hattie was desperate to find out more about what

had happened between the pair of them, but she didn't dare ask. On one hand, Mrs Scott was far too stern and formal to even think of broaching the subject, and on the other hand, she couldn't face seeing that sad look in her uncle's eyes again – so she kept her mouth shut.

Less than an hour later, Hattie couldn't help but wonder if the delicious scent of the Pebble Street pudding had wafted to all four corners of Seabury rather than just around the hotel, as a steady stream of visitors appeared in the kitchen.

Lionel had just made himself comfortable with a dish full of pudding when Charlie and Ethel both turned up. Charlie came bearing a string of onions that one of the other growers had sent down as a gift for Hattie.

Of course, Hattie was more than happy to reward the messenger with some fresh pudding. The first bite made Charlie come over all weak at the knees, and he settled gladly onto a chair next to Lionel. Ethel bustled around making them all a fresh pot of tea.

As soon as she sat down next to him, Ethel argued that she'd only try one "little spoonful" of pudding - which Charlie grudgingly allowed her to pilfer from his bowl. Ethel promptly stole half of Charlie's portion, earning herself a decidedly mournful look.

Hattie gladly dished him up a second helping - followed by a third - to make up for the fact that

Ethel kept coming back for "just another little spoonful". Hattie took all this as a massive compliment to the chef and stored it away to share with Mrs Scott the next time she saw her.

Next to appear at the door looking hopeful was Lou. Hattie invited her to try a bit of pudding, but this time she made sure that Lou's weapon of choice was a teaspoon rather than a serving spoon.

Just as the kitchen was starting to feel like it was hosting a Pudding Club revival party - with everyone sitting around the table discussing the merits of the delicious dessert - Ben appeared. Sneaking over to Hattie, he wrapped his arms around her waist and demanded to try the pudding before it was all gone.

He fed Hattie a spoonful before trying some himself. Hattie quickly closed her eyes – mainly to block out the fact that everyone else had stopped talking and were now doing wolf whistles (Lou) or giving her little winks (Lionel) and nudging each other in excitement at this rare public display of affection (Charlie and Ethel).

Hattie felt her cheeks flush several degrees warmer than usual as she simultaneously tried to enjoy the moment with Ben while batting him away so that the others would quit their teasing.

In the end, she gave up. Frankly, she didn't really *want* to stop Ben from wrapping her up in his arms and kissing her cheek as she savoured another spoonful of pudding – and trying to stop the others from giggling like a bunch of teenagers was clearly impossible.

Doing her best to ignore them all, Hattie enjoyed what she promised herself would be her last mouthful of pudding. It really was a mysterious concoction. It tasted so much better than the sum of its parts – but she knew that what Mrs Scott had said was right – it was the honey that *really* made it work.

Mrs Scott had promised to deliver the extra jars she had stashed away so that Hattie would have enough to make the pudding for everyone on opening night. Hattie knew that after that, she'd need to find the elusive Mr Eaves who owned the hives if she wanted to keep the pudding on the menu… but that was a problem for another day. Right now, she had a more pressing issue.

Opening her eyes, she couldn't help but laugh. There was a fierce spoon-battle going on as the others concentrated on scraping the last of the pudding directly from the baking tin into their mouths.

'Alright you lot,' she said, 'before you all pull a disappearing act now that the grub is gone, I've got a question for you…'

Lionel turned to her, raising his eyebrows. 'If the question is *should Hattie make more pudding*, then the answer's yes!'

'Hear hear!' cried Charlie, licking the back of his spoon and then taking a great big slurp of tea.

'I agree!' said Ben, leaning back against the edge of the counter and grinning at her. 'That's going to go down an absolute treat on opening night.'

Hattie couldn't help but roll her eyes at them. 'Yeah yeah - I agree with that - but it *wasn't* the question I had in mind!'

'So?' said Lou, who now had her fingers in the tin, hunting around for the tiniest crumbs. 'Out with it!'

'The question is, what should I serve it with?' said Hattie.

'Custard!' said Ben promptly, without missing a beat.

'Don't you want to hear the options?' laughed Hattie.

Ben shook his head. 'Custard,' he said again.

'What *are* the options?' asked Ethel, rolling her eyes at Ben.

'Cream, ice cream or… custard,' said Hattie.

'What sort of cream?' said Lionel. 'That thick stuff that spreads like butter or the stuff you pour?'

'The pouring kind,' said Hattie.

'What flavour ice cream?' he pressed.

'Strawberry!' said Lou.

'Eew!' said Hattie. 'Absolutely not.'

'I second the yuck on that!' said Charlie. 'That would spoil it!'

'What then?' said Lou.

'Vanilla. Proper vanilla,' said Hattie.

'Hmm,' said Lionel, 'and the custard… would that

be hot or cold? And would it be homemade or from a tin?'

'You lot are impossible,' said Hattie with a sigh.

'Well, these *are* very important questions,' said Ben, poking her playfully in the ribs.

'Fine,' said Hattie, wriggling away from him and getting all flustered as Ethel gave her a knowing wink. 'The custard would be hot and homemade!'

'My favourite kind,' said Ben, his voice low as he gave her a naughty wink.

'Behave!' she muttered.

'It's definitely custard for me,' said Lionel. 'As long as it has skin on it like I remember from school!'

Hattie bit her tongue. She was desperate to point out that skin on custard wasn't exactly a sought-after trait in a fine-dining setting. 'I can't promise anything,' she said trying to keep a straight face, 'but I'll see what I can do.'

'That's all I can ask!' said Lionel with a contented nod.

'Charlie? Ethel?' Hattie prompted.

'As long as I get a dish full of that pudding, I don't really mind what comes with it!' said Charlie, licking his lips.

'I agree,' said Ethel, 'though I like the idea of something hot – so custard, I guess.'

Hattie nodded. 'Lou?' she asked, vaguely dreading the answer following the strawberry ice cream suggestion.

'Ice cream. No – cream...' Lou bit her lip. 'No – custard!'

'You're a great help!' laughed Hattie.

'Well... it all depends what you're going to serve it on, doesn't it?' said Lou.

'Does it?' said Hattie.

Lou nodded. 'If it's on a plate with a piddling spoonful of whatever and half a tasteless strawberry as a garnish and a dusting of icing sugar...' she wrinkled her nose.

'There'll be none of that nonsense!' said Hattie, earning herself approving nods from around the table and a little cheer from Ben.

'In that case,' said Lou, 'I'd go for custard too - as long as it comes in a nice big bowl with high sides.'

'So – to recap – another one for custard?' said Hattie, trying to keep up.

Lou nodded. 'In a *big* bowl. And I hope the main course won't take up too much room because I want to have lots of space left for dessert.'

Ethel let out a little laugh.

'Lou – I hate to remind you,' said Hattie, 'but you won't actually be eating it on the night... you'll be too busy waitressing!'

Lou looked crestfallen for a moment but then brightened up again. 'Ah-ha!' she said with the air of someone who'd just spotted a loophole, 'but if there's any left over in the kitchen after everyone's been served – that's mine then, right? I mean – perk of the job and all?'

Sensing that she might have a one-woman mutiny on her hands from her one and only precious member of staff if she said no, Hattie promptly agreed. She didn't actually hold out much hope that there *would* be any leftovers if today's success was anything to go by. She just hoped that Lou would deal with the disappointment on the night!

'Ben,' she said, 'what about you? Still set on-'

'Custard,' said Ben without missing a beat, earning himself a gale of laughter from the others.

'What?' he demanded. 'There's nothing better than proper custard – as long as it's not the piddling dollops you offered me when you cooked for me the first time though! I'm with Lou – there needs to be plenty. Think of a vat of the stuff and then double the amount.' He let out a dreamy little sigh. 'I've always loved custard – and blancmange, not that anyone makes the stuff anymore. Maybe I'm just old fashioned.'

'Maybe you are,' said Hattie, 'but in a good way.'

A way that she was falling in love with a little bit more every single day. She couldn't help herself. Ben's energy and enthusiasm for life was infectious.

'Right,' she said, giving her head a little shake as she tried to get back on track. 'So – custard it is.'

∽

Eventually, the others wandered off. Ben was the last to leave, treating Hattie to a lingering, toe-curling kiss that left her head in a spin. If there hadn't been so much left for her to do, she'd have seriously considered skiving for the rest of the afternoon and convincing Ben to go for a long walk somewhere seriously secluded.

As it was, she ushered him out of the kitchen, re-barricaded the door and splashed plenty of cold water on her face. She needed to come back down to earth long enough to clear up the remnants of the impromptu pudding party.

As soon as everything was neat and tidy again, Hattie started to search the kitchen cupboards. She'd have to make a huge cauldron of custard for opening night if there was going to be enough to serve everyone – after all, she'd hate to run out of the stuff. Plus, there was the added benefit that the bigger the pot she used, the more likely it was that there would be some skin around the edges for Lionel's special request.

With a great deal of clanking and crashing, Hattie rummaged right to the very back of one of her newly reorganised cupboards. She knew she'd stashed a massive pan in there somewhere. She remembered Ethel scrubbing it clean when they'd sorted out the kitchen, and she'd wondered if there'd ever be a reason she'd need such a massive old thing.

Drawing it out with some difficulty, Hattie

plonked it down onto the table. Folding her arms, she gave a little nod of satisfaction and smiled. It would be perfect. For a second, she wondered if it might be the same pan that Mrs Scott's mother had used all those years ago.

Just the thought of it made her smile grow wide. The tingling feeling was back – that strange sensation that she was becoming a part of the ongoing story of The Pebble Street Hotel. She just hoped that she would make Mrs Scott – and more importantly, Mrs Scott's mum - proud.

CHAPTER 14

Dear Mrs Mary Scott,
Please accept this invitation to be our guest of honour
at the grand re-opening of The Pebble Street Hotel
restaurant.
Join us for an informal evening of celebration to mark the
launch of our new menu.
Lionel & Hattie Barclay
RSVP

Hattie couldn't believe it. The big day was here at last, and they were about to find out if all their plans for Pebble Street's opening night were going to work out.

It felt like months ago that Lionel had invited her to take the position of Head Chef here at the hotel. At the same time, it felt like it was just yesterday that she'd arrived in town on the ancient bus – completely dazed and confused by the twist her life had taken.

The last thing Hattie had ever expected was to be back here in Seabury after all these years. And yet, here she was... about to make one of her dearest dreams come true.

Hattie looked around the kitchen and nodded before allowing herself a contented little sigh. Everything was exactly how she wanted it. The fish and vegetables were prepped and ready to go, the much-anticipated puddings were already cooked to perfection, and the custard would only take a matter of minutes to pull together when the time was right.

There was only one thing that was worrying Hattie right now, and that was the fact that she wasn't nervous. At all. That couldn't be right, could it?

She felt... at home. Completely in her element. After all, she'd been working towards this moment for years. All those stupidly long shifts, putting up with idiots throwing tantrums while she learned her craft - it had all been leading to this moment. Now that it was almost here – she found that it wasn't fraught with drama like she'd expected. Instead, there was a strange, serene kind of *rightness* to the whole thing.

This was exactly where she was meant to be.

Lionel, she had to admit, wasn't quite so calm. He'd been dashing around all day like an excited six-year-old. What felt like the entire town had booked a table for the evening – and Lionel was both touched and surprised.

It didn't surprise Hattie, though. Not when it came down to it. Everyone adored Lionel - so it made sense that they were all turning up to support him. The fact that they were supporting *her* just as enthusiastically took her breath away every time she thought about it. In fact, she'd made the conscious decision *not* to think about it too much. It was the only detail about the whole affair that she was finding more than a little bit overwhelming.

Mrs Scott had sent word to Hattie that she would be delighted to attend, and Hattie was thrilled. In spite of all her help and kindness, Hattie had wondered if such a public outing to Pebble Street might be more than Mrs Scott could handle. Hattie had reserved a small table for her by the window. In her view, it was the best one in the house.

Tonight, the breakfast lounge would be full to capacity, but with the help of the allotment holders and the local fishermen – not to mention Lou and Lionel - Hattie felt like she was totally in control.

Well... *mostly* in control. Hattie grinned as she fitted a little key into the door of the walk-in kitchen pantry and firmly locked it. She'd spent most of the afternoon trying to stop both Lou and Lionel from picking at the two enormous Pebble Street puddings she'd stashed in there.

She pocketed the key with a smile. That would stop the blighters sneaking any more while she wasn't on guard duty! It was time for her to head into the breakfast lounge to see how the last-minute preparations were getting on.

Hattie padded out into the hallway and peeped into her new restaurant. Those two words set her heart racing with excitement. She couldn't believe that this was actually happening!

The room looked nothing short of amazing. The old photographs on the newly painted walls gave the place just the right hint of nostalgia. Lou had cleaned the curtains and it had made such a difference. It looked elegant, fresh and stylish – and was practically unrecognisable from the dowdy, disgusting breakfast lounge she remembered from when she'd visited the hotel as a kid. Thank heavens!

The deal she'd made with Lionel to wipe all hints of Veronica Hughes from the soon-to-be-open Pebble Street restaurant was on course.

'How you doing, boss?' asked Lou as she sidled up next to Hattie.

Hattie nodded and smiled. 'I'm ready.'

'I don't get it,' laughed Lou, 'how come you're not a total, quivering wreck?'

Hattie shrugged. 'I've got you on my side'

Lou blushed and then elbowed her in the ribs. 'You soppy git!' she laughed, making Hattie grin.

The pair of them took a moment to amble around the room, checking that everything was in place – but there really was no need. Lou knew exactly what she was doing – the tables were all beautifully laid, the little vintage condiment sets that Hattie and Ben had discovered on their treasure hunt were placed *just so* – and everything was pristine and spotless.

'You've done an amazing job,' said Hattie. 'Everything's immaculate!'

'As long as you're happy, then so am I,' said Lou. Clearly, she wasn't one to let praise go to her head. 'I've just got to place a wine list on each table and I think that's it.'

'Has Lionel brought them down yet?' asked Hattie. Lionel had chosen the wines for each course and then taken himself off on a little jolly to pick them up from his old friend at Upper Bamton vineyard.

'Got them right here, my dear!' said Lionel, appearing behind the pair of them.

Hattie looked her uncle up and down. It was meant to be an informal evening, but he looked incredibly grand in a tweed suit and waistcoat.

'Don't you look every inch the gentleman!' said Hattie approvingly.

'Very spiffy, Mr B!' said Lou.

'Thank you, ladies!' said Lionel, tugging on the hem of his waistcoat and then patting his pocket.

'You okay?' asked Hattie, curiously.

'Just checking I've still got my speech in there,' he said sheepishly. 'I keep going over it and I think I've pretty much got the thing memorised… but I thought I'd better have a copy with me just so I don't forget anything important.'

'And your glasses?' said Hattie.

'Well ahead of you!' laughed Lionel, drawing them out from his jacket pocket. 'Thought it might be a good idea if I could actually *see* what I've written!'

'Sounds like you've thought of everything,' said Lou, giving him a little pat on the arm before taking the wine lists from him and pottering off to set them out on each table.

'You doing okay, my girl?' he asked Hattie in a low voice.

'Better than okay,' she said, taking his hand and giving it a squeeze. 'Thank you.'

'And you,' he said with a soft smile. 'Right, I'm planning to greet everyone at the door and welcome them into the hotel… so I guess I'd better go and loiter in reception in case of any early arrivals!'

'You know where I am if you need me,' said Hattie.

'Right where you belong,' said Lionel in a low voice, smiling at her gently. 'Right ladies, best of luck!' he said in a ringing tone, earning himself a thumbs up from Lou before he disappeared.

Hattie figured that she'd better get back to the kitchen – the last thing she wanted was to get caught up chatting with any early arrivals. She let her eyes roam over the room one last time, checking everything was exactly as it should be.

'Erm, Lou?' she said, frowning.

'Yeah?' said Lou, turning to her with her eyebrows raised.

'Did you put that there?' she pointed at a tiny crystal vase that had appeared on the table that was reserved for Mrs Scott. In it sat a single red rose.

'Not me,' said Lou in surprise.

'Oh, okay,' said Hattie.

It must have been Lionel… no one else had been in the room.

'Hattie?' said Lou, a warning note in her voice. 'I can hear voices out in reception.'

'Blimey!' said Hattie. The mystery of the rose would just have to wait! 'I'd better get out of here, the guests are starting to arrive - catch you in a bit!'

Hattie dashed for the doorway and peeped around the corner. Lionel was chatting with a guest. She was about to slip back into the kitchen unnoticed when she heard someone call her name.

Damn – so close!

Hattie turned, only to find that the unknown

guest was actually Ben - she just hadn't recognised him.

'Hey, Hattie,' he said, taking a couple of steps towards her.

Hattie blinked. He was wearing a tailored suit with an open-collared linen shirt. She let her eyes sweep over him, taking in everything from his shiny leather brogues to the fact that he'd brushed his hair for a change.

Oh, holy hell!

Hattie was pretty sure that her heart had just skipped a beat or twenty. He'd even shaved. He looked gorgeous... practically edible...

Ben leaned in and kissed her on the cheek, and Hattie did her best not to come over all Victorian-heroine and go into full swoon-mode.

He smelled amazing too.

Someone fetch the smelling salts... she was a goner!

'Hi!' he said.

'You... erm,' Hattie paused and cleared her throat. 'You look nice.'

'Thanks!' said Ben, grinning at her. 'I've come ready to help out... I thought you might need someone else to give Lou a hand?'

Hattie nodded, feeling slightly dazed. She was horrified to find that her voice box seemed to have gone on strike.

'I definitely wouldn't mind a hand when it gets busy!'

came Lou's voice as she appeared behind Ben, bustling out of the breakfast lounge towards the pair of them. 'That'd be great, wouldn't it Hattie?' she prompted.

Hattie was too busy ogling Ben for her brain to be functioning fully. It was only when Lou's sharp nudge connected with her ribs that she snapped out of it.

'Right. Yes. That would be great. Thanks,' she said, forcing a smile onto her face.

Focus, idiot!

Hattie shook her head slightly. She needed to get with the program. She needed to stop taking long, deep breaths as if she was trying to breathe Ben in. It was opening night. She'd done this a hundred times before – just not with a gorgeous man walking in and out of the kitchen all night.

'Ben,' she said, finally pulling herself together, 'can you handle the wine?'

'I thought you'd never ask,' he said, producing a corkscrew from his pocket.

'Oh my god,' said Lou, giggling. 'Is that a corkscrew in your pocket or are you just pleased to see me?'

Hattie let out a snort of laughter that felt like a release valve going off. Then she suddenly realised that the three of them were still standing in the hallway and that there were, in fact, actual guests starting to arrive.

She grabbed both Lou and Ben by the wrists and dragged them into the kitchen.

'Right team – focus,' she said in a low voice. 'Ben – you're on wine duty – that'll take that pressure off Lionel and leave him free to mingle and chat with his guests.'

Ben gave her a little salute.

'When you're not doing that, you can chip in with whatever Lou needs?'

Lou nodded and wiggled her eyebrows at Ben, making him laugh.

'Alright then,' said Hattie, taking a deep breath in and then releasing it slowly. 'Let's get this show on the road.'

CHAPTER 15

The last sneaky peep she'd taken had shown Hattie a breakfast lounge that was filled to the brim. She'd hastily ducked back inside the kitchen and set to work.

There was something comforting about being able to hide away behind the scenes like this... half listening in on the proceedings but not actually being expected to take part in them herself.

Hattie was in her element - stirring, checking, ducking and diving around the space - performing the debut of her solo dance to an invisible audience. As she worked hard to bring all the elements of this evening's menu together in perfect time, she kept one ear on the rumble of the guests as they chatted away to each other – all clearly eager for the evening ahead.

The moment Hattie paused for a breather, a sharp

spike of nerves punched her in the gut for the first time. It had just dawned on her that the one thing their guests were all waiting for was the perfect meal…

The one thing they were all waiting for… was her!

Shit!

Thankfully, her little spiral of panic was interrupted by the sound of Lionel clearing his throat. Then came the chiming of a spoon against the edge of a wine glass. He was clearly ready to make a start on his opening speech.

Hattie took a deep, calming breath and got back to the job at hand. After all, this was her cue that it wouldn't be too long before service should start.

Hattie hefted a pan and moved over to the lit burners, all the while keeping her ears peeled for what her uncle was saying. She smiled as she listened to him welcome everyone back to the hotel, or *his old girl*, as he was so fond of saying.

'It's so nice to see so many of you here after so long. I know most of you haven't been through those doors in a while – and I know that you've had your reasons. Or – *reason* – I should say.'

A ripple of knowing laughter followed, and even Hattie had to grin at that. Veronica had certainly left an awful lot of bad feeling behind her.

'Now then, I want to keep things brief – I know you're all here for the food, not me…'

Hattie laughed as she heard a resounding round of applause and cheers greet this statement.

'Okay, okay,' said Lionel with a chuckle, 'no need to rub it in! But I do have a few thank yous I'd like to make before you all tuck into our amazing menu.

'Firstly, I'd like to thank Ben for all his help in getting the old girl back into shape. I know it hasn't been easy with such a tiny budget to play with – and I can't believe how much he's managed to do. The kind of care and attention that young Ben has shown this old building… well, it warms my heart!'

There was more cheering and even a few wolf whistles at this. From her hidey-hole in the kitchen, Hattie bet she could attribute the whistling to Lou. Still, she was glad Lionel had mentioned Ben – he deserved it after everything he'd managed to achieve in such a short space of time.

Hattie froze in place for a second as she heard Lionel mention her name next.

'Of course, my wonderful great-niece deserves all my thanks for coming back to Seabury and making my dreams of reopening the kitchen here come true. I'm truly honoured to have such a great chef running the ship.'

Hattie smiled. That hadn't been too bad. She just hoped that Lionel didn't expect her to make an appearance this early on in the evening – because until the food had been served and scoffed, her place was back here behind her pots and pans.

She breathed a sigh of relief as she listened to the clapping die down again and her uncle continue with his speech without demanding that she put in an appearance.

'Lastly – I would like to say a very special thank you to my guest of honour, Mrs Mary Scott. Mary has very graciously shared the original Pebble Street Pudding recipe with Hattie – and I'm delighted to say that it will be the crowning glory of this evening's meal.

'Thank you, Mary, for trusting us with such an important family heirloom – we're both really excited that the recipe has come home to The Pebble Street Hotel. I know I speak for Hattie too, when I say that we both hope that we'll do the memory of your dear departed mother proud this evening.

'So – I hope you all enjoy tonight's food – and make sure you leave enough room for pudding!'

There was an enormous, resounding cheer from the direction of the breakfast room, and Hattie felt the hairs on the back of her neck stand up in response.

'Here we go, then!' she muttered to herself. It was time to start plating up.

Hattie was vaguely aware of Lou making an appearance in the kitchen behind her, ready to begin service, but right now nothing could break Hattie's concentration as she swiftly dished up plate after plate of perfectly prepared food.

There was baked fish – painstakingly filleted herself and scattered with a light pinch of fresh herbs – nothing overpowering because she wanted the sweet, flaky flavour of the sea to stand for itself. It was served with a tiny drizzle of peppercorn butter – and there were little jars of extra for each guest to help themselves from if they wanted it.

To this, she added sautéed leaves and roasted root vegetables. Other than the lightest seasoning, she left these plain. The vegetables from the allotments were so tasty that there was no point smothering them in some kind of rich sauce. She wanted the flavour of the local produce to speak for itself.

It had taken quite a lot of encouragement from Lou before Hattie had been brave enough to stick to her convictions. This meal flew in the face of everything she'd learned whilst working with Marco. In the end, it was the memory of the review of his new restaurant that had convinced her once and for all, that when it came to Pebble Street – she should trust her own instincts.

After all, the review had been true - the man approached cooking like some kind of abstract concept instead of something that should bring enjoyment to the people who ate it. Marco completely missed the point – and she'd almost made the same mistake. Luckily, she'd had Seabury on her side to help her see sense.

'Ready,' she muttered to Lou, pointing to the first line of plates.

Lou swiftly stepped forward just as Ben joined them in the kitchen, and between them they began to move backwards and forwards seamlessly, taking the plates out to the breakfast lounge as Hattie finished off plating up the next batch.

As soon as Ben had finished helping Lou, he settled straight into his role of filling their guests' glasses.

'Time to get the dishes of extra veg out to the tables!' said Lou, dancing back through the kitchen doors.

'Already?' gasped Hattie. It had only been seconds since Lou had delivered the last of the plates.

'Yep – doesn't look like anything's going to last for long.'

'But… but… they were pretty substantial portions!' said Hattie, feeling slightly defensive as she remembered the ridiculously tiny plate of food she'd tried to serve Ben the first time she'd cooked for him.

Lou laughed at her kindly. 'Blimey woman, stop fretting and take it as a compliment. They're absolutely loving your food and can't get enough of it.' She picked up two laden platters filled with extra veg and headed for the door. 'It's a good thing!' she added, winking at Hattie before she disappeared again.

'Ben – everything okay?' Hattie asked as he reappeared.

Ben nodded. 'Any idea how many bottles of wine Lionel actually bought for tonight?' he asked, looking mildly flustered. 'They're getting through the stuff pretty quickly.'

Hattie smiled. 'It's okay - there should be plenty, but Lionel told me that if we start running out, he's got a few bottles in reserve up in his rooms.'

'A few bottles?' said Ben, still looking concerned.

'You know Lionel,' laughed Hattie. 'By a few bottles, he probably means a few crates.'

'Thank goodness for that!' said Ben. 'I mean, we're not quite at that point yet – but I don't think it'll take long!'

'It's good you gave everyone extras of that buttery stuff – all the little pots are empty!' laughed Lou, reappearing and snatching up the next two platters of veg. 'And by the way – bravo on the fish filleting!'

'Eh?' said Hattie.

'Not a bone in sight. Not a single one.'

'Phew!' For a second, she sent a quick prayer of thanks to Marco for hating handling fish so much. All that practice had clearly paid off!

∽

It wasn't long before the empty plates started to appear in the kitchen – and every single one of them had been scraped clean.

'Good thing too!' laughed Lou when Hattie marvelled at it. 'Less washing up as far as I'm concerned.'

'Right... here we go with the emergency stash,' said Ben, reversing into the kitchen carrying a crate of wine.

'We're not on Lionel's bottles already, are we?' said Lou, her eyebrows shooting up.

'Certainly are,' said Ben.

Hattie paused in her custard making duties to eyeball Ben as he bent to place the crate carefully on the floor. The man had just run right to the top of the building and lugged that lot down numerous flights of stairs, and he wasn't even out of breath.

'Remember Lionel wanted skin, won't you?' laughed Lou, peering at Hattie's custard and interrupting her mildly lecherous thoughts just in time to get her head back on the job.

The custard was ready. It was silky and smooth – but sure enough, there would be a nice bit of skin from the sides for Lionel by the time she'd finished dishing up.

Hattie took the little key from her pocket and retrieved the two giant Pebble Street puddings from the walk-in larder.

'Right – I'll cut and divvy this lot up – you ladle

on the custard to the side like we agreed?' said Hattie, peeping up at Lou who nodded, ladle at the ready.

'Thank goodness there's someone sensible in charge of custard quantity,' laughed Ben. 'Remember now – no little dollops!'

'I'll give you little dollop!' muttered Hattie, not taking her eyes off the first tray of pudding as she sliced it ready to portion out.

With Lou's help, they soon had dozens of dishes with a generous turret of pudding peeking out from a sea of custard. Old school and -hopefully - delicious!

'Right Ben,' said Hattie, 'you're off wine duty until this lot's all sitting in front of our guests.'

'Yes boss!' said Ben, giving her a salute and then diving into action with Lou.

Hattie leaned back against the worktop and took a deep breath. This was the moment of truth. She watched Ben and Lou work quickly and efficiently to get the bowls out to their guests and had to ignore the temptation to help them. It was still too early for the chef to leave the kitchen.

Perhaps this strange feeling in her stomach was nerves? She wasn't sure. All she knew was that the jury was out, and all she could do now was wait.

All the bowls were gone. This was it.

Hattie took another deep breath, straining to see if she could hear anything that might ease the knot of uncertainty in her chest. But there was nothing. Everything had gone completely quiet.

Oh goodness, what on earth had she got wrong? See, this was the problem with working on a recipe out of her head. It was complex… tricky. But she'd been so sure she'd got the blasted thing right both times.

Hattie wracked her brain, trying to think what her mistake might have been. She knew the honey was in there… maybe she'd used too much… or too little…

See, this was what came of trusting your instinct, wasn't it? The whole night, which had started out so well, was busy ending in silent, excruciating disaster.

CHAPTER 16

*H*attie couldn't stand the suspense any longer. She wiped her hands on a tea towel, flung it down on the kitchen table and tiptoed over towards the door. Peeping out into the hallway, she checked that the coast was clear.

Pushing lightly on the door, she snuck out of the kitchen and peered around the doorway into the breakfast lounge. Hattie's breath caught at the sight, and she did her best not to let out a surprised giggle of relief.

Everyone was digging into their pudding bowls with what could only be described as giddy delight. No one was talking – they were all too busy savouring every mouthful.

Hattie watched in amusement. At every table, friends were sharing knowing looks with each other in between blissed-out sighs. Unless she was very much mistaken, the looks translated to something along the lines of *this is soooooo good* and tended to be followed up by little hand gestures of pure delight.

Hattie's gaze travelled across the room. More than one person had their eyes closed in delicious contemplation of their pudding, but there was only one person whose reaction she truly cared about right now. She sought the table bearing the single red rose and her eyes met Mrs Scott's.

A spasm of nerves gripped Hattie for a moment as she watched Mrs Scott place her spoon down slowly into her bowl – but then she kissed her hand and blew it to Hattie before mouthing a silent *well done*.

Hattie swallowed hard, desperately trying to fight the swell of emotion as she grinned her appreciation back to Mrs Scott. That was all the feedback she really needed.

The eery, blissed-out silence in the breakfast lounge was soon broken by a strange chorus that sounded a bit like birds twittering. It was actually the sounds of dozens of spoons scraping eagerly at the remnants of custard and pudding. Hattie took it as her cue to hot-foot it back to the kitchen. She scurried away from the breakfast lounge, closely followed by Lou.

'Time to dish up a second-round,' laughed Lou.

'Just as well I made a second pudding, eh?' said Hattie, her smile wide now that she knew the evening was a success. She'd hoped they'd love it enough to want more... and it had actually worked.

As Lou and Ben delivered a full second sitting of the pudding, Hattie scraped out the last, thick, rubbery layer of skin that had formed around the custard pan and added it to a bowl with a generous second helping of Pebble Street Pudding.

'That one's for Lionel,' she said, handing it over to Lou.

'Aw – I got my hopes up there!' said Lou, sticking her lower lip out in mock dismay.

'Sorry Lou – they've cleaned me out – there's not even a crumb of leftovers in this kitchen right now!'

'I'll get over it!' said Lou, beaming at Hattie. 'Congratulations boss!'

'Thanks,' said Hattie, grinning at her. 'And don't you worry – I predict plenty more pudding in our future!'

The future? As Hattie watched Lou disappear out of the kitchen yet again, she couldn't help but marvel at that thought. She hadn't believed for one second that her future might really be here in Seabury.

Her life had taken a sharp right-hand turn just when she'd least expected it. But looking around at the devastation of a kitchen that had just served up a spectacular opening-night feast, Hattie knew for certain that the unexpected twist had landed her exactly where she needed to be.

For just a second, she thought about how differently things could have worked out. She could have turned down Lionel's offer and stuck it out in London. She would have found a job somewhere. Eventually. For no money – with stupidly long hours – living in her tiny flat she couldn't really afford. Having to travel across the city by bus.

Nope.

No. No.

Nope.

Hattie rolled her shoulders. Just the thought of London made her feel tired. No – scratch that! She *was* tired. Totally exhausted. But she didn't care. All she had to do at the end of the night was climb the stairs to her room and tumble into bed.

The thought of her comfy bed nearly made Hattie go weak at the knees. It was so tempting to sneak off right now and disappear for a snooze. Maybe she could sleep for two days straight like she did when she first arrived! She certainly felt like she could do with the rest – her whole body was throbbing with the delicious tiredness that only came from cooking for a full house.

It was so, so tempting!

She loved nothing more than drifting off to the sound of the waves, but she couldn't. At least – not yet. The kitchen needed cleaning down – and of course, tonight was just the beginning. There was prep to be done for tomorrow. And shopping lists to be written. Then there were certain things she still needed to source for the kitchen and more ingredients to get for the puddings. Now that she knew they were going to be a popular addition to the menu, she'd have to track down more honey – and of course, she'd promised Mrs Scott that she'd spread her shopping around the district.

It was just as well Lionel had given her Veronica's old car! Perhaps tomorrow, Lou might be up for going shopping with her after she'd finished her morning shift over at The Sardine – at least that way she might be able to find her way back to Pebble Street without Ben having to come to the rescue again.

Ben was probably right, though – she *did* need to make the car look a bit different somehow – especially after hearing the reaction of their guests this evening at the slightest mention of Veronica. The woman was gone for good and there was no point reminding people of her all the time. Hattie had the hotel reputation to think of, after all.

Her mind drifted back to the menu and what she'd like to try out next. Maybe there would be some gurnard in the next catch, or perhaps some pollock – either of those would work brilliantly. Maybe she'd add a fish stew as another option too – something light and simple where the flavours from the freshest fish could shine through.

Hattie grabbed her little notebook and a pencil from the windowsill and started scribbling notes as the ideas came in thick and fast. After all – she hadn't even touched on shellfish yet – and there was so much potential there!

The possibilities for Pebble Street were enough to make her head spin and, for just a moment, she grinned down at the page, unable to bottle up the sheer joy that somehow – miraculously – it was her job to explore them all in a place she loved so much.

A sound at the door of the kitchen made Hattie's head snap. It was Lionel, watching her work on her list with a gentle smile on his face.

'And?' she said, straightening up, a little wriggle of nerves in her stomach as she waited for his verdict. 'How did it go? Are you happy?'

Lionel didn't say a word but walked straight towards her and wrapped her in a big hug.

Hattie couldn't help but let out a sound that was halfway between a laugh and a sob. Lionel just patted her on the back and continued to hold her tight – because he knew what this moment meant to her more than anyone.

The pair of them eventually stepped away from each other - beaming with the joy that only a successful dream come true could produce.

'There are still a few people in the breakfast lounge,' he said. 'The ones who wanted to say hello.'

'Oh,' said Hattie.

A few people? She could handle that, couldn't she?

It wouldn't be like having to stand there while Lionel made his speech. 'Okay,' she said, 'two secs!'

She took her apron off, removing the splatters of custard and smears of pudding with it, leaving her in her relatively clean and tidy chef's whites. Not that any of her friends would really care what she looked like, but she had to keep up appearances a little bit, didn't she?

Getting the sense that she was now stalling, Lionel gave her a gentle push towards the door, and Hattie reluctantly left the safety of her bolthole. She was comfortable out of sight amongst the dishes. She always had been.

'Come on, you,' laughed Lionel, giving her another gentle shove towards the door of the breakfast lounge.

Hattie took two steps into the room, staring awkwardly at the gleaming floorboards. As Lionel came to stand beside her, she let her eyes drift upwards, and her mouth dropped open in shock.

The room was still packed. They were *all* still there, waiting to see her. She couldn't believe it.

As one, every single guest in the place got to their feet and started to clap and cheer. Hattie couldn't help but break into a huge smile as she let her eyes travel across the room – taking in the fact that they were all on their feet – cheering for her.

Ben and Lou were standing next to Mrs Scott – who couldn't stop beaming at Hattie as she clapped along with the others. Over on the corner table, stood Kate from The Sardine, along with Mike, Sarah, Charlie and Ethel.

A particularly rowdy cheer drew Hattie's eyes to a table that was surrounded by the women of Seabury's WI – along with Rose Blanchford who was banging her walking stick against the floor with abandon.

Hattie turned, her eyes seeking Lionel's, and there he was, standing right behind her, a huge grin on his face as he clapped and cheered along with the others. He took a step forward, and as he wrapped an arm around her shoulder, the cheering ramped up another notch. It was pretty overwhelming, and she felt it steal her breath away.

Hattie's eyes met Ben's across the room, and she watched as his grin softened. He gave her a little wink, and she smiled back. There would be time to catch up with him later - after all, there was no hurry now – this was Seabury, and she had all the time in the world.

What a wonderful place to call home.

THE END

SURPRISES IN SEABURY

SEABURY - PART 6

CHAPTER 1

Hattie cursed her alarm and buried her head under her pillow in an attempt to drown it out. It did nothing to deaden the annoying, cheerful chirruping coming from her phone. Now she was just uncomfortable as well as awake and irritated.

Keeping her eyes closed tight, Hattie re-emerged with a grumble. Flinging out a hand, she repeatedly slapped her mobile in an attempt to make it stop sounding so damned happy about interrupting what had been a rather wonderful dream.

Epic fail. Her wild flailing sent the phone tumbling off her duvet.

'Balls,' muttered Hattie as it hit her bedroom carpet with a dull thud before continuing to bleat its happy little tune.

Letting out a weary sigh, Hattie cracked her eyes

open, heaved herself upright and reluctantly relinquished the duvet. It felt like she'd fallen into bed just five minutes ago and she was absolutely wiped.

Kneeling on the floor, she reached under the bed, feeling around blindly for her phone. Gross! It seemed to have skidded to a halt amongst a veritable nest of dust bunnies. Wincing as she drew it out, she blew off a handful of lint before hastily silencing the alarm.

Hattie scrambled back to her feet and eyeballed her rumpled bedding. Ten more minutes? No, she'd better not risk it. No matter how much she wanted to snuggle back down under the covers and sleep for Britain, there simply wasn't time for all that. She had too much to do down in the kitchen to allow herself the luxury of a lie-in.

With another huge sigh, Hattie zombie-walked across to her bathroom in the hope that a shower might breathe life into her weary bones. It was a brand-new day, after all. She should be happy, excited… raring to go! Another day meant another full house of bookings in the restaurant. A buzzing, busy evening full of eager dinner guests. The thought was almost enough to send her straight back to bed.

The Pebble Street Hotel's restaurant was proving to be a huge hit. People were travelling from all over the country to sample her food. It seemed that fresh fish - simply prepared and presented with local, seasonal vegetables had a huge fan base! But that was nothing compared to the Pebble Street Pudding. It was the first dish Hattie had ever known to have its own groupies… and it had already earned itself a permanent spot on their menu.

They were selling out of the stuff every single night, and diners were having to pre-order seconds if they wanted them the minute they sat down. Hattie would put good money on the fact that there'd probably be a waiting list for the crumbs if she suggested it.

Hattie held out her hand and waited for the water to run warm in her over-bath shower before clambering over the side. She closed her eyes and raised her face to the gentle stream of warmth, doing her best to relax and wake up at the same time.

Hattie was happy – of *course* she was happy - that they were so busy. It was totally mad and wonderful fun. Even so, she had to admit that she was starting to feel the pressure a tiny bit. There was just no let-up, and although she wouldn't have it any other way, working on her own in the kitchen meant that it was down to her to pull off a perfect service every night.

She'd noticed that Lionel and Lou were both starting to get a bit ragged around the edges too, what with front-of-house being so much busier than they'd anticipated. A few days ago, Hattie had decided that it was time to have a little chat with Lionel before they all burned out. They had a change of menu coming up, so they decided to make the most of the opportunity and grab a couple of days off before launching into the next round of insanity.

One more day... and she'd be free.

Hattie gave in to a full grin for a second. She knew exactly what she was going to do with her time off! She fully intended to spend every waking second with Ben... and every sleeping second too, if she could get away with it. In fact, if she had her way, they'd get as far away from Pebble Street as they could manage. Maybe even somewhere other than Seabury!

Hattie stepped out of the shower and wrapped herself in a huge, fluffy towel before padding back to her bedroom. She went straight over to the window - the huge smile still plastered on her face and her head full of Ben.

Hattie threw open the curtains, her smile stretching even wider. She'd done this every morning since she'd arrived all those weeks ago, and she didn't think she'd ever get bored of this view. Taking several long, slow breaths, Hattie took a few moments to drink in the wonderful panoramic sight of sea, sea and more sea. From her bedroom window, she could see West Beach, North Beach *and* The King's Nose. This was her little slice of heaven.

Hattie loved Seabury – but she'd not really seen much of the surrounding coastline or countryside yet. She simply hadn't had the chance. It was no wonder that she was craving a break - she was

SURPRISES IN SEABURY

desperate to get out and about and explore a bit further afield. The twenty-minute dashes she managed to grab during her breaks meant that she rarely made it any further than the town itself and its two beaches.

Of course, Hattie didn't really mind. Getting Pebble Street on its feet simply had to come first. It had been so crazily busy – an unexpected wildfire of a success – but it did mean that she hadn't been able to catch her breath since opening night.

Speaking of which – she'd better get a wiggle on rather than ogling her view any longer - she was due to meet Lionel for breakfast. It had become their daily ritual. Lionel liked to give her feedback and comments from the previous evening's service while they both mainlined toast and coffee as though their lives depended on it.

Hattie turned away from the window and grabbed her clothes with a sigh. One more day and then she'd be free.

∽

'Morning sleepyhead!'

Hattie tried to return her uncle's greeting as she ambled into the breakfast lounge, but couldn't force the words past the huge yawn that had just body-snatched her.

'Coffee!' said Lionel, quickly pouring her a mugful

from the cafetière on the table, adding a glug of milk and pushing it across to her as she took the seat opposite him.

'You lifesaver!' she said, stifling another yawn that was threatening to follow up her first. Hattie wrapped her hands around the mug and took a huge gulp of scorching coffee, willing the caffeine to lift her brain fog.

'You not sleep well?' asked Lionel with a frown of concern.

Hattie smiled at him. 'Too well. I think I was asleep before my head hit the pillow last night.'

'I know how you feel,' he laughed. 'Thank heavens we've got a few days off coming up.'

Hattie grabbed a couple of pieces of toast from the rack in the middle of the table and started to smother them with marmalade. 'So – any feedback from last night?'

As they weren't yet in a position to hire any additional staff, Lionel was still helping Lou every evening - mostly when it came to doling out wine and clearing away the empty plates. It meant that he was perfectly placed to chat with their guests and had actually worked out a treat. Lionel had managed to secure several bookings for later in the season when the hotel would be fully open at last. Her uncle never missed a trick.

'Well, my dear,' said Lionel, his eyes twinkling. 'It

seems that news of your fantastic pudding has reached your old stomping ground!'

'Eh?!' said Hattie.

'A couple of the diners last night told me that they'd travelled all the way down here from London – would you believe it? They came all this way just to taste your pudding!'

'Wow,' said Hattie. 'That's insane!'

'Insane?' he said shaking his head. 'I think it's brilliant! Anyway, they said they weren't disappointed. They loved it and had such a good time I think they'll be coming back when they can stay over for a few nights. They said they wanted to bring a big party down – so that's exciting!'

'It is,' said Hattie. She couldn't help it – the idea that people were travelling so far just to eat at *their* restaurant was a bit overwhelming. 'They didn't drive all the way back up to London after eating, did they?'

Lionel shook his head. 'Staying in Bucklepool for the night, apparently. But they said they can't wait to come back here!'

'That's wonderful!' said Hattie, nibbling at her toast.

'Anyway,' said Lionel with a warm but weary smile, 'things are definitely looking up. Finances are back on track and we're all paid up so far with the allotments and the local fishermen. So… at long last, we can look at finishing off the guest rooms on the top floor and fully reopen in the summer!'

Hattie nodded, smiling at her uncle as she mainlined her coffee. She was thrilled that the restaurant was doing so well this early on. She'd never dared to dream it would be a financial success so soon after opening. And, of course, it wasn't just Pebble Street that was benefitting.

The allotment holders had come up trumps. Hattie never found herself short of delicious fresh vegetables to cook with – and in return, Lionel was paying them a fair price. Even so, their overheads were way down compared to when Veronica had shopped at the supermarket. More than one fresh coat of paint had appeared on the sheds up at the allotments – along with new tools and seeds, raised beds and polytunnels.

The local fishermen also seemed to be thrilled to be supplying them again – especially as Hattie was busy branching out with her menu. She was adding new dishes all the time and wasn't afraid to experiment with their *catch of the day* recommendations. The whole town was benefitting from The Pebble Street Hotel's success.

'My dear, are you okay? You can hardly keep your eyes open!' said Lionel, a note of concern in his voice as he watched Hattie's head bobbing over her coffee cup.

She stifled a yawn behind her hand and nodded as a wave of tiredness hit her full in the face.

'S-s-sorry!' she said. 'I'm fine. Just a bit wiped out.'

'I'm not surprised!' said Lionel, nodding. 'You've barely left the hotel for the last few weeks. If you're not in the kitchen you're up in your room!'

Hattie nodded. It was true – in the few moments she wasn't working, she was desperately trying to fit in an extra nap.

'How are things going with Ben?' Lionel asked, his voice light.

Hattie took a bite of toast to delay the need for a response. She smiled and nodded and chewed... but Lionel wasn't to be put off – he knew her little diversionary tactics far too well.

She swallowed. 'Great,' she said, eventually.

'Really?' said Lionel, his bushy eyebrows lifting.

Hattie nodded. 'Yeah...' she let out a long sigh. 'I mean – yes, they really are great but... well, you know what it's been like. We haven't really managed to spend too much time together. I work late into the evening, and he never seems to stop during the day. Even if he does manage to wangle an hour or two off between jobs, I'm usually busy with prep. We're lucky if we manage to grab a cup of coffee together, let alone...'

Lionel held up his hands, clearly not requiring any further explanation.

Let alone anything more intimate!

Hattie finished the sentence off in her head. Yes, definitely best she didn't say *that* out loud to Lionel – it wouldn't do his blood pressure any good.

The thing was, Hattie had to admit that it was bugging her. A lot. In fact, if she was being honest, she wasn't sure the situation was all that great for *her* blood pressure. Not least because she fancied the pants off Ben. Every time she saw him - even if it was just in passing – she just turned into complete mush. But he still hadn't invited her around to his place – not once since they'd got together.

In a way, she could understand why… they were so busy that by the end of the day, they were both dropping with tiredness. But she couldn't help but admit that it *would* be nice to stay somewhere overnight other than here at the hotel. Together.

'I get it!' said Lionel, watching her closely. 'You're both very busy – and it's not as though you have much private space for any time-out together.'

Hattie stared at her uncle. She really, *really* hoped that he hadn't learned how to mind-read all of a sudden – because that would be… uncomfortable.

'I love my room!' she said quickly, not wanting him to think that she was ungrateful for everything he'd done for her.

'I know, Hattie love. You don't need to explain. But I *do* understand that you can't live in a hotel forever.'

SURPRISES IN SEABURY

Exactly,' said Hattie, breathing a little sigh of relief.

She'd been thinking exactly the same over the last few weeks. She loved it here at Pebble Street but, now that she was considering staying in Seabury longer than she'd originally anticipated, it would be good to have somewhere more settled that she could call home. Preferably somewhere that didn't share the same roof as her work.

Lionel picked up the newspaper that lay on the table next to him, unfolded it, and disappeared behind it giving Hattie a brief moment to collect her thoughts.

'I just wish Ben would share a bit more of his life with me,' she muttered, surprising herself.

Lionel lowered the paper again, shooting her a surprised look over the top of it.

'Sorry,' muttered Hattie.

'Don't be!' said Lionel.

'It's just... he's really vague about his life outside of Seabury. Other than his work, and the allotments and all the stuff he does for people... he's hardly told me anything. I mean... I don't even know exactly where he lives. What's he got to hide?!'

Lionel watched her for a moment, a curious expression on his face. Hattie couldn't make it out.

'What?' she said eventually.

'Erm...' said Lionel, giving up on the newspaper and carefully refolding it before brushing toast crumbs from his waistcoat. He was clearly trying to buy himself a bit of time. Hattie was just as familiar with her uncle's stalling tactics as he was with hers.

'*What?*' she said again.

'He hasn't introduced you to Sylvie yet, I take it?'

'Who?!' demanded Hattie.

'Ah,' said Lionel, looking awkward. 'Oops. Maybe I wasn't supposed to say anything.'

'Tell me!' pleaded Hattie, her heart thumping, all traces of lazy sleepiness forgotten.

Lionel shook his head. 'There's a time and a place for everything. I don't think it's my place… pretend I didn't say anything, okay?'

'But-'

Lionel shook his head, clearly set on keeping his mouth shut. 'I'm sure he's just not got around to telling you yet… that's all.'

Hattie watched in surprise as her uncle gathered his cup and plate before getting quickly to his feet.

'Right – best get on, eh, my girl?!'

Hattie gave him a half-hearted smile and watched as he strode out of the room, giving her one last awkward, backwards glance.

What on *earth* had that been about? And who the *hell* was Sylvie? One thing was for sure – Ben had some serious explaining to do… as soon as she could find five minutes to actually pin him down!

CHAPTER 2

Hattie threw the chopped potatoes into the large silver pan with rather more force than was strictly necessary. The chunks of veg did the wall of death around the gleaming sides and promptly flew back out, before bouncing merrily off the kitchen table and skidding across the floor.

That pretty much summed up the kind of day she'd had, and Hattie slammed her knife down on the table before stooping down to pick up the errant veg, muttering a fluent stream of her choicest swear-words while she was at it.

Lobbing the rescued chunks of spud into the bin, Hattie turned to the sink and scrubbed her hands with a little more vigour than was necessary.

The kitchen was meant to be her sanctuary – where everything fell into place - somewhere she could forget about whatever else was troubling her.

Not today, though. She was tired, angry and out of sorts, and she couldn't shake it off. Hattie knew *exactly* what was wrong, of course.

Sylvie.

She'd spent the entire day wondering who the hell this mystery woman of Ben's was. She'd run through pretty much every scenario, and none of them had made her calm down in the slightest.

What if Ben had been married before? She *would* have thought that he might have mentioned it… but then, perhaps not. Maybe he didn't think that whatever they had going on between them was that big a deal? Maybe he didn't see a future together, so couldn't be bothered sharing his past with her.

Oh god – what if he was *still* married?! But no – surely not. This was Seabury! There was no way her uncle - let alone the rest of them -would have let her get this far with a married man. Would they? No. Definitely not. She hoped.

The only thing Hattie felt certain of right now was the fact that Ben had never so much as breathed the name Sylvie around her.

Oh god, what if he had kids? Not that it would have been a problem for her in the slightest… it was only an issue if he'd decided to keep it a secret from her! But surely he would have told her something so important?

Maybe that was why he was so cagey when it came to talking about anything other than work or random Seabury gossip. But no – it couldn't be that. Someone else would have mentioned if Ben had kids, wouldn't they? The Seabury gossip mill wasn't exactly known for its tact!

Hattie had been preparing for a showdown with Ben since breakfast. She'd waited with bated breath for the fish van to turn up. As soon as she'd glimpsed it from the kitchen window, she'd marched out to greet it, hands on her hips, ready to do battle… only to find that it was one of the other drivers doing the round.

When she'd demanded why Ben wasn't working his usual shift, she'd received a tight-lipped shrug in response. The poor bloke had lugged her boxes inside for her, looking petrified the entire time. When he'd finished, he'd practically dived back into the van and pulled away with an impressive wheel spin.

Hattie had then fully expected Ben to turn up sometime in the afternoon – like he normally did. They usually managed to squeeze in a coffee together before she had to get cracking on prep for the evening. But there had been no sign of him.

She couldn't help but wonder if Lionel had been in touch with Ben. Maybe he'd called to warn him that she was on the warpath because he'd put his foot in it over breakfast.

In the end, Hattie had to have a stern word with herself in the store cupboard. She was just getting paranoid. She was exhausted and getting everything blown out of proportion. That's all it was, wasn't it? Yes. It had to be… but then…

Sylvie…

Sylvie…

Sylvie…

The name echoed in her head with every slice of her knife, driving her to distraction. Man, she was tired. That's all this was. She was exhausted and not thinking straight.

Right. Maybe it was time for some positive thinking before she went loopy – because she had loads of things to be grateful for… didn't she?

For one thing, she wasn't half as tired as when she'd first arrived in town. Despite her long hours in the kitchen, she had a little bit of colour to her skin for the first time in ages. She felt healthier too – and that was just from the snatched walks along the beaches with Ben – usually with a much-needed coffee in her hand from The Sardine.

Hattie knew she was lucky in so many ways. She was living somewhere she loved - somewhere she could get a lungful of fresh sea air just by stepping outside. She loved her room. As much as she'd had a whinge about it to Lionel earlier, it would be a wrench to leave it when somewhere more permanent became available. And – of course – she had Ben.

But *did* she have Ben? Or did Ben actually belong to Sylvie?

'Gah!'

Hattie put down the knife again, rolled her shoulders and decided that maybe she needed a couple of minutes out of the kitchen. Before things got out of hand. She needed to clear her head – she couldn't be worrying about this right now – not when she had a full restaurant to cook for again this evening.

Hattie wandered towards the breakfast lounge where Lou was busy setting the tables.

'Hey boss!'

'Hi,' said Hattie.

Her voice came out dull and flat. That wouldn't do at all. Lou had an excellent grump radar. She'd once explained to Hattie that it was because her ex was the grumpiest-git imaginable towards the end of their relationship. Now she could smell a bad mood brewing at a hundred paces.

Either way, it wasn't fair to take out her bad mood on Lou just because she was the only person around. It wasn't Hattie's style, and no matter how bad things got, it was a promise she'd made herself from the start. Her staff would always be treated with respect. It was time to put a brave face on things.

'Looking good in here!' said Hattie, glad to hear her voice coming out much lighter.

'You okay?' asked Lou, pausing to look at her curiously.

Hattie nodded quickly. Damn Lou and her superhuman bullshit sensors.

'Sure! I'm grand!' Hattie added, forcing a smile

when Lou's eyebrows went up. 'Just – you know… looking forward to some time off!'

'Oh, me too!' said Lou, nodding enthusiastically. 'My feet are killing me after this week – it's been manic. And The Sardine's busy too! Don't get me wrong, I'm loving it here – but I'm glad you and Lionel have decided to take a bit of a break before the new menu launches!'

'Yeah, I think it'll do us all good to have a bit of a breather!' Hattie nodded. It seemed that they were all running on empty.

'Got anything nice planned?' asked Lou, grabbing a tray of wine glasses from her little cart and beginning to place them on the table she was working on.

'Well… spending some time with Ben… I hope.' She wasn't half as excited about the idea as she had been just yesterday – not after the revelations of the morning.

'That sounds lovely,' said Lou, completely oblivious to the agonising jumble that was going on in Hattie's head.

'Yeah,' Hattie nodded. It *should* be lovely… though, in reality, Hattie wasn't so sure. She doubted they'd actually want to spend any quality time with each other after she'd confronted him.

'I'd better get back to it,' she sighed. 'We're a full house again tonight – let's keep it together for one more night and then we're free!'

'Right you are, boss,' grinned Lou, giving her a little salute.

∼

This was a total nightmare. Hattie was having to pinch herself every five minutes to stop herself from burning everything. She wasn't usually like this. She was used to being focused... calm... confident in every move she made in the kitchen.

There was no doubt about it, the ghost of Sylvie was following her around the room, distracting her. This ghost had somehow acquired Jessica Rabbit style curves and a mane of honey-blonde hair since she'd first heard about her that morning. The harder Hattie tried to push thoughts of Ben's mystery woman away, the more she pictured the pair of them together.

On top of that, she was desperate to hold it together enough so that Lou wouldn't notice anything was up.

'Ready!' she said as she finished plating up the first batch of main course meals.

Lou stepped forward, loaded up four plates and headed for the door. Two seconds later, she turned around and set them back down in front of Hattie.

'What?' Hattie demanded in surprise.

'You've forgotten the potatoes... and the peppercorn butter,' said Lou, her voice light.

Hattie peered at the plates. Lou was right. Without saying a word, Hattie quickly rectified her mistake.

'Ready,' she said again. 'Sorry Lou.'

'No worries,' said Lou, picking the plates up again and heading out.

Hattie took a moment, straightening up and taking a deep breath. This wasn't *like* her – she was making mistake after mistake tonight. Luckily, she wasn't the kind of person that flew off the handle when something went wrong - that had been her old boss Marco Brooks' signature move. Even so, she couldn't help but admit that she was getting rattled.

It was a good thing that her menu was pretty simple. At Marco's old restaurant, she'd have had to move everything around with a ruler and a toothpick on the plate to make sure it was all perfect. She didn't cook that type of food, so at least the mistakes so far had been an easy fix.

Even so - easy fix or not – forgetting the sauce *and* the potatoes would have had Marco pulling out his hair and screaming obscenities by this point. Not that Marco *had* that much hair – just an orange top-knot paired with those silly glasses that he didn't really need to wear.

She still couldn't believe that she'd worked for such an epic plonker for so long. In a way, he'd done her a favour when he'd ditched her and buggered off to his new restaurant. If the foodie grapevine was to be believed, the move hadn't worked out well for him. His new restaurant, Number 14, had only lasted a few weeks before running into financial difficulties. The last she'd heard, it had already closed its doors for good.

'Sucks to you,' she muttered as the ghost of her ex-boss joined the ever-present one of Sylvie. Clearly, both her past *and* her future were intent on ganging up on her this evening. Distracted didn't even cover it.

Hattie took another deep breath as Lou reappeared through the door.

'All good?' she said, shooting Hattie a concerned look as she surveyed the table, clearly surprised not to find the next round of plates already good to go.

'Sorry, yep. Two secs,' said Hattie, pulling herself together and swiftly beginning to plate up the next round of meals.

She was here in Seabury. She was doing something she loved. She was living her dream, serving food to a sold-out Pebble Street every night. And she had Ben. Or she thought she did…

Things could be worse, couldn't they?

Sylvie…

Sylvie…

Sylvie…

Hattie gritted her teeth, trying to focus.

'Ready?' she said to Lou, sounding a lot less sure than usual.

Lou raised her eyebrows in surprise, glanced at the plates and then nodded. 'Looks good,' she said, the relief evident in her voice as she picked them up and swung back through the kitchen door.

Hattie quickly got to work on the next batch. One thing was for certain – when she *did* finally manage to catch up with Ben, he was going to be on the receiving end of a damn good talking-to!

CHAPTER 3

'Urgh!'

Hattie scrubbed her tired face with her fists, doing her best to wake up. She'd thought she'd been tired yesterday, but that had been *nothing* compared to this morning. Thank heavens it was the first of her much-longed-for days off. She was so tired, even her fingernails ached.

Typically, she'd woken up as soon as the sun had stained the sky a peachy orange. No matter how desperately she'd tried to get back to sleep, she'd failed spectacularly. Things got even worse when the birds on The King's Nose decided to tune up and treat her to a rousing morning chorus.

Of course, thoughts of Ben and this mysterious Sylvie had promptly bombarded her weary brain. She twisted around and around in a vain attempt to escape the unwelcome images – ending up tangled in her stripy duvet that suddenly felt more like a straight jacket than a comforting cloud of bedding.

Hattie tumbled out of bed, stroppily shaking herself free of the constricting cotton, stamping on it as it fell to the ground.

'Take that!' she muttered, before stomping through to the bathroom for a nice, relaxing shower.

Well… *a* shower. She had a feeling the *relaxing* part wasn't exactly going to go to plan. In fact, Hattie was pretty sure all chances of being able to relax were going to remain firmly out of reach until she'd had the chance to speak to Ben.

'Great, *thanks* Ben!' she muttered, rinsing the last of the shampoo roughly from her hair before clambering back over the side of the bath without bothering with any conditioner. What was the point?!

Just Ben's name on her lips made Hattie let out a little growl. She vigorously rubbed herself dry with her towel and then twisted her damp hair into a messy plait to save herself the bother of blow drying it.

She was gutted that thoughts of Ben – usually the source of uncontrollable smiles – were now making her heart sink like a lump of lead. This was not the way she'd imagined starting her precious few days off, and the thought of hunting him down so that she could get to the bottom of the whole *Sylvie* thing made her shudder.

Hattie knew she needed to get outside. In fact –

she needed to get out of Seabury. That's what she'd do. She'd hop in the car and take herself off somewhere nice for the morning. Maybe she'd head over to Bucklepool and grab a coffee. Perhaps it'd help her calm down a bit... get the whole thing in perspective so that when she *did* finally catch up with Ben, she'd be able to initiate a calm, adult conversation.

Calm.

Yeah.

Right.

She needed to get out of here! Hattie quickly grabbed her jacket and her handbag and pausing only to lock her bedroom door behind her, made her way quietly through the early-morning hotel. She padded across the gleaming kitchen and let herself out through the back door.

The cool, morning air felt like a balm on her jangled nerves. Hattie sucked in a deep breath, willing her tight shoulders to drop down away from her ears where they'd been hovering ever since yesterday morning. Yes – a morning away from here would definitely do her good!

She wandered towards the old garage where the car was stashed. It would be nice to get some time to herself for a change. She'd take the coast road to Bucklepool – it should be absolutely glorious at this time of day. Maybe she could even get the old radio in the car working. A little singsong with the window down would help her get her mind off everything.

After all, she didn't want to spend the entire day obsessing over-

'Ben!'

Hattie came to an abrupt halt in front of the garage. The door was wide open and Ben was standing there in his overalls.

'Hey Hattie!'

His wide smile felt a bit like a slap in the face this morning... especially after its owner had cost her a precious night of sleep. The anger that she'd been busily trying to tamp down rose up in her throat. But that could wait for just a couple of seconds longer. Right now, she had a more immediate issue to discuss with him.

'You've painted my car!' she said in pure disbelief.

It wasn't really *her* car. The boxy old estate had belonged to Veronica before she'd buggered off to Australia, leaving the hotel in financial chaos. Lionel had given Hattie the car not long ago – but everyone had agreed it would be a good idea for her to change its appearance. Veronica was universally loathed in Seabury and the surrounding area. The terror caused by her catastrophic driving style still loomed large in people's memories – especially when confronted with her old vehicle.

'Well – yes!' said Ben with a grin. 'You said yourself it'd be best not to remind everyone of Veronica all the time. Anyway, I did it yesterday. Sorry I didn't

get the chance to come in and see you, but I wanted to get it finished as a surprise.'

Hattie stared at his proud smile in disbelief. In that moment - with a mixture of anger and exhaustion swirling around in her head like a toxic fog - she wanted nothing more than to wipe the grin off his face.

'Daisies? You thought it would be a good idea to cover my car in daisies?'

Hattie didn't like how her voice came out. It was all whiney and mean and so unlike her. She didn't like the dejected look that landed on Ben's face either. But what *right* did he have to make her feel bad?

'They're not daisies,' he said quietly. 'They're supposed to be marigolds.'

'Flowers, Ben?' she spat. *'Really?!'*

The tired old car Hattie had become ridiculously attached to in such a short space of time was covered in bright petals.

'What?' he said with a shrug. 'You wanted something quick, colourful and – above all – cheap. I used some of the leftover gloss paint from re-decorating the guest bedrooms…'

He paused and looked from the Hattie to the car and then back again, clearly confused and hurt by her reaction. Hattie just crossed her arms and stared at him hard. She wasn't about to give in to those cute freckles and pleading eyes – not today.

'Look – you just needed to make sure no one thinks it's Veronica's old car,' he sighed. 'I only had a couple of hours to spare. But honestly, I thought you'd like it. I thought it was fun… and… happy?'

Hattie was feeling anything but fun and happy right now – but she knew it had absolutely nothing to do with the car. In fact, she loved it. It was bright and jolly and she couldn't wait to hop in and get the hell out of here.

No… she was angry about something else entirely.

'Who's Sylvie?'

She'd blurted out the words without even meaning to. Their effect on Ben was instant. She watched in horror as he went completely still. The colour seemed to drain from his face, before returning as a furious blush on his cheeks.

'Oh… erm…' He ran his fingers through his sandy hair, tucking the waves obsessively behind his ears. 'I guess Lionel said something?'

Hattie didn't reply. She just raised an eyebrow and gave him a terse nod.

'I know I should have said something sooner,' said Ben in a quiet voice. 'I just didn't know how to tell you.'

'Tell me what?' said Hattie, her voice dangerous.

'Oh!' said Ben, sounding surprised. He watched her for a long moment as if he was trying to work something out.

It was as much as Hattie could do to keep herself from turning and walking away. Now that they were finally on the subject of Sylvie, she wasn't really sure she wanted to know what was going on after all.

'Right... well...' said Ben at last, 'I think maybe it's time the two of you met.'

'*Met?!*'

Hattie winced. That had come out as a shriek and Ben was looking more than a little bit nervous. It was as much as she could do not to hot-foot it back up to her room, lock the door behind her and hide under her duvet for several days.

'Yeah – come on,' sighed Ben. 'It's definitely time... though I think maybe I should drive.'

Hattie froze for a couple of long seconds. She wasn't really sure she was up for this right now... but then, she wasn't going to be able to focus on anything else until she got some answers, was she? And if that meant she had to come face to face with a Jessica Rabbit impersonating ghost that had ballsed up last night's dinner service as well as her much needed night of sleep... then so be it!

'Fine,' she snapped, marching around to the passenger side of the old car. She caught Ben watching her in confusion – but there was no way she was about to start apologising. No flippin' way. He could roll his eyes all he wanted.

Ben took his place behind the wheel. The rumble of the ancient engine broke the awkward silence that had descended between them as he carefully navigated his way out of the garage.

Hattie stared fixedly ahead through the windscreen. She'd only agreed to Ben driving because he knew where they were going. Frankly – she wished she'd just insisted on driving anyway – at least it would have given her something to focus on. Her nervy fingers were busy worrying away at a thread in her jumper, and at this rate, she'd manage to pick a hole in the hem before they'd even reached the road.

Hattie had no idea what she'd find out when they reached their destination. She wasn't even sure she *wanted* to know anything about the mythical Sylvie anymore. Why Ben thought she'd want to meet the woman was beyond her. Still – she couldn't back out now!

She did her best to keep the stern expression on her face as they drove along the seafront towards North Beach – but it was proving difficult. Everyone they passed pointed at the car and waved - grinning as they drove by. Ben's flowers were obviously proving to be a great hit with Seabury's residents.

Ben let out a snort of laughter, and it was as much as Hattie could do not to join him. It was getting ridiculous out there. Every single person they saw stopped to have a good look, and passing cars were honking their horns and flashing their lights as the drivers waved furiously at them.

Ben waved back, grinning away like a lunatic –

seemingly without a care in the world. How could he be so calm about everything right now? Didn't he realise that what was going on between the two of them was serious? Didn't he understand that this morning was basically make-or-break time for them?!

No matter how hard she tried, though, Hattie simply couldn't keep her hands in her lap. She had to wave back too – because it was rude not to, wasn't it?! Especially as the latest pair of locals to stop, grin and wave were Charlie and Ethel... quickly followed by Kate from The Sardine, who was out on an early morning stroll with Stanley.

Hattie caught Kate's grin and smiled back at her, blowing a little kiss to Stanley. For just a moment, she wanted to beg Ben to stop the car so that she could hop out and have a cuddle with the big bear of a dog. That would definitely help her feel better!

But, before she knew it, they were climbing the narrow lane out of Seabury, leaving all the smiling, waving people behind them. Hattie instantly stopped smiling and crossed her arms tightly over her chest.

Whatever this not-so-magical mystery tour was all about, it had better be good. Ben had better have a damn good explanation waiting for her at the other end. If not, she had a feeling that this could be it for their relationship. The thought made Hattie's lip tremble, and she bit it hard, doing her best to swallow down the swell of emotion.

Hell, they hadn't even managed to have a proper argument yet. How could it be over before they'd had an argument?! Not that she wanted to argue with Ben. Nothing could be further from the truth. He was one of the best things that had ever happened to her... or at least, that's what she'd thought before the name *Sylvie* had dropped like a hand-grenade into their cosy little bubble.

Hattie frowned hard, doing her best to man up. She needed to pull herself together. The last thing she wanted to do was to meet this Sylvie when she was an emotional, blubbering mess! But now they'd left the hotel and everything familiar behind them, Hattie was feeling more than a little bit wobbly.

In fact, as she stared out of the window, blinking hard and willing the hot swell of unshed tears to clear off, Hattie realised that she didn't recognise a single thing they were passing. She had no idea where Ben was taking her... but it was dread, not excitement, that was currently filling her heart.

CHAPTER 4

Hattie was steeling herself for action. It felt like they'd been driving for ages, and she was about to demand that Ben turn the car around and take her back to Seabury. She'd been on the verge of saying something for the last ten minutes.

Give it thirty seconds more… and she'd say something.

Or maybe when they passed that tree…

Nope, not yet… maybe that gatepost instead…

Hattie bit her lip and let out a sigh. The more time she had to think about it, the less agreeing to meet up with the mysterious Sylvie seemed like a good idea. But her common sense was waging a fierce war with sheer curiosity. Curiosity was definitely winning.

For what felt like the millionth time, she decided

not to say anything until Ben came clean about exactly what was going on.

She'd just changed her mind *yet* again and was about to ask Ben to turn around, when he took a right-hand turn and began navigating his way downhill along a decidedly wiggly lane.

Staring stonily ahead, Hattie caught a flash of silver through the trees. There it was again - water dancing and glimmering in the sunlight. As Ben followed a curve in the road, Hattie gasped. Ahead of them was a wide stretch of river. They were winding their way down the side of a steep valley towards the water.

'Almost there,' murmured Ben as they continued to trundle down the hill.

Just a minute later, they rolled up in front of pair of high metal gates. They weren't in the best repair and almost looked like they'd grown out of the greenery that surrounded them.

Hattie raised her eyebrows as Ben yanked at the handbrake. Then he got out of the car and went over to heave the rusty old things open. She knew she should offer to help, but she stayed glued to her seat in confusion.

Hattie had absolutely no idea what was going on, and the sign she'd just spotted to one side of the gates didn't do much to clear up the mystery. It was ancient and weather-stained, but she could just about make out the words "Bamton Boatyard".

What on *earth* were they doing at a boatyard? Maybe this Sylvie woman worked here? Or perhaps she was coming here to meet them? Either way, Hattie definitely wasn't comfortable with the idea of being out in the middle of nowhere - not when she was expecting some kind of showdown! She really, *really* wanted to be back in her nice, comfy bed enjoying the day off that she deserved.

Hattie squeezed her eyes closed for a second. She'd give anything right about now to rewind to yesterday morning - she'd simply wander off before Lionel had the chance to let the cat out of the bag. That way the name Sylvie wouldn't mean a jot to her... she wouldn't have been grouchy with Ben... and they'd be just getting ready to enjoy a lovely few days together with no worries at all.

Hattie forced herself to open her eyes and face reality. Even if she was granted her fantasy version of events, it wouldn't help her in the long run, would it? If her relationship with Ben was going to go any further, he needed to be honest and upfront with her...

...and she needed to scratch this Sylvie's eyes out.

No. No, of course she didn't. She was being ridiculous. Okay, maybe not that ridiculous...

She jumped slightly as Ben got back in the car. He shot her a sheepish little smile and then, without a word, set off again leaving the rusty gates in the rear-view mirror.

There was something decidedly eery about this place. Hattie stared as they passed various ancient wooden boats standing up on chocks all around them. There were piles of knackered scrap wood, oversized chains and weathered buoys everywhere.

Ben seemed to know exactly where he was going, but Hattie wasn't enjoying the mystery tour one little bit. Their surroundings felt strangely gothic and removed from reality... like they'd suddenly found themselves on a film set... of a horror movie.

She shivered. She hadn't spotted any other signs of life since they'd driven through the gates. The hairs on the back of her neck were starting to stand on end.

Hattie took a deep breath, realising that she was obsessively lacing and unlacing her fingers in her lap – a classic nervous tick. She was over-tired and wound as tight as a watch spring. Her imagination was running away with her, and she needed to calm down. Preferably right now. The last thing she needed was to get herself worked up into a lather before she'd even had the chance to meet this Sylvie character.

Ben drew the old car to a halt in front of a large heap of rusty scrap iron. Without a word, he killed the engine and climbed out. Hattie removed her seatbelt and paused for a couple of seconds in a vain attempt to regulate her ragged breathing, before following him.

Bugger it. No matter how scared she was feeling right now, there was no way she was going to let it show. Hattie folded her arms and jutted her chin out defiantly.

Whatever explanations or excuses Ben was about to throw at her... if he thought that bringing her to the back end of beyond was going to get him off the hook... well, he had another thing coming!

A chilly breeze whipped her hair into her face, and Hattie had to resist the impulse to wrap her arms around herself or - even worse - wrap her arms around *him.* But no, there would be no snuggling into Ben for warmth today. In fact, she wasn't sure that was going to be an option ever again.

Just the thought of the huge loss she was now facing made something crack deep inside Hattie's chest. She couldn't bear this wonderful thing coming to an end. Especially not here - surrounded by the skeletons of old boats with the threat of a ghost called Sylvie hovering close by.

Hattie gave another involuntary shudder – but she knew it didn't really have anything to do with the chilly breeze. She glared around at the wide expanse of water and the old, rotten boats. It was time to get this over and done with so that she could go back to Seabury and lick her wounds in private.

'Ben... what-?' she started.

'Over here,' said Ben, beckoning for her to follow him. He held out his hand for her to take, but she simply stared at him coldly until he dropped it again with a shrug. She followed him over to a half-rotten boat that had a small wooden ladder leading up to the deck.

Hattie finally decided that enough was enough. She wanted to go home and disappear under her duvet. She needed to get over the fact that her dream of living happily ever after in Seabury with Ben had come to a very weird end.

'Ben, what are we doing here?' she sighed.

'Exactly what I promised you.' Ben paused and cleared his throat. 'Hattie - meet Sylvie.'

Hattie frowned in confusion until Ben pointed upwards towards the stern of the ancient boat. Grudgingly, she peered at the spot he was pointing at. Even though a great deal of the paint had peeled off, she could still just about read the name of the boat.

Sylvie.

Hattie's jaw dropped. With a strange rush of relief, anger, confusion and the desire to give in to hysterical laughter, she turned to stare at Ben.

'Sylvie's a boat?' she said – a bubble of laughter fighting its way out despite her complete confusion.

Ben shrugged. 'She's a bit more than that…'

'Oh?' said Hattie.

'Well, she's my home. This is where I live.'

Another laugh escaped her lips – this time, it was one of pure disbelief. There was no way that he lived *here!* The boat was a soggy wreck. Then she noticed the look on Ben's face – as if he was willing her to look again.

She turned back to the great hulk, her eyes combing every inch of Ben's "other woman." Sure enough, she started to notice that at least some parts of the old boat had been repaired.

'Oh!' she said again, unable to hide the surprise in her voice. He really *lived* here?

'I bought her a few years ago,' said Ben, looking unusually anxious. 'I've been living on board for the last twelve months – it's cheaper that way. It means I can use all the money I'd waste on rent to do her up and… well… I get to keep an eye on her too.'

Hattie's eyes flicked to the boat again. She nodded, even though she couldn't really see that there was any need to keep an eye on the old thing – after all, it didn't look like it was about to go anywhere any time soon.

'She's going to be beautiful when she's finished,' said Ben. With a soft smile, he moved to pat Sylvie's side.

Hattie could feel the layers of anger and fear and worry that had been building ever since she'd first heard the name Sylvie begin to peel off and blow away in the breeze. She could breathe again. It was like someone had cut through strings that she'd become caught up in.

There was another feeling there too. She felt…

well… kind of stupid if she was being honest. Yes, Ben was in love with someone – or *something* – else, but in true Ben-style, it wasn't another woman - it was a broken-down old boat.

Hattie could feel reality shifting around her. She felt like she needed to buy herself a bit of time to digest everything.

'Where are we?' she asked, peering around her at the other boats all waiting for some TLC.

'That's Bamton Estuary!' said Ben, pointing to the sweep of slow-moving water. 'If you follow it just around the bend there, you get to where the river Bamton meets the sea.' He paused and beamed at her then gave Sylvie's side an excited pat. 'When I get this old girl finished, I'll be off in that direction!'

'Wait!' said Hattie, feeling the strands of fear pull tight again. 'You're leaving?'

'Well, obviously not for a few years yet!' said Ben, shaking his head and pulling a face as he picked at a bit of rotten wood. 'There's so much to do and it all takes time – especially as I'm living on board too. It's very slow and very expensive. Just the cost of getting the timber for the repairs is enough to make you weep.'

'I bet!' said Hattie, still willing her brain to catch up.

'That's why I have to work all the time,' said Ben. 'I need to keep busy so that I can earn enough extra cash to keep the project going... but she'll be worth it in the end... you'll see.'

Hattie nodded vaguely and stared up at Sylvie's less-than-svelte form. She still couldn't believe that Ben actually *lived* in there!

'So,' she said faintly, 'this is why you've never invited me to your place before is it?' She couldn't help the residual accusation in her tone – she was having a hard time letting go of the ghost of Sylvie that had been plaguing her since the day before.

'Well,' said Ben, scuffing his feet awkwardly in the gravel and glancing at the ladder that led up to the deck, 'it's hardly a suave, sexy bachelor pad is it?!'

Hattie let out an involuntary snigger. 'Sorry!' she muttered.

Ben shrugged. 'Add to that the fact that you live in that swanky room at the hotel... I just wanted the chance to do her up a little bit more before I brought you here, that's all... I just... I didn't want this to be a deal-breaker.'

He paused and took a deep breath. 'Anyway, I guess this is as good a time as any. Do you want to take a look inside?'

Hattie gaped at him. Not because of the invitation, but because he'd been worried that he might lose her. As *if* something like a knackered old boat was going to put her off Ben Yolland! Sure... the *other* kind of Sylvie she'd been busy imagining might have but-

'Hattie?'

'What?'

'Do you want to go up?' said Ben.

Hattie stared at him. The poor bloke was clearly on tenterhooks and here she was letting her imagination run away with her. Again. She looked at the rickety old ladder that led up to the deck and forced herself not to pull a face.

Really Hattie?

Was she really going to let a little bit of fear put her off this adventure and hurt Ben while she was at it?

For just a second, Hattie hovered, remembering what she'd been like when she was younger. Fearless. Sure – other people in Seabury might use different words for it like *out of control,* or *feral,* or *human tornado* – but Hattie definitely preferred the term *fearless*.

Where had all that spirit disappeared to? Drummed out of her while she worked for idiot chefs with huge egos, she guessed. It was a shame – but just because her fearlessness had gone awol didn't mean that it had to stay away, did it?!

'Absolutely!' said Hattie at long last, turning to grin at Ben. 'Sylvie and I need to get acquainted. The two special women in your life…'

She petered out, suddenly wondering if she'd gone a bit too far, but Ben grinned at her.

'You've got that right,' he said in a low growl.

Hattie swallowed a swoop of nerves.

You're meant to be fearless remember – dumbass!

She stepped forward and grabbed the wooden rungs of the ladder, giving them a sneaky tug just to check that Sylvie wasn't about to dump her on her behind. After all, she was the interloper here – and Sylvie might not like the idea of having a rival for Ben's affections.

Much to her relief, the ladder didn't budge. She could see that the top was tied down safely, and as she scaled up the first few rungs, it barely even shuddered under her weight. Shame really – she'd have rather liked the feeling of Ben's strong hands getting a firm grip on her bum to stop her from falling! Ah well – you couldn't be fearless without having to make a few sacrifices here and there, could you?

When she reached the deck, Hattie climbed aboard and then turned to wait for Ben to follow her up the ladder.

'Sorry about the mess!' he said, his grinning face appearing over the edge. 'If I'd have known you were coming for a visit, I'd have tidied up a bit!'

CHAPTER 5

There were tools and ropes, cans of paint and scraps of wood lying everywhere. Hattie did a very slow circle on the spot, trying to take it all in while at the same time trying to avoid breaking her neck. There was a relatively clear pathway across the deck towards both the cabin and the cockpit with its antiquated controls - but it looked like that might well be the only clear space on the entire boat.

'What do you think?' asked Ben, running his fingers through his hair distractedly and peering around as if he was surprised to find them both standing there.

'Honestly?' said Hattie, feeling wrong-footed. 'I've got no idea!'

Ben grinned at her. 'Okay, well, I'm not surprised. I guess it *is* kind of a shock.'

Hattie nodded. Maybe not the *worst* kind of shock, though. She might not have imagined this in her wildest dreams, but she definitely preferred it to what had been running through her head since yesterday morning!

'Come on, let me show you around a bit!' said Ben.

He led the way down into the cabin. Hattie ducked her head and followed. When she reached the bottom of the steps, it took a while for her eyes to adjust to the dim light after the brightness of the morning sunshine outside.

As she became more accustomed to the gloom, she found herself standing in a wonderland of wood and brass. The low ceiling gave the impression that they were in some kind of timber-lined cocoon.

Hattie looked at the rows of little round portholes that ran down either side of the hull, letting shafts of light into this little wood-lined haven. Dust motes danced in the air, and it felt a bit like she'd stepped back in time. It really was rather beautiful… in a very Ben sort of way.

'It's all pretty basic,' said Ben, sounding decidedly nervous. 'Somewhere to sleep. Basic galley…'

He gestured vaguely around him, inviting Hattie to have a good look - which she was glad to do without feeling like she was somehow prying into his private little world. Her first impression was that it was hard to believe that anyone was actually *living* here. Camping over for a night or two she could just about imagine – but living here full time? She just couldn't picture it.

And yet, there were little clues everywhere she looked – a plate covered in crumbs and an empty coffee cup left over from Ben's breakfast. Stacks of books were piled up on every surface – and one sat cracked open and face down on a little wooden table.

Hattie took a sneaky peek at the spines on the nearest stack, only to find that they were all books about restoring historic wooden boats.

There was a very basic kitchen – or *galley* as Ben had called it - to one side of the space. It boasted an empty jam-jar full of cutlery, a few random pieces of crockery stacked on a rough worktop, and what looked very much like a single-ring camping stove.

Most of the cabin was dominated by a large, double bed, which stood right in the middle. Hattie couldn't help but stare at it. It was heaped with layer upon layer of bedding - mostly old sails by the look of it, but there were definitely several blankets in the mix too.

Ben followed her gaze and grimaced. 'It... erm... gets a bit cold in here so you need plenty of layers. The sails are good for keeping the warmth in and any stray drips out - and a hot water bottle is essential!'

Hattie nodded, doing her best to keep a mildly horrified look off her face. She couldn't help but compare her warm, cosy bed at the hotel with Ben's sleep set-up – which sounded more like an endurance test than a relaxing rest after a long, hard day at work.

Ben watched her for a moment and then, clearly discomfited by her continued silence, continued to witter.

'I mean, the sails are a bit rough, but they really do the trick. Especially when icicles form in the winter. That's a bit rubbish, but – they do that sometimes. See that gap there?' he pointed over the bed. 'You get some epic icicles form on the edge. Usually when it snows outside.'

Ben fell quiet again, but still, Hattie didn't say anything. She had to tear her eyes away from the bed. Ben standing in front of her, looking so vulnerable and incredibly cute was causing havoc in her slightly befuddled brain. It would be so easy to grab him and just… topple… onto the bed… sail cloth and icicles be damned!

Hattie shook her head, doing her best to clear the unexpected X-rated images. She needed to rein herself in before her overactive imagination started to run away with her. She turned deliberately away from the bed and stared around the rest of the space again.

There were several piles of what looked like scrap metal on the floor, and Hattie bent to have a closer look.

'I've stripped all the useable brass from the

masts and other parts of the boat,' said Ben. 'Thought it'd be best if I salvaged as much as I could to use for later. Brought them down here for safe keeping.'

'Okay...' said Hattie, straightening back up again.

She listened as he filled her in on the various repairs and renovations he'd already managed to make a start on. His talk of galleys and masts, cockpits and hulls made it sound like he was speaking a foreign language, but Hattie loved how animated his face had become. He started to point out various bits and pieces in the jumble of scrap metal that he had earmarked for jobs that needed doing.

'How long is it going to take you to finish doing her up?' asked Hattie.

Ben ruffled his hair again, looking around with a slightly bewildered expression on his face.

'Well, it's just me working on her at the moment,' he said with a little shrug.

Hattie watched him closely. If that was a hint for some help, it was about as subtle as a brick in the face.

'Plus, living here at the same time as doing her up really slows things down. I mean, I'd love a place in town really – but this just made sense with it just being me... so... with that in mind... and the fact that I've got to get the funds together to pay for it all as I go along... maybe four years. I'd like to get her back in the water in five, tops!'

'Maybe I could help you with some of the work?' said Hattie.

The words were out of her mouth before she could stop herself and she cringed slightly - she wasn't sure how Ben would react. This project was his baby. It clearly meant the world to him and she hadn't exactly made it easy for him to introduce her to Sylvie!

Hattie watched Ben's face nervously, and a great whoosh of relief hit her as he broke into the most gorgeous, beaming smile.

'You know, every time I imagined this moment – me showing you around for the first time - I always fantasised about you saying something like that!' said Ben. 'I usually spend a ridiculous amount of time out here with Sylvie – and… well… I'd hate it if that was a problem or… I don't know, maybe I'm being stupid… but it would be awful if you were jealous of Sylvie for taking up all my time!'

'I'd never do that!' said Hattie, giving another huge, inward cringe. After the way her imagination had run rampant since yesterday, saying that she could *never* be jealous was ridiculous. She'd already thoroughly demonstrated that when it came to Ben Yolland – she *could* and she *would.* It wasn't something she was particularly proud of… but hey – guys like him simply didn't come around very often. In fact, so far, he was the one and only guy like him she'd ever met.

'What can I do to help?' she said, grinning at him as she started to roll up her sleeves. Sure, it was a diversionary tactic – she didn't really want to have to talk about her jealous streak right now. She had a feeling that Ben would find it very difficult to turn down the offer of a bit of help... sneaky but necessary!

'I thought it was meant to be your day off,' laughed Ben. 'I was hoping to show you around the area a bit. You've been so busy, I thought you'd like to see the local sights so that you could get your bearings?'

Hattie stepped forwards, careful not to trip over one of the many piles and wound an arm around Ben's waist, snuggling into the warmth of his tatty jumper.

'Well,' she said, 'we're here now... surely there's something that needs doing?'

Ben grinned down at her and then looked around them. 'Erm... everything needs doing!' he laughed. 'There's a really long way to go before I'm done here.'

'Right then,' said Hattie, reluctantly pulling away from Ben again. 'We'd better get started! It's still early – we could get loads done!'

'Are you sure?' said Ben.

Hattie smiled at the look on his face – it was somewhere between hopeful and gobsmacked. Yes - she was sure. There was nowhere else she'd rather be than right here with this gorgeous man. After feeling like she was about to lose him… Hattie had to admit that her feelings for Ben were *way* more complex than she'd previously given them credit for.

Not that she was about to admit anything of the sort out loud just yet though!

'Yes, I'm sure!' she said with a grin, playfully thumping him on the arm. 'But first things first, where's the kettle?'

Ben let out a hoot. 'That's my girl!'

He pointed her in the direction of the little camping stove, complete with an old metal kettle that was already full of water. Hattie busied herself getting it lit, and by the time it had started to steam merrily, Ben had managed to dig out a couple of relatively clean mugs – even though they rather chipped and cracked.

'Aren't they the old things I threw away when I was sorting out the kitchen at the hotel?' said Hattie in surprise.

Ben nodded. 'Yep. Proud Pebble Street rejects! Lionel said I could have them as they were only destined for the bin. One of his many contributions to Sylvie!'

'You know,' said Hattie, carefully lifting the kettle and splashing hot water onto a couple of tea bags, 'I can't believe he knew all about Sylvie and kept it from me for so long!'

Ben shrugged. 'He's a good friend. He knew I wanted to introduce the pair of you in my own time.

I should have known he'd let it slip eventually though – that man is an open book!'

'Sorry it didn't happen the way you wanted it to,' Hattie mumbled. She was starting to feel pretty rubbish about the way she'd reacted.

Ben shook his head. 'Don't be silly, I'm chuffed you're here now. It's a real weight off my mind if I'm honest. Now I just want you to love her as much as I do.'

Hattie handed Ben his cup and the pair of them made their way back up onto the deck, blinking in the daylight after the relative gloom of being in the cabin.

'You know,' said Ben, plonking his bum down onto a coil of rope, 'Lionel's promised to come and paint Sylvie for me when she's in a better state. As in – on a canvas... with oil paints!' he laughed.

'I wouldn't have put it past him to come and actually *paint* paint her,' chuckled Hattie.

'I'm sure he would offer to help if I asked him,' said Ben. 'He's been doing everything he can to support me even though this is a completely mad project. It's why I've had so much work renovating and redecorating the hotel. Without Lionel's support, I wouldn't have been able to get the place in a decent enough state to move in.'

'Sounds like Lionel,' said Hattie, a warm glow lighting in her chest. The man was one of the kindest people she'd ever met. And it was clear that Ben was one of his biggest fans.

She wandered over to the side and stared out across the boatyard, then her eyes lit upon her old car with its snazzy new paint job. She felt another jolt of horror go through her at how badly she'd behaved that morning. She'd been so scared of losing Ben... and when she added that to the weight of tiredness she was carrying around with her...

'I love the marigolds, Ben!' she said, turning back to him with a smile.

'You do?' he said in surprise. 'I got the impression... that... maybe you weren't keen... or something?'

'Erm... it was definitely "or something",' mumbled Hattie. 'I wasn't in the best frame of mind and I took it out on you. Sorry.'

Ben shrugged. 'That's okay... are you okay now?'

Hattie nodded. Sod it, she might as well come clean.

'I thought you had someone else.'

'Eh?!' said Ben, plonking his cup down on the deck and scrambling to his feet.

Hattie nodded miserably. 'When Lionel mentioned Sylvie but then completely refused to tell me anything else... my brain went into overdrive. And... well... I'm really sorry.'

'I'd never-' started Ben.

'I know!' said Hattie.

Ben stared at her. 'So that's why you were... erm... not quite yourself earlier?'

Hattie nodded again, watching as he picked his way through the piles of scrap towards her. Much to her surprise, he took her mug of tea out of her hands, popped it onto the side and took her hands.

'Just so you know,' he said, squeezing her fingers, 'there isn't anyone else.'

Hattie swallowed and stared down at the deck.

'Why would there be when you're here? You're one of my favourite people. Actually... you're my favourite person,' Ben paused and gently titled her face up with one finger under her chin, then grinned down at her. 'Even when you're delirious because you're sleep deprived!'

Hattie returned his smile and snuggled into the warm arms that were suddenly wrapped around her.

～

The rest of the day disappeared in a happy haze of sanding and drinking tea and then sanding some more. Just as Hattie had thought she was going to drop from hunger, Ben called time on the nautical DIY, disappeared down into the cabin and reappeared with a stack of Tupperware.

'What ya got in the boxes?' she asked, doing her best to wipe the dust and grime from her face using the equally grubby sleeve of her jumper.

'Cake, mostly,' said Ben with an apologetic grimace. 'I know it's not much, but I had planned on nipping to the shops before coming back… but obviously, there was a bit of a change of plans!'

Hattie smiled sheepishly. 'Sorry about that!'

Ben just shrugged. 'It's no bother to me… as long as you don't mind cake for your tea.'

'Honestly,' said Hattie, eyeballing the boxes in his hands, 'I'm that hungry I'd be happy to scrape the mould from an old crust and gobble it right now!'

'Classy bird!' laughed Ben. 'Sorry to disappoint – no mould here! I keep everything in these tubs so that they stay fresh and dust-free… I did have some Pebble Street Pudding, but that was breakfast!'

Hattie grinned. 'That's probably a good thing – I'm not sure I want that on my day off!'

'Well, there's plenty of Ethel's finest rhubarb streusel cake on offer, if I can tempt you?'

'Hand it over!' said Hattie, making grabby hands at him.

'Maybe start with a pack of wet wipes?' grinned Ben, lobbing them at her so that she could wipe her hands and her face clean. 'I'll grab our cups of tea.'

Balancing the boxes of cake on an old crate, Ben ran back down to the cabin while Hattie cleaned her hands and then helped herself to a huge slice of cake before slumping to sit on the deck, with her back against the side. She took a huge bite of cake and then rested her head back with her eyes closed.

It really had been the most wonderful, dusty day together. As the sugary sweetness gave her a much-needed energy boost, Hattie felt full to the brim with the sheer joy of spending proper time with Ben, helping him with a project he loved so much. Considering how wretched she'd felt when she'd first woken up... well, she couldn't believe what a difference a few hours could make. It was the perfect day. In fact, she didn't want it to end.

'You know,' said Ben, reappearing at her side and popping the cup of tea down on the deck before sitting down next to her, 'once we've finished this, we'd better start thinking about getting you back to Seabury!'

Hattie turned her head to face him and brushed the cake crumbs from her fingers. 'I could always stay,' she said slowly.

Ben stared at her and for just a moment, he didn't say anything. Hattie kept her eyes glued on his.

'It can get really cold,' he said with a frown. 'It's going to be a clear night...'

'I'm sure we'll figure something out,' said Hattie, still not taking her eyes off of his as she watched a smile curve on his lips.

Fearless.

It was all coming back to her.

CHAPTER 6

Hattie cracked her eyes open as the familiar sound of Ben's little motor boat woke her. She was still snuggled up in his bed, weighed down by layer upon layer of blanket and sailcloth. She reached out and laid a hand on the still-warm sheet next to her where Ben had lain just ten minutes ago.

Hattie let out a sigh of pure bliss as she wriggled down a bit further, tucking her chin under one of the blankets as she thought about yesterday evening. Talk about the perfect end to an unexpectedly perfect day. If only Ben had been able to stay on board Sylvie a little longer this morning and join her for a lie-in! That would have been the extra dusting of sugar on top of the cherry on top of the cream on top of the… jelly?

Hattie let out a snort.

Whatever!

It had been perfect, and she couldn't be grouchy about poor Ben having to dash off to work.

After she'd *finally* managed to convince him that she wasn't a total princess and that *yes* - she really *did* want to spend the night with him on Sylvie, Ben had been very apologetic about the fact that he'd have to do an early-morning disappearing act.

It hadn't put Hattie off in the slightest – especially when she'd discovered that she'd be able to laze around in bed even if Ben couldn't. It turned out that Ben had cycled into Seabury the day before - abandoning his bike at Pebble Street when she'd accosted him. His little motorboat was tied up here at the boatyard, so she wasn't required to play taxi driver to get him back into town in time for work.

Still – it would have been even better if he'd been able to stay in bed next to her and keep her warm! Hattie was sure Ben must have mentioned which of his many jobs he was off to – but she couldn't really remember. To be fair, he did several… and she'd been more than a little bit distracted when he'd mentioned it.

It might have been something about to do with the fish van… or mending someone's toilet… or some repairs that he needed to help his dad with… or maybe doing something for Kate at The Sardine?

Either way, he said he definitely had to go to Pebble Street later to hang some curtains for Lionel in the newly redecorated guest bedrooms, so the pair of them had made plans to meet back up there later.

As the sound of the boat began to fade into the distance, Hattie realised that the warmth of the bed was beginning to fade away too, now that there was one less starkers body keeping it toasty.

They hadn't even been slightly chilly last night! In fact, just thinking about it made a blush start at her toes and sweep all the way up to her face. It was time to get up. There was no point lying around, daydreaming about Ben when he wasn't there to keep her company.

Pushing back several layers of sailcloth, Hattie began to struggle out from under the pile of blankets that were holding her captive. She had to admit – the bed was way more comfortable than it looked. She still didn't want to imagine what it must be like trying to get to sleep down here when it was icy and blowing a gale outside though. As cosy and romantic as it had been last night, she'd bet anything that it could get pretty unpleasant in the depths of winter.

Hattie couldn't help but admire Ben's determination to do everything in his power to get the work done on Sylvie though. All those jobs and the mad hours he worked, only to come back here and put in just as much time and effort on his pet project.

Hattie had no doubt that Sylvie was going to be an absolute stunner when she was finally finished. She just hoped that Ben didn't reach the bottom of his seemingly endless supply of energy before that happened!

Quickly yanking her jeans up, Hattie got dressed as fast as she could. Considering that her clothes were still littered in a seriously blush-inducing trail around the cabin – it took rather longer than normal. She was desperate for a coffee to warm her up a bit by the time she was fully decent.

'You sweetheart!' she murmured as she hopped her way over to the little galley kitchen, pulling on her socks as she went.

Ben had already boiled the kettle and laid out everything she'd need to make coffee – including some sachets of milk that looked like they'd been half-inched from the train station at Dunscombe Sands. Clearly, Ben was just as much of a dab-hand at stretching a tight budget as he was at DIY!

Hattie poured boiling water into the one-cup cafetière and then carried it over to the tiny table along with one of the chipped cups from the hotel. She plonked herself down onto the rough, wooden stool and eyeballed the breakfast offering hungrily.

Ben had set out the last piece of Ethel's cake for her – the only slice they hadn't demolished the day before. She took an enormous bite and let out a groan of pleasure as the rush of sugary, rhubarby goodness made her tastebuds tingle. As she pushed the plunger on her coffee, she realised that she was munching away and smiling to herself like a complete idiot. Thank heavens she was on her own!

But then, who cared what she looked like?! This was a practically perfect breakfast. The only thing that would have made it better would be if she was eating it with Ben. Hattie slurped at her coffee, sighing with relief as the warmth and caffeine made their way into her bloodstream.

She hated to admit it, but she was absolutely shattered after all that sanding yesterday. But then, it was a much nicer tiredness than the sheer exhaustion she'd been experiencing for the last few days. There was something sweet and delicious about the way her muscles twinged unexpectedly... Hm, okay, maybe that wasn't just down to the sanding! Clearly spending time with Ben was good for her.

As Hattie broke off another chunk of moist, gooey cake and popped it in her mouth, she spotted a bit of paper tucked under the side of her plate. Brushing the crumbs from her fingers, she tugged it out and opened it up.

It was a note from Ben. Actually – it was more of a map than a note - so that she'd be able to find her way back to Seabury. Hattie studied it with a smile. Ben's pencil squiggles made it look a lot easier to get back than the wiggly-waggly mystery tour they'd taken on the way over here yesterday. That said, she'd been in such a foul mood that she hadn't been paying much attention at the time. She'd been too busy getting ready to have a showdown with the mysterious Sylvie.

'We're all good now though, eh Sylv?!' she murmured.

As she said it, a beam of early sunlight made its way through one of the dusty portals. It kissed her face and spilt across the table, lighting up her breakfast. Hattie grinned. She'd take that as a sign of friendship from the old boat.

Looking back down at the map, she followed Ben's erratic pencil lines with a sense of relief. This made it look like she could just drive out of the gates, turn right at the junction and then stay on the same road all the way back to town. According to this, as long as she pointed herself in the right direction to begin with, she couldn't help but bump into Seabury eventually.

There was a little note at the bottom of the map in Ben's childlike scrawl.

Don't worry about locking up when you leave – no matter how gorgeous my Sylvie is, no one is going to steal a half-rotten, twenty-six-foot boat. There's no lock or key anyway – so no point even trying! Ben X

Hattie read the note and then let her eyes linger on the big kiss at the end. She broke into a huge, goofy smile, her mind suddenly full of all the kisses they'd shared the previous night. There was no doubt about it – Hattie could *definitely* do with more days off if they were all going to work out like this!

Finishing her coffee and cake at warp speed, Hattie slipped Ben's note into her pocket and began to hunt around for her shoes. She eventually located them - kicked into one of the random piles of scrap metal.

Making her way up the steps into the daylight, Hattie took a moment to reconcile herself to the fact that she was standing on the deck of a boat. In a boatyard... in the middle of nowhere. As she peered around, the place looked a lot friendlier than it had the day before. Its eery, gothic vibe had disappeared and instead, it felt warm and friendly.

Hattie broke into a huge smile. She couldn't believe that she was even thinking this - but she was already looking forward to spending more time here with Ben! Yesterday definitely went down in the history books as one of the weirdest days of her life. And one of the best too.

Letting out a happy sigh, Hattie made her way towards the edge of the boat and then eyeballed the rickety ladder. Hmm... it looked a bit more daunting from this angle than it had from the ground. Ah well – here went nothing.

Taking a tight hold of the ancient wood, Hattie swung one leg over the side, feeling for a rung. As soon as she was confident that she wasn't about to step out into nothingness, she swung right out over the side.

Easy peasy. Don't be a scaredy-cat!

Hattie made it down to the ground without incident and gave a triumphant little skip. Right. Time to get back to Seabury. She turned and made her around to the other side of Sylvie, heading towards the car. As it came into view, she let out a laugh. Ben's flowers really were very sweet! She hadn't really been in the right frame of mind to appreciate all the work he'd put into them yesterday.

While they'd been munching on yet more cake, Ben had told her that he'd originally wanted to paint dolphins all over it – but they'd turned out to be too tricky. In true Ben-style, he'd given it a go, but apparently, the first attempt had ended up looking more like a slightly deranged swan, so he'd washed it off before the paint had the chance to dry. That's when he'd changed the plan to marigolds.

Hattie stared at the car, a wide grin on her face. She still thought they looked more like daisies – but who was she to argue?! Either way, the old thing looked bright and cheerful – and, more importantly, no one would mistake her for Veronica!

Hattie opened the door, slid into the driver's seat and crossed her fingers before turning the key. It started the first time, and she let out a sigh of relief. Yup – it was official, she loved this old thing. As much as she'd enjoyed hanging out here with Ben, she didn't much fancy the idea of being stranded in the boatyard on her own for a whole day – especially as her phone had precisely zero signal down here!

Fiddling around in her pocket, Hattie drew out the map, smoothed it out over the steering wheel and then placed it carefully on the passenger seat next to her. It was time to find her way back to Pebble Street.

It looked simple enough – though Ben's idea of important landmarks were things like rickety gates, stone walls with graffiti... and a funny shaped tree. At least - those were the ones she could make out. Much like his marigolds, some of his drawings could be any number of things.

Ah well – if she ended up getting lost, at least she'd get the chance to see some more of the countryside around Seabury. Hattie couldn't really seem to get worked up about anything much this morning. She still had a massive smile on her face – and thanks to Ben – she had a feeling it would take rather a lot to make it disappear!

Putting the car in gear, Hattie drove a little way towards the main gates and then paused. Winding down her window, she leaned her head out and waved at the old boat she'd spent such a memorable day on board.

'Bye Sylvie!' she called, blowing a kiss. 'See you again soon I hope!'

CHAPTER 7

'Unbelievable!' laughed Hattie, shaking her head.

She glanced down at Ben's map and then back up at the gnarled tree that graced the sharp right-hand bend in front of her. Sure enough, the real thing was just as lopsided as the one he'd drawn. When she'd first studied the map, Hattie had thought it looked like Ben had been drunk in charge of a pencil, but this was practically an exact replica of the real thing. The little sketch perfectly captured the old tree's tortured boughs and branches - blown into shape by the prevailing wind.

In fact, Ben's map was proving to be remarkably accurate so far. All his signs and landmarks had been exactly where he said they'd be – and all his sketches had turned out to be ridiculously lifelike. The rickety fence was, indeed, very rickety, and the stone wall with the smiley face spray-painted on it was glaringly obvious. It seemed that Ben's map-making skills were just as impeccable as his many, *many* other skills…

Hattie wriggled in her seat and let out an embarrassed little snort as heat flooded her cheeks again. She quickly opened the window a crack to let some air in. When that did nothing to cool her down, she started to hum in a bid to distract herself from the naughty flashbacks her brain had just decided to play like a slideshow. Blimey, it was still a bit early in the day for this kind of thing!

Not helpful, brain, not helpful at all!

Hattie had a feeling that it wasn't particularly safe to spend too much time thinking such thoughts – not when she was doing her best to navigate these unfamiliar, meandering lanes in her massive hulk of a car. The last twenty-four hours with Ben had turned out to be *quite* the eye-opener, and if she wasn't careful, she was going to end up getting distracted… okay - *more* distracted. The last thing she wanted to do was plough into a hedge and scratch her brand-new flowery paint job!

Quite frankly, if she ended up having to be dragged out of a ditch just because she was too busy thinking naughty thoughts about what the pair of them had got up to in Sylvie's cabin last night, she wasn't sure how she'd explain everything to her rescuers. She could just imagine the police report…

and the epic amounts of gossip that would spread around Seabury. Nope – she needed to keep all thoughts of naked Ben out of her head and focus on the wiggly waggly country lanes!

Wiggle waggly!

Hattie started to giggle. Getting her head out of the gutter was clearly going to be much harder than she thought. She quickly wound the window down the rest of the way – just in case it helped!

It didn't take long before Hattie spotted the lighthouse in the distance. She was back on the coast road now, and as she began to make her way down the steep hill towards the sea, Seabury itself came into view. However much she adored the place - it had been fantastic to have a day away. Just that short break had been enough to give her a good rest and find a fresh perspective on everything.

It was hard to believe that just a matter of a few weeks ago, Hattie had been convinced that her future was back in London. She'd thought cooking for Marco – and eventually owning her own restaurant in the city – was how her life was meant to go. She thought that was what success looked like – and that anything else meant she'd failed to achieve her dream.

Staying in Marco's shadow would have been a total disaster. She knew that now. Hattie hadn't realised it at the time, but it had been a blessing in disguise when he'd buggered off to his new restaurant and sacked her along with the rest of his staff.

That wasn't to say that it hadn't been a complete gut punch. However, now that she had time and perspective on her side she knew that, even if he'd taken her with him to Number 14, things would have ended badly anyway. She'd been exhausted, and completely caught up in his ridiculous notions about what constituted good food. It had been a recipe for disaster and Hattie could now see that things would have blown up between them before too long.

Hattie sighed. She hated to admit it, but there was still a tiny part of her that was gutted her original dream hadn't worked out… but there was no point in dwelling on that now, was there?

Even if there had been a job for her at Number 14, her life would have still imploded – just a couple of weeks later. Apparently, the restaurant had already closed its doors – the place had been a disaster from start to finish and she'd have had to find a new job anyway. There was no doubt about it, coming from a failed venture like that would have made it harder still to find a new position. London might be a big city, but the foodie scene up there was a tiny world and news spread fast!

Hattie gave herself a little shake, peering through the windscreen at the beautiful view – Seabury unfolding below her and the sea stretching away into the distance. Just look how lucky she was!

The job offer from Lionel had come at the perfect time. Of course, it might have taken her longer than it should to realise it - but it had changed her life for the better. She would never have met Ben again if she hadn't come back to Seabury. He would have just remained a distant, childhood memory of a freckly, smiley face who'd made her holidays magical. Not that there had been much time for revelling in happy childhood memories when she'd been working every hour god sent in Marco's old restaurant. Sure, she was just as madly busy here – but the big difference was that she was loving every second of it.

Of course, she'd only planned on staying in Seabury for a very short time – just long enough to help her uncle get Pebble Street back on its feet and find someone decent to run the kitchen for him. It hadn't taken her long to start changing her mind, though.

Now, just the thought of someone else taking over from her at the hotel made her shiver. It was her happy place – somewhere she was making a dream come true – even if that dream looked a little bit different these days. Was it really such a stretch of the imagination to think about settling down here? Living here forever? Maybe not...

She had friends here. Real friends. People who cared about her and supported her. People who made her laugh. People who fed her cake and checked in on her. There was Lionel, of course, and Kate and

Stanley over at The Sardine. Then there was Ethel and Charlie, and all the plot holders up at the allotments. They were like her extended family now that she was working with them so closely to supply Pebble Street's kitchen.

She'd even formed quite a bond with the proper, irascible ex-headmistress Mary Scott. They'd connected over puddings and recipes and old stories about The Pebble Street Hotel back when Mary's mum had been the cook.

Then, of course, there were the Chilly Dippers too. She was getting to know them all, slowly but surely. They hadn't given her too much of a hard time about joining them on one of their swimming adventures just yet, but Lou had assured her that it wouldn't take long before they did.

Hattie broke into a wide grin as she thought about Lou - who was quickly becoming so much more than just a colleague. Hattie had never had a best friend before, but she was pretty sure that Lou qualified. Either way, the slightly bonkers woman in question insisted that she was getting used to her chilly dips in the cold water now... though she claimed she was still doing it against her better judgment and wasn't quite ready to admit that she was enjoying it just yet!

Just last week, Lou had bounded into Pebble Street, full of the joys of spring because she'd just discovered that she could fit into her old swimming costume. Hattie couldn't imagine her life now without regular doses of Lou's peculiar brand of insanity.

She let out a happy sigh. The road was now comfortingly familiar, and Hattie knew that it was a matter of minutes and she'd be back in Seabury itself. She'd only been gone for the best part of a day, but she was happy to be back.

Seabury was so reliably sleepy and unchanging that there was something comforting about it. Not like London where everything changed so fast that it constantly felt like the rug was being pulled out from underneath you. At long last, she could understand why Lionel had chosen to stay here, wrapped up in the cosy blanket of the town he loved so much. As he'd once said to her over their shared breakfasts – "what a wonderful, charming, sleepy little backwater to spend your days in."

There was rarely any drama here... unless you counted stories about the town Christmas tree being blown away... or Stanley appearing at your door, wanting a biscuit and a snooze on your rug. Oh – and Veronica's infamous disappearing act... but that really was about it as far as she could tell.

Navigating a tight bend in the road, Hattie watched as North Beach spread out in front of her. The tide was high, and only a narrow strip of the pebbly beach was visible right at the top next to the wall.

Hattie trundled gently along the seafront road and then grinned when she spotted Ethel beetling along the pavement towards her. Ethel promptly started to wave and Hattie waved back. It looked like she was going to have to get used to this level of enthusiastic arm-waving – the flowers Ben had painted on the car were clearly at work again. No doubt people would get used to them eventually… she hoped.

As she pulled past Ethel, her friend's waving became more frantic – raising both hands over her head and looking a bit like a deranged windmill as she stepped out into the road. Hattie watched her in surprise in the rear-view mirror… and promptly realised that she wasn't waving at all. Ethel she was trying to flag Hattie down.

Slamming on the brakes, Hattie leaned her head out of the window and watched as Ethel marched up to the car.

'What's wrong?' said Hattie, her voice laced with concern. She suddenly felt like there was a puncture in the perfect happy bubble she'd been floating around in since leaving the boatyard. 'Is it Charlie? Lionel? Is everything okay? Oh god, it's not Ben is it?'

'Where have you been?' demanded Ethel, ignoring her questions. 'I've been looking everywhere for you since yesterday! So's everyone else, come to that! Lionel said you were probably with Ben, but-'

Hattie nodded. 'Yes, he was right – I was with Ben over at the boatyard. Why? What's happened!'

'Well Hattie,' said Ethel, her eyes twinkling, 'if you will go off gallivanting with your fancy man, what else can you expect?'

'Eh?! I don't understand…'

Ethel grinned at her widely. 'You've missed all the fun!'

CHAPTER 8

The minute she stepped out of the car, Ethel grabbed Hattie's hand and towed her towards the entrance of New York Froth. She'd insisted that Hattie just pull the old thing in and leave it at the side of the road, swearing they wouldn't be too long. Hattie wasn't so sure about this... but Ethel had been pretty adamant that whatever this was couldn't wait a moment longer.

'Come on, love,' said Ethel, 'let's get inside.'

New York Froth wasn't exactly Ethel's usual haunt, but it was right there on North Beach and much easier than going all the way over to The Sardine. Hattie was both alarmed and intrigued – what on earth was going on? This was certainly urgent gossip if it had Ethel breaking out of her usual routines like this!

Hattie stared around, admiring the beautiful café

while Ethel ordered a pot of tea for them to share. She hadn't had the chance to spend much time in here yet – preferring to grab a takeaway from The Sardine and take it down onto West Beach whenever she could get away from the kitchen for five minutes. It really was a lovely place, with its low lighting, walls of bookshelves and well-worn sofas.

It didn't take long before they were ensconced at a relatively private table towards the back of the café. Ethel glanced around to make sure there was no one close enough to eavesdrop and then leaned in.

Hattie couldn't help but mirror her, eyes wide as she waited for her friend to finally give up the goods.

'He was here!' Ethel muttered. 'Turned up yesterday!'

'Who?' said Hattie. She couldn't help but note that her heart was hammering. She was feeling decidedly anxious, even though she was yet to work out what this drama was all about. 'Who was here? She repeated, forcing her voice to stay as steady and calm as possible.

'Your old boss, of course!' said Ethel, rolling her eyes as if she was willing Hattie to catch up with her.

'Wait… what?' Hattie shook her head slightly. Of all the scenarios running through her head, this one hadn't even featured. 'Marco Brooks is in Seabury?'

'That's the fellow!' said Ethel, nodding. 'I'm not sure about now… but he definitely *was* in Seabury.'

'But wait… what?' Hattie gawped at Ethel, then

she quickly looked around the café again, her eyes raking the dark corners in case Marco was loitering in one of them. Just the idea made her shiver. Surely there had been some kind of mistake? Maybe she was still stuck inside her own imagination on the back lanes outside of Seabury somewhere. She surreptitiously pinched her leg under the table.

Ouch! Nope – not imagining things!

'See, it was like this,' said Ethel, casting a glance behind her, as if she was checking that the man himself wasn't standing there, listening over her shoulder. 'I went to take some cakes round to one of my neighbours yesterday morning, and this idiot had parked their silly big car right outside my cottage. And I mean *right* outside. I couldn't even get out through the front door. You know how narrow it all is along there. I mean, I guess I could have squeezed down the side… though it would have been difficult with my cake tins. But then, why should I?'

Hattie raised her eyebrows, but Ethel clearly wasn't finished.

'Didn't the inconsiderate so-and-so notice that there are double yellow lines all along my road for a good reason? Surely he noticed that he was blocking access to an entire house. I mean to say – that was my *front door!*'

Hattie nodded, wincing slightly as Ethel's voice headed up an octave or two as she became more and more irate.

'Anyway,' she continued, 'I squeezed down the side and went to have a quiet word with this *person,* and I recognised Mr Brooks. I mean, who else could it be? He was the spitting image of his picture in the papers.

'I didn't use to get that paper, you know, but ever since you came to town, we all like to have a read of it. Now that we've got our very own posh London chef, we like to keep on top of what those bigwig restaurants are up to. Of course, everyone wanted to read that review for Number 14 after the way Mr Brooks treated you. I've loaned my copy to *that* many people, I've lost track!'

Ethel patted Hattie's hand, and Hattie had to bite her tongue. Of course, she appreciated the crazy amount of support that the whole town was showing her but, right now, she *needed* to know what on earth Marco was doing in Seabury.

'And you're sure it was him?' said Hattie quickly, hoping to nudge her friend back on track.

'Oh yes,' said Ethel with a determined nod. 'I mean, who else could it be? Short, silly glasses, and a tuft of orange hair right on top of his head... if you can call it hair. I thought it was a feather or something that had just landed on him and got stuck there at first. But I recognised him from that picture in the paper... he really *does* like to be in all the photos, doesn't he?'

Hattie nodded morosely. What on earth was

Marco doing in Seabury? She didn't want him here in her new life. She'd left all that behind her in London. Or at least, she was doing her best to leave it all behind. Him being here was just going to stir it all up again – just when things were starting to fall into place, too!

'I still don't understand what he's doing here,' said Hattie, her voice sounding strained.

'Give me a sec,' said Ethel, 'I was just getting to that bit...'

Hattie bit her lip, willing herself to stay calm. There was clearly no point trying to hurry Ethel – not when her friend was relishing telling the story quite so much!

'Like I was saying – I went out to give him a piece of my mind for blocking my front door. I *am* an elderly resident, after all. I had to leave my cake tins behind and squeeze down the side of the silly great car. And then *he* started to complain about there being nowhere to park!' Ethel paused and let out a gusty sigh. 'The cheek of the man! Turns out he'd already been told to move when he was parked up in a gateway.'

'What gateway?' said Hattie, trying to keep up.

'The one up at the allotments!' chuckled Ethel. 'He was going on and on about how he thought people in the country were meant to be friendly. Anyway – when he described it, I could only imagine that it had been my Charlie who spoke to him. I mean, I don't think Charlie would recognise Marco like I did – because he's too busy with his nose in his seed catalogues to read the Sunday papers like I do. But he *hates* it when people block the gateway to the allotments. It's the only time I've seen him properly riled. He does *try* to be polite, but it's not really his strong suit. Salt of the earth, that man... salt of the earth!'

Hattie was nodding along, praying that Ethel might eventually get to the point and tell her what Marco was doing here.

'Anyway!' said Ethel. 'What does it matter if my Charlie was rude to Mr Brooks? The man deserves it!'

Hattie nodded again, crossing and uncrossing her fingers compulsively under the tabletop.

'And here's the good part,' said Ethel, her eyes twinkling, 'he said he was looking for The Pebble Street Hotel. That's what he told me... like it wasn't right there in front of him – the bloomin' great big building right in the middle of town, and he couldn't even find it. Probably couldn't see past his own ego!

'Anyway, I certainly wasn't about to give him directions, was I? I told him to move his car.' She gave a satisfied huff. 'Silly great thing it was,' she added as an afterthought.

'Then what happened?' asked Hattie faintly.

'Well, he moved his car, didn't he?' said Ethel, her lips pursing in dislike.

Hattie wanted to laugh in spite of herself. She

could just imagine Marco's reaction at being told what to do by someone like Ethel. Still, it would take a much braver man than him to argue with Ethel Watts when she got going!

'I don't think he was all that happy about it, to be honest,' said Ethel. 'But I just crossed my arms and waited for him to leave. I guess he was in town looking for you – but you were nowhere to be found.'

Hattie shook her head but didn't manage to get a word in edgeways.

'I mean, I looked for you everywhere. Don't worry, I waited until he'd driven off so he couldn't follow me – I didn't want to lead him to you by mistake. I saw his car driving around the town though – looking for somewhere legal to park I suspect. But every time I saw him coming, I ducked into a doorway and hid until he'd driven past…' she paused and rubbed her nose with the back of her hand. 'It was quite exciting really!'

'Did you see where he went in the end?' asked Hattie, feeling none the wiser for Ethel's story.

Ethel shrugged. 'He found the hotel eventually – I'm afraid I couldn't really help that. I mean, it's the biggest building in town and pretty hard to miss – even for an idiot like him.'

'Yeah, I guess,' sighed Hattie.

'He talked to Lionel. I'm not really sure about what, but I think your uncle tried to call you afterwards – said he couldn't get through.'

'I didn't have any signal over at the boatyard,' said Hattie. 'Now I feel terrible – I didn't mean to worry Lionel.'

Ethel shrugged. 'I don't think he was worried, love – like I said, he was pretty sure you were off somewhere with Ben. I think he just wanted to fill you in about Marco.'

'But *what* about him?' asked Hattie, desperately.

'Beats me! Marco was in the hotel for quite some time yesterday. I stayed in a doorway over the road until he came back out again… but I don't know what they talked about. I could have gone in and tried to eavesdrop, of course, but there aren't really any decent corners for hiding in at Pebble Street, so I thought better of it. And I didn't want to be rude and pick Lionel's brain about it when I saw him…'

'Probably best,' said Hattie, biting back a laugh. She couldn't help it - the image of Ethel creeping around Pebble Street like a spy, diving into doorways and trying to eavesdrop was one that was proving pretty hard to take very seriously.

'Hmm,' said Ethel with a frown, 'I still wish I'd given it a go. But then, Mr Brooks would have probably caught me at it, and I didn't really fancy getting into another argument with him… silly little man.' She paused and a huge grin lit up her face. 'Actually, maybe I wouldn't have minded *that* much. If anyone deserves a good shouting at, it's him!'

'Who deserves a good shouting at?'

The male voice from behind her made Hattie jump and spill her tea.

'I'm so sorry!' said Robbie, the young barista, hurrying to mop the spill with the tea towel he had slung over his shoulder. 'I'm so sorry... I was just coming over to ask if you ladies fancied anything else!'

'It's fine,' said Hattie with a tight smile. 'I thought you were... someone else!'

Her head had been so full of the image of Marco Brooks striding around Seabury, that she'd been sure she was about to turn in her seat only to be faced with her worst nightmare. Frankly, she was so happy that Robbie *wasn't* him, she could hug the boy.

'Anyway,' said Ethel, smiling at Robbie as he straightened up, looking sheepish, 'the answers to your questions – in no particular order are - Marco Brooks and a hot buttered teacake!'

CHAPTER 9

It took Hattie ages to peel herself away from Ethel. Her friend was full of righteous indignation about Marco's arrival in Seabury – and she'd wanted to share it... at length.

In the end, Hattie had to make the most of Robbie's appearance and had left Ethel relaying the whole tale to him from scratch, clearly delighted with her fresh audience. New York Froth's young barista had shot desperate *save me!* vibes at her as she struggled to her feet - but Hattie hardened her heart, made her apologies and headed for the door without a backwards glance. Poor Robbie - she'd have to go back later and apologise to him for throwing him under the Ethel-shaped bus.

Once outside, Hattie sucked in a deep breath in an attempt to calm her racing mind. Huh - no chance of that until she got to the bottom of what was going on. She needed to pin Lionel down and find out exactly what he knew about the whole Marco situation. She had a sneaking suspicion that he was bound to be able to give her a fuller picture than Ethel.

Praying that she wouldn't incur the wrath of Seabury's elusive but ever-present parking warden, Hattie made the snap decision to leave the car where it was. She was desperate to get to Lionel as quickly as possible and, for some reason, she decided a quick dash to Pebble Street on foot would be simpler than going back to retrieve the car first. Wrong. Very, very wrong.

Hattie put her head down and attempted to hurry along the seafront towards the hotel. Unfortunately, trying to hurry anywhere in Seabury was an art form she hadn't quite managed to master yet.

The problem was, everyone she knew had the delightful habit of stopping for a chat - and this being Seabury - she knew *everyone!* It was something that Lionel called the *Seabury effect* - a rare and wonderful thing that meant a trip outside to buy a pint of milk could take all morning if you didn't watch out.

Hattie quickly realised that she was in for the *Seabury effect* on steroids this morning. Due to her long days in the kitchen combined with the fact that she liked to spend every spare second she had sneaking off somewhere with Ben - the locals didn't actually get to see her out and about very often.

As it turned out, everyone wanted to stop and say

hello. Ten minutes after leaving New York Froth, Hattie had only taken about twenty paces and felt like she was at bursting point. She was torn between her desperation to reach Lionel and wanting to be friendly and polite. After all, these people weren't just her neighbours - they were her customers too. Plus - they were all being lovely! How were they to know that she felt like her brain was going to explode if she didn't get to the bottom of this Marco-shaped mystery as soon as was humanly possible?

So, she smiled and nodded and chatted, all the while pacing from foot to foot, desperate to leg-it to Pebble Street. There were just three topics of conversation this morning. Half of the town seemed to want to talk about her car's new paint job, having spotted it the day before or heard about it on the gossip vine. Then there were the ones who wanted to tell her that they were *sure* they'd seen Marco Brooks in town. And the rest... well, they just wanted to talk to her about food.

Most of Seabury's residents had eaten at the hotel by now - many of them more than once as they tested out the different dishes the menu had to offer... and they wanted to show her their appreciation – at length! Normally, this would have absolutely thrilled Hattie, but right now, she was struggling to react with the appropriate balance of grace and enthusiasm.

What did Marco want?

She needed to get back to Lionel!

As Doris from the post office laid a hand on her arm. Hattie had to take a deep breath and stop herself from just turning on her heel and running off. She clenched her teeth and forced a polite smile to her face as Doris waxed lyrical about the Pebble Street Pudding.

'Mary Scott's mum was a genius for inventing that one, and no mistake,' said Doris with a sigh. 'Of course, I've no doubt that it must take an enormous amount of skill to make it...' she petered off, and Hattie noticed a look in her eyes. Uh oh... she'd come to recognise that look as a warning sign. A recipe wrangling attempt was on its way.

'I mean...' said Doris casually, 'how on earth do you keep it so moist? Obviously, there's sugar and flour and... treacle?'

'Ah now,' said Hattie, 'you know my life in Seabury wouldn't be worth living if I let that cat out of the bag!'

'Top secret, eh?' said Doris, tapping her nose.

Hattie nodded. Doris knew full well that it was top secret... but that didn't stop her from prodding for hints and tips whenever she bumped into Hattie.

Hattie was pretty certain that most of the ladies of the Seabury WI had tried their hand at recreating the popular pudding in their own homes. She also knew - as the only one person to be let in on the secret for decades - that there was no way anyone could simply guess and get it right. The recipe was just too complex for anyone to stumble upon it using trial and error... even if they happened to get most of the ingredients right. Besides, the top-secret ingredient was King's Nose honey - something that was incredibly difficult to get your hands on these days!

All in all, Hattie felt pretty happy that her secret was nice and safe - as she didn't end up blurting it out just so that she could get away from Doris. Speaking of which-

'Sorry Doris,' she said, 'I've got to dash. Lionel needs me!'

She waved her hand and shot Doris a grin before dashing away, leaving Doris staring after her. She didn't want to be rude, but she knew from previous experience that she could be there for at least another twenty minutes if she didn't extricate herself!

As Hattie spotted yet another local smiling at her from across the road, clearly eager to chat about what fish she was planning on including on her new menu or something similar, Hattie winced. This was turning into a total nightmare! She really should have just jumped straight back in the car after escaping Ethel and driven around to the hotel garages. At least that way she'd have avoided the crowds.

She quickly made a show of yanking her mobile out of her jacket pocket and pressed it to her ear, shooting an apologetic grimace along with a little wave at the elderly lady. Sure, her phone might be out of battery and as dead as a dodo - but she could still use it as a shield, couldn't she?!

Hattie beetled along the last stretch of North Beach, pretending to be deep in conversation with someone about something very important. She nodded and frowned and tutted and agreed with all her might. She loathed herself on principle for doing this, but after passing at least half a dozen more people who simply smiled and nodded rather than stopping her in her tracks, she quickly decided that in this case, it was the lesser of two evils. Especially if it meant that she might make it back to Pebble Street before dark!

Her imaginary conversation wasn't doing anything to stop questions running through her mind on a loop, though. What the hell was Marco doing, coming down here anyway? And how did he even find out where she was?

Actually, the answer to the second question was probably fairly simple. It was one thing keeping in touch with her old friends from London and getting them to act as spies so that they could fill her in on what Marco was up to – but it was always going to be a two-way street, wasn't it?! Most of her old colleagues knew where she was – even if it was hard to find Seabury on a map. They also knew that Pebble Street was turning out to be a surprise success. Maybe that was why Marco was here?

Ethel had said that he was looking for Pebble Street. She hadn't mentioned anything about him asking for her. Interesting... maybe he'd just come to town to check out the food. Huh – he'd be lucky! The restaurant was booked solid for weeks. Knowing Marco, he'd probably try to jump the queue and squeeze himself in somehow. That would be classic Marco. He'd probably think they'd all roll over and do anything for him because he was a "celebrity chef!"

Yeah.

Right.

Hattie tried not to growl at the thought. He'd have to wait for a last-minute cancellation – and there were very rarely any of those. In fact, they'd only had one of them since they'd opened their doors, and that had been when old Mrs Easterbrook was rushed off to hospital with appendicitis. According to local gossip, she'd spent the entire time in the ambulance complaining. She'd been convinced that there was nothing wrong with her, and she didn't want to miss out on her piece of the Pebble Street Pudding!

Lionel had managed to squeeze her in as a special addition the following week. An emergency operation wasn't going to keep Mrs Easterbrook away from her long-anticipated Pebble Street treat!

If Marco thought that he could just rock up and expect to get a table though, he had another thing coming. Mrs Easterbrook had been a different matter entirely - that had been about looking after one of their own.

What if Marco *had* come to Seabury to find her, though? Perhaps he'd figured out that she'd actually been an important part of his business. Maybe it had taken the failure of Number 14 to open his eyes. What if he'd decided that he couldn't carry on without her and the kind of dedication she was willing to pour into her work? It was a stretch to imagine it, but what if he'd finally realised that it was her and the rest of the team that had been the magic ingredients to his success.

Hattie could feel her breathing speeding up. What if he asked her to go back to London with him? What if he wanted to start over again at some new restaurant… the pair of them cooking together again? What would she say? What would she *do?!*

Hattie came to a grinding halt. Her grip on the dead mobile phone still at her ear was iron-tight and clammy. What if that really *was* it?! She stared at The Pebble Street Hotel just ahead of her, her heart hammering - half in fear, half in excitement. If she said yes, they'd have to start at the bottom again and build on their original success. It'd take some doing to distance themselves from the disaster of his failed venture – but with hard work…

That really *could* be it, couldn't it? He'd come all this way – in his big, silly car, according to Ethel - to take her back to London. To give her the chance to start her career – and his – all over again. Another shot at achieving her dream…

Hattie let her arm drop, giving up the pretence of the phone call as a bolt of electric excitement ran through her at the prospect of being back in the kitchen of a London restaurant again. *Her* restaurant. Because this time, Marco would realise that it would have to be a partnership – not a one-man show… wouldn't he?

What was she even *thinking?!* Reality dumped itself on her head like a bucket of icy water. *Even* if that's what Marco wanted to talk to her about, it would mean leaving Seabury.

Leaving Pebble Street.

Leaving Ben.

Hattie suddenly felt like she was untethered and starting to float away from everything she'd come to love so dearly. She brought a hand to her chest. It felt like a crack had just formed across her heart. She wasn't sure she could bear the pain. Suddenly, she realised that she had a new dream - and she was already living it - here in Seabury, surrounded by so much love.

Hattie wasn't about to walk away. Not now. It was essential she found out what the hell was going on and what mischief Marco had managed to achieve in her absence. She upped her pace, determined to get back to the hotel.

CHAPTER 10

Hattie darted through the front door and practically trotted across the reception and down Pebble Street's wide hallway in search of Lionel. Screeching to a halt, she peered around the door to the breakfast lounge and let out a gasp of relief. She'd found him!

It looked like he was enjoying the tail end of a late breakfast. Hattie paused, watching as Lionel took a leisurely sip of coffee, looking like nothing could possibly ruffle him.

Hattie felt a powerful rush of love for her uncle. He'd been there for her when she'd been at her lowest. He'd given her a job, a place to live and – more importantly – he'd given her the chance to find herself again. And now, just when he was enjoying a few well-earned, lazy days off, her London life had caught up with her and intruded on Lionel's peaceful existence.

Hattie felt awful. She didn't need to know the ins and outs of Marco's visit to Pebble Street to know that he would have made a royal pain in the behind of himself - because that was just the kind of person he was.

As she watched, Lionel got to his feet, stacked his dirty dishes into a pile and swept a bunch of toast crumbs from the table cloth onto the floor.

So that's what he got up to when he thought no one was watching, eh?! Hattie let out a chuckle.

'Caught you!' she grinned.

'I don't know what you mean!' he said, shooting a sheepish smile at her, promptly trying to make it look like he was sweeping the crumbs into his hand instead. 'Nice to have you back!' he added, reaching for a tray and piling crockery onto it. 'Did you have a nice time with Ben?'

'How did you know that's where I was?' asked Hattie curiously.

'He sent me a text!' said Lionel with a good-natured eye-roll. 'Didn't want me worrying.'

'Sorry I pulled a disappearing act,' said Hattie, suddenly feeling incredibly guilty. 'I got to meet-'

'Sylvie!' said Lionel with a grin. 'What did you think?'

'She's going to be beautiful… in a few years!' she said.

'So, fancy moving in with Ben then?' asked Lionel lightly.

'Honestly - I'd live with Ben like a shot,' she said, surprising herself. 'We had the best time - and I can't pretend it wasn't good to get away from Pebble Street for a while - but Sylvie's barely fit for one person to live on… let alone two.'

Lionel nodded. 'I know… I do worry about Ben living out there.' He let out a long sigh. 'Anyway - things all sorted with you both now?'

Hattie grinned, doing her best to ignore the blush that spread over her cheeks. 'All good. Anyway, I hear you had a visitor while I was gone?' said Hattie, getting back to the issue at hand.

'Oh, you already know about that, eh?' said Lionel, pulling a comical face.

Hattie nodded. For some reason, she suddenly felt like her entire life in Seabury was dangling by a thread. Yet here was Lionel, pottering through his sedate morning routine, looking completely unruffled.

'Odd little man, isn't he?' said Lionel, picking up the tray and leading the way out of the breakfast lounge into the kitchen.

Hattie followed hot on his heels, still not saying anything. She wanted to hear Lionel's account of what had happened without colouring it in any way by her questions or responses… at least, not until she'd figured out what Marco had been up to!

'He told me he was your boss in London?' said Lionel. 'Fascinating hairdo - I have to say, that orange tuft had me mesmerised for a second. Is it real hair?'

Hattie couldn't help but snort at the sarcasm in Lionel's voice. Her uncle was usually the epitome of kind, calm and accepting. She didn't dare think how rude Marco must have been to elicit this kind of response. It didn't come as much of a surprise though – the man had always been a bit of an obnoxious git. It was certainly quite a stretch of the imagination that his recent failure might have softened him at all.

'I'm really sorry, Lionel,' she sighed. 'If I'd known he was coming, I would have made sure that I was around. At least that way I could have dealt with him.'

Lionel yanked open the door to their snazzy new dishwasher and began to load it with slightly more force than was needed. Clearly, he was more rattled by the behaviour of their unexpected visitor than he was letting on. When he was finished, he straightened up and turned to Hattie.

'I showed him the menu,' he said. 'He actually sneered. I've never seen anyone do that before in real life! I mean, you read about people sneering in books, but it's really quite something to see it happen in front of you.'

Hattie frowned but didn't say anything. Her uncle was mid-rant – which in itself was an unusual phenomenon. She figured it'd be best to let him get it out of his system.

'Apparently, the man doesn't like fish. He said it's unphotogenic. Whatever that means!'

Hattie sighed and nodded. She was right - he was the same old Marco. Nothing had changed. To think she'd been excited by the thought of working with him again - even for an instant. What on *earth* had she been thinking?!

'You know what he said next?' demanded Lionel. 'He said that our menu was *probably* alright for a provincial little town like ours, but anywhere else it would be a disaster. He actually said that. I couldn't believe it!'

Lionel ground to a halt, his bushy eyebrows bristling.

'He can be a bit... much,' said Hattie, reaching out and patting Lionel gently on the arm.

Inside, she was seething. She hated the fact that Marco had been here and done this. Lionel was so proud of everything they'd already achieved together. The idea of anything tarnishing that for him made her want to hit something... or at least throw a potato at someone. Still – she needed to know the answer to the question that had been plaguing her ever since Ethel had accosted her.

'Erm – Lionel... what did Marco actually want?'

Lionel puffed out an annoyed breath before answering. 'To be honest, I'm not really sure. After he'd pulled that awful face at the menu, turned his nose up at the décor in the breakfast lounge and generally acted like an unpleasant little so-and-so, he demanded to see the recipe for the Pebble Street Pudding. Odd little man.'

Hattie's jaw dropped. She sat down heavily on one of the kitchen stools. The pudding? Could that be it? She watched as Lionel reached for the kettle and filled it before preparing the cafetière for another round of coffee. Hattie watched him counting out spoonfuls and raised her eyebrows as he added an extra one. Clearly, the subject of Marco had left her uncle in need of an extra-strong hit of caffeine!

'What did you tell him?' Hattie asked eventually when she realised that Lionel had ground to a halt.

'About the pudding?' he asked, turning to her and blinking as if he was coming out of a daze.

Hattie nodded.

Lionel shrugged. 'I told him that I didn't have the recipe. You wouldn't believe it, but he got quite shirty with me. He said that it *must* be written down somewhere. When I told him that it wasn't, he went all red in the face and looked like he was going to explode.'

Hattie rolled her eyes. She'd seen that reaction many times before – usually directed straight at her for placing a mung bean sprout in the *wrong quadrant of the plate* … or upside down. She'd never quite managed to figure out which way up a mung bean sprout should go! The thought of Marco turning beetroot red in front of Lionel at Pebble Street was actually pretty funny.

'I told him that only two people in the entire world know how to make our famous pudding...'

'Famous?!' laughed Hattie, shaking her head.

'What?! I felt completely justified in upping its credentials a bit... given the circumstances.'

'Fair enough!' said Hattie.

'I mean - whether it's *actually* famous or not is up for debate... but it's obviously famous enough to bring Marco Brooks all the way down from London to try to get his grubby mitts on the recipe. Sadly for him, he had to go away empty-handed.'

'Hah!' said Hattie. 'Good for you, Lionel.'

'Well... thankfully I couldn't have given him the recipe even if I'd wanted to... but it's not all good news, I'm afraid.'

Hattie raised her eyebrows and studied the worried look that had just appeared on her uncle's face.

'Why?' she asked, a new spike of worry catching her off-guard.

'I mean... I don't think I should have told him *who* knew the secret recipe. I couldn't help myself though – he was getting under my skin a bit by that point and it just slipped out. I'm not usually that easy to annoy – I lived under the same roof as Veronica for years after all – but there's something about this Marco character, isn't there?'

Hattie rolled her eyes and nodded emphatically. 'Yes, there really is. Don't worry – Marco has that effect on pretty much everyone. Anyway, I don't think any harm's been done – it's common knowledge I'm the only chef here, and everyone in town knows the recipe came from Mary Scott. I think it was even mentioned in the newspaper when they covered opening night, wasn't it?'

'You're right,' said Lionel, looking relieved. 'They did mention it in that section about the history of the hotel - along with a copy of the photo of her holding the pudding! I guess it's still not brilliant that he knows, but at least I wasn't the one who let the cat out of the bag.'

'Nah. It wouldn't have taken much for him to get that bit of info anyway,' said Hattie, her mind travelling down the river to her friend Mrs Scott. 'In fact, if it really *is* the pudding recipe he's after, I'd bet that he already had a copy of that article. Marco might be an idiot, but he's not stupid. I just hope that he doesn't bother Mary - she's already had more than enough grief over that recipe from Veronica over the years. I'd hate to be the reason that happens to her again.'

Lionel nodded but didn't say anything.

Suddenly, Hattie felt awful. She wasn't exactly sure how things now stood between her uncle and Mary Scott, but it couldn't be easy for him, could it? After all, they'd only just become reacquainted - decades after Mary had broken Lionel's heart. She had a feeling that neither of them had said a word to each other since the opening night feast. It was a shame – but Hattie didn't really know how to tackle the void between them. If she was honest - she didn't think it was any of her business. Still - maybe she should try a bit harder to keep mentions of Mary's name down to a minimum.

'Erm,' she said, desperate to change the subject as quickly as possible, 'so… Marco didn't ask to see me at all while he was here?'

It was the one thing that was still bothering her - and she knew it was because her own ego was ruffled. Even if *she'd* decided that she was staying in Seabury - no matter what - it would still be nice to be *asked* back to London, wouldn't it?! In fact, a bit of begging would go down a treat… even if it was by one of the biggest idiots she'd ever met!

'Not that I remember,' said Lionel with a shrug. 'If anything, I'd say he actually seemed rather relieved that you weren't here. I think he expected to be able to give me the slip and sneak into the kitchen to have a sniff around - obviously much easier without you in the building!'

'He *what?!*' said Hattie, looking around her domain as if it might be invaded at any moment.

'Don't worry,' laughed Lionel, leaning forward and patting her hand. 'He ran into me before there was any chance of him letting himself in here. In fact, I think I rather scuppered his grand plan - I don't think his visit to Pebble Street went quite as he'd intended.'

'Good!' said Hattie.

'Indeed,' chuckled Lionel. 'You know, he actually huffed as he stomped off! I haven't seen anyone do that since a court case back in the late 1980s.'

Hattie giggled. Marco's huffs were legendary. She'd actually seen a kitchen porter sacked for doing an uncanny impression of it. Unfortunately for the lad in question, Marco had appeared right behind him while he'd been entertaining the entire waiting staff. Marco had let him dig his own grave for several long minutes before saying anything. The porter couldn't work out why his audience had fallen silent and started to slink away - until the temper tantrum started in his right ear!

'He's certainly got quite a temper on him!' said Hattie.

'Well, I stand by what I said – that's one very odd little man,' said Lionel.

Hattie nodded. 'You're right there.'

'Are you sure that hair isn't stuck on?'

CHAPTER 11

Hattie sped up until she was practically jogging back through town towards her car. She had her fingers crossed that there wasn't going to be a rude note waiting for her, or worse - a parking ticket!

Hattie smiled and nodded as she zoomed past people but resisted the urge to do the polite thing and stop for a chat. She'd be there all day otherwise and she didn't want a re-run of earlier. She was on a mission.

Everything was just starting to sink in - and instead of the nice, gentle day pottering around the town that she'd been planning on, Hattie was now hell-bent on visiting Mrs Scott. There was no way she could rest easy until she knew whether Marco had attempted to make contact with her irascible friend - and it certainly wasn't something she wanted to deal with by phone.

It was also just beginning to really hit home that Marco had come all this way without the slightest intention of making things right with her. Hell, it didn't look like he'd even mentioned her name while he'd been rampaging around the town. All he was after was the Pebble Street Pudding recipe.

Hattie was both gutted and relieved all at the same time. Gutted because she wasn't going to get the chance to turn him down when he begged her on bended knee to go back to London with him (yes, she *might* have embellished that fantasy a tiny bit since it had first popped into her head!). And relieved... for the same reason, really. Hattie didn't want or need the kind of drama Marco took with him wherever he went. Not anymore. She loved the simplicity of life here - sheer hard work cemented together by lots of love, friendship and fun. Frankly, Marco and his ill wind could take a running jump.

Which was exactly why she needed to check in on Mrs Scott. Hattie might know that Marco's bark was worse than his bite - but she was certain that he would have given her friend a really hard time while he was busy trying to get what he wanted.

If she was being honest, Hattie was still marvelling that the notoriously lazy Marco had really come all this way for a recipe. Then again... the pudding might not exactly be famous as Lionel had made out, but people *did* love it. And the London foodie lot were an odd bunch… the Pebble Street Pudding could be just the sort of thing to relaunch Marco's flagging career if he got his paws on it.

'Nope!' she panted. 'Not if I can help it!'

Still, she couldn't believe Marco had come all this way just to get his hands on something that didn't belong to him. It was all about getting another shot at being a "bright light in the culinary firmament". That's how the review had described his early rise to fame… but even that had been based on other people's hard work and determination. *Her* hard work and determination.

Hattie huffed and puffed her way along the seafront, getting more and more irate as she went. It was all classic Marco, wasn't it? All drama - all show - zero substance.

She felt really stupid now - to think that she believed for a moment that he might have been here to apologise to her. As if he'd ask her to work with him again! The man was simply incapable of such a huge transformation… only a personality transplant would have made something like that a reality. It had all just been her overactive imagination at work.

One good thing had come out of all this though, hadn't it? It had made her realise that she didn't want - or need - his apology. Just like she didn't want - or need - to go back to London to fulfil her dream. She was already living it, right here in Seabury.

Needing to catch her breath, Hattie paused for a moment. She wasn't used to all this dashing around! She grabbed the railings and turned to stare out across the pebbles, down to the waves as they lapped at the shores of North Beach. Yes, there was no doubt about it - if she ever had to choose between London and Seabury… well, the answer would be Seabury. Every time.

There were plenty of reasons, of course, but the most important one was that she was happy here. She definitely couldn't say that about her time in the capital - working every hour god sent to build up Marco's restaurant for him.

Now that she'd had a little bit of distance, she could see that her day-to-day life had been pretty miserable. She'd been overworked and underpaid and - at the time - she'd believed that had been the only way to achieve her heart's desire.

Why on earth would she consider giving up everything she had here to go back to that? Her life in Seabury was pretty special. She had a lovely room in a gorgeous hotel. Sure, at times she was desperate for somewhere a bit more… settled… but she was sure that would happen eventually. Then, of course, there was the fact that she got to work with her amazing uncle every day. She had complete creative control of Pebble Street's menu and a kitchen she'd been able to set up just how she wanted it!

Add to all that the fact that she was surrounded

by incredible people - and she was basically in heaven. Sure, her new friends and neighbours could drive her to distraction at times, but that was just because they cared for her. Hattie could feel it deep in her bones - she was already part of this tiny, close-knit community – and that in itself was a huge honour.

Not to forget Seabury itself, of course. She could walk barefoot on the beach any time she liked. Okay, so there hadn't been much time for that so far because she'd been so busy getting everything up and running at Pebble Street – but there would be all the time in the world when things settled down a bit.

Hattie sucked in a deep breath of sea air and let it out slowly. She spotted the Chilly Dippers piling onto the far end of the beach and watched as they all set out their towels on the pebbles before legging it down to the sea and splashing straight into the water.

The squeals of pure joy reached her all the way up on the pavement, and she let out a little chuckle. She could see Lou splashing around in the middle of the group. It looked like her friend was thoroughly enjoying her precious time off just as much as Hattie had been - until Marco Brooks had appeared to spoil her fun.

No matter how much Lou liked to complain about her cold water exploits when they were working together, she was doing a damn good job of looking like she was having the time of her life out there. As she watched, Hattie decided that maybe she *would* join this bunch of nutters before too long. That said, she might wait for August… and then make sure she was wearing a wetsuit too.

Pushing away from the railings, Hattie tore her eyes away from the Chilly Dippers and set off again. She was almost back to her car when she was sure she heard someone calling her name. Spinning around, she saw Kate hurrying along, trying to catch her up, Stanley lumbering along at her heels.

'Hey!' puffed Kate. 'Blimey – you walk fast! I swear you were completely lost in your own thoughts there for a minute. I started calling you when you were standing by the railings, but you were miles away!'

Hattie grinned. 'Sorry! It's been an insane morning. I had a bit of an Ethel-shaped emergency earlier and left my car on the double yellows. I've already left it there way longer than I meant to - hence the semi-jog!'

Kate nodded and clutched at a stitch as Stanley wafted his feathery tail in excitement and promptly sat on Hattie's feet. He stared up at her with melting brown eyes, bumping his head back against her thighs, demanding tickles.

'Hello boy,' said Hattie, smiling down at Stanley and stroking his huge head.

'Stanley even barked… I thought he was trying to help me get your attention… though let's face it - he probably just wanted to go for a swim with the Dippers.'

'More than likely!' laughed Hattie. Stanley's penchant for a good dip was legendary and Ben had told her he'd had to head out in his boat to collect him more than once. No wonder Kate had such a tight hold on his lead. 'Anyway, what's up?'

'I need to apologise, I'm afraid,' said Kate, pulling a face.

Hattie's eyebrows shot up. 'Why? What's happened?'

'Your old boss is what's happened…'

'Uh oh,' sighed Hattie. 'Has he been bothering you too? He's managed to get Lionel all riled up.'

'Seriously?' said Kate. 'I didn't actually think that was possible. Mind you, now I've met the man… if anyone was going to manage it…'

'Quite!' said Hattie. Stanley chose that moment to bump his head against her leg again and she smiled down at him briefly. This dog really did know the exact moment you needed a comforting hug, didn't he?! 'Anyway… what did Marco want?'

'Well… I'm not sure how it happened. I mean, I really didn't mean to tell him, but I didn't recognise him at first… but then when he'd gone, Sarah told me who he was.'

Hattie shook her head, trying to follow Kate's garbled apology. 'But… what *did* you tell him?' she said, her laugh masking the sinking sensation in her chest.

'I managed to tell him where Mrs Scott's house is! I'm so sorry… he was really sneaky about it. He made it sound like he was on his way to visit her and was lost… It wasn't until after he'd gone that Sarah pointed out what he'd probably been up to. I wouldn't have said anything if I'd have had my head screwed on – but it all happened so fast. I'd only popped into The Sardine to pick Stanley up and wait with Sarah until Ethel turned up.'

'It's… it's okay!' said Hattie, her mind racing. Her worst fears had been confirmed - Marco had been on a mission to find Mrs Scott. The question was, what should she do now?

'It's not okay. I'm so sorry,' said Kate, interrupting Hattie's panicked train of thought. 'I was just really worried and in a bit of a hurry and I didn't stop to think until it was too late. Stanley hasn't quite settled in at the lighthouse yet. He keeps wandering back down into town and turning up at The Sardine wanting to be let in!'

'Poor old boy,' said Hattie, looking down again at the big brown eyes and ruffling his ears, earning herself a panting, toothy smile in return.

'I'm hoping he'll calm down soon - I get so worried when he goes wandering. We close the gates, we've fenced the garden… but it's like nothing can keep him in. It's not so bad when the café's open because they always call me to tell me that he's there, but when it's closed, he just sits outside the door to the empty flat.' Kate paused. 'It's breaking my heart a bit!'

Hattie reached out and patted Kate's arm. 'He'll get there,' she said gently, her own worries forgotten for a brief moment. 'And everyone in town knows him – he'll be okay.'

Kate smiled and nodded. 'I know, you're right. It's just quite a lot to get used to – and one of us seems to be constantly driving down into town to pick him up at the moment. Anyway, I'm really sorry. If it wasn't for Stanley, I might have had my wits about me yesterday.'

'Stop worrying,' said Hattie, wishing she could take her own advice. 'I'm sure it'll all be fine.

'Look,' said Kate with a rueful grin, 'even Stanley feels bad'

Hattie looked down into Stanley's pleading brown eyes – and then she started to laugh as the big bear flopped down onto the pavement and started to chew his fluffy tail.

CHAPTER 12

Hattie let out a huge sigh of relief as she reached her ridiculously cheerful car. No rude notes. No nasty, yellow stickers on the windscreen. Phew!

She hastily unlocked the door, slid inside and turned the key in the ignition. Just as she was about to pull off, she heard the sound of another vehicle pulling up alongside her. Half expecting someone who was about to have a go at her for her illegal parking, she turned to face them slowly only to find Ben grinning at her from the fish van.

Hattie quickly wound down the window, returning his smile with a beaming grin of her own. The butterflies in her stomach promptly woke up and flew into full kaleidoscope-mode as images from last night started to bombard her again. Blimey – as if she could *ever* consider heading back to London and leaving this gorgeous man behind her. Nope - just not a possibility!

'Hey stranger!' said Ben. 'Found your way back into town okay then?'

'Thanks to your map!' said Hattie with a nod. 'And thank you for breakfast.'

'Maybe next time we'll actually get to eat it together,' he laughed. 'Anyway, I've just finished my stops up this end of town and I've got a few minutes before I've got to head off again – do you fancy going for a coffee? I need to pop into The Sardine anyway…'

Hattie bit her lip for a second. She'd love nothing more than to hang out with Ben and make the most of a few stolen moments together… but she was on a mission, and she'd already delayed it for longer than she'd have liked.

'Sorry,' said Hattie, shaking her head, 'but I've got to get over to Mrs Scott's as soon as possible.'

'Marco Brooks?' asked Ben, raising his eyebrows.

'You know about that?' said Hattie in surprise.

Ben nodded. 'Everyone's talking about him being in town. It's not every day an odd-looking stranger appears in a silly, big car.'

'By that description, I'm guessing you've been talking to Ethel!' laughed Hattie, recognising the exact phrase from Ethel's rant earlier.

'Yeah – she popped around to the van to buy a bit of pollock for Charlie's tea. I don't think I've ever heard her have quite such a long outburst before,' he laughed. 'I swear she was going for a full ten minutes before she ran out of puff!'

'Yeah,' sighed Hattie, 'Marco has the innate ability to try the patience of a saint!'

As she said it, she couldn't help but wonder again what kind of damage Marco might have caused over at Mrs Scott's. Suddenly, the idea that she could have inadvertently led that kind of distress to her friend's door made her feel sick.

'Hattie... is everything alright?' said Ben, looking concerned.

'Erm... I'm not sure yet, to be honest,' she said. Then she watched in surprise as Ben's jaw tightened. Maybe he was worried that Marco was here to try to convince her to return with him to London. After all, that had been her first thought.

'Don't worry,' she said quickly, 'it's not me he's after... not in *any* way! He just wants to get his hands on the Pebble Street Pudding recipe.'

The tightness disappeared only to be replaced by a look of pure confusion.

'I promise I'll fill you in later,' she said. 'I'm really sorry – but I've got to get over to Mrs Scott's!'

'Okay,' said Ben, nodding. 'Actually, I've got to dash too - I promised I'd pop into The Sardine to talk to Kate about... erm... about some work up at the lighthouse.'

Hattie nodded, narrowing her eyes at Ben for a

split second. Okay - that was odd. Very odd. He'd just come over all shifty!

Suddenly, Hattie was absolutely certain that there was something Ben wasn't telling her. There was nothing particularly strange about him catching up with Kate about a bit of work… after all, he'd worked in pretty much every single house in the town at some point or other. But Hattie was sure she wasn't imagining the fact that he'd just started squirming in his seat.

'I saw Kate just now, actually,' she said lightly. 'She's just walking Stanley.'

'Oh,' said Ben, his eyes darting this way and that, looking mildly panicky. 'Did she… erm… say anything?'

Hattie's quirked an eyebrow. The more fidgety Ben got, the cuter he became!

'Yes,' she said, 'more Marco Brooks stuff.'

The moment she said Marco's name out loud, Hattie decided that whatever Ben was up to - whatever he wasn't telling her - it was a mystery that was going to have to wait until later.

'I'm sure Kate will fill you in,' she said. 'I'd better get going.'

'Is there anything I can do?' he asked, his face full of concern.

'Nah – I've got this,' said Hattie, beaming at him. 'See you later, though?'

Ben nodded and grinned at her. 'Definitely. We'll

catch up later. Text me when you're on your way back, and I'll meet you at Pebble Street?'

'I don't know how long I'll be,' sighed Hattie.

'I've got all the time in the world,' said Ben.

She watched as he pulled away, and just as she was about to wind her window back up, Hattie caught faint words drifting back to her down the road...

'Love you!'

Wait.

WAIT...

It took a moment or two for those two precious words to actually register. By the time they'd sunk in, Ben had gone – rounding the gentle curve of the seafront.

Wow. Did that just really happen? Or was it just her hopeful imagination? Blimey - this was turning out to be one of those days she wasn't going to forget in a hurry.

Well... there was no point sitting here like a dazed fool, was there? Ben was gone, and there wasn't anything she could do right now about what he had... or hadn't... just shouted to her out of his window.

Shaking her head like a confused dog, Hattie did her best to clear her thoughts. She was on a mission. She could talk to Ben about this later... or maybe not *talk...* but... whatever! She needed to get going!

As Hattie executed what felt like a rather ungainly nine-thousand-and-twenty-three-point turn in the big old car, her head was filled with a riot of colourful, shiver-inducing flashbacks of the night before. She cracked the window back open, desperate for some fresh air to soothe her flushed cheeks. Who would have thought that a bed principally made up out of old sails and blankets - in the hull of a half-rotten old boat - could be quite so comfortable… let alone the scene of such naughtiness!

As she began the steep climb out of Seabury, back up the hill she'd descended not more than an hour ago Hattie gave a wriggle of pure excitement. So much had happened in such a short space of time - but it was just starting to sink in that this morning had confirmed something once and for all – Seabury was going to be her home for the foreseeable future. And that meant that there could be many, many more moments spent with Ben and Sylvie.

Frankly… the sooner, the better! The next time she was invited for a visit though, Hattie was planning on taking a sandwich with her for breakfast. Cake was lovely and all, but it did seem to pave the way for a decidedly excitable morning! Perhaps she could even talk Lionel into making it for her – he was good at sandwiches, provided that they had cheese in them.

SURPRISES IN SEABURY

In fact, it probably wouldn't hurt to grab a box of cereal to take over too. She could pour it into a Tupperware box to stop it from getting damp. And some cutlery... and maybe a bowl or two. Of course, it might not be a bad idea to pop some curtains up at the portholes – they let in a lot of light in the morning, and she shuddered to think about the eyeful anyone would get if they happened to be exploring the boatyard at night.

Hattie snorted at the thought and opened the car window even wider to let more fresh air into the car. She was being ridiculous, of course... as if anyone would be pottering around that scrapyard at night! Besides, the portholes were pretty high up... still... it might not be a bad idea if she could talk Ben into it.

Doing her best to drag her mind back out of the gutter, Hattie forced herself to concentrate as she whipped past the high, green hedges that lined the route out of Seabury. Mrs Scott's schoolhouse stood in a secret cove a little way along the coast from the town. She'd driven there a few times since her first visit in Ben's boat, and she still couldn't get over how much longer the journey took by road than by sea!

The first time she'd decided to take the car, Ben had come with her, insisting that she'd never find it without a guide. He'd been right. The twists and turns of the tiny lanes were mind-boggling – and the breath-taking view had the habit of stealing your attention away from where you were going every few feet.

It still didn't beat travelling by boat though. Hattie hadn't been so sure the first time Ben had taken her out, but she'd quickly got used to it. The pair of them had been out a couple more times since then, and the coastline was simply beautiful. There were places where the water was so clear, Hattie had been able to see all the way to the seabed as she'd watched fish flitter beneath the boat. It was magical… and the captain wasn't too bad either!

Now that she was sure she wasn't about to plunge overboard at every rise and fall of the little boat, she could enjoy the feeling of the salty spray on her face and the wind in her hair. They were certainly experiences you didn't get in a kitchen! They'd spotted cormorants, seals and even dolphins. All she'd ever got to see in London were the ever-present, ragged pigeons.

Hattie held her breath as she navigated her way around a particularly sharp bend in the road. Her mind flew back to her old kitchen in London… and from there, it hopped straight on to Marco. She couldn't help but hope that he might have got lost in these lanes and given up before he found Mrs Scott's house. Even with Kate's directions, the schoolhouse was very tucked away… it would be pretty hard for a stranger to find.

On top of that, Hattie knew for a fact that Marco

would take issue with the idea of the hedges scratching his car's paintwork. Plus, losing a wing mirror on the corner where the lane got really tight was a definite possibility for such a big vehicle...

As Hattie navigated her way slowly towards Mrs Scott's house, she kept a close eye out for any *silly big car* parts stuck in the bushes. Sadly, she couldn't spot anything... but then, maybe that was a good sign. Perhaps Marco hadn't even made it this far. With any luck, he'd given the whole thing up and disappeared back to London where he belonged.

CHAPTER 13

Hattie pulled the car into a weedy, gravelled patch under a stand of old oaks. Hurrying towards the old school gates, she crossed her fingers and sent up a little prayer that Marco had never made it here. She couldn't bear the idea of that git terrorising her friend.

Mary Scott had kept her mother's pudding recipe secret for years – ever since she'd died. She'd not given into Veronica's relentless demands and had only decided to share the recipe with Hattie so that she could bring the pudding back to life for their recent reopening.

The whole thing was an incredibly delicate subject, and just the thought of Marco rocking up with all the delicacy of a rhino on a skating rink made her cringe from her fingertips right to her shoelaces. She was dreading what state her friend would be in.

Hattie made her way through the gate, her eyes on the front door of the old school as she crossed the defunct playground with its faded games and tufts of grass pushing through the tarmac. Just as she was about to reach up and ring the bell, she caught the sound of a pair of garden shears hard at work. Hattie made her way around the side of the building only to find Mrs Scott hard at work in the bright, flower-filled patch of garden that flanked the school.

'Hello Hattie!' said Mrs Scott, pausing for a moment to glance in her direction before continuing the rather vigorous pruning of an unsuspecting bush.

'Hi, Mrs Scott!' she said, wondering how to broach the subject now that she was here.

'How many times do I need to tell you to call me Mary?' she tutted, raising an eyebrow. 'It's bad enough being the ex-headmistress of most of the people around here – and they *will* insist on keeping things formal and sticking to my *teacher* name - but you? Well, no need for you to fall into the same habit!'

Hattie shot her a rueful smile. 'Sorry… Mary.'

'That's more like it!' said Mary with an approving nod. 'Anyway, to what do I owe the pleasure… as if I couldn't guess! I have to say, I thought I might be seeing you at some point today.'

Uh oh, that sounded ominous. 'Actually, I came to

apologise... for any, erm, unexpected visitors you might have received yesterday.' Hattie wrinkled her nose.

Mary continued to calmly chop away at the bush until she'd trimmed the entire length of it. Then she placed her shears down on the grass, pulled a seriously sharp pair of secateurs from her apron pocket and started to deadhead a plant in a huge terracotta pot.

'Well,' she said eventually, 'you're right. I did have a caller yesterday. Odd little man.'

Hattie had to bite back a smirk. It seemed that everyone around here had exactly the same opinion of Marco.

'He said he was your old boss,' she continued without looking up, 'up there in London. He told me that you're close friends and that he taught you everything you know.'

'I'm not so sure about that!' Hattie snorted.

'Which bit?' said Mary, quirking an eyebrow at her.

'Both!' said Hattie, prickling with indignation. 'The whole *teacher* bit is decidedly far-fetched. He hasn't got the patience to teach anyone anything. Frankly, I learned more about cooking in the places I worked before ending up with Marco - even right back at the beginning when I was just washing dishes. I did learn something from him though... I learned from him how *not* to behave. And the friend thing is a definite no-no.'

Hattie ground to a halt and rubbed her nose awkwardly, realising that she'd just gone off on a bit of a rant. Clearly, she'd caught the tendency from Ethel!

'Now that I've had the *pleasure* of meeting him, I can just imagine,' said Mary.

'Yeah. Well.' Hattie blew out an irritated breath, still unable to believe that he'd dared to come here to try to muscle in on her new life. 'I've learned more in the time I've been here in Seabury than I did in the whole eighteen months in his kitchen. And - I mean - about *real* cooking. I've definitely learned more about myself, too.'

Hattie wondered as she said the words, whether this was really true. How could muddling along by herself in the kitchen at Pebble Street have taught her more than a chef who, despite being a total gobshite, had been a rising star at the time?

The answer was fairly simple – yes, it was true. She'd learned more here because she'd had to listen to her own instincts. Because it was all about food that would delight their guests and fill their bellies – not about how it would look in a photo and how many new followers it might gain on Instagram.

Today wasn't about her, though. She quickly turned her attention back to Mary.

SURPRISES IN SEABURY

'I'm guessing that he wanted to ask you about the pudding recipe?' said Hattie.

Mary paused for a moment in her clipping, tilting her head to one side as she thought about it.

'Ask?' she said eventually. 'I'm not sure that *asked* is quite the way I'd put it. I'd say that *demanded* might be nearer the mark.'

'Oh no,' sighed Hattie.

'Yes. He demanded that I tell him what was in the pudding. He really does have a rather unfortunate manner.'

Hattie winced. 'What did you tell him?' Hattie, feeling the nerves rise in her throat. She just hoped that Mary hadn't fallen for his lies about them being friends.

'I told him, of course!' said Mary.

Hattie's jaw dropped. 'You... you-'

'I told him that it was a family secret and that I'd only ever shared it with one other person – you. But he said he was your friend, so I thought it'd be okay.'

Mary had moved on to the next flowerpot now and was calmly tying a tall spire of pale blue flowers to a stick so that they wouldn't get blown over. She was acting as if she didn't have a care in the world - but Hattie's mind was reeling.

She'd *told* him?

'Wait... you gave Marco your mother's recipe? For the Pebble Street Pudding?' she practically whispered in disbelief.

Mary's expression flickered. It was only for a split second, but Hattie caught it. She was clearly trying to keep a straight face as she grabbed her secateurs and renewed her deadheading with increased enthusiasm.

'I gave him *a* recipe,' she said, not meeting Hattie's eye. 'I didn't give him *the* recipe,'

Hattie let out a surprised snort of laughter, and Mary glanced at her, a flicker of a smile just starting to appear on her face.

'It must have sounded about right because he wrote it all down. But I left out a few key ingredients,' she said.

Mary's grin was out in full force now, and Hattie was beaming back at her, shaking her head in slow disbelief. It was official - Mary Scott was her hero.

'Oh, and I might have got a few of the quantities wrong too. And popped in a couple of… interesting additions. And overcooked it by twenty-five minutes… on the wrong shelf… at the wrong temperature. But other than that – yes, it was the pudding recipe!'

Hattie was laughing so hard her shoulders were shaking and she could feel all traces of anxiety leaking away. She should have known that everything would be okay, shouldn't she? Mrs Mary Scott had been a headteacher for years… she was one wise lady! There was no way she was going to be fooled by an obvious, spoiled little brat like Marco, was there?

As for Marco, he'd gone off with a recipe that was completely useless – after coming all this way to steal it. Ah well – it couldn't have happened to a nicer guy.

'You know,' said Mary with a frown, 'he didn't even stop for a cup of tea. Or say thank you. He just drove off. I think he might have lost his wing mirror in the hedge over by the gates too – he had one of those silly big cars that you don't see down here too often.'

'Have you been talking to Ethel?' said Hattie, already guessing the answer considering the *silly big car* comment.

Mary nodded. 'Of course. She brought me my cake subscription box from The Sardine and told me all about Marco blocking her in. I didn't tell her about his visit here though... it didn't seem fair on you. You know what she's like... it would have been around the whole town in seconds.'

Hattie nodded. 'You've got a point there. Thanks!'

'No problem,' said Mary. 'Besides - I wanted to see the look on your face myself!' she added, her eyes twinkling. 'Priceless!'

Much to Hattie's surprise, Mary dug her in the ribs with a friendly elbow.

'Now then, I don't suppose you fancy dipping into that cake box, do you? Perhaps with a nice pot of Darjeeling?'

'How can I refuse?' laughed Hattie.

'Wonderful!' said Mary, starting to strip off her gardening gloves. 'I'll get the kettle on.'

It had been quite a morning... sure, it would be her second helping of cake for the day – but that hardly mattered right now. She was still on one of her precious days off, and now that the whole Marco situation seemed to be under control and he was back where he belonged, she thought she deserved a treat. Besides, Ethel made the best cake in the county – she'd be a fool to miss it!

CHAPTER 14

'And you're absolutely sure that Marco was planning on heading straight back to London?' said Hattie.

Although Mary had reassured her several times that she was absolutely fine and had rather enjoyed sending her unwelcome visitor away with a flea in his ear, Hattie was still rather keen to confirm that he was gone. She wanted to know for sure that he'd left her perfect patch of the world.

She watched as Mary poured boiling water into an ornate teapot, gave it a brisk stir and then popped it onto the tray she was preparing.

'Quite sure,' said Mary with a tut. 'But let's not talk about him anymore. He's not important. I want to hear how you've been getting on.' She placed a sugar bowl onto the tray, followed by the box of cakes from The Sardine and then added a couple of linen napkins.

'Here, I'll grab that,' said Hattie, picking it up. She followed Mary down the hallway and back out of the old schoolhouse into the sunshine.

'Let's go down to the beach,' said Mary.

Hattie grinned at her friend and nodded. Now *that* sounded like an excellent plan.

They ambled together across the old playground and then Mary led the way down towards the private beach that sat a little way along the path from the old stone quay where Ben liked to moor his boat.

'Ooh – deckchairs!' said Hattie as they wandered onto the pebbly shore.

Two old-fashioned, red and white striped affairs were already set up facing the sea. Between them sat a low, folding camp table.

'Well,' said Mary, 'as I said earlier, Ethel dropped by, and you know what she's like – she simply *had* to stop for a natter while she was here. The weather's been so lovely, and we both said that it would be a shame to waste it by sitting indoors. We had plenty to talk about, so we thought we'd do it in style. Then when she left, I didn't think there was much point putting them away again as I was fairly certain that you'd turn up at some point to find out what was going on.'

'I'm nothing if not predictable!' laughed Hattie.

'That's what I told Ethel. She was all of a dither

about you going walkabout - but I told her it was pretty obvious that you wouldn't have got very far and that you were probably be with Ben somewhere!'

'You're right. I spent yesterday over at Bamton Boatyard with him,' said Hattie. She placed the tray carefully down onto the table and eased herself into one of the chairs – glad of the excuse to hide the blush that had just appeared on her face.

'Ah – I assume that you've been introduced to Sylvie then?' said Mary, raising her eyebrows in question.

Hattie nodded in surprise. Did *everyone* know about Sylvie apart from her?

'The other love of Ben's life!' laughed Mary, hefting the pot and pouring a cup of tea for both of them.

'You know about Sylvie?' said Hattie.

Mary nodded, picking up her cup and saucer and settling back into her deckchair with a sigh of contentment. 'Oh yes. Ben dragged her out of the mud where she'd been left to rot, and he's been trying to make her seaworthy ever since.' She paused and sipped her tea while Hattie stayed quiet, hoping to hear more. 'Of course, a job like that takes an awful lot of time. Ben's certainly got the energy and the drive... but even for someone like him, it's a massive undertaking.'

'Yeah, I can see that,' said Hattie, thinking of Sylvie with her piles of scrap metal, random bits of wood, oily rags and paint cans strewn all over the place. 'I'd get overwhelmed just trying to figure out where to start – especially if I was living there while trying to do it all!'

'You and everyone else!' said Mary. 'But if anyone can do it, it'll be Ben. Of course, I believe work has slowed down rather a lot since you came along!'

Hattie caught the twinkle of mischief in Mary's eye as she turned to wink at her, but frowned, feeling suddenly guilty. 'That's not good.'

'Oh, but it is,' said Mary with a decisive nod. She took a sip of tea before continuing. 'Ben's been a lot happier since you arrived back in town, you know.'

'Really?' said Hattie in surprise. 'He has?'

She hadn't really thought about her appearance in Seabury having that much of an effect on anyone else's life. She'd just assumed that Ben was Ben – whether she was around or not. Sure, they'd shared some lovely, snatched moments together, but they'd both been so busy. Until yesterday, they hadn't exactly managed to talk much about their relationship and where it might be going. In fact, they hadn't exactly *talked* about it yesterday either!

'Trust me,' said Mary, watching her closely over the rim of her teacup, 'I've known Ben even longer than you have – since he was a little tacker starting school - and that was well before you started running riot together every school holiday!'

Hattie grinned at the memory of the pair of them

enjoying long, wild days together, exploring Seabury under the hot summer sun.

'Anyway,' Mary continued, 'I've never seen him as happy about anything as when you reappeared in town. If I'm honest, he seemed... a little bit lost before then. He was always working so hard to get Sylvie fixed – but I think he was in desperate need of someone to tell about it all. He was missing a key piece of the puzzle - someone to share the adventure with. Maybe even someone to sail away into the sunset with at the end of it all!'

'That's a long way off,' laughed Hattie, shifting in her seat uncomfortably at the thought of Ben disappearing into the sunset. What if he went without her?

'Maybe so, but it's all part of the dream, isn't it? And I'd say that you're busy making our Ben's dreams come true.'

Hattie couldn't think of anything to say to that, so she sipped her tea, her mind full of Mary's words. She hadn't really thought about it like that before. But then, considering she'd only met Sylvie for the first time just yesterday, it wasn't really that surprising, was it?

She realised that she desperately wanted it to be true, and yet... what if it wasn't. What if this was just a case of their mutual friend wanting to matchmake them both. But then – hadn't she caught those words drifting back to her from the fish van just that morning? She was certain that he'd told her he loved her – even if it was by mistake.

'You know,' said Hattie quietly, 'I thought there was someone else when Lionel mentioned Sylvie a couple of days ago. I only saw her for the first time yesterday. I just wish Ben had felt like he could share it with me before now.'

'Well, you've had an awful lot on your plate, getting the restaurant up and running,' said Mary.

'Yes but-'

'And he was embarrassed, wasn't he?' said Mary, cutting her off.

'But why?' said Hattie. 'That's ridiculous!'

Mary smiled and took a bite of chocolate cake with relish. She chewed, swallowed and then dabbed at her mouth with her napkin before answering. If Hattie hadn't known better, she'd have sworn her friend was rather enjoying this!

'No, it isn't ridiculous. Ben was worried about sharing his living quarters with you in case it put you off.'

'What?' said Hattie, marvelling at this insight into someone she thought she knew pretty well. 'As if it would put me off!'

'I told him that,' said Mary, rolling her eyes. 'I said he was being ridiculous. He talks to me quite a bit when he comes over to do odd jobs for me, you see. Ben's always been an open book – there's no side to him. That's why I always liked him so much. Even when he was a kid you didn't get any kind of performance, there was no act. He's just one of those people who's happy to help out in any way he can and shares everything about himself freely.'

'It's one of the things that I really like about him too,' sighed Hattie. 'I just wish he'd felt like he could share this with me before he was basically forced to. Maybe he doesn't trust me. I mean, he's not exactly been an open book with me, has he?'

'It was only because he cared so much about what you'd think,' said Mary. 'And believe me when I tell you that he spent a good amount of time beating himself up about it too. He was desperate to share Sylvie with you… but he was scared. Plain and simple.'

Hattie let out a little huff of disbelief as she stared out at the gentle waves lapping the pebbly shoreline.

'Hattie, listen to me - you might have known each other well as kids, but all this is all very new to you both. You've come from a fancy job, living a life in London that is so alien to the way Ben lives down here… and he just wasn't sure that he'd be… enough.'

Hattie winced inwardly – because even though she'd never admit it out loud, until very recently, she had been questioning exactly the same thing. Would Seabury be enough for her? Would Ben? The answer, of course, was blindingly obvious.

She turned to Mary only to find that her friend was watching her closely.

'Ben's the person most people in Seabury call if they've got a problem,' said Mary. 'He will always turn up to help – always. But when it comes to hoping that someone might do the same for him... well, I think he's only just learning that that's a possibility. Not just a possibility, but a reality now that you're here.'

Hattie swallowed hard as a lump of emotion lodged unexpectedly in her throat. The idea that generous, kind, lovely Ben might ever doubt that he deserved love and friendship and help when he needed it made her heart squeeze. Things were *way* more complicated than she'd given them credit for, weren't they? And she was already in *way* deeper than she'd realised.

Who had she thought she was kidding, anyway? Hadn't her reaction to the tiniest possibility that there might be someone else in Ben's life taught her anything?

'You know – Kate's very similar to Ben in many ways,' said Mary, staring out into the little bay.

Mary was clearly changing the subject to give Hattie a moment to collect herself – and Hattie was intensely grateful.

'Seabury does seem to grow good uns, doesn't it?' Mary continued.

Hattie nodded her agreement, willing her swirling emotions to settle down.

'You know – I've always thought that's why The

Sardine is so popular. Kate's kind, and that draws people to her. She'd do anything for anyone too. I have to say, it makes me so happy that she's getting her own happy-ever-after. It seemed pretty unlikely with Mike Pendle, of all people... but all her dreams have come true, what with moving up to the lighthouse with him and Sarah.' Mary paused and turned to Hattie again. 'And now, maybe it's Ben's turn. With you.'

Uh oh!

Hattie had just about managed to get control of herself, but suddenly her lip gave a treacherous wobble. She was just tired. That was all it was. Not surprising after last night, really.

Head out of the gutter, Hattie! Now's definitely not the time!

Hattie cleared her throat, willing herself back down to earth.

'How do you think Kate's doing with the move?' she said, determined to change the subject to something safer again. 'I was talking to her earlier and apparently, Stanley keeps turning up at The Sardine, wanting to be let in!'

'Darling Stanley,' laughed Mary. 'He appeared here a few days ago too. But then, he's always had the run of Seabury, really – it all started when his original owner died, and the family abandoned him.'

'What?' said Hattie in horror. 'How could anyone do that?'

Mary shrugged. 'Some people are *not* our kind of people. Anyway, the point is, I'm sure Stanley will settle, and the same goes for Kate. Though I can imagine that moving up to the lighthouse after being on her own for so long in that little flat will take some getting used to. But I think she'll be very happy there - she finally has the family she's always craved.'

'I like Kate,' said Hattie. 'She always seems so sure of herself and her place in the world. She doesn't seem like the kind of person to ever make a mistake.'

'Don't you believe it,' laughed Mary. 'She got married to someone... less than suitable, shall we say... and she moved to London to be with him. It lasted three months before she realised what a mistake she'd made and that she belonged back here – back in her little flat with her lovely café.'

'Wow, I didn't know,' said Hattie in surprise.

'Oh yes. It was lucky that your uncle was able to help her – her awful ex went after the café you know?'

Hattie's eyes went wide as she stared at Mary. 'I had no idea Lionel had done that!'

'Yes, well, the point is... we all make mistakes.'

Mary went quiet, her face taking on a mask-like quality as she stared out at the bay, clutching her teacup as if her life depended on it. Hattie frowned at her in concern. Clearly, she still found it difficult to talk about Lionel. Hattie watched her for a long moment, wishing she could do something to heal the rift between them. And just as she'd done with her uncle, she promptly decided that it was none of her business.

'I've been working on my new menu,' she said, grabbing a napkin and wiping sticky chocolate icing from her fingers, 'and I was wondering if you happened to have any more of your mother's recipes up your sleeve?'

Mary turned to her in surprise and smiled, clearly grateful for the change of subject.

'Well, as you know, you're not the first person to ask me about recipes recently… the difference is, I like you!'

Hattie let out a chuckle, glad to see her indomitable friend was quickly recovering her pepperiness.

'Thank you,' she beamed.

'I can certainly show you a thing or two,' said Mary, 'but it might take a little time.'

'Perfect,' said Hattie. 'It's my day off - actually, my second day off - so I've got all the time in the world if you'll have me?'

'I'd be delighted!' said Mary. 'I hope you won't mind the kitchen though, it's a little bit old-fashioned.'

'You've seen Pebble Street,' laughed Hattie. 'Old fashioned is just the way I like things!'

CHAPTER 15

It was fairly late in the afternoon by the time Hattie pulled into the garages of The Pebble Street Hotel. She'd texted Ben to let him know that she'd be back much later than anticipated and he'd promised to meet her at the hotel when she returned. Hattie'd forgotten to send him another message before she'd set off as her brain had been too full of the most incredible new dessert recipe Mary had taught her. Never mind - she'd nip into the hotel and if he wasn't already there, she'd give him a call.

Hattie had spent the most wonderful afternoon with Mary in her kitchen. It had been the best kind of therapy - just what she needed after a whole morning of dashing around in the wake of the Marco-shaped tornado that had whipped through Seabury.

Now that the drama was all over though, she was

actually quite looking forward to filling Ben in on the whole story. Hattie was rather hoping that Lionel would be around too - she wanted to reassure him that all was well after her ominous whirlwind of an appearance that morning.

Hattie let herself in through the back door of the hotel and then stopped dead to listen. Complete silence. Huh - if she had to guess, it looked like Pebble Street was currently deserted. She knew that was ridiculous of course. It was a massive building so there was no way of knowing what was going on upstairs from all the way down here in the kitchen… but there was a different quality to the silence somehow when you were the only one there.

Hattie peeped around the kitchen. All was calm, peaceful, and ready to jump into action the next day when service resumed. They would be launching the new menu to a full-house. She grinned - excited at the prospect. All she'd needed was a tiny bit of time off. Hattie made a mental note to remember that the next time her energy levels disappeared through the floor!

Right… well, considering there was no one around and Ben didn't know she was on her way back yet… maybe she could sneak in a quick shower before she called him! A night on Sylvie had been lovely - but that, closely followed by a wild goose chase all over town had left her in need of a good soak and some scented bubbles! Right - decision made. She'd nip upstairs, grab a shower and then call Ben.

Hattie made her way over through the hallway towards the sweeping staircase and began to heave herself up towards her room. She realised with every step she took that she was knackered... but in a nice way.

She'd just had the craziest two days off she'd ever experienced - from meeting Sylvie, to spending the night, to following Marco's trail of havoc all over town. Thank heavens it had all worked out in the end. Marco had turned tail and trotted off back up to London, triumphantly clutching an incorrect recipe. Somehow Hattie doubted that the corrupted Pebble Street Pudding he was about to bake would make him famous.

There was a small part of Hattie that still couldn't help wishing she'd been around to confront the idiot herself - she could certainly think of a few choice words that she'd have liked to share with him! Just the idea of him coming to Seabury just to steal her pudding recipe made her grind her teeth - the nerve of the man!

Then again, maybe it was better this way. Hattie wondered how long it would take for Marco to twig that his prize for all his effort was completely useless? Probably quite a while, if she knew him - he'd refuse to believe he'd been beaten!

As she reached the top of the staircase, Hattie

paused for a moment. Despite her lovely, chilled afternoon, today had yielded one surprise after another and she felt like her head was spinning with it all. She hadn't really had the chance to digest everything yet… especially what Mary had shared with her about Ben. Then, of course, there were those words she'd caught floating back to her on the breeze. Blimey - she needed to get back to her room, grab that shower and get a blast of normality. Maybe then everything wouldn't feel quite so overwhelming and… life-changing!

Hattie set off again, keen to reach her own space - even if it was just a room in a hotel. But - it *wasn't* just a room she had here, was it? It was an entire town. An entire community. Everyone here had stuck up for her - Ethel, Kate, Lionel. Mary Scott. Just the thought of her new friends rallying around to send Marco on a wild goose chase that had led nowhere made her feel all warm inside. She couldn't believe that she had such amazing friends here. Hell, they were more than friends, weren't they? They were family.

Hattie was practically dragging her feet by the time she rounded the corner onto the stretch of corridor that led to her room. The feeling of lethargy didn't last long though - it was pierced by a shard of concern as she spotted her bedroom door - which was standing ajar.

Pausing, Hattie listened intently. Perhaps Lionel

SURPRISES IN SEABURY

was in there for some reason. He did like to pick wildflowers for her as a surprise sometimes… there wasn't a sound coming from inside though.

Hattie frowned. She knew she'd closed and locked the door when she'd left yesterday morning. She was always careful about that, given the number of people that could end up pottering through the hotel in a day. They might not be fully open to the public yet, but there were always workmen, delivery drivers and even curious random visitors having a look around as Lionel drummed up interest the nearer they got to their opening day. Her uncle viewed everyone he met as a prospective hotel guest these days!

'Hello?' she said quietly, nearing the partially open door.

Still no sound.

Surely Marco hadn't managed to find out which of the rooms was hers? She wouldn't put it past him to sneak in and snoop around up here on the off chance that she might have left the Pebble Street Pudding recipe lying around.

But no - that couldn't be the case. Lionel had said that he'd kept tabs on him the entire time he'd been in the hotel yesterday - and there'd be no way for him to know that the recipe Mary had handed over wasn't the real deal.

Hattie approached the door tentatively. There didn't seem to be a light on inside.

'Hello?' she called again, this time a little louder -

but there was no answer. She reached slowly around the frame and, flicking the light switch, she pushed her way inside.

'Oh no!'

Hattie didn't recognise her own voice as it tumbled from her lips in a horrified squeak. Her room had been completely cleared. All her things were gone - there was, quite literally, nothing left.

It wasn't just things like her laptop and jewellery that were missing either. All her shells, driftwood, little gifts from Ben and Ethel and Charlie… things that were more dear to her than anything else. Hell, even her clothes were missing.

She peered around the doorway to her bathroom and gasped - that had been completely emptied too. Even her toiletries were missing.

What the hell?!

She'd been robbed… by the world's tidiest thief. They'd even remade her bed. It was like she'd never set foot in this room before.

Hattie dashed back out into the hallway, thinking fast. She *had* to find Lionel. Maybe he was up in his rooms… but no - she didn't remember seeing his jacket on the pegs in the kitchen where he tended to hang it there whenever he was in.

So… maybe he was over at The Sardine? Or out on one of the beaches… though she hadn't seen anyone down on North Beach when she'd driven past on the way back to the hotel. West Beach, then? She'd start over on West Beach.

Hattie hurried down the stairs, taking two at a time as her heart pounded in her chest. It was a rare moment these days when she took the stairs rather than sliding down the bannisters - but whizzing down to the ground floor was strictly reserved for *good* days - and having all her possessions stolen did not make this a good day.

Running into the reception, Hattie pulled herself up short as she came face to face with her uncle.

'Hattie!' he said, grinning at her. 'Sorry - I didn't hear you come in-'

'Everything in my room has gone!' said Hattie, not letting him finish.

'Yes, I know,' said Lionel in a calm voice. 'That's what I wanted to talk to you about.'

Hattie felt herself deflate slightly. She was pretty sure that was a twinkle in her uncle's eye. What on earth?

'You're not kicking me out or something, are you?' said Hattie, suddenly worried that Marco's sudden arrival had made her uncle reconsider their arrangement.

'Well, in a manner of speaking, I am - yes,' he said, his voice still calm as he smiled serenely back at her.

'What?' gasped Hattie, tears springing to her eyes.

'Don't go fretting, now,' said Lionel, patting her

on the elbow. 'You know how I said a couple of days ago that you can't go on living in a hotel forever?'

Hattie nodded. She still thought that it was a bit rich coming from the man that had commandeered a hotel suite for decades!

'Well,' said Lionel, 'I think we might have found the perfect solution. Follow me!'

In complete confusion, Hattie let Lionel lead her out through Pebble Street's front door and as soon as they reached the pavement, he turned their steps towards West Beach.

'Where are we going?' said Hattie, her heart pounding with a nervous unease that she didn't quite understand. 'And who's taken all my stuff?!'

'Come on, Hattie, let's not spoil the surprise!' chuckled Lionel.

Hattie raised her eyebrows. Something decidedly fishy was going on here - she just couldn't quite figure out what it was. If Lionel wanted to have a chat over a coffee to break some news, surely they could have just gone down to the kitchen at Pebble Street?

'It's closed!' said Hattie, pointing in confusion at the front of The Sardine. The gates were across the little yard and the brand new, brightly painted wooden shutters had been pulled across the windows.

'I know,' said Lionel, distractedly rummaging through his various pockets. 'Ah-ha!' he said, finally pulling a set of keys out of his trouser pocket and holding them out for Hattie.

'What-?' she said, staring at them but making no move to take them from him.

'These are yours now, my girl!' he said with a grin. He reached out, grabbed her hand, turned the palm upwards and then forced her to accept the bunch of keys. 'Come on!'

With a nudge, Lionel bustled her around the side of the closed little café until they were standing at the side door that led to Kate's old flat.

Hattie turned to him again, feeling lost.

'Open up, Hattie - you've got the keys!'

She opened her mouth again as if she was about to start demanding answers, then thought better of it and fitted the key into the lock. Sure enough, it turned easily, and she pushed the door open.

'Up we go, then!' said Lionel happily, gesturing towards the staircase inside.

CHAPTER 16

'Surprise!!!'

Hattie jumped so violently that both her feet left the floor for a second, and she let out a yelp.

'Sorry, sorry!' gasped Ben, rushing out of the little living room.

Hattie stared around, trying to get her bearings as her heart pounded in her chest. She was intensely grateful for Lionel's steadying hand right in the middle of her back - she had a feeling she'd have toppled straight back down the stairs otherwise!

'Ben?' she said, staring at him in confusion. 'What's going on?'

Ben reached out and grabbed both her hands. 'Come on!' he said impatiently, drawing her into the living room, closely followed by Lionel.

Hattie's mouth dropped open. She was sure that it

wasn't a particularly good look - but she couldn't help it. So, *this* was where all her things had disappeared to!

'What do you think?' said Ben, his voice quivering with the level of excitement usually only reserved for six-year-olds. 'I hope you love it… do you love it?'

'Let the girl breathe, lad!' chuckled Lionel. 'You *did* just nearly give her a heart attack after all.'

Staring around the room, Hattie felt like she'd entered some kind of alternate dimension - one where she'd lived in this little flat for at least a year. All her most precious things had been perfectly placed, making it feel as familiar as her own room back at Pebble Street.

'Hang on… Stanley?' she laughed in confusion, as the big bear got up from the rug in front of the unlit wood burner and padded towards her. He sat on her foot, leant his head back and promptly demanded a tickle.

'Erm - he was feeling a bit homesick again,' said Ben. 'Turned up at the door just as we were bringing the last of your boxes over. I've already called Kate - but I said he could stay for the night. I hope you don't mind?'

Hattie looked up from Stanley's melting eyes and met Ben's hopeful ones. 'I… I don't understand,' she said.

'Maybe I can help?' said Lionel, plonking himself down on one of the two dining chairs that had clearly been pilfered from Pebble Street's dining room.

Hattie looked from her uncle to Ben and back again. 'Okay...' she said. 'I'm all ears!'

'Well, I've been talking to Kate about this place for a little while now. I'd had the idea that it might be the perfect opportunity for you to put down some roots... but only if you really made up your mind that Seabury was going to be your home long-term.'

Hattie shifted her weight awkwardly. She hadn't really realised that her uncle had been fully aware of her inner struggle when it came to Seabury versus her career.

'Don't look so worried!' he laughed. 'It's natural that there's been a bit of adjusting for you to do. Anyway - when I saw you this morning - beaming away after spending some proper time with this one,' he said, nodding at Ben, 'well... that's when I knew it was time.'

'Time for what?' demanded Hattie.

'Time to rope young Ben here into the plan and ask him what he thought.'

'And I liked the plan,' said Ben, grinning at her. 'A lot.'

'So that was that part settled,' said Lionel. 'Kate's hated leaving the flat standing empty, but she didn't really want to let it out to anyone she didn't know - especially not to holidaymakers. And she'd already heard that you'd want to move out of the hotel at some point when I first broached the subject.'

'How did she hear that?' said Hattie faintly.

'Erm... I told her,' laughed Ben.

Lionel nodded. 'Yes - and Kate suggested that maybe you and Ben might like to live here. Together. Get you out of the hotel for some privacy and your own space!'

'And obviously, Lionel and Kate both already know what conditions on Sylvie are like... and that I'd get the work on her done a lot quicker if I wasn't living on board at the same time!' said Ben.

Hattie stared at him, wide-eyed and completely speechless. Then she turned back to Lionel, who was grinning at her, looking very much at home.

'I'm sorry for shocking you with your empty room,' he said. 'But you'd said that you'd text Ben before you set off. We'd really hoped to catch you before you saw it like that!'

'But how did you... I still don't understand how you managed to do all this behind my back!' breathed Hattie.

'Easy. Ben saw you heading over to Mary's in the car. He reported back to Kate. Kate phoned Mary to give her the heads-up and asked her to keep you occupied for as long as possible.'

Hattie shook her head in disbelief. 'You were all in on it?'

'Well - to be fair, I only found out about the plan this morning,' laughed Ben. 'But yes!'

'I hope we've done the right thing, Hattie,' said Lionel gently. 'We tried to make the place look as much like home as possible!'

Hattie felt the tingle of the shock beginning to calm down, and as she stared around the gorgeous little living room with all her things arranged on the shelves, she couldn't help the smile that started to spread across her face.

'You've made it pretty much perfect,' she said quietly.

Lionel broke into a relieved smile. Next to her, Hattie could swear that she felt Ben sag with relief.

'I wouldn't want the pair of you moving too far away,' said Lionel, beaming at her. 'At least this way I can keep an eye on you! Anyway, I've taken up far too much of your time already. I'll head off and let the pair of you settle in. If there's anything you've forgotten or anything you need Hattie dear, you know where I am... it's the big building just up the seafront! You know, I've got no idea why some people can never seem to find Pebble Street!'

Ben chuckled and Hattie stepped forward and kissed her uncle on the cheek. 'Thank you - for everything. I'll see you really soon, okay?' she said, horrified to feel a lump forming in her throat.

'That you will,' said Lionel, gently patting her cheek, 'we've got a full house tomorrow night!'

With a little salute to Ben and a final pat of Stanley's head, Lionel made his way out of the living room, and they heard his footsteps disappearing back down the stairs.

In the silence that followed, Hattie turned to look around the room again. She could feel Ben's eyes following her every move. He was clearly waiting for her to take the lead, but she just needed to take a moment to let everything sink in.

All her shells and odd-looking bits of driftwood were laid out along the shelves. A few of Ben's shipbuilding books that she recognised from Sylvie had already made their way over too, and now sat nestled next to her tiny collection of antique Austen novels.

'I went back to the boatyard after agreeing everything with Kate earlier and collected a few things,' said Ben, clearly unable to stand the silence any longer.

Hattie just nodded, not saying anything as she tried to adjust to this new reality.

'I know I should have asked you about all this first... but I guessed that you and Mrs Scott would have a lot to talk about... and it was your day off... and... well...' he stopped, and Hattie heard him swallow nervously. 'Look, if you hate it, you can tell me. It's not a problem. We can just go back to how things were, no problem at all, but...'

Hattie still couldn't get any words out. Instead, she reached out and took one of his hands. Ben paused, smiled and took a deep breath as she squeezed his fingers in hers.

'Lionel has supplied us with fresh sheets for the bed... and pillows... and there are new curtains coming tomorrow because Kate had already taken the ones from here over to the lighthouse. She's obviously taken most of the furniture with her too... but I can deal with that. I'll make you anything you want!'

He grinned at Hattie, and she smiled back, a bubble of undiluted happiness growing in her chest.

'Obviously, I'll have to slot it all in between the other jobs,' said Ben, shooting her a cheeky wink, 'like the bus and the fish van and other people's toilets... and working on Sylvie of course... but I'm sure I'll find some time for you in there... somewhere.'

'Oh really?' said Hattie, suddenly finding her voice. Letting out a laugh of pure joy, she tugged him towards her and wrapped her arms around his waist.

'We'll have to return these chairs to Pebble Street, but I'll do my best to rustle something up to sit on in the next few months... if you're lucky...' he said, closing his arms around her and nuzzling into her hair, making her wriggle.

'You know when I saw you this morning?' said Hattie.

'Mmm?' Ben mumbled.

'You said you loved me.'

Ben pulled back and looked her dead in the eyes.

'I'm not sure about that,' he said, his eyes twinkling. 'You must have misheard me or something.'

Before Hattie could say a thing, Ben pulled her into a kiss.

'Huh,' he said as he drew back again, smiling at her, 'you're right, it's all coming back to me.'

Hattie dug him in hard in the ribs, and he laughed.

'Of course I love you,' he said, 'isn't it obvious?'

Hattie grinned up at him, taking in his untidy, sandy hair, the little freckles she'd loved for so long, and the ever-present smile.

'Me too,' she said simply, reaching up to kiss him again. 'You know,' she added, 'I think we'd better get an early night.'

'Hattie,' laughed Ben, 'it's only about seven o'clock.'

'Yes,' she said, her face becoming serious, 'but I've got a very long commute to get my head around in the morning. I mean… it's going to take a lot more energy than just sliding down the bannisters, isn't it?'

'You do have a point,' he said with a grin. 'The bed's all made up. I brought over some of my old sails… just in case we get cold.'

Hattie felt the hairs on the back of her neck tingle. 'I don't think there's much chance of that.'

'Let's go, then,' said Ben, taking her hand and pulling her towards the hallway. 'Sorry, Stanley old boy, we're abandoning ship!'

Stanley didn't even bother to lift his head off of his bed - he was already sound asleep in his favourite spot.

Leaving the snoozing dog curled up on the rug behind them, Ben led Hattie up the stairs towards their new bedroom. Hattie followed, her cheeks aching from far too much smiling.

Suddenly Ben paused and looked back down at her. 'You seriously want to live with me?'

Hattie raised an eyebrow. 'Are you going to make me sleep under any dripping icicles?'

Ben grinned and shook his head.

'In that case - I can't imagine anything I'd love more.'

THE END

ALSO BY BETH RAIN

Little Bamton Series:

Little Bamton: The Complete Series Collection: Books 1 - 5

Individual titles:

Christmas Lights and Snowball Fights (Little Bamton Book 1)

Spring Flowers and April Showers (Little Bamton Book 2)

Summer Nights and Pillow Fights (Little Bamton Book 3)

Autumn Cuddles and Muddy Puddles (Little Bamton Book 4)

Christmas Flings and Wedding Rings (Little Bamton Book 5)

Upper Bamton Series:

A New Arrival in Upper Bamton (Upper Bamton Book 1)

Rainy Days in Upper Bamton (Upper Bamton Book 2)

Hidden Treasures in Upper Bamton (Upper Bamton Book 3)

Time Flies By in Upper Bamton (Upper Bamton Book 4)

Standalone Books:

Christmas on Crumcarey

Seabury Series:

Welcome to Seabury (Seabury Book 1)

Trouble in Seabury (Seabury Book 2)

Christmas in Seabury (Seabury Book 3)

Sandwiches in Seabury (Seabury Book 4)

Secrets in Seabury (Seabury Book 5)

Surprises in Seabury (Seabury Book 6)

Dreams and Ice Creams in Seabury (Seabury Book 7)

Mistakes and Heartbreaks in Seabury (Seabury Book 8)

Laughter and Happy Ever After in Seabury (Seabury Book 9)

Seabury Series Collections:

Kate's Story: Books 1 - 3

Hattie's Story: Books 4 - 6

Writing as Bea Fox:

What's a Girl To Do? The Complete Series

Individual titles:

The Holiday: What's a Girl To Do? (Book 1)

The Wedding: What's a Girl To Do? (Book 2)

The Lookalike: What's a Girl To Do? (Book 3)

The Reunion: What's a Girl To Do? (Book 4)

At Christmas: What's a Girl To Do? (Book 5)

ABOUT THE AUTHOR

Beth Rain has always wanted to be a writer and has been penning adventures for characters ever since she learned to stare into the middle-distance and daydream.

She currently lives in the (sometimes) sunny South West, and it is a dream come true to spend her days hanging out with Bob – her trusty laptop – scoffing crisps and chocolate while dreaming up swoony love stories for all her imaginary friends.

Beth's writing will always deliver on the happy-ever-afters, so if you need cosy… you're in safe hands!

Visit www.bethrain.com for all the bookish goodness and keep up with all Beth's news by joining her monthly newsletter!

facebook.com/BethRainBooks
twitter.com/bethrainauthor
instagram.com/bethrainauthor

Printed in Great Britain
by Amazon